The al-Andalus series

Book Three

**THE RING OF FLAMES**

The Scottish novelist Joan Fallon, currently lives and works in the south of Spain. She writes both contemporary and historical fiction, and almost all her books have a strong female protagonist. She is the author of:

FICTION:
Spanish Lavender
The House on the Beach
Loving Harry
Santiago Tales
The Only Blue Door
Palette of Secrets
The Thread That Binds Us

The al-Andalus series:
The Shining City (Book 1)
The Eye of the Falcon (Book 2)

NON-FICTION:
Daughters of Spain

(all are available in paperback and as ebooks)

www.joanfallon.co.uk

**JOAN FALLON**

# THE RING OF FLAMES

**Scott Publishing**

© Copyright 2017
Joan Fallon

The right of Joan Fallon to be identified as the author of this work
has been asserted by her in accordance
with the Copyright, Designs and Patents Act 1988

All Rights Reserved

No reproduction, copy or transmission of this publication
may be made without written permission
No paragraph of this publication may be reproduced,
copied or transmitted save with the written permission
of the publisher, or in accordance with the
provisions of the Copyright Act 1956 (as amended)

Any person who commits any unauthorised act in
relation to this publication may be liable
to criminal prosecution and civil claims for damages.

ISBN 978 0 9955834 1 2
First published in 2017
Scott Publishing
Windsor, England

## ACKNOWLEDGMENTS

My sincere thanks to my editor Sara Starbuck for helping me to create an exciting novel out of a turbulent period in history, to Lawston Designs for the cover, and Angela Hagenow for going through my manuscript and removing all the typos. Their advice and support have been invaluable.

The Ring of Flames

## LIST OF MAIN CHARACTERS

**The ruling class**
Al-Hisham II, Caliph of al-Andalus 976 - 1009 AD and 1010-1013 AD
Al-Mansur, Regent and ruler of al-Andalus 976 - 1002 AD
Abd al-Malik al-Muzaffar, (son of al-Mansur) ruler of al-Andalus 1002 -1008 AD
Abd al-Rahman Sanchuelo, (son of al-Mansur) ruler of al-Andalus 1008-1009 AD
Muhammad II 1009 Caliph of al-Andalus
Sulayman ibn al-Hakim Caliph of al-Andalus 1009 -1010 AD 1013 -1016 AD

**The falconer's family**
Ahmad ibn Makoud a falconer
Aisha (his wife)
Rafiq ibn Makoud, (his brother) a soldier
Qasim ibn Makoud, (his brother) a doctor
Fatima and Bayda (his daughters)
Makoud ibn Ahmad (his son)
Amina (his mother)
Layla, (his aunt)
Salma (Layla's granddaughter)

**Friends**
Simon a Christian monk
Rachel a Jewess (friend of Salma)
Isaak a Jew (Rachel's father)

**The army**
General Tayyub
General Wadhi
Asif, Hannad, Hasan and Isa - quaids (friends of Rafiq)

The Ring of Flames

# PART ONE

# Córdoba
# 1008 - 1010 AD

## CHAPTER 1

Ahmad couldn't believe his eyes. He always came straight to the Falcon House after he'd been to the mosque. Being with the falcons prolonged that feeling of peace he got from his early morning prayers. But not today. He looked at the empty perches, at the feathers covering the floor, at the drops of blood that led to a dirty sack in the corner of the room. Who had done this? Who had killed his beautiful birds? His legs felt weak with shock. He squatted on the floor and looked around him. If he were a woman he'd weep and wail, he would tear at his clothes and howl his grief to the skies. But he was no woman. All he could do was hold his grief inside himself and feel it turn to anger.

A whirring of wings made him look up. A peregrine falcon flew in through the open door and landed on its perch. So some of them had got away. Thanks be to Allah. Maybe it wasn't as bad as he'd first thought.

He held out his hand and the bird flew straight to him.

'Good boy,' he said, pulling a titbit of meat from his pouch and handing it to the bird.

The bird held it in its claws and regarded it quizzically before gulping it down. He'd been hunting for his own breakfast today. Carefully Ahmad placed the falcon on one of the perches and tied his jesses to it. He should check on the rest of the falcons to see if they'd been attacked too. But where was everybody? It was well past dawn.

He unlocked the door to the inner part of the mews, where they kept the rarest of the royal falcons and the most expensive. Everything seemed as it should. Some of the birds started making

# The Ring of Flames

a fuss at the sight of him, the morning's harbinger of food. Others stretched their wings or were busy cleaning themselves. Whoever had caused the devastation in the first room hadn't been able to get in here.

'Ahmad. I've just heard. Young Dirar brought me the news. So there's been a break-in. Have they done much damage?'

A rotund man in an expensive white djubba and wearing an Arab style turban, bustled into the Falcon House. It was the new Grand Falconer, Abdul Nasir. Ahmad didn't like him very much. He hardly ever came near the Falcon House and was reluctant to even touch the birds. Al-Mansur had appointed him when the previous Grand Falconer, Ahmad's grandfather, had died. It had been a most surprising appointment; the falconers had talked about nothing else for months. There were many better candidates, himself included, but there was nothing anyone could do about it. Nobody argued with al-Mansur. However if there was one big advantage in having Abdul Nasir as their boss it was that he left them completely alone.

'I haven't checked right through yet, but it looks as though there are about thirty birds missing. Some of them may have escaped. If so, they'll turn up again when they're hungry,' Ahmad replied, locking the door behind him. 'Luckily they didn't manage to get this door open, although it looks as though they tried.'

He pointed to the long scars in the wooden door, where someone had attempted to prise off the heavy iron padlock.

'Well clean up this mess, and let me know exactly how many birds have been taken. We need to inform the Palace Guard to be on the lookout for anyone trying to sell the royal falcons.'

'Do you think they stole them to sell them?' Ahmad asked. 'Look at this.' He pulled the dirty sack out of the corner for the Grand Falconer to see. 'They've killed some of them. Now why would they do that if they wanted to sell them? And why would they leave them here for everyone to see?'

13

## The Ring of Flames

The Grand Falconer tipped the birds out of the sack onto the floor. How insignificant they looked lying there, their magnificent plumage blood-stained, their bodies, normally so graceful in flight, limp and motionless, and their piercing eyes, vacant. Again Ahmad felt the anger burn inside him.

'Maybe it was an accident. Maybe they just couldn't handle them,' continued the Grand Falconer.

'I'm sure you're right. They obviously didn't know what they were doing. That's why I think some of the birds escaped. But why kill them? If they wanted to sell them then why kill them?' Ahmad repeated. He still couldn't believe that this had happened.

'Is it a message? A warning perhaps?' Abdul Nasir asked. He looked uncomfortable. 'Remember that falcons symbolise the power of the Khalifa.'

'What? A sign that something will happen to the Khalifa?'

'Or to the caliphate.'

If this was the case then it was much more worrying than the death of a few falcons, however beautiful they were.

'No. It's probably nothing more than some drunken louts thinking they could make some money by stealing the Khalifa's falcons,' the Grand Falconer said, kicking the sack out of his way. 'Just get it cleaned up and I'll speak to the Chief of the Guard.'

As Ahmad watched him leave, he thought about what the Grand Falconer had said. It wasn't as unlikely as all that. Times had been turbulent lately. Al-Mansur had been a ruthless ruler it was true, but his strength had held the caliphate together. He'd removed all power from the Khalifa, al-Hisham, but he'd let him keep his title.

Now that al-Mansur was dead there was no strong man to rule the caliphate. His son, Abd al-Malik al-Muzaffar, had succeeded his father and for six years had reigned uneventfully, but he was nothing like his father.

Ahmad groaned. What was he going to tell al-Hisham about the birds? The falcons were the only thing that the Khalifa was interested in these days, apart from his harem of young men and the forbidden wine that he drank in his secluded palace. Would he too see it as a sign that something awful was going to happen?

If the death of the falcons was a warning then it could only be against the ruler of al-Andalus. But which one? Abd al-Malik or the Khalifa? Whichever it was Ahmad knew that troubled times lay ahead.

## CHAPTER 2

The general had summoned the entire corps to the parade ground at first light. Rafiq was puzzled—unless they were about to go into battle, this never happened. Minor instructions were always relayed to the leaders of each of the five contingents, and then they in turn told their men. So what was going on? Now Rafiq took his place next to the other four quaids who reported to General Tayyib.

'What's Chuckles want with us now?' his friend, Hannad whispered.

Rafiq shrugged. He knew no more than the rest of them. Their General, unlike his name suggested, was not a light-hearted man. On the contrary, he was a dour man who took life very seriously and met every disobedience from the men in his charge with a severity that sometimes seemed unwarranted. But at least he was of Arab stock, born and bred in Córdoba. Their corps was one of the few in Abd al-Malik's army which was not made up of entire tribes of Berbers. Rafiq looked across at his own men. They were the elite, the cavalry. They sat astride their magnificent horses, their rounded helmets gleaming in the sunlight. His contingent of a thousand men was a force to be reckoned with when they rode into battle, swords drawn, their battle cries ringing. There were very few Berbers amongst his soldiers, who were a mixture of conscripted men from the provinces, Christian prisoners-of-war who preferred to fight for their old enemy rather than submit to whatever fate awaited them, mercenaries, slaves and local men who, like himself, still believed in the caliphate and would fight to the death to protect it. Their loyalty was to themselves—he couldn't deceive himself otherwise—but he knew that when the heat was on, they could be relied upon to fight bravely and protect the backs of their colleagues. And they knew they would be well rewarded.

Five thousand men were lined up on the parade ground that morning and the only sound that could be heard was the occasional exhalation as one of the horses blew through his nose to indicate his impatience. In front of them, on a raised dais, stood General Tayyib, in full dress uniform, and the imam—stranger still, because the imam only led them in prayers before a battle.

'Good morning men,' said the General, his voice carrying to the furthermost corners of the parade ground. 'I have called you all together today to give you some sad news. Our Supreme Commander, Abd al-Malik al Muzaffar is dead.'

He waited a moment for his words to sink in then raised his hands and said, 'Allah akbar. Allah is greatest. To Allah we belong and to Him is our return.'

The soldiers repeated his words, their heads bowed in respect. Then the imam called them to prayer. Five thousand men prayed for the soul of their departed Supreme Commander.

As Rafiq listened to the familiar words of the imam and the voices of the soldiers, praying in unison, his mind began to wander. Al-Malik had ruled for only seven years and in that time they had engaged in four major campaigns against the Christians, and numerous smaller skirmishes. He had fought in them all—Catalonia, Castile, León and Aragon. Al-Malik hadn't been the charismatic leader that his father was, but he'd been a fair man, and a good Muslim. Rafiq was sorry to hear of his death, not because he had particularly admired the man but because he feared that it was the start of a period of great uncertainty for the country. There were too many people who believed they had the right to rule. He sighed. If only al-Hisham were a stronger khalifa.

The imam concluded the prayers then the general, always a man of few words, announced, 'The funeral will be in three days' time. Our new commander is al-Malik's brother, Abd al-Rahman Sanchuelo. I have no doubt he will wish to address his troops at some time in the near future.'

Having said all that he intended to say, General Tayyib wheeled his horse to the left and trotted away from the surprised soldiers. Rafiq wondered what he felt about the death of his commander. Maybe nothing. Maybe he'd seen so much death that one more meant nothing to him.

\*

Once the men had been dismissed and everyone had returned to their duties, Rafiq joined the other quaids in the Dar al-Jund.

'Well there's no surprise there,' said Hannad. 'We've known for some time that his brother's had his eye on the throne. So he's in charge now, is he?'

'I doubt there'll be any change,' said Asif, who'd been a soldier even longer than Rafiq. 'His father set the scene, infiltrating the government and the army with Berbers. Al-Malik just continued what his father started. I don't imagine that idiot Sanchuelo will do anything different.'

'I can't see Chuckles letting him mess about with his corps, so we'll be all right,' Rafiq said.

'Always so optimistic, Raf,' said Hannad. 'Who knows what this one will do? Sanchuelo's not the man his father was. Not even as clever as al-Malik. They at least took the power and left the Khalifa with his title.'

'And that's all they left him,' added Rafiq. 'Shut away in his palace all his life. What existence is that for an Omayyad khalifa? What does the rest of the world think when they come to Córdoba and instead of seeing the Khalifa in his throne room, they're presented to al-Mansur's son? The son of a civil servant.'

'He may have been a civil servant but al-Mansur was a strong man. That's what a country needs. Strength. What good is the Khalifa if he's a weak, degenerate who hides away in his palace

## The Ring of Flames

and spends his time with his whores and his toys? He's never even been in battle. I doubt he can even ride a horse, never mind wield a sword,' said Asif.

'Well, I can guarantee that this new one will be intent on making his mark. I'll wager we'll be marching north before the end of the month,' said Hasan, the quaid in charge of the archers.

'He'll have to fight a lot of battles to beat his father's record. What was it, fifty battles al-Mansur fought?' said Asif.

'Fifty-seven.'

'Well he'll never beat that.'

'Makes no difference to me. I'm too old to try to beat records. I just want to live long enough to retire to a little place in the country,' said Rafiq.

'Don't let our new Supreme Commander hear you say that,' said Asif. 'He'll kick you out right away and put in another of those Berber bastards.'

'What on earth would you do in the country? You'd be bored out of your skull,' Hannad said. 'You're a soldier and that's all you'll ever be. How many soldiers do you know that live to retire to the country? No, the best you can hope for is a quick and honourable death on the battlefield.'

'Maybe.'

His friends were right. They were moving into troublesome times. Who knew what would happen. He hadn't liked al-Mansur. The man had been ruthless and manipulative but he had held the country together. They'd been constantly at war with one faction or another—usually the Christians in the north—but the general populace had lived in peace and prosperity. Would this new ruler be able to maintain the peace? And would Rafiq ever get to realise his dream of breeding horses? Or was Hannad right? All that awaited him was death.

As a soldier you never thought about death. You saw it all around you but you didn't let it touch you. Once it touched you, once you accepted that you were mortal, you were finished. He'd been lucky all through his career, serving under brilliant commanders who won battles and rewarded their men well. Was this going to change under Sanchuelo? Well, if Hasan was right about him, then he'd know soon enough.

'Where have you been?' asked Asif. Their other companion, Isa, had joined them. He was the youngest among the general's quaids. His father had been one of the Slavs in the Palace Guard and Isa was as blond as his father had been. Today his face was flushed red with excitement.

'Have you heard the news? He was poisoned. Al-Malik was poisoned. And they say it was his brother who did it,' he said, the words tumbling out of his mouth in his haste to tell them what he'd learned.

'I'm not surprised but how do you know?' asked Asif.

'I spoke to someone in the Palace Guard. He says he even knows how it was done. Sanchuelo put the poison in a jug of wine and had someone slip it into al-Malik's house. He died in agony. The guards say his screams could be heard all round the alcázar.'

'But I thought al-Malik didn't drink alcohol?' said Rafiq.

'Oh, that was when his father was alive. Al-Mansur forbade his sons to break any of the laws in the Haddith. But once he died, neither of them bothered any more,' said Asif. 'You mean you never saw the barrels of wine he always took with him on a campaign?'

Rafiq shook his head.

'Well now we know. He was murdered,' said Hasan. 'What's Sanchuelo's next step going to be?'

'He won't be satisfied with being Supreme Commander,' said Asif. 'He will want to be Khalifa. You mark my words.'

# CHAPTER 3

Al-Hisham II, the Omayyad Khalifa of all al-Andalus, son of al-Hakim II and grandson of the great Abd al-Rahman III sat in the gardens of his sumptuous palace. A magnificent peregrine falcon sat on his hand while he fed it small pieces of rabbit. He'd named him Shamal—the wind that comes from the north—because he was bred in the north of Portugal. Al-Hisham murmured softly to the bird, fragments of poetry he remembered from his childhood. His father had read the works of many of the poets to him when he was a child and encouraged him to commit them to memory. At barely nine-years-old he'd been able to recite the entire works of ibn Abd Rabbihi. What a long time ago that had been. Now he could barely remember a complete stanza. Why did he feel like this? He wasn't an old man, only forty-three. Yet his joints ached and he was plagued with headaches. Those accursed doctors seemed unable to help him. They'd given him an ointment made of myrrh to rub on the sores on his feet but it did nothing; they'd given him oil to rub into his joints but they remained stiff and sore. He was tired of the concoctions he was made to drink: black seed in warm goats' milk every morning, and copious glasses of za'tar—he hated the taste of thyme—plus anise to relax him and God knows what else. He'd lost count of the medicines the doctors prescribed him. And none of it did any good. Whatever it was that ailed him, it was invincible. It had to be a punishment from Allah.

He hadn't been a good Khalifa. He knew that. But it wasn't his fault. He'd only been a boy at the time, and nobody had told him what to do. He twisted the ring on his finger. This was supposed to be the symbol of his power but what good had it done him? Why was he being punished for something he couldn't help? How was he supposed to have grasped his power back from al-Mansur? Even Mama had told him it was for the best and he'd believed her. At the thought of his mother, Hisham's eyes filled with tears. If only she were still alive, she would help him. She would find a cure for whatever it was that was devouring his body. He poured some wine into a glass and drank it down quickly.

'Your Majesty, there is someone here to see you,' said his servant, Umari.

'To see *me*?'

Nobody ever came to visit him. Months would pass and the only person who came to see him was Ahmad, to bring him a new falcon. Ahmad, his dear friend, had remained true to him, despite everything.

'Is it Ahmad? he asked, feeling slightly more cheerful at the prospect of seeing his first, if unrequited, love.

'No Your Majesty, it's Abd al-Rahman Sanchuelo, the new Grand Vizier and Supreme Commander of the armed forces.'

'The new what? What's happened to the old one? That boy, the son of al-Mansur?'

'Abd al-Malik. He's dead, Your Majesty. This is his brother.'

'Another son of al-Mansur. How many more are there I wonder?' Would he never be free of that man and his offspring?

'Shall I show him into the throne room, Your Majesty?'

'What? Oh, yes. I suppose I have to see what he wants. I am the Khalifa after all.'

'Would you like me to send someone to help you get dressed?' the servant asked.

'Do I need to get dressed? Is that what you recommend, Umari?'

'As you said, Your Majesty, you are the Khalifa. Let me send Musa to help you. In the meantime I will show the Grand Vizier into the throne room and give him something to eat and drink while he waits.'

'Pour me some more wine first,' al-Hisham said.

'Is that wise, Your Majesty? You will need a clear head when speaking to the Grand Vizier.'

'Maybe you're right. Later then. I'll have some later.'

Umari had been his servant for some time now. He couldn't remember exactly how long. He was Gassan's son. Gassan, who'd served al-Hisham since he was a boy. It was Ahmad's father who had suggested that Umari take his place. Ahmad's father had said that it was important to have people he could trust around him. In those days his personal guard had checked out all the palace staff before letting them near al-Hisham. There was no-one to do that now. Al-Mansur had sent a handful of the Palace Guard to guard him and the rest he'd taken to his own, new palace in Córdoba. Al-Hisham had never been there. He'd never left his own palace grounds, not for years. At first he'd felt that he was prisoner and wanted to be free, but not now. Now he felt too tired to have anything to do with all that pomp and public display. He wasn't well enough for all that fuss.

'Your Majesty, I have brought your white robes and a gold embroidered cloak. Will that do? Would you allow me to help you?' asked Musa.

He was a delightful boy, not more than eighteen and with skin like honey. If only al-Hisham felt stronger, he would take him into his harem and make love to him, but as it was, he had to make do with just enjoying the pleasure of seeing him each day, when he came to dress him.

'They will do very well, Musa.'

\*

Al-Rahman Sanchuelo was not pleased to be kept waiting, even if it was for the Khalifa. But he knew he mustn't show his impatience. It was important that he persuade al-Hisham to accept his proposal, freely. Force was out of the question. He may be a pathetic excuse for a man and completely useless as leader of this great country but there were still people in al-Andalus who regarded the Khalifa as the successor to the prophet Muhammad. It wouldn't do to antagonise them.

He sipped the mint tea that the servant had brought him and looked around him. He'd never been inside the alcázar before. The throne room, with its marble columns and gold ceiling, was still magnificent even if the rest of the royal palace was showing signs of neglect. Still what could you expect? It was years since Madinat al-Zahra had been the centre of power. His father, al-Mansur had seen to that when he moved the government bit by bit to Córdoba. He had been a shrewd man. He hadn't rushed in and seized the throne as many would have done, no, he had carefully insinuated himself into a position of unassailable power, cutting the Khalifa off from the populace and assuming his role in everything but name. It was Sanchuelo's duty, as his son and heir, to hang on to that power, to finish what his father had started. It would be up to him to make sure that their names were never forgotten.

A handful of Palace Guards, in their immaculate green and gold uniforms, stood at the back of the throne room, casually chatting amongst themselves. They looked across at him from time to time but didn't appear to recognise him. There was obviously no discipline here at all. Well that would soon change once he was Khalifa. And where was the bloody Khalifa? Was he keeping him waiting deliberately? Or was he too incapacitated to see him? Sanchuelo had never met al-Hisham—well there had been no need to—before today. He'd heard all about his debaucheries and his failing health, but even that gossip had not prepared him for the pitiful specimen of manhood who now entered the throne room, leaning on the arm of his servant.

At the sight of the Khalifa the guards quickly stood to attention and Sanchuelo reluctantly rose to his feet. He waited until al-Hisham was seated on his throne before approaching him in the traditional way, advancing part way and then bowing low to the ground before advancing closer. Al-Hisham didn't speak;

he was staring at him in bewilderment. Despite being dressed as a khalifa should be, in a pure white djubbah, a white turban swathed about his head, a magnificent gold cloak around his shoulders, the royal sceptre in his right hand and the famous Omayyad ruby glowing on his left, he looked like an imposter. There was nothing regal about him at all. All that Sanchuelo had heard said about him appeared to be true. He was a sick man. You only had to look at his blotchy red face and his skimpy beard to see that something was wrong. His servant carefully arranged his cloak about him and stood to one side.

'As-salama alaykum, Your Majesty,' Sanchuelo began as it soon became obvious that al-Hisham was not going to speak first. 'May I introduce myself, I am Abd al-Rahman Sanchuelo, the Grand Vizier.'

He bowed once more and waited. At last a thin reedy voice spoke, 'As-salama alaykum. How can I help you, Abd al-Rahman Sanchuelo?'

'I merely wished to call on you to pay my respects and to ask if there was any way in which I could be of service to Your Majesty,' Sanchuelo replied.

'You are the new Grand Vizier?' al-Hisham asked.

'I am, Your Majesty, and Supreme Commander of the Army.'

'Indeed. Is that so?' al-Hisham said. 'Supreme Commander of the Army?'

Sanchuelo didn't know what to say. He waited for the Khalifa to continue.

'That used to be the Khalifa's job,' said al-Hisham, at last looking straight at Sanchuelo as though he could now see him clearly. 'When did it become the responsibility of the Grand Vizier?'

'Your Majesty, I do not know all the history of these things. My father took over that responsibility when you were a boy. My brother, may Allah rest his soul, succeeded him and I now follow my brother. Is it a position you would like to resume?' He asked, safe in the knowledge that al-Hisham would never accept responsibility for the armed forces. A more unlikely soldier he had never clapped eyes on.

Al-Hisham lifted his arm and waved it dismissively. 'No, no. I have no intention of doing so. I am not well, you know.'

'I am sorry to hear that, Your Majesty. It must weigh heavily on you that you have no family to care for you, no son to succeed you.'

'That's true. I have no heir. That is the will of Allah. What can I do about it? One day I will die and there will be no-one to follow me. To Allah we belong and to Him is our return,' he quoted.

'Forgive me for my presumption, Your Majesty, but that is what I would like to speak to you about. The country needs a ruler, not just a ruler but a Khalifa. There can be no caliphate without a Khalifa.'

'I know that. But what can I do? Allah has not blessed me with progeny, not a son, not even a daughter. That is His will.'

'I have a proposal for you, Your Majesty. If you will permit me to speak.'

Al-Hisham nodded his approval.

'Appoint me as your successor,' continued Sanchuelo. 'You will continue to be Khalifa until your death and then I will take over. In that way your life will remain unchanged but you will be protecting the caliphate for the future. The people of al-Andalus will be forever grateful to you for preserving their way of life. If the caliphate were to fall, then who knows what would happen to the country? There are Christian forces in the north waiting for their chance to invade and take over. They would destroy everything we hold dear. And not just the Christians. There are Berber tribes in north Africa who would fall upon al-Andalus and take it for their own. You owe it to your people to keep the caliphate strong, to protect them and their culture.'

Sanchuelo waited, wondering if he had said too much too soon. He wasn't known for his patience and now was regretting his haste in broaching such an important matter. Still better now

## The Ring of Flames

than later, before someone else took advantage of their weak Khalifa or, worse still, murdered him.

'For you, Your Majesty, nothing would change,' he continued. 'You would still live here in your palace, in Madinat al-Zahra. And I would make sure that you were well protected.'

Politeness forbade that he looked at the Khalifa while he waited for his answer. Instead he focused his gaze on the tank of mercury that hung suspended from the ceiling. He'd heard of this spectacular ornament, whose only function was to impress visitors with the Khalifa's wealth. Sunlight bounced its rays off the tank, dazzling him with its brilliance. When he was Khalifa he would install one in his own palace at al-Zahira.

'I have listened to you, Abd al-Rahman Sanchuelo and I will think about your words. Now I must rest,' said al-Hisham, signalling for him to leave.

'Very well, Your Majesty. Ma'a salama,' Sanchuelo replied. He bowed and left.

So what now? The man was so vague that he couldn't really gauge his reaction to the proposal. The Khalifa hadn't seemed offended nor had he been angry. Maybe, given time, he would come to see the advantages in Sanchuelo's offer. And if not? There was an alternative but it was one he preferred not to take.

\*

Al-Hisham remained sitting in the throne room long after Sanchuelo had left. He was trying to work out the real significance of the new Supreme Commander's visit. It was conceivable that he really was concerned for the future of the caliphate but could he believe him? He twisted the magnificent ruby ring round his finger—it was something he wore every day, whether he had important meetings or not. It was much too big for him now—his body was diminishing daily. How ironic. Here was he, the Khalifa of all al-Andalus, the richest country in the West, and he couldn't even command his own body to be well.

He coughed and there was the taste of blood in his mouth. The sun was higher in the sky now, and its rays caught the tank of mercury suspended from the ceiling and were deflected down onto his hand. The ruby glowed and flickered in the light, as though there were flames inside it. Was that why it symbolised the Omayyad dynasty—a dynasty founded on bloodshed and death? It had belonged to Abd al-Rahman III, his grandfather and the first Khalifa of al-Andalus, a warrior who had united the country into one caliphate. He had given it to al-Hisham's father and now it was his. More than anything else it symbolised who he was. They might call him weak, they might say he was degenerate, that he was not fit to rule but while he wore the ring, he was Khalifa.

His thoughts turned to Sanchuelo's proposal. What choice did he have? If Sanchuelo wanted the throne he would take it. However, if al-Hisham did as he suggested then there was at least a chance that he could continue with his life undisturbed. It was not as though he wanted to rule or go on all those dreadful campaigns; he just wanted to stay here in the alcázar with his friends and his falcons. If Sanchuelo wasn't trying to trick him then it was an excellent idea. He didn't care who ruled once he was dead. Yes, he would send a messenger to tell Sanchuelo to come again tomorrow and this time to bring a lawyer. It would be written down formally. He wasn't so naive as to believe in a verbal agreement with someone who wanted to succeed him.

'Umari,' he said to his servant. 'Help me back to my rooms. Then I want you take a message for me.'

## CHAPTER 4

Aisha was preparing the vegetables for their evening meal when her son, Makoud, rushed in, his face flushed and gasping for breath.

'Mama, Mama. Uncle Rafiq is coming. He has something to tell us,' the excited youth cried.

'All right. Makoud, calm down. I don't expect the world is about to end. Is it?'

'No, Mama, but he says it's important. He wants to know if Baba is home.'

He'd barely finished speaking when her brother-in-law appeared. He looked very official in his uniform, with a chain mail vest over his tunic, and his red cape. He was even wearing his helmet and had a short sword tucked into his belt. She didn't often see him dressed like that; normally when he visited them, he wore a brown tunic and djellaba, which he referred to as his off-duty clothes.

Rafiq was a frequent visitor to their home and Makoud worshipped him. Her son was determined to be a soldier as soon as he was old enough, like his uncle and the grandfather he was named after. She was not very happy at the idea. She had only borne Ahmad one son, and he'd arrived late in life, after their two daughters. Mothers with only one son didn't like giving them up to the army and she was no exception.

'Where are you off to?' Aisha asked, giving her brother-in-law a broad smile. 'Another campaign?'

'That's right. We leave tomorrow at first light. That's why I must speak to Ahmad right away.'

'He's not home yet but I don't expect he'll be long. Sit down and I'll make you some tea. You look as though you need something to calm you.'

She was dying to know what was so urgent that he had to speak to her husband before leaving. One of her own brothers was a soldier and she was well acquainted with pre-campaign preparations. Rafiq should be in the Dar al-Jund right now, making sure that everything was in order before they left. He would be in serious trouble if his commander knew he was visiting his brother instead.

'You might as well go up and see your mother, while you're waiting. She's in her usual place. I'll bring the tea up when it's ready,' she said, filling a pan with water and setting it to heat on the stove.

Her mother-in-law, Amina, spent much of her time up on the roof terrace. She liked to sit there and do the chores that her daughter-in-law gave her: some mending, repairing the sleeping mats, or like today, smoothing the damp clothes so that they could dry in the sunshine. Amina was in her seventies now but her fingers were still nimble and although she didn't have the energy she'd had when Aisha first met her, she still contributed to running their household.

Aisha would often go and sit with her there in the evening, when the swifts flew low over the river and they could watch the sun setting over the distant hills. They would sit there until they could hear the imam calling the faithful to prayer in the Great Mosque then they would pray together before she would go down to prepare her family's dinner.

'She'll be pleased to see you,' she added. Rafiq was Amina's favourite son, mostly because he looked so much like his father, al-Jundi, with the same broad back and square head.

Amina watched as Rafiq climbed the stairs to the flat roof, closely followed by Makoud.

'Where are you going to this time, Uncle Rafiq?' her son asked.

'León. Our new Supreme Commander has decided to teach that Christian king, Alfonso a lesson.'

'I wish I could go with you,' the boy said, wistfully.

'One day, when you're older and stronger.'

'Baba wants me to join him in the Falcon House. He says it's what my grandfather would have wanted.'

Rafiq looked at him and laughed. 'Which grandfather? The one who was a soldier or the Grand Falconer? Either way one of your grandfathers would be pleased. Would you like me to speak to him for you?'

'Oh, would you, Uncle Rafiq? He would listen to you. Everyone listens to you.'

'Not everyone, unfortunately.'

Aisha sighed. She wished Rafiq wouldn't encourage her son, but she couldn't say anything without offending him. It was understandable that Makoud looked up to his uncle—he was a very dashing figure in his uniform. She'd ask Ahmad to speak to him about it.

'Fatima, have you collected the bread yet?' she asked. Her daughter was sitting on the patio, chopping herbs for their evening meal.

'I'll go when I've finished this,' she replied. 'Ali was very busy this morning. He said he couldn't bake our bread until later.'

Ali was Amina's great-nephew and only a few years older than Fatima. They had known each other all their lives, gone to the same school, shared the same friends. Now Aisha was worried that her daughter was becoming too close to her cousin. She'd tried telling her that what was perfectly all right when she was ten years old was not appropriate now she was almost eighteen. She would have to ask Ahmad if he'd decided on a suitable husband for her yet. If only his head wasn't so full of those damned birds. It had been a hard enough battle to get him to choose someone for their eldest daughter, but at last Bayda had become betrothed to a nice young man from a good family. He was still a student so the wedding was to be in the Spring, when he had finished his studies. She would miss her daughter when she left.

'Leave that. I'll finish it. You run along and collect the bread. And tell that cousin of yours that I don't want to wait half the day for my bread, next time. If there's no room in his oven for my bread, then I'll get it baked somewhere else.'

'Mama. That's not fair.'

'And no loitering. I want you straight back. It's no time to be hanging about the streets with all these soldiers about,' she snapped. Her husband was too soft with his daughters. Here they were, eighteen and twenty and neither one married yet. Most girls were promised as soon as they entered puberty, some even earlier. But no, Ahmad wanted to keep his girls at home; he wanted them educated. Didn't he understand that the older they were, the harder it would be to make good matches for them?

\*

His mother was sitting in the sun, her eyes closed and a slight smile on her lips, when he opened the door to the roof terrace. Her face, relaxed in that way, looked younger. Her grey hair was pulled back into a bun and her headscarf lay round her shoulders.

'Is that you Rafiq?' Amina asked, opening her eyes and sitting up. 'What are you doing here? Has Aisha offered you something to eat?'

'As-salama alaykum, Mama.'

'Wa alaykum e-salam, my son. Come here and kiss your mother. Are you keeping well? What about some food? There're some almori downstairs. You like almori.'

'I am well, Mama and I'm not hungry. Don't fuss.'

'Why are you here?' she asked, looking at him suspiciously.

'Do I need a reason to visit my mother?'

Amina took his hand and squeezed it. 'Of course not, son. Are you sure you're not hungry? You look as though you've lost weight. I don't think you get enough food in that place.'

'The alcázar, you mean, mother? Oh yes, we get enough food. You don't need to worry about me.'

## The Ring of Flames

'So tell me what you've been doing. Sit down, sit down.'

'I can't stay, Mama. We're leaving in the morning for León. I have a lot to do to get the men ready. You understand how it is.'

'Yes, dearest son. I was married to a soldier for thirty-five years,' she said. 'I know exactly how it is.'

'Baba is home,' said Makoud. 'I can hear his voice.'

'Mama, I'm sorry I must go.'

'But you'll stay to eat, at least, Rafiq. Everyone needs to eat.'

'Sorry, Mama, I can't stay. I shouldn't really be here now.' He bent down and kissed her on the forehead. 'I'll see you soon. Take care now.'

'May Allah go with you, my son.'

\*

Ahmad was in the courtyard, washing himself before prayers.

'This is a nice surprise, brother. Have you come to say goodbye? Aisha says you're leaving in the morning.'

'I am, but before I go I must tell you something. Where can we talk?'

'Here's as good as anywhere,' Ahmad said, rubbing himself dry and sitting down on a rush mat. 'Makoud, go and see to the goats and tell Mama to bring the tea out here.'

'Yes, Baba.'

'So what's this all about? You're very mysterious today.'

'You know we have a new Commander-in-Chief?'

'Yes, I heard. Sanchuelo. Not the most trustworthy of men, in my opinion. They say he poisoned his brother.'

'Exactly. Well that's not all. He's been to talk to the Khalifa and now he's telling everyone that al-Hisham has made him his successor. I thought you should know as soon as possible. You do still see him? Al-Hisham. You still see him?'

'Yes. Not very often. But I go if I have a new bird to show him and sometimes he sends for me. He's very unwell, you know and the doctors don't know what ails him. I was planning on going later this week to tell him about the birds.'

'What about them?'

'Someone broke into the Falcon House and killed some of the falcons. I can't understand why anyone would do that. It was terrible.'

'I'm sure it was, but why would you want to tell the Khalifa about it?'

'Because I think someone is trying to tell us something. I think the Khalifa's life might be in danger.'

'Ahmad, sometimes I despair of you. Of course the Khalifa's life is in danger. Never mind the damned birds. Weren't you listening to me? Sanchuelo will become Khalifa when al-Hisham dies. Now you've just said that the Khalifa is a sick man. How long do you think it will take for his health to deteriorate and for him to die? Not long, I can tell you. If our new Supreme Commander is capable of poisoning his own brother then he is certainly capable of orchestrating the death of a sick man. Al-Hisham's days are numbered. You need to warn him and to make sure he is guarded day and night.'

'But why me? Surely the Palace Guard are the people to speak to? I'm not a soldier.'

'No, but you're the only one who cares what happens to him. And you're able to come and go as you please. You will be able to speak to al-Hisham without alerting any suspicion.'

'I knew something like this was going to happen as soon as I saw the dead falcons. It's an omen,' Ahmad groaned. 'I knew it.'

'It's no such thing. However it may be a warning and in which case you should take notice of it.'

'That's why I was going to tell him about the falcons. I *was* going to warn him,' Ahmad said, insistently. 'I know we're no longer friends. It's hard to be friends with him these days—he's not the same person he was when he was a boy—but I wouldn't like anything to happen to him.'

'No, of course not. Our father made it his life's work to protect the Khalifa, so the least we can do is to try to help him,' said Rafiq.

'You're right of course,' Ahmad said. 'I will go tomorrow, first thing. Well after I've been to the Falcon House, anyway. And you, when do you leave?'

'Tomorrow. Sanchuelo is desperate to emulate his father, and his brother, on the battlefield. He's been two minutes in the job and already he's decided to ride north. He won't last long. Mark my words. He's too stupid. If I was in his shoes, I'd be staying here and making sure that my position was safe before I'd worry about what the Christians were doing.'

Aisha could hear everything that the two brothers said and she wasn't happy. Why did Rafiq want Ahmad to be the one to warn the Khalifa? If anyone found out then Ahmad would be killed too. Ahmad was no soldier. He loved a quiet life, his home and his falcons—all this political intrigue was beyond him. She wanted to rush in there and tell Rafiq that he should do it himself but she knew she would offend them both if she did that—Rafiq for making him appear to be hiding behind his brother and her husband for making him out to be less than a man. No, she had to hold her tongue—for now. She picked up the pot of tea and took it out to the patio.

'Stay for supper with us,' she said, pouring the tea into two small cups. 'There's plenty of food and it will please your mother if she can see you eating.'

'No, I must go now. I just came to tell you the news. But thank you,' Rafiq replied.

'Don't worry. I'll go to see al-Hisham in the morning. I have a couple of beautiful goshawk chicks for him,' said Ahmad.

'Good.'

Rafiq drank his tea quickly and got up to leave. 'Ma'a salama, dear brother.'

'Alla ysalmak.'

The brothers embraced and Rafiq added, 'Take care, Ahmad, and don't trust anyone. We're living in dangerous times.'

Aisha felt her stomach contract at his words. If Rafiq said such things, then it must be true. What else did he know that he wasn't telling them?

## CHAPTER 5

Ahmad remained sitting on the patio, sipping his tea. It was as he had feared. The Khalifa was in danger. He must act, right away.

'Aisha, I'm going out. I won't be here for dinner tonight.'

He picked up his cloak and threw it around his shoulders.

'You're going to see the Khalifa?' she said, standing in his way. 'Don't go, Ahmad. It's too dangerous. You of all people should know that.'

'Don't worry, my dear one. No harm will come to me. I'm just going to take him the chicks and perhaps give him a word of caution. I won't leap between him and an arrow again,' he said, rubbing his shoulder where the old wound still ached from time to time.

There had been an attempt on the Khalifa's life when he was just a boy—rumour had it that al-Mansur was behind it but nothing had ever been proved—and the arrow that was destined for him had wounded Ahmad.

'You said you'd go to see him in the morning,' she said. 'Wait until then. Don't rush off now, please Ahmad.'

So Aisha had been listening to them. It didn't surprise him—his wife didn't miss much; she always knew the latest gossip.

'Don't worry, wife. I won't be long.'

'Well, take this with you, just in case,' his wife said, thrusting a sword into his hand.

'Where did this come from?' he asked. 'We don't keep weapons in the house.'

'Rafiq left it for you when he called in to see Amina. He said we might need it to protect ourselves.'

'Why didn't he give it to me, himself?'

'Because he said you would refuse to take it.'

'What a fusspot he is. I swear that sometimes he's more like an old woman than a soldier.' Nevertheless, despite his words he took the sword and slipped it into his belt. 'Now, does that make you feel better, dearest one?' he asked.

'Not really. I'd prefer it if you kept well away from the Khalifa altogether.'

'Baba, can I come with you? I've never met the Khalifa?' said Makoud.

Ahmad looked at his handsome young son, with his thick black hair and his perfect profile. At thirteen there were still a look of the child to him, soft smooth skin and wide innocent eyes. No, there was no way he was going to introduce Makoud to the Khalifa. Ahmad knew his taste; he had seen the young men, no more than youths many of them, wander out from al-Hisham's personal quarters. No, he wasn't going to put temptation in the Khalifa's way.

'Another time. For now I need you to stay here and look after your mother and sisters. We should heed Rafiq's words and be extra careful.'

'Very well, Baba,' the boy said, pulling himself up to his full height. 'I'll take care of them. You can depend on me.'

'I know I can, son,' Ahmad said, hugging Makoud to him. It had been the happiest day of his life when Aisha had given birth to a baby boy.

*

When Ahmad arrived at the alcázar, all looked as usual. He had picked up the two goshawk chicks from the Falcon House and now carried them in a wicker basket where they never ceased to protest at their confinement.

'I've brought something for the Khalifa,' he told the guard who lounged at the main entrance to the alcázar.

He lifted the lid of the basket so that the man could see the tiny squawking birds.

'Oh, it's you Ahmad. Well go on in. You know the way,' the guard replied, chewing on a hunk of bread.

## The Ring of Flames

Ahmad could swear that the man had been drinking on duty. That would never have happened when his father worked there. Al-Jundi had been a quaid, in charge of a contingent of a thousand men. When he died his men had said that he'd been a strict officer but a fair one. That's exactly how Ahmad remembered him being as a father.

He walked through the deserted corridors until he reached the Khalifa's rooms. It was possible that al-Hisham was in his harem right now, so he went straight to find his servant.

'Umari, I've something for the Khalifa. Can you tell him I'm here.'

'Of course, Ahmad. Please be seated. Will you have a cool drink? Wine? Mint tea? I can give you a lovely drink made from honey and anise. It's very refreshing. The Khalifa likes it very much.'

'Thank you, Umari. Some water will do.'

Ahmad never touched wine. It was forbidden for Moslems to drink it, but many did, especially the members of the Court.

'I will tell the Khalifa that you're here,' he said. The servant bowed and disappeared into al-Hisham's private quarters.

Moments later, a very bedraggled al-Hisham appeared, hurriedly tying his robe around himself. Ahmad tried not to imagine what he'd been doing when his servant announced Ahmad's presence.

'Ahmad, my dear friend. How good it is to see you. I've not been well, you know. I am a sick man. But I am a happy man now that you have come to see me.'

He would have hugged his friend but Ahmad was too quick for him and bowed low, in the manner of any other subject.

'As-salama alaykum, Your Majesty. I am sorry to hear that you are unwell. Do the doctors not help you?'

'Doctors. They are useless. What do they know of the torments that I suffer? What do they care? All they do is devise extra tortures for me to endure. If I had the energy I would send them all into exile.'

39

Ahmad smiled. The Khalifa always started their conversation with a tirade against the medical profession, even though he knew that Ahmad's brother was a doctor.

'Well I have brought you something to take your mind off your ailments,' he said, handing the wicker basket to al-Hisham. 'These are from Byzantinium. The best that you can get. Worthy of a Khalifa, Your Majesty.'

He lifted the lid of the basket and the chicks at first went quiet, then realising there was still no food on offer, set up a series of high-pitched squawks. They were very young, nothing more than balls of white fluff topped by two very angry faces.

'They will need some food, Your Majesty. Here, I have brought some tiny pieces of quail for them.'

He handed the bag with the chopped-up meat to al-Hisham, who was now transfixed, his attention solely on the birds. Carefully he selected the smallest piece of quail and dropped it into the first chick's gaping beak. One gulp and it was gone and the squawking resumed.

'Lovely. You have done well, Ahmad. They are lovely,' al-Hisham said, feeding the second bird.

'They will be great hunters, Your Majesty.'

'We will keep them in the Falcon House here, not in Córdoba.'

'That's a good idea, Your Majesty. Then you will be able to see them whenever you want.'

He watched the Khalifa continue to feed the baby birds. He was a different man when he was handling his hawks, gentler, more alert, happier. It seemed a shame to make him face the threats that were hanging over him—Ahmad had no doubt that his brother was right; al-Hisham had placed a target on his head when he told Sanchuelo he could succeed him. How was he to make him understand the danger? Sometimes talking to the Khalifa was like handling a difficult child—you could try to make him understand the risks he was taking but you never quite knew how he would react.

'Your Majesty.'

'Yes, Ahmad? What is it that's bothering you? I can see something is wrong.'

'I am very concerned for your safety, Your Majesty. I heard that you have nominated Abd al-Rahman Sanchuelo as your successor.'

'That is true, my friend. As you know I have no heirs. I have not been blessed with any children, so who is to be Khalifa after me? I cannot leave the position empty. That would lead to bloodshed as there are many who feel that it is they who should rule al-Andalus. I cannot do that. It was Abd al-Rahman Sanchuelo himself who alerted me to this danger and he is right. Everything will go more smoothly when I die, if I have named a successor. Then there can be no dispute.'

Ahmad was no politician but even he could see the naivety of this reasoning. 'But, Your Majesty, that means that Abd al-Rahman Sanchuelo cannot become Khalifa until you are dead.'

'Naturally. He has already said that he is happy for me to continue as Khalifa for the time being. It seemed a perfect solution.'

'They say that he murdered his brother,' Ahmad said, tentatively. 'Does that not worry you?'

'I didn't know that. But it makes no difference. No-one would dare to murder a Khalifa. The people would not allow it.'

Al-Hisham's words were bravely spoken but Ahmad could hear a tremor in his voice. Even in his isolated world he must have heard of the dead bodies that had strewn the path of his previous Grand Vizier, al-Mansur. No-one had been allowed to stand in his way. Who was to say that his son was any different?

'Well I just wanted you to know, so that you could be careful,' Ahmad said. 'Don't put your trust in him.'

'Don't worry, Ahmad. He will not harm me. I am no obstacle to what he wants to do—he has all the power and I have none. Why would he murder me?'

'Just be careful, Your Majesty.'

'I know it's late but will you come with me to see the falcons? One of them looks a little sick, and that young man in charge of them, just tells me not to worry. I would be happier if you would look at it for me.'

'Of course, Your Majesty. I am happy to do that for you,' said Ahmad, realising that there was nothing more he could say about the danger hanging over al-Hisham. Before he left he would make sure to speak to Umari about it. The man was very loyal to the Khalifa and could be trusted to look out for his best interests. In the meantime he must stay alert and listen for any loose gossip among the falconers.

## CHAPTER 6

They'd been camped outside the city of León for two weeks and so far, apart from a couple of skirmishes, nothing had happened. King Alfonso V of León was not much more than a boy, but he had good advisors who knew how to wait it out. This was the city that al-Mansur had sacked twenty years previously but once again it had been necessary for the Muslim armies to return to León, a Christian city which had no intention of accepting their rule. No matter what they threw at it, the city did not crumble. It was obvious that Sanchuelo had expected the young king to surrender quickly to the Muslim forces but he'd been wrong and so here they were, with the biting north wind bringing flurries of snow that froze their feet and turned their faces to ice.

Rafiq's men were getting restless. They had come expecting a battle and instead they were sitting around with freezing bums waiting for their enemy to emerge from his fortified castle. This wasn't what they were used to. They wanted action. They wanted to hear the call to attack. Instead their lily-livered Supreme Commander didn't seem to know what to do. Even the horses were restless. Like the men, they weren't used to this cold weather; their coats had grown long and shaggy and they'd lost weight. The camels, hardy creatures that they were, didn't like the cold either and their drivers had draped them with thick rugs to protect them from the snow. The only ones who seemed happy, both with the freezing temperatures and the long rest period, were the pack mules. They grazed on the hay that their handlers fed them and seemed quite content to do nothing. Rafiq did what he could to keep the men's spirits high. He had them doing drills each and every morning. He sent scouting parties out to see if anything was changing. The men scoured the surrounding countryside for food and ate well from rabbits from the fields, geese that they trapped and even goats that they bought from local people. They would have been happier stealing them, but General Tayyib was an old soldier—he had served more experienced commanders than Sanchuelo, commanders who knew how important it was to keep the local populace on your side. Just as it had been laid down by al-Hakim and his father before him, the local people had to be treated with respect and were to receive payment for any food or livestock that they took. Not that Sanchuelo would care about such things. He treated them all the same—civilians and soldiers, they were all the enemy to him.

Rafiq looked at his own contingent of men. Most of the time they sat polishing the horses' harnesses or sharpening their lances and swords. The animals were growing lazy with so little action. They were beautiful steeds, all of them from pure-bred Arabian horses, born and reared on the Khalifa's stud farm. They were the envy of the world. He walked across to a light grey mare with a white blaze on her nose. She was his horse, broad in the back and hind quarters but capable of a fast turn of speed. Her agility had got him out of more than one tight corner. He'd named her Antarah, after the mighty warrior, because she was fearless in battle. He would ride no other. But now even Antarah was restless. When she saw him approach she pawed at the ground in excitement.

'There, my beauty. Patience. It won't be long now before you see some action,' he whispered in her ear. 'Patience, my beauty. Patience.'

Yes, something had to happen soon. He'd already heard that some of the archers, mostly Berbers, had up and left in the night. They'd decided that there would be no spoils from this campaign and so had deserted. Now there were rumours that other tribes of Berbers, recruited as foot soldiers, were planning to desert as well. Two men had been executed as an example to the rest but it hadn't had much effect—they couldn't execute an entire corps and the soldiers knew it. By now it was obvious to them all that Abd al-Rahman Sanchuelo was not the skilled commander that his father had been, nor was he even as able as his murdered brother. If only he would hand over command to one of the generals or listen to their counsel, but he doggedly followed his own plan, which was to wait it out until the young king became so frightened of their immense army—thirty thousand men—that he opened the gates and surrendered. Rafiq had grave doubts about this plan.

'My men are getting restless,' said Hasan. 'They do nothing but grumble.'

'Can you blame them? They were hoping for some bounty from this campaign and they won't get anything just sitting here,' added Asif.

'They'll be lucky if they see any action at all, at this rate. They're more likely to die of old age than get killed in battle,' said Hasan.

'Or boredom,' added Rafiq. He joined the other officers in a tent not far from Sanchuelo's, where they were eating a frugal meal of bread and cold beans.

'Or frost-bite,' said Asif, stamping his feet on the frozen ground in an attempt to warm them.

'Doesn't our esteemed leader realise that you can't keep thirty thousand armed men sitting around wondering what will happen next? They want action. Some of them are going to explode if we don't fight soon,' continued Hasan.

'You heard about the deserters?' asked Rafiq.

'Yes. Some of Hannad's men. They were gone before anyone was the wiser,' Asif replied. 'Mark my words, there'll be more if Sanchuelo doesn't give the order to attack. We could breech those walls in a few days, if only he'd give the word.'

'Exactly What was the point of lugging those bloody great siege machines all this way if we don't get the chance to use them?' complained Isa. His men were responsible for transporting and operating the huge wooden catapults that were capable of breaking down the strongest of fortress walls. The machines were so large and so heavy that they needed four oxen to drag each one along. They had kept to the plains as much as they could, even though that meant sometimes making a circuitous detour. Even so they couldn't travel any faster than eight or nine Arab miles a day. It had been a slow journey.

Suddenly there was a commotion outside. A rider galloped into their camp, pulling his horse to a standstill outside Sanchuelo's tent. He leapt down and rushed inside. Despite the cold, sweat was running from his forehead and he looked as though he hadn't slept in days.

'What's going on?' Rafiq asked, moving outside to get a better look.

'Someone's in a hurry,' said Hannad. 'Come on, let's see what all the commotion is about.'

The quaids abandoned their food and hurried out to join the crowd that was forming outside Sanchuleo's tent. They elbowed their way through the curious soldiers and entered their commander's tent. The messenger, his clothes dishevelled and dirty from his long, hard ride stood with his head bowed while Sanchuelo read the missive he had brought him.

'What is it?' asked General Tayyib, who had also seen the messenger arrive. 'Bad news?'

'There's been a coup in Córdoba. People are rioting. It says that Muhammad al-Mahdi has declared himself Khalifa,' said Sanchuelo. 'That bastard thinks he can usurp the Khalifa and his named successor? Not while I have breath in my body, he won't. Pack up. We're leaving. Now.'

'But, my Lord, what about the campaign?'

'To the devil with the campaign. Our campaign is back in Córdoba, against that treacherous al-Mahdi. Your true Khalifa has been arrested and imprisoned in Córdoba. It is our duty to rescue him and put him back on the throne. Then we will deal with the traitor.'

'But, my Lord, what about the city of León? The Christians will think we're running away.'

'Do as I say, damn you. Don't stand around like a load of stupid, old women. Get your men together. We leave at first light.'

They all knew it was too late. Córdoba was almost four hundred Arab miles away. It would take them weeks to get back with all the siege machinery in tow and by then al-Mahdi would have secured control of the city. The traitor had chosen the perfect moment to strike.

'You heard the Supreme Commander,' said General Tayyib. 'Get to it, men.'

This was disastrous. The men would be even more dispirited than ever when they heard the news. There would be no bounties, no looting, nothing to show for the campaign. There had been promises of great riches inside the city of León which boasted many Christian churches and wealthy merchants. Now they would return with nothing.

It was as Rafiq had thought. The news spread quickly among the disgruntled soldiers and they were becoming rebellious. Rafiq felt fairly confident in his own cavalry but he knew Hannad was worried about how he could keep the rest of his men together and Isa too. Most of the army was made up of mercenaries who fought for the highest return. Even if they didn't desert now that didn't mean that they would stand by Sanchuelo when they arrived in Córdoba. It would all depend on whom they decided to follow, Sanchuelo or al-Mahdi. And what of the Khalifa? Was it true that he'd been imprisoned? No, things did not look good.

## CHAPTER 7

Rafiq had been right to say that the Khalifa was in danger but, in the end, the danger had come from an unexpected source. Whatever Sanchuelo's plans might have been for al-Hisham, they would never know now. Instead it was Muhammad al-Mahdi who'd had the Khalifa arrested and thrown into a dungeon in Córdoba. He had proclaimed himself the new Khalifa, Muhammad II, by virtue of being a member of the Omayyad dynasty and the great-grandson of al-Rahman III. Ahmad didn't care about all that. Politics had always been something he could never understand and, as long as it didn't affect him and his family, he wasn't interested. But this was different. This was the true Khalifa of al-Andalus who'd been arrested, a man he considered in a strange way to be his friend. He was worried about him and he had to find out if he was still alive. People were often thrown into prison and then never seen again. Nobody asked too many questions about what happened to them.

Ahmad set off for the prison at first light. He wound his cloak around himself to keep out the cold, pulled the hood of his djellaba over his head to disguise his identity and tucked the short sword that Rafiq had given him into his belt. He had no idea whom he might come across in the city now, who might be roaming the streets using the coup as an excuse to attack and rob any casual passerby. It was as well to be prepared. Aisha was still sleeping when he left. He hadn't told her of his plan to visit the Khalifa—she would only have tried to stop him and he didn't have time to argue with her. He would explain later.

The prison was a dark and gloomy place, with its stone walls and thick wooden doors. It loomed against the skyline menacingly, a warning to all. Cautiously he approached the

## The Ring of Flames

sentries guarding the main gates. He prayed that there would be someone who remembered his father, someone who would recognise him and let him pass.

'Halt. What is your name and what business do you have here at this hour?' the first sentry asked.

He was a burly man, who, by the look of the long scar down the side of his face, had seen plenty of active service.

'I need to see the Khalifa, al-Hisham. I am in charge of his falcons and I need to speak to him about them. It is very urgent.'

'Falcons?' he boomed at Ahmad. 'What the hell can be so urgent about bloody falcons? Off with you. Be on your way before you feel the end of this pike,' he said, thrusting the lance close to Ahmad's face.

Ahmad was undeterred and stood his ground. The sharp point of the lance was very close to his face—one slip and it would pierce his eye. He took a deep breath to calm himself. 'You look as though you've been a soldier for many years,' he began tentatively.

'I have indeed. What's that to you? Be off, I say.'

The guard absentmindedly touched the scar on his face; he seemed proud of it.

'You will remember my father then. He was al-Hisham's personal bodyguard. His name was Makoud ibn Qasim. Everyone called him al-Jundi,' Ahmad said, boldly. This would work or he would receive a clout round the ear for his trouble. At that moment he wasn't sure which it would be.

But his words intrigued the guard, who lowered his lance and leaned forward to take a closer look at Ahmad. 'Step into the light, where I can see you,' he said.

Ahmad lowered his hood and allowed the flickering light from the oil lamps on the wall to fall on his face.

'Al-Jundi's boy are you? I thought his son was a soldier,' he said suspiciously.

'That's my brother Rafiq. He's away on campaign at the moment. I'm the youngest, Ahmad. I work in the Falcon House.'

'Yes I remember you. You were always coming to the alcázar with those damn birds. Weedy little scrap, if I remember. You've grown a bit since then, I see. So you're still working with the falcons, are you?' The guard's attitude had changed; now he seemed inclined to chat. Ahmad supposed it was a break for him from the monotony of standing guard. 'Yes, I remember your father well. He was an honourable man and a good soldier. There're not many like him these days. My father fought alongside him in Salim. Back in forty-eight I think it was. A good commander, my father said, and a just and generous man.'

The guard paused, his mind drifting back to tales his father had told him.

'So how can I help you? What do you really want with our degenerate Khalifa?' he asked. His tone had mellowed.

'I just need to see him. To see that he's all right. I've known him since he was a boy,' Ahmad explained.

'Well he's not the Khalifa now, you know. We've a new one. Although I wonder how long he'll last?' the guard said, opening the door and letting Ahmad through into a dark dingy corridor. 'Wait a minute and I'll take you along to him.'

He spoke briefly to the other sentry, then locked the doors behind them.

'Follow me,' he said, taking an oil lamp from the wall and holding it up so that a beam of light lit up the filthy passage.

It was the smell that hit Ahmad first, that rank odour of faeces and bodily fluids. Immediately he was a prisoner again, cowering in the corner of his cell. He shuddered, trying to cast off the memories.

'Are you all right?' the guard asked him.

'Fine.'

The prison looked even worse in the lamplight. Water dripped down the walls and the floor was covered with what looked like animal droppings. It was no place for the Khalifa. But as the guard had said, he was no longer Khalifa, he was just an ordinary man who stood in the way of Muhammad II. Well, at least he was alive, for now.

'This is it. You can have five minutes, no more, because the guards are due to change very soon. I could lose a week's pay for doing this, you know.'

'Thank you,' Ahmad said, as the guard unlocked the metal door to the cell.

'What is it? Who's there? Papa? Is it you? Mama? Have you brought me any food? Who is it?' a querulous voice asked.

Food? In his haste to get here Ahmad had never given any thought to bringing the Khalifa food, or anything else for that matter. If he'd told Aisha what he intended doing, she would have told him—after berating him for being so foolish— to take some food with him in case.

'Your Majesty, it's me, Ahmad.'

'Ahmad. Praise be to God. Have you come to take me home? I have to get out of this stinking hole.'

The Khalifa was a sorry sight. His white robes were stained. His turban had come loose and dangled over one shoulder and his face was bruised from some altercation, probably during his arrest.

'Are you all right, Your Majesty? You look tired,' Ahmad said, despair making his voice croaky. Here was the Khalifa of al-Andalus, successor of the prophet Muhammed, ruler of the richest, most cultured country in the western world, brought low by some upstart, thrown into a dungeon with common cut-throats and thieves.

'I am not well, Ahmad. My ailments torment me daily. The doctor has not been to see me since I was incarcerated in this dreadful place. I have been neglected and forgotten by all except my faithful servant, Umari. If it wasn't for him, I would have to eat this dog-shit that they serve up as food.'

Ahmad looked around to see if the guard had heard these words, but he was further down the corridor, talking to someone else.

'I will ask my brother, Qasim, to come and visit you, Your Majesty. He is an excellent doctor. He used to work with Abu al-Zahrawi before that eminent man retired through ill-health. He will help you, if he can,' Ahmad said.

'Have you brought me any wine?' al-Hisham asked. He held out his hand and looked pleadingly at Ahmad. 'A little wine to ease my pain?'

'I am sorry Your Majesty. I haven't brought anything. I thought you would have all that you needed.'

'All that I need? What I need is to be out of here as soon as possible,' the Khalifa snapped. 'I am left here in the cold and the dark, with not a decent morsel of food and nothing to quench my thirst. I have no music to soothe my soul, no company to ease my spirit. I am in hell.'

'I am sorry, Your Majesty. I will see what I can do to help you,' Ahmad said, although he knew his words were hollow. There was little he could do to change the situation. 'Sanchuelo will be back any day now and he will release you and put you back on the throne. Try to be patient until then.'

The Khalifa turned away from him and curled himself into a ball. He began mumbling to himself in a low voice.

'What is it?' Ahmad asked.

'Take no notice. He's always talking to himself, or to those phantoms he sees,' said the guard.

Ahmad looked at the Khalifa huddled in the corner on a straw pallet. It was a far cry from the silk covered sofas and richly woven carpets that decorated his palace.

'You must leave now,' the guard added.

'Very well.' Ahmad turned to the Khalifa once more and said, 'May Allah protect and bless you, Your Majesty.'

The Khalifa did not reply but continued to mumble to the unseen ghosts from his past.

'Is there nothing we can do to make his life more comfortable?' Ahmad asked the guard.

## The Ring of Flames

'What's the point? He'll be dead before the week's out. I've seen it all before. The arrest is just for show. Tomorrow or the next day, some cut-throat will be sent here to bribe the guard and he'll slip into the Khalifa's cell and then it will be all over. And an end to his incessant complaining, thanks be to Allah.'

Ahmad looked at him in horror. Was this al-Mahdi's plan? To eliminate any threat to himself by murdering al-Hisham? Rafiq had been right. The Khalifa's life was in danger, but from more than one source. What could he do about it? How could he prevent it? If only Rafiq were here, but he was hundreds of miles away in León. He looked down the damp, narrow corridor that led to the bleak dungeon which was the Khalifa's present home and shuddered. The walls seemed to be pressing in on him. He was struggling to breathe and his heart was banging wildly in his chest. He had to get out. He had to get out into the fresh air. He turned and ran towards the locked doors.

'Let me out,' he cried to the guard. 'Let me get out of here. Open up, I say.'

'Take it easy now, my man. Let me get the door unlocked first,' the guard said, then added in a genial tone. 'Don't worry. You're not the first to feel the terror of being inside this prison. My advice to you, my man, is to go home to your family and your falcons and forget the Khalifa. You can do nothing for him, now.'

Ahmad didn't reply. He had to get away from that awful place before he collapsed. It brought back too many dreadful memories of his own experience.

Once he was outside in the street, he threw his head back and breathed long and deeply to clear his lungs of the stench of imprisonment. Gradually he felt his heart slow and his breathing become normal. Dawn was breaking and a sliver of pale light lay along the horizon. Already the clouds were taking on a pinkish hue and the stars were fading fast in the once velvet night sky. It was good to be outside, to be standing there, a free man. He had been falsely accused and imprisoned once, when he was a young boy. It had been the worst experience of his life and he had languished there in his cold cell in total despair until his father had found proof of his innocence. After a few weeks he had been released, but the horror of that time stayed with him. The Khalifa would never know what an effort of will it had been for him to visit him today.

The air was still cold, so he pulled his cloak around him and set off for home. He needed to see Aisha and his family before he could face the world again. Then he must decide what, if anything he could do to help the Khalifa.

## CHAPTER 8

Salma hurried through the poorly lit, narrow alleyways towards the Dar al-'ilm, her cloak pulled over her head. Since the coup the streets were not safe. The city was crawling with soldiers, al-Mahdi's men. They said that the Khalifa had been arrested and thrown into prison and Muhammad al-Mahdi had declared himself the rightful ruler of al-Andalus, Muhammad II. He was the fourth Omayyad Khalifa, but unlike his predecessors he was intent on destroying their beautiful city rather than improving it. The enormous palace that al-Mansur had built by the river— which Sanchuelo had claimed for himself— had been razed to the ground. It had taken three years to build his magnificent home and three weeks for al-Mahdi to obliterate it. She felt sick when she thought about the devastation. Salma had never visited it herself, but one of her colleagues in the university had gone there once. He had been a young professor at the time, a man of science summoned there by al-Mansur along with other eminent professors. He told her what a traumatic experience it had been for him to hear al-Mansur order them to burn all the science books in the library and, on top of that, to be forbidden to study his beloved chemistry. Nevertheless, despite all that, he could still relate what treasures he had seen in the new alcázar. It was a palace to rival all others. The doors were of carved ebony, the gardens filled with marble and ivory statues. He said the ceilings were of gold, that the walls were painted with the most beautiful designs and Persian rugs covered the floors. Even the Khalifa's palace in Madinat al-Zahra could not compare, he said. And now it was gone, in a vengeful gesture executed by this new pretender. The buildings were in ruins, gutted, their treasures looted and the servants killed. All that would await Sanchuelo's return was a pile of smouldering rubble. The fire they had built had burned for three days and even now the air was acrid with smoke and a film of ash covered the surrounding streets. She pulled her scarf over her face to cut out the smell, and quickened her step.

It was the people of Córdoba who wanted to get rid of al-Mansur's son. They were astonished and very angry when they heard that he was to be al-Hisham's successor. They said he had taken advantage of al-Hisham, a simpleton steeped in debauchery. They wanted an Omayyad to rule, but this time they wanted a strong man, one who would be a true Khalifa. So they had risen up against Sanchuelo and chosen Muhammad al-Mahdi to lead the coup.

Salma had no personal opinion on the matter. As far as she could see they were all as bad as each other, driven by a lust for power and personal greed. Why didn't people understand that these men cared nothing for their city nor their heritage. They acted out of private gain and nothing else. Why couldn't people see that? The days of al-Hakim II—the man who had made their libraries the byword for knowledge in all the civilised world—were gone. Nowadays the men who wanted to govern their country cared for nothing more than power and riches.

'Salma, is that you?' A young woman, wearing the distinguishing yellow sash of the Jews, emerged from a shop doorway. It was Rachel, a friend who worked in the library, translating books and manuscripts from Hebrew to Arabic.

'Rachel. As-salama alaykum.'

'Wa alaykum e-salam, dear friend. Have you heard? They pulled a body out of the river this morning,' Rachel said, pulling the door to the shop closed behind her.

'Who was it? Do you know?' Salma asked, already walking on.

'No. A slave, a eunuch, they say. Nobody of any importance. Anyway, why the hurry?' Rachel asked, hurrying to catch up with her.

'I want to get to the library to make sure everything is safe. This looting makes me fearful. Now they have taken all they can from Sanchuelo's palace they might turn to the university and the libraries. We need to protect the books,' she replied.

Salma was a scribe. She had a natural talent for calligraphy and illustrating and when she'd finished her schooling, had been lucky enough to get a job in one of the many libraries in the city. She loved her work. To her it was like being in heaven to enter that cool, quiet space each morning and sit and copy the texts she'd been given. She never tired of it and she was never bored. The books were her life. When the elderly professor had told her about the destruction of all the books of science, she had felt as though a dagger had been plunged into her heart. The thought of such a treasure of knowledge going up in flames—not just chemistry, but physics, astronomy, astrology, logic and many more—had horrified her and left her with a fear that other books would one day suffer the same fate.

'Why would they want to loot the university? What on earth would they want with a load of books they probably can't read or understand?'

'You're thinking logically, Rachel. Looters don't think logically. They just take what they can. And if they don't want it, they destroy it.'

'Well, we're here now. So you can stop worrying,' her friend said. 'It looks like it will be a clear, bright day. Plenty of light to work by, not like yesterday.'

The previous day the sky had been dark with heavy rain clouds and, inside the library, it had been hard to see what she was copying. She had lit the oil lamp but the wick was poor and flickered so much that it was better without it, so in the end she spent most of the day paring nibs and hollowing pens and making up the mixture of oak galls, gum and vinegar to prepare the ink. Today she would be able to get on with what she really loved, the actual calligraphy.

The library where she worked was part of the university and contained all the most important works on medicine—a science that, fortunately, al-Mansur had spared from the flames. It was a large building, topped with a magnificent tiled dome and inside it was divided into an upper and lower storey. There were rooms especially set aside for readers, who came to sit cross-legged on the thick Arabian carpets that covered the floors and studied their particular specialisms, rooms filled with shelves and shelves of books and manuscripts, some made of vellum, some of parchment and even some books imported from Baghdad, made from paper. She worked in one of the rooms on the ground floor, in the area dedicated to scribes and copyists.

The two young women walked through the gardens that surrounded the library and past the ornamental lakes. It was a place of tranquility and learning and seemed far removed from the chaos outside the walls.

'As-salama alaykum, Salma, Rachel. I trust you are both well?' an elderly man with a long white beard said, bowing slightly. He was the Chief Scribe and the one who directed their work.

'Wa alaykum e-salam,' the women responded. 'Very well, thank you.'

'And Rachel, how is the treatise on The Use of Herbs for Cooling the Blood proceeding?' he asked.

Rachel was in the middle of translating the manuscript from Hebrew to Arabic. It was a slow and laborious business.

'It is going very well, Hajj. Thank you.'

'Good, good. And your work, Salma? Is it completed yet?'

'Yes, Hajj. I will bring it to you later this morning,' Salma replied. The book she'd been copying was finished but yesterday, on the very last page, she'd made a mistake. She blamed it on the poor light. Now she had to scrape away the offending area and make it good before he saw it.

'Good, good. Bring it to me when you are ready. Mmn. Yes. Well done.' He walked away, nodding his head in approval.

The young women looked at each other and giggled.

'I'll see you at mid-day, in the garden,' said Rachel. 'You can tell me how your romance is going with the young Anglo-Saxon monk.'

Salma said nothing, but couldn't prevent the blush that spread up her neck and covered her face in seconds. Rachel was referring to Simon, a man who had come here to study a few years previously and never returned to his native land. She and he had become close friends, but she hesitated to call it a romance. For one thing it was forbidden, and besides which her father, before he died, had had someone else in mind for her as a husband. He had been the son of a colleague of her father, but he had tired of waiting for her and married his childhood sweetheart. Her grandmother said he'd probably still take her as a second wife if they approached the family. Salma didn't want that to happen.

She went to her workplace and sat down. The book she'd been working on was called 'Bones of the Human Foot.' She had found it very interesting and spent many hours since staring at her own feet and tracing the bones with her fingers. The Chief Scribe had given it to her because she was particularly accurate at what she drew and the book contained many anatomical drawings. She took her penknife from the pocket of her robe and scraped carefully at the last few words in the book. It was tiring work copying, and yesterday with the dingy light, she had written the same word twice. She could have left it and probably nobody would have noticed it until some student read it, weeks or years hence, but she liked to do her job well. She took great pride in her work and couldn't rest until her error had been corrected. She had to be careful or the knife would dig into the parchment and tear it. Gradually, bit by bit she removed the offending words, then she took her pumice stone and sanded the surface until it was smooth.

'Salma.'

She looked up. It was Simon. He was so different from the other men she knew—tall, fair-skinned and very blond. His

## The Ring of Flames

golden hair was shaved at the front and he wore the same zunar as all the other Christians, in a blue so vivid it matched his eyes. He'd told her he was from a monastery in Wessex, in the land of the Anglo-Saxons. He'd travelled many thousands of miles to study here in the university of Córdoba and now he didn't want to leave.

'As-salama alaykum,' she said shyly, bowing her head so that he wouldn't know she was looking at him.

'Wa alaykum e-salam,' he replied. His command of their language was excellent. That was why he'd been sent here to see what the monks could learn from the writings of antiquity. He should have left last year, taking with him copies of the books he'd been instructed to find. Instead he'd stayed, and now worked in the library, not only translating works from Hebrew and Arabic into Latin but also from Latin and Greek into Arabic.

She secretly hoped that it was because of her that he hadn't returned to his native land.

'This is for you,' he said, handing her a reed pen.

'Thank you,' she said, taking the pen and examining it. It was hollowed perfectly and the point had been sharpened and split to form a perfect nib. 'It is a fine pen.'

'Fine penmanship deserves a fine pen,' he said, solemnly.

'Thank you,' she said again and added, 'I must hurry now because I have something to finish for the Chief Scribe.'

'Of course. Please don't let me delay you.'

He seemed embarrassed and hurried back to his desk.

Salma laid the pen on the writing table. She wouldn't use it now. It would look odd to finish the book with a different pen. Anyway, she always used pens made from falcon's feathers—supplied in great quantities by her second cousin Ahmad—because she found them lighter and more flexible. But this was a present and she would cherish it, even if she didn't use it very much.

Carefully she wrote the missing words on the last page of the book and sat back and admired her handiwork. You couldn't tell

## The Ring of Flames

there had been any corrections. She was pleased with it. It had taken many months to copy this book and, although Salma had enjoyed doing it, she was glad it was finished. She was looking forward to doing something different. Only this year she had been promoted from a junior copyist to a scribe. She still had plenty of copying to do but she also had things to write for the library—small things, nothing too important, compiling new catalogues for the bookshelves and writing simple instruction manuals. It made her feel important and her grandmother had been very proud when she rushed home to tell her of her promotion.

Salma closed the book and put it to one side. She had to check on the ink she'd prepared the previous day. She walked into the area everyone called 'the kitchen' where pots of ink in various stages of preparation were standing. The iron-gall ink took several weeks to be ready but it was important to stir the mixture each day. She picked up a spatula and stirred at her own pot. The smell was obnoxious. Whether it was the vinegar or the bitter galls that it contained, she didn't know, but something smelled rancid. Maybe it was the gum they added to make it stick to the parchment. Luckily by the time it came to use the ink, the smell had usually disappeared.

Another of the copyists came in to check on the progress of his own ink.

'Have you heard the latest news, Salma? Sanchuelo has been seen approaching the city. Our illustrious Chief Scribe has recommended that everyone go home and that we lock up the library until we know it's safe. Who knows what will happen when his army enters the city?' he said.

'But what about our work?' Salma asked. It was hard to be fearful in this serene environment but she knew he was right. Anything could happen when the two armies met.

'It will still be there tomorrow. Go home and stay indoors. That's what I'm going to do. I expect it will be all over by the morning.'

He gave his own pot of ink a quick stir and was gone.

## The Ring of Flames

By the time she got back to her desk, most of her colleagues had already left. Only Simon was waiting for her.

'Thank goodness,' he said. 'I thought you'd already gone. I'll walk along with you.' He handed Salma her cloak and ushered her to the door. 'We must hurry. It's not safe to be out on the streets.'

'Thank you,' she said. 'But I must find Rachel before we leave.'

She ran the length of the scribes' room and there was Rachel, head down, oblivious to all around her.

'Rachel, come quickly. The soldiers are coming. We must leave. They're going to lock up the library. Hurry.'

Rachel got up slowly, looking dazed at what Salma was saying. Her head was obviously still full of Hebrew phrases and Salma's words were taking a while to sink in.

'Now, Rachel. Come on. Everyone's gone already. Hurry.'

The two girls ran back to where Simon was agitatedly waiting for them. 'Come on,' he said, grabbing Salma's hand and almost dragging her to the door. 'If we don't go now, they'll lock us in.'

Salma took one last look at her desk, a place of so many happy hours. The book she'd just finished was still lying there. She had to put it away before she left. She pulled away from Simon and ran to get it.

'Just a minute. I must put the book in a safe place,' she said.

'There's no time. Just bring it with you,' Simon said. 'Hurry. I can see them locking the doors.'

Salma tucked the book into her satchel and together they ran out into the street.

Outside it was chaos. People were running in all directions. Their fear was tangible. Everyone was desperate to get home, to leave the city or at least to find a safe place to hide from the soldiers. No-one would be safe when the armies met.

Salma lived with her widowed grandmother, close to the river —her parents had died of a disease that had swept the city when she was a child and she had been lucky to survive. Their house

## The Ring of Flames

was not far from that of her mother's cousin Ahmad. She would collect her grandmother and they would both go there.

'Come in here and stay with us,' Rachel said as she arrived at the gate to the Jewish quarter. Her house was just inside the walls and Salma could see Rachel's father busy boarding up the front of his shop.'You'll be safe here until tomorrow.'

Salma shook her head. 'No, I must get home to my grandmother. I can't leave her on her own.'

'Very well, but take care, dear friend,' Rachel said, putting her arms around her and hugging her.

'And you. See you soon,' Salma called. She would have said more, but Simon was pulling at her arm to hurry.

She began to feel frightened. The adrenalin was ebbing away and now all she could feel was the danger around them. Were things ever going to be the same again? She hoped the municipal police would be patrolling the streets, although they were usually more interested in how much was being charged for a loaf of bread. Somehow she didn't think the police would be taking on Berber soldiers.

'Come this way,' Simon said. He had tight hold of her hand now and it made her feel a little better to know he was with her. He pulled her down one of the alleys that led away from the mosque and the river. 'There'll be soldiers guarding the bridge. It's safer if we skirt round the back of the Jewish quarter.'

At first the alley was deserted, then just as they approached the corner, at the point where it split into two separate passageways, they ran straight into two of Sanchuelo's soldiers. The men were on their own and they'd been drinking; she could smell the wine on them before the soldiers even opened their mouths.

'Where do you think you're going?' one of them said, grabbing Salma by her cloak.

'Just trying to get home,' she said, her voice trembling.

'And who's this?' The second soldier asked. He had a recent scar across his face and was in a very aggressive mood. 'A

Christian is it? Holding hands with a lovely young Muslim girl? What are you playing at? Breaking the law, are you? Trying to abduct her?'

He grabbed Simon by the shoulders and shoved him hard against the wall. Salma heard a loud crack as her friend's head came in contact with the stone wall. Blood started to run down his face and she thought he would faint.

'Well, lost your tongue, have you?' the soldier continued. 'What are you up to? Where are you taking this woman?' He pulled the injured man roughly towards him and pushing his face close to Simon's, said, 'Well? Speak up, man or it will be the worse for you.'

Scarface unsheathed his sword and pointed it at the recumbent figure. 'Speak now or I'll run you through.'

Simon opened his mouth but only managed to groan before he slumped to the ground.

'We work in the library,' Salma gasped, wriggling free from the other soldier's grip. It was all she could do not to scream. 'We're going to deliver some books to a bookseller. The Christian is just a servant. He carries the books for me. Look, here's the one that I have to deliver.'

She picked up the satchel, which Simon had been carrying for her and opened it so that the soldiers could see what was inside.

'Books? Devil's work,' the first soldier muttered and tipped up the satchel so that everything fell out onto the ground. He kicked at the contents but there was nothing of interest to him.

Salma felt in the pocket of her robe for the penknife that she always carried with her. It wouldn't be much use against their swords but it made her feel better to know it was there.

The soldier with the scar, swayed towards her and leaned so close that she thought she would gag at the smell of his vile breath. 'You shouldn't be in the streets, you know. A pretty little woman like you,' he slurred, waving his sword at her. Then he turned back to Simon and said, 'You get her home and no funny

# The Ring of Flames

business or we'll come looking for you. Mark my words.' He lifted his sword and pressed the point against Simon's chest.

This time she couldn't contain it, her scream echoed down the narrow alleyway, bouncing off the stone walls and as the sound gradually died away she could hear instead the noise of a battle in the distance. It was coming from the direction of the Great Mosque and getting closer. More soldiers. More danger. They had to get away. They had to get home.

Luckily the soldiers heard it as well. 'Leave them. Come on, this way,' said the first soldier. 'We've got more important things to do than worry about a Christian servant and a screeching woman. Quick. Let's get going.'

He lurched off in the opposite direction to the battle but Scarface remained. He turned back to Simon and pointed his sword at his recumbent form. 'Well, the little lady can carry her own books from now on,' he said.

Before he could thrust his sword into Simon's chest, Salma had leapt at him and dug her penknife into his neck. The soldier dropped his sword and turned, bewildered, clutching at his wound. Blood spurted from his neck like a fountain. Salma was horrified. What had she done? The soldier staggered towards her. He tried to speak but could only make a gurgling sound before falling to his knees. He knelt at her feet, his blood continuing to spurt through his fingers. There was nothing he could do to stem its flow. It soaked into the gravel road and it stained the hem of her robe. She stared at it. She stared at the soldier, at her robe, at the blood-stained knife in her hand. She had done this to him. She had stabbed him. Now he was going to die. She wanted to help him but she couldn't move. Then it was over. The soldier toppled to one side and lay there, his unseeing eyes open, accusing her.

'Salma,' a weak voice called.

Simon. She rushed over to him. 'Are you all right?' she asked. Blood was dripping from the cut on his head and he still seemed rather groggy but he was conscious.

## The Ring of Flames

Salma pulled him to his feet. 'Can you walk? Simon? We have to leave, right now. Simon?'

At last he focused his eyes on her and nodded.

'Come on. There's no time to waste. We must go now. There're more soldiers coming. We have to go, Simon. Now,' she almost screamed at him. They had to get away from the dead soldier before they were caught. They would show them no mercy if they found out what she had done.

She wiped her hands on her skirt to remove the blood. Then she stuffed the book back into her satchel, slung it over her back and put her arm around Simon's waist. Together they stumbled down the alleyway towards the river. It was hard going. Simon had difficulty in keeping his balance and more than once had to stop and rest. He was very pale and the blood from his head was dripping onto his tunic. He looked ghastly but she knew they had to keep moving. She did what she could to hold him up but it wasn't easy. He was a tall man—but luckily sparse of frame—and she was short and plump. Her father used to call her 'his little churros,' because she was very sweet and round, he said. Thinking of her father made her want to cry but there was no time for tears. She had to get Simon to safety.

The sound of fighting was getting louder. She hoped that Simon had been right and that the battle was concentrated on the Roman bridge that crossed the Guadalquivir. It was in the opposite direction to her grandmother's house and all they would have to do was follow the riverbank until they reached safety.

*

They passed no more soldiers, although the sounds of fighting were all around them. Allah was protecting them, Salma was sure of it. When she got home she would say some extra prayers of thanks to him and ask for his forgiveness. She had taken a life today. That was a sin. But was it a sin if she did it to protect someone else? She couldn't see that it was. She pushed the thoughts from her mind. For now the most important thing was to get Simon to safety.

At last they arrived at the river bank. She could see the battle in the distance, raging by the main bridge into the city, but ahead of them all was peaceful. They turned west and walked as close to the reeds as possible. She would have liked to climb down the bank and make her way under cover of the riverside vegetation but the ground was too uneven for Simon and she knew she would never be able to support him down there. So they took their chances and walked in plain view of any passersby. Not that there was anyone about. Everyone had disappeared off the streets; even the usual stray dogs were nowhere to be seen.

At last Simon began to regain a sense of where they were and what had happened to them; he no longer leaned against her like a sack of corn but managed to walk beside her, slowly but at least unaided. She moved the heavy satchel from one shoulder to the other. The strap was cutting into her neck.

'We're almost there now,' she told him, encouragingly. 'Then you can rest.'

The Christian didn't reply. All his energy seemed to be focused on putting one foot in front of the other. Salma whispered up a prayer, 'May Allah keep us safe from harm.'

'It's just round that bend,' she said. 'My grandmother's house.'

'Thank you,' Simon whispered. These were the first words he had spoken since the attack.

\*

Salma's young cousin Makoud was there when she arrived at her grandmother's old stone house.

'Salma. Thank goodness. We've been so worried about you,' he said, hugging her to him. 'I've come to persuade Teta that she should come and stay with us for a while. You'll come too, won't you?' He looked at Simon. 'Who's this? What's happened to him? Why has he got blood all down his tunic? And you, your robe is covered in blood? Are you hurt too? Why are you shaking so?'

'In a minute, Makoud. I'll tell you everything in a minute.' She turned to her grandmother. 'Teta, can you help him? He's lost a lot of blood.'

Now that they were safe at home, the tears started to flow. It was stupid but she couldn't stop them. She brushed them off her face, angrily, but still they came. She cried as though her heart would break. What had she done?

'My dear Salma. What has happened?' Layla asked her. 'Here, come and let your grandmother comfort you, my poor child.'

Salma laid her head on her grandmother's shoulder. 'He would have killed us, Teta. I thought we were going to die. I had to do it. I had to do it. I know it was a sin but what else could I do?'

'Hush child. You're safe now. Don't cry, dearest one. Whatever you did, Allah will know you did it with a pure heart.'

'But I didn't, Teta. I hated him. I wanted him dead. Oh, what will happen to me? Will they lock me up?'

'Come now, no-one is going to lock up my sweet granddaughter. Enough of this nonsense. I expect you did what you had to do. Now let me have a look at that young man. He doesn't seem at all well. Makoud, put some water to boil, so I can clean up his wound,' Layla said, opening some large stone jars. 'I have just the thing to cure him.'

While Salma told her grandmother about the attack and what she'd done to save Simon's life, Layla unwrapped Simon's turban and began to examine the extent of his injuries.

'So this is the young man from the library that you talk about so much?' she asked, wiping away some of the blood so that she could see the wound.

'Yes,' replied Salma wiping her tears from her face. 'This is my grandmother, Simon. Her name is Layla. She used to be a pharmacist and she knows everything about herbs and potions. She'll make you better.'

'I'll try to,' said Layla with a smile.

'As-salama alaykum,' Simon said, trying to sit up. 'Thank you for helping me.'

'It is what I do. There is no need to thank me. Just lie down and keep still while I clean this up.'

'Why was he wearing a blue zunar?' Makoud asked. 'Is he a Christian?'

'Yes, he's a visiting monk who works at the library.' Salma explained. 'They've closed the library because of the soldiers, and sent everyone home. Simon wanted to walk with me to make sure I was safe. And it's a good job he did or I might not be here now.' She didn't like to think about what might have happened if she had met those two soldiers on her own.

'He has a bad wound to the back of his head,' Layla said.

'Yes, that's where one of the soldiers banged him against the wall. He lost consciousness for a while.'

'Oh dear, That's not good. Makoud, is the water ready?'

'Yes, Teta. Here it is.' The boy place the jug of hot water on the low table beside Simon.

'Good. Now, go and chop these up for me as finely as you can,' Layla said, handing him a bunch of calendula flowers.

She poured some of the water into a shallow bowl and sprinkled a handful of thyme into it. 'This will help stop any infection,' she explained to Salma.

'Can I help?' Salma asked.

'Yes, hold his head still while I cut away some of his hair. I need to see exactly how badly he's hurt,' she said, beginning to chop at his hair with some iron scissors.

'Why don't I do that, Teta?' Salma asked.

'All right, but be careful you don't dig them into the wound.'

Carefully Salma began to remove Simon's hair from around the injury. She had never seen this instrument before; it was like two knives joined together. 'Where did you get these, Teta? They're much better than a knife.'

'My nephew Qasim gave them to me. He got them from the hospital. But don't tell anyone—I'm not sure he was allowed to take them.'

'Qasim is a doctor,' Salma explained to the patient Simon. He was beginning to look a little like a plucked chicken. 'We will ask him to take a look at you later, when he gets back from the hospital.'

'He'll be busy today,' Makoud said, handing the chopped calendula to Layla. 'Is that fine enough, Teta?'

'Excellent. You will make a fine pharmacist,' she said, tipping all of it into the jug of hot water.

'I'm going to be a soldier,' he said. 'Like uncle Rafiq.'

'Oh, are you? And what does your father say about that?' Layla said, with a smile.

She left the calendula to infuse while she began to bathe Simon's head. There were bits of moss and crumbled stone in the wound but the damage wasn't as bad as it had first seemed. She took some tweezers out of her pocket and carefully picked the debris out of the wound.

'So, young man, why are you here in our beautiful city?' she asked Simon.

'I'm a student,' he replied, 'I was a novice monk in England and I came here to learn. That was four years ago.'

'And do you like living in Córdoba, a Muslim country?'

'Yes, I am very happy here,' he replied, wincing as she pulled a particularly large piece of grit from his head.

'Until today,' said Salma. She had put the scissors away and was sitting watching her grandmother work.

'Today was exceptional,' he said. 'I'm sorry I wasn't able to protect you more, Salma.'

'It sounds as though she was the one doing the protecting,' said Makoud, with a big grin. 'But then, I don't suppose monks are taught how to fight.'

'That's not fair,' said Salma. 'Simon had no weapon and the two soldiers were armed.'

'And drunk, by the sound of it.'

Her cousin Makoud could be so annoying at times.

'But you must find life much more restrictive here than in your own country?' Layla continued. 'I don't suppose you have to wear a zunar, for instance, so that you can be recognised as a Christian?'

'No, I don't, but being a monk has its own restrictions. I have to wear a brown robe and my hair is cut in a tonsure, so everyone knows that I'm a monk. I'm not allowed to marry.' As he said that, he looked across at Salma and smiled.

Salma felt a jolt of surprise. Was that why he was still here? Did he think that he could marry her? Surely he knew the law?

'It's not so different here,' she said. 'People cannot marry whomever they please. A Christian may not marry a Muslim woman, for example. Most Muslim women marry someone whom their father choses for them.' She could feel herself blushing as she spoke.

'But the Chief Scribe is married to a Christian woman. He told me so himself,' Simon said.

'Oh yes, a Muslim man may marry a Christian, but not the other way about.. The only bride you will find in Córdoba is a Christian one, I'm afraid,' Layla said. 'There that's clean now. I'll just put a touch of myrrh on it and then I'll bandage you up.'

'I'll do it, Teta,' said Salma. She took the strips of white cloth from her and began to wind them around his head.

'Now I want you to drink this infusion. It should help your wound heal. Not my first choice, I'd sooner put some dried hare's blood on it—that's more effective. I'll ask Qasim if he has any to spare when he comes back from the hospital.'

'Please don't concern yourself,' said Simon. 'I feel much better already.'

'Well you need to rest. We'll walk round to Ahmad's house with you and once we're there I'll give you something to make you sleep. Sleep is the best cure of all,' she said, putting her precious herbs back in their jars and tightening the lids.

Salma was only half listening. She was thinking about Simon. If only there was some way they could marry, but he would have to renounce Christianity and become a Muslim. Somehow she couldn't imagine him doing that. And then there was her family. What would they say? No, it was never going to happen and when he realised that he would return to his own country. She felt her heart sink at the thought.

## CHAPTER 9

It had been a complete disaster. The campaign had been abandoned and Sanchuelo had ordered them all to return home. Half the army deserted, slipping away during the night to look for other paymasters. Then Sanchuelo made his biggest tactical error. Irritated by their slow progress, he split the depleted army into two, so that he could hurry on ahead to regain control of Córdoba. This meant leaving the slower moving artillery, the siege engines and all the pack animals laden with provisions and extra weapons, to trundle on at their own pace. Rafiq and the jinetes were in the vanguard, along with some of the infantry. The remainder of General Tayyib's corp made up the rear. As the days passed, the distance between the two parts of Sanchuelo's army became greater and the few provisions that Rafiq's men had with them began to run out. By the time they reached Córdoba, the men were hungry, frustrated and exhausted from the forced march. Not surprising then that as soon as they reached the city, many of the soldiers were disinclined to fight. The battle was all over in a couple of hours.

Rafiq had taken the remainder of his jinetes and their horses to Madinat al-Zahra and left them there. Now they would wait for instructions from General Tayyib. After all they were the Khalifa's army. The problem was that al-Hisham was in prison and al-Mahdi had declared himself Khalifa. Who were they supposed to follow? And how long would the situation remain like that? If one thing was clear, it was that nothing was certain these days.

He took the Nogales road from the old city to Córdoba. It wouldn't take him long to reach Ahmad's house. He would stay there until he received word from the general.

As he approached the city walls, he veered off towards the river. No need to go through the west gate; he could reach the house by following the Guadalquivir. He dismounted and walked, leading Antarah by the bridle. It was wise to be cautious. The city would be full of soldiers and many would still be spoiling for a fight. Once their adrenalin was up, it couldn't just be turned off like a tap. Whichever side they were on, these men would be frustrated and angry. They would be scouring the city, looking for someone to take it out on. Suddenly Antarah stopped and lifting her head, whinnied softly.

'What is it girl? What can you see?' he asked, pulling his sword from his belt.

The night was dark; what little moon there was temporarily shrouded in cloud. Just the night for an ambush. Carefully he walked on, keeping close to the city wall. There was the smell of burning in the air and the westerly wind was blowing it right at him. Sanchuelo's palace. It had still been smouldering when they'd arrived. Their Supreme Commander had been furious when he'd seen the pillars of smoke coming from the remains of Medina Azahira. He had lost all control and charged straight for the bridge. They'd had no chance. Al-Mahdi's archers picked them off one by one as they attempted to cross into the city. General Tayyib had tried to reason with their commander, but Sanchuelo was beyond reason. Then suddenly it was all over. He remembered the shame he felt when Sanchuelo was captured. How powerless he was. But there was nothing he could do. General Tayyib did the only sensible thing in the situation, he retreated and led him men away. Looking back at the bridge Rafiq saw them hoist Sanchuelo's head up on a pole above the city gates, a bloody, unrecognisable blob. The image had stayed with him.

Someone was waiting for him. He could feel it in his bones. And Antarah knew it too. He could hear her blowing softly through her nose. He stroked her gently, trying to calm her but he could feel her tension beneath his finger tips. She was a war-horse. She could sense danger. All at once a figure emerged from the shadows, followed by another and then a third. Three men, all armed. Soldiers. They'd been hiding in the reeds by the water's edge.

'Stop, in the name of the Khalifa,' one called out.

Rafiq could tell from his accent that this was a Berber, recently come to their land. Were they al-Mahdi's men? Or were they deserters from Sanchuelo's army? He didn't bother to answer. Surprise was everything in battle. He leapt up onto Antarah's back and charged straight at them, his sword raised to strike. The men scattered but not before one of them had lunged at Rafiq with his sword. The blow caught the pommel on his saddle and the sword spun out of the soldier's hand and landed in the river.

'Damn and blast,' the soldier exclaimed, scrabbling in the reeds.

'Grab his legs,' shouted one of them. 'Pull him down.'

But Rafiq was too quick for them; he dug his heels into Antarah's sides and urged her on. Before the soldiers could regain their wits, he was out of sight.

He let Antarah have her head for a bit, then reined her in to a walk. There was no sign of the three soldiers but that didn't mean that there was no more danger. There would be dozens of these groups of soldiers, leaderless and lawless. He must get to Ahmad's house as quickly as possible.

\*

The entrance to Ahmad's house was barred and bolted. Rafiq knocked loudly. There was no reply. He knocked again. Surely there must be someone home, his mother at least and Aisha. He tried knocking again and still there was nothing.

'Ahmad. It's Rafiq. Open up. It's bloody cold out here,' he called.

At last there was a creaking and scraping as someone pulled back the heavy wooden bars. Then the door opened and there was his brother.

'About time too. I'm freezing my balls off out here.'

'Nice to see you too, brother,' said Ahmad, opening the door just wide enough for his brother to get through.

'I've left Antarah outside.'

'Better bring her in too. I'll send Makoud to get some hay for her. Just take her through to the outer patio.'

Since there had been so many disturbances in the city, Ahmad had built an extra part onto their house, where they could keep their animals safe. Once those heavy wooden doors were locked for the night, all his family, including the animals, were securely inside. Like all their neighbours' houses, this one faced inwards onto a number of open-air patios—one for cooking, one for sleeping in the summer and now one for their animals. In the latter, there were two goats, a few chickens, a dog and now Rafiq's horse. He stroked her nose.

'You'll be safe in here, my beauty,' he said.

The squawking of some tiny hungry birds came from a box in the corner. It seemed Ahmad also used the patio for the falcon chicks that he sometimes brought home with him.

'As-salama alaykum, brother-in-law,' Aisha said. 'This is a pleasant surprise. Your mother will be so happy to see you.'

'Wa alaykum e-salam, sister-in-law.'

He looked around the room. There were more people than usual. All Ahmad's family were there: Rafiq's nieces, Bayda and Fatima, young Makoud, Qasim's wife and children, and Aisha. Yes, and there were Layla and her granddaughter. And a man he didn't recognise, with an enormous bandage around his head. He greeted each of them in turn, assuring them that he was well, that he was uninjured and that no, he didn't know what was happening out there.

'As-salama alaykum, my son,' said Amina, coming from her room, her sleeping robe wrapped tightly around her. 'Praise be to Allah that you are safe.'

He hugged her. How thin she was now. She felt like a twig that would break in his hands.

'Are you well, Mama?' he asked.

'As well as can be expected for an old woman like me,' she replied with a broad smile. 'And all the better to have you back with us, alive and well.'

'Are you hurt, Rafiq?' asked Salma. 'Is that blood on your sleeve?'

He looked at where she was pointing. She was right. That bloody idiot's sword must have nicked his arm.

'It's nothing. Just a scratch. I was attacked by three men on the way here,' he said.

'That's done,' said Ahmad, re-locking the door. 'Your beautiful mare is settled in, with her supper of hay and water. Now what about you brother? You look like you could do with some nourishment yourself.'

'I wouldn't say no to some food. We've been on half-rations for days and I haven't eaten anything yet today.'

'Sit down and Layla will dress your arm while I heat up some lamb tagine for you,' said Aisha.

'That sounds wonderful,' he replied. He was beginning to feel faint with hunger. 'So Simon, you work in the library with Salma, do you?'

'I do.'

'What happened to your head? Did a book fall on it?' he laughed and turned to Salma, 'I've always said that too much learning was dangerous and it seems I was right.'

'Don't be silly, cousin. We were attacked, the same as you, but we didn't have a big horse to escape on,' Salma replied.

He'd offended her. She didn't like him joking about something that must have been a very frightening experience for them. 'Sorry. I suppose it's become a habit, making light of danger. I couldn't be a soldier if I thought of all the perils that are out there.'

'Keep still. How can I clean this up if you keep fidgeting?' Layla said. His aunt was wiping the blood away from the wound. 'You're right. It's just a scratch. But that doesn't mean that it couldn't become infected. This should clear it up,' she added, smearing his arm with a gooey substance.

'So what has happened to Sanchuelo?' asked Ahmad.

'He's dead. Executed.'

'What happens now?'

'Your guess is as good as mine. In fact you probably know more than I do. Remember I've been out of the city for months,' Rafiq said.

'Well, as you probably have heard, al-Hisham is in prison and al-Mahdi has declared himself Muhammad II. But what will happen now, I have no idea. Your idea that al-Hisham would be murdered wasn't quite right, but the danger is still there.'

'It will always be there. He is, after all, the rightful Khalifa. Even though he's less than useless, he will always be a threat.'

'He's not useless,' protested Ahmad. 'He was never given a chance. I know. I was there. I saw how he was ignored and isolated and he was younger than my Makoud.'

Now he'd upset his brother as well as Salma. Maybe it was time he went to bed. Lack of sleep always made him too outspoken.

'Here eat it up while it's still warm,' Aisha said, putting a plate of lamb and aubergines in front of him. 'It's your mother's recipe, in case you're wondering.'

'I don't care who's made it. It looks wonderful,' he said, putting an enormous forkful into his mouth.

Well, at least tonight he would sleep soundly, in a soft bed, with a full stomach and no need to worry about the next day. It wasn't over. He knew that. But for the moment he could rest. Tomorrow he would face the future. Tomorrow there might be word from the General.

'This is the best meal I've had in a long time,' he told Aisha, his mouth full of the succulent lamb.

## CHAPTER 10

Muhammad al-Mahdi couldn't sleep. He had defeated one enemy —his head was rotting on top of the entrance to the city—but now there was another contender for the throne. He thought he'd been safe with al-Hisham locked up and Sanchuelo dead, but now this. The rumours had been flying around the court for some time. He knew of him. A distant cousin who by some tenuous link claimed kinship with al-Mahdi's grandfather, Abd al-Rahman III. A tiny drop of Omayyad blood and he thought that was enough to claim the throne? No he would have to quash this before it got out of hand. But who could he trust? Not any of those thieving Berber tribes for a start. They'd slice your throat just for the pleasure of it.

He got out of bed and threw his robe around his shoulders. Winter was approaching and despite the fire that burned in the hearth, his room was cold.

'Abdul, bring me some hot tea and then send for General al-Wahdi. I need to speak with him. Apologise for the early hour and tell him it's urgent,' he said. 'Take him to the throne room when he arrives. I will speak to him, there.' General al-Wadhi had served in the army a long time. He'd been a slave who'd risen to the position of general through hard work, bravery and above all, complete loyalty. Now he commanded an army of freed slaves. Men who were loyal to Muhammad II and men who would follow their general anywhere.

His servant bowed. 'Very well, Your Majesty.' He backed out of the room.

Your Majesty. Muhammad II. He loved the sound of it. He loved the way everyone bowed to him, how they jumped to his every command. He had harboured dreams about becoming

Khalifa for years, since childhood. He'd listened to his father talking about al-Hisham and saying what a disgrace it was to have an Omayyad Khalifa like him, how he should relinquish his position for someone else in the family, how even little al-Mahdi would make a better ruler than he was. Of course as he grew up he realised that al-Hisham wasn't just weak, he was completely powerless. All the power lay with the Grand Vizier, al-Mansur, and nobody felt capable of dealing with him, least of all his father. But that had all changed.

Another of his servants approached. 'Would you like me to help you get dressed, Your Majesty?' he asked. 'It is very cold today.'

'Yes, Jazuli. Bring me my white woollen djellab. The thick one. And a silk turban.'

\*

General al-Wahdi was waiting for him when he arrived in the throne room. As al-Mahdi looked about him he felt a pang of regret that he'd ordered the destruction of Medina Azahira, al-Mansur's palace. It was precipitous of him. There had been an occasion once when he had visited the throne room of the palace with his father, and he remembered how magnificent it had been in those days. Well, first things first. He would secure his position as khalifa, eliminate the opposition and then he would start thinking about building a palace for himself. And it would be bigger and more sumptuous than anything the people of Córdoba had ever seen.

'As-salama alaykum, dear friend,' he said when the General had finished the elaborate bowing ritual that protocol expected and which gave him such pleasure to witness.

'Wa alaykum e-salam, Your Majesty. I am honoured to be of service,' the General replied.

He was a man whose grizzled grey beard made him look many years older than al-Mahdi, although there were only ten years between them. He was short in stature, with strong arms and a barrel-like chest. He always gave al-Mahdi the impression that he was fearless, that there was nothing he would not tackle. Just what he required in a soldier. He had never enquired where the General was from; it was good enough for him that he was a Slav and had no Berber blood in his veins.

'I have a mission for you, General al-Wahdi. You have heard the rumours?'

'Yes, Your Majesty. Sulayman ibn al-Hakim is planning to seize the throne.'

'Exactly. We must stop him.'

'He relies on the Berber soldiers,' the General said. 'It is they who have nominated him as their Khalifa. There are thousands of them these days. There are entire contingents in the army made up of complete Berber families, so their loyalty is to themselves, to their tribe. I doubt if they even care for Sulayman, even though he has some Berber blood in his veins. They are good fighters, fierce and brave, but loyalty? No, the only loyalty they know is to their own kith and kin.'

'So how do we defeat them?' asked al-Mahdi.

'With respect, Your Majesty, the first thing you should do is to expel all the Berbers from the city. Córdoba is not safe with so many of them wandering around the streets.'

'Very well. See to it at once. Then what else? If that is the first thing, then what is the second?'

'We must attack them and kill Sulayman, as soon as possible. Use troops you can rely on, men you can trust.'

'Where is he now? Have your spies told you his location?'

'Yes, Your Majesty. He is in Calatrava, not far from the city of Toledo. It is rumoured that he has made a pact with Sancho Garcia of Castille. They have joined forces against you.'

'Then we will march there as soon as the troops are ready. Who can you rely on?'

'There is General Tayyib. I think most of his corps is still here in the city. And there is General Bishr. He can be relied upon. And your own militia, of course.'

'Very well, General al-Wahdi. Let me know when everything is prepared.'

'Yes, Your Majesty.' The General bowed as low as his stocky body would allow him and backed from the room.

*

Expelling the Berbers from the city had been relatively painless. The Palace Guard rounded them out and drove them through the gates like a flock of goats. It was reported that they headed north, no doubt to join Sulayman. The people of the city were glad to see them go. Now at last, they could move about freely and get back to their work.

Preparations for the campaign were almost complete and tomorrow at first light, al-Mahdi would ride out at the head of his army to defeat the Pretender to his throne.

'Your Majesty,' Abdul said, coming in and waiting with bowed head.

'What is it, Abdul?'

'The Chief Assayer is here with your new coins.'

'Excellent. Excellent. Send him to the throne room and I will meet him there.' Al-Mahdi insisted on only meeting his ministers in the room he had designated as his throne room. He wanted them to acknowledge who he was. He wasn't an upstart, like Sanchuelo or a sham like Sulayman. He was the grandson of al-Rahman III and he wanted them to remember that.

The assayer was an old man, bent as a reed in the wind. He had a servant with him, carrying the box of coins.

'As-salama alaykum, my good man. What have you brought me?'

He could hardly contain himself. These coins would have his name on them.

'Wa alaykum e-salam, Your Majesty. I have brought you the coins which you ordered to be cast.'

He signalled for one of the servants to open the box and then he took out a round silver coin and handed it to al-Mahdi. It was beautiful. It nestled in his hand, this perfect dirham, the width of

# The Ring of Flames

his finger. He held it up to the light and read the inscription on the front of the coin: 'There is no deity except God alone. He has no equal.' Then he turned it over. 'The Imam Muhammad Commander of the Faithful' and there below it, his name: 'al-Mahdi by the grace of Allah.' It was truly beautiful. Now he would be remembered as one of the Omayyad khalifas. Maybe the best yet. Who could tell?

'You have done very well,' he told the Chief Assayer, as he continued to rub the coin between his fingers. There was an intricate annulet on the reverse side. All in all, it was excellent. 'You may leave now. Take the coins to the Royal Mint and replace some of the old ones with them.'

In time all al-Hisham's coinage would be removed and melted down and only his would remain. But now it was time to turn his mind to other things— the battle against Sulayman. Once he had defeated him he would return and get rid of al-Hisham. Then there would be nobody to stand in his way.

## CHAPTER 11

Salma walked as far as the Grand Mosque then turned away from the river towards the Jewish quarter. Now that the soldiers had gone she could resume her old habits, one of which was her early morning stroll by the riverbank. She always left her grandmother's house at first light, and walked directly into the sunrise so that she could watch the sun begin its daily climb and see the city gradually come alive in its rays—the cold dark walls turning to warm shades of pink and gold, the mosaics glinting and sparkling. Today was no different although the morning was cold and Layla had forecast snow before the day was out. She hoped her grandmother was right. Salma loved it when the city was covered in its white coat—something that happened only a few times each winter.

The library was open again and today she could go back to work. Yesterday Simon had returned to his lodgings near the university and she and her grandmother had moved back into their own home. They said it was safe now, but she was not so sure. Rafiq had been sent for by General Tayyib and was on his way north to fight for Muhammad II against another pretender. She didn't understand it. One day Rafiq was fighting against al-Mahdi and now he was fighting for him, against someone else. Her cousin had tried to explain it to her. He said that he was a simple soldier. He fought where and when he was told. He didn't care much for al-Mahdi but he trusted his General. That was what mattered to him. And anyway what choice did he have? She understood that. If he refused to fight then he would be labelled a deserter and executed.

It wasn't the fact that there was a battle that frightened her—battles were a way of life here. They were constantly fighting

## The Ring of Flames

campaigns against the Christians in the north, and had been for years, but this was different. This was a battle for the throne, between opposing sides of Muslims and it affected everyone, not just the soldiers. Last time the battle had been in Córdoba itself and this time Córdoba was the prize once more. This was where the victor would come to claim his throne. If al-Mahdi lost then the city would be in turmoil again. No it wasn't safe yet.

She turned down the narrow walled road where Rachel lived. Her friend was standing in the doorway talking to her father. She noticed that the door to the shop was damaged, as though someone had tried to break it open.

'As-salama alaykum, Rachel. Are you ready?' Salma asked, unable to take her eyes off the splintered door.

'Wa alaykum e-salam, Salma.' Rachel kissed her father on the cheek and said, 'Don't worry Baba. I will come straight home.'

She took her friend's arm and together they walked down the alley. 'You saw the door?'

Salma nodded.

'Someone tried to break it down last night, but they didn't succeed,' she whispered. 'My father is very worried. He thinks something bad will happen to us. He didn't want me to go to work today. He says it's still not safe.'

'He could be right,' said Salma. 'But at least there aren't any soldiers on the streets. Not now, anyway.'

'So, tell me all that's happened,' Rachel said, smiling at her. 'Have you seen Simon since he walked you home?'

Salma explained how they'd been attacked on the way to her house.

'So he stayed with you all this time?' she asked, her eyes wider than usual. 'What did your grandmother think of him?'

Salma remembered how her grandmother had taken her aside that first evening and said, 'Don't let him fall in love with you, Salma. It's not fair. I've seen him looking at you. You will only break his heart. You know you can never marry him.'

But all she said to Rachel was, 'She thought he was nice enough, for a Christian.'

'But didn't she wonder why he had walked you home?' Salma could see Rachel was determined to find out all she could.

'It was obvious. He was a colleague escorting me home because of the danger. What else would she think?'

'Come on Salma. Surely something happened. You were with him for five days. Did he try to kiss you?'

'No, of course not. I told you; he was injured. That was why he stayed. He wasn't well enough to leave.' She couldn't tell her about her suspicions because then Rachel would never leave it alone. 'Anyway, what about you? Have you met the young man your father has chosen for you yet?'

'I don't want to talk about that. He's awful. And he's not young. He's old and pompous,' Rachel said, pulling her pretty face into a scowl. 'I've told them I'd sooner not marry at all than marry an old man.'

'I'm sorry. You seemed very excited about it last time we spoke.'

'He lives in Seville. I would have to leave Córdoba and all my family and friends. I won't do it, even if he is rich. I told my father.'

'What did he say?'

'He said he would look for another husband for me, but I must try not to be so choosey, next time.' She laughed. 'I knew he didn't really want me to leave Córdoba.'

By now, they had reached the library and it was time to go their separate ways. Salma's first job was to take the book 'Bones of the Human Foot' to the Chief Scribe, but before she could do that she had to check how much damage had been done when the soldier tipped it out onto the road. If the Chief Scribe discovered she'd taken the book home with her he'd dismiss her instantly.

'I'll see you at lunchtime,' she said to Rachel.

When she got to the Scribes' Room, she carefully unwrapped the book and took it out. Luckily it was hardly damaged at all, just a tiny scrape of mud on the cover. She'd have that cleaned up in no time.

As she worked away at removing the stain, gently scraping and sponging it until it had gone completely, her thoughts went back to Rachel. Her friend had declared she would sooner not marry than marry an old man. Salma wanted to marry for love. It wasn't usual—most children, both boys and girls, took the advice of their parents—but it wasn't unheard of either. She was sure her grandmother would agree to her marrying for love, but nobody was going to let her break the law. Nobody was going to allow her to marry a Christian. Well, perhaps she wouldn't marry at all. She had her work. That would be enough for her. But even as she thought it, she knew it wasn't true. She wanted Simon. She wanted him as her husband.

\*

Simon's head still ached from the attack. He was supposed to go to the library today and resume his work, but he couldn't focus. The medicine that Layla had given him made him drowsy all the time—she'd said that was a good thing, that what he needed was lots of rest—but he wanted to get back to work. And more than that he wanted to see Salma again. He was certain she cared for him. The way she blushed when he spoke to her, the way she avoided looking directly at him, and when he caught her eye unexpectedly, how she would look away in embarrassment. When they met at work, it was much more natural; they were colleagues and could talk about the books. There in her home, with her family watching their every move, he felt her withdraw from him. He had to know how she felt.

Simon had loved her from the first moment he'd seen her. She had been sitting at her desk, a book open before her, a quill in her hand and a look of the deepest concentration on her beautiful face. She was an angel. Even if he was a monk, a servant of God, how could it be wrong to love such a perfect creature? He had wanted to stretch out his hand and touch her long, black silky hair, to make her smile, to stroke her downy cheek. This feeling that lit his life and filled him with joy was a gift from God. It was no sin. As he listened to his heart beating wildly in his chest, he knew that he could never go back to the monastery. His life was here, by her side. Even if they could never marry, it was enough for him to be close to her, to know that she loved him.

'Simon, the barid has brought a letter for you,' a fellow lodger said, handing him a rolled-up piece of parchment.

Simon had a room in a house owned by a widow who made her living renting rooms to visiting Christians. Most of them stayed a year or two before returning home. A devout Christian herself, who delighted in giving shelter to priests, monks and scholars, she had asked Simon on many occasions when he would be returning to his monastery. He had never given her a straight answer.

'Thank you, Nicholas.' He knew without opening it, what it was. It was from the abbot. Again. Each year he wrote to Simon to ask when he would return. It was obvious from his words that he feared Simon would abandon his religion and turn to Islam. Many others had done it. 'I'll read it later,' he said. He slipped the missive into the pocket of his robe and went back to his room.

The abbot was far more outspoken this time. He made it very clear that if Simon did not return before the end of the following year then he would have no choice but to excommunicate him, as he was sure that the reason for Simon's absence was an ungodly one.

This was serious. Simon was a true believer in Christianity and the Christian Church. Leaving the monastery was something he could tolerate but the thought of excommunication filled him with fear. He didn't doubt for one moment that the abbot would carry out his threat if he didn't return. But how could he leave without Salma? Perhaps he could persuade her to go with him. If not, was he prepared to risk his immortal soul and stay here with her? It was an impossible choice. How could he choose between his faith and the woman he loved? He felt as though his heart was being torn in two. He needed time. Time to find out if Salma really loved him. All he could do at the moment was to send a reply to the abbot to appease him and to ensure he didn't do anything hasty. In the meantime he would think carefully about his future and which way his path would lead.

He sat at his desk and began to write:

'*Esteemed Lord Abbot. I am in receipt of your letter and I hasten to assure you that I will make my return next summer, when the roads are easier for travel and the mountain passes are open. Forgive me for the delay in returning but I have been working very hard on behalf of the monastery, translating many interesting works from the ancient Hebrew to Latin. I am sure that when I return you will agree that my time away, although longer than originally expected, has been well spent. I remain, in God's faith,*

*Your humble servant,*

*Simon of Norwich.*'

He sprinkled sand on the letter to dry the ink, gently shook it clean, then read it once more before rolling it up and addressing it to the abbot.

'Nicholas. Has the barid gone?' he asked. 'I want to send a reply. It's urgent.'

'He'll be at the tavern by the mosque. You should catch him if you hurry,' said the landlady, who was hovering, no doubt wondering what was so urgent about his reply to the abbot.

'Here, let me take it for you,' said Nicholas. 'You don't look as though you could walk there, never mind run.' He grabbed the letter from him and was out of the door before Simon could object.

Oh well, there was no changing his mind now. He'd promised to return in the summer and now he would have to do it. But would Salma go with him?

## CHAPTER 12

Ahmad and a few of his companions had been out all morning, training the falcons. They were excellent birds, swift and ready to return to the glove after only a few weeks. He felt very pleased with their progress. As usual he returned from working with the falcons feeling reinvigorated and refreshed. The air up on the sierra was clean and cold, unlike in the city where a pall of smoke still hung over everything and grey ash covered the ground like a dirty blanket. He rubbed his hands together to warm them.

'There'll be snow tonight,' he said to another of the falconers. 'Mark my words. The birds could sense it.'

'You and the birds. You think they talk to you,' the falconer replied. 'They're just wild creatures. What they sense is a good meal, a nice fat rabbit running across the field, or a plump pigeon they can catch unawares.' He picked up a piece of leather and began working it into a jesse for one of the birds.

'What news of the Khalifa?' asked one of the older falconers, as he tethered a huge gyrfalcon to its perch. The bird had been a gift from a northern king to al-Hisham and was the only one in the Falcon House. A beautiful white rarity, it was as fierce as it was lovely.

'The one in Calatrava or the one rotting in a dungeon?' Ahmad asked bitterly.

'There's only one true Khalifa. You know that as well as I do.'

'He's not a well man. They won't need to assassinate him, he'll be dead soon anyway,' Ahmad replied. He had no intention of telling his friend that he was going to visit al-Hisham again that evening. He had told no-one of his visits, not even Aisha. He knew that he could be arrested and accused of treason if news of it got to al-Mahdi's ears. No point in implicating anyone else.

## The Ring of Flames

Well that had been his original plan, but now he had to involve his brother, Qasim. It was true what he'd said, al-Hisham was very sick. The doctor at the jail had given him a cursory look and said immediately that there was nothing he could do for him. Not only that, he'd painted a very black picture of what the Khalifa's last days would be like—blindness, hallucinations, tremors. It sounded a terrible way to die. Ahmad couldn't accept that. There had to be something that could be done to alleviate his pain at least.

'I have to go out,' he said. 'I need to see my brother but I won't be long. I'll be back in time to see to the birds this evening. If Nasir comes by, tell him I'm still up on the sierra.'

'Do you really think he'll come by? He's been here twice this month already. I don't think we'll see him again for a while,' said his friend with a laugh.

'No, you're probably right.'

\*

Ahmad headed straight for the hospital where Qasim worked. His brother was one of the senior doctors there now and had a small house in the hospital grounds, where he lived with his wife and three children. Ahmad had said it was about time he built himself a bigger house but Qasim was happy where he was; it was very convenient for his work, he said.

It was a long time since Ahmad had been there but the building was just as he recollected. He approached it from the North Gate and made his way to the entrance. From outside it was simply a large stone building with high walls but inside there were many rooms and gardens with fountains and sweet smelling plants—these he remembered very well. The previous time he'd been there was when he was a boy, as a patient. They took him there after he'd been wounded with an arrow, fearing that he would not live. That was something else he didn't want to think about. And again it was to do with al-Hisham—the arrow had been meant for him. He and the Khalifa were bound together by a shared past. It was not something he could dismiss lightly. That was why he felt that he should do something to help the unfortunate man—after all now that Queen Subh was dead, there was nobody else who was going to do anything for him.

The main door was open so he walked straight in. Immediately a male slave, wearing loose trousers and a grey tunic, came up to him and bowed. His head was shaved and his skin was the colour of ebony.

'As-salama alaykum, sayyad. How can I help you?' he said.

'Wa alaykum e-salam. I am here to see my brother, Doctor Qasim. Please tell him.'

'I am sorry, sayyad. He is with a patient at the moment. Can I get someone else for you?'

'No. It must be my brother. I will wait.'

'Very well, sayyad. I will send word that you are here.'

The slave opened another door and spoke quietly to someone. The gentle music of lutes playing somewhere inside the building floated through the open door along with those distinctive hospital smells that he remembered, sweet smelling anise, fragrant thyme, the pungent smell of frankincense and garlic. Instantly Ahmad was back there, lying in that hospital bed, gazing up at a ceiling covered in thousands of tiny stars that twinkled and sparkled by the light of the oil lamps. He'd fallen asleep thinking he was in the garden and that it was the night sky above him. That or he had died and gone to Heaven. The next morning when he woke with his shoulder on fire from the arrow wound, he realised he was in the recovery ward.

The door swung shut and instantly he was back in the present.

His brother had worked at the hospital since he was a student. He had studied under one of the most famous doctors of the age, Abu al-Zahrawi, who for many years had been al-Hisham's physician. The learned doctor was now retired, but he had passed on his skills to many other doctors, including Ahmad's brother. If anyone could help al-Hisham it had to be Qasim.

It took quite a while for his brother to finish whatever he was doing but at last the door opened and there stood Qasim. He looked quite different dressed in his doctor's robes. He wore a long grey tunic and had a grey turban wound around his head, hiding his hair. There was a stain down the front of his tunic— blood perhaps?

'Ahmad? What is it? Is everyone all right? Are you all right?' asked Qasim. 'Why are you here? Has something happened to Mama?'

'As-salama alaykum, brother. Yes, we're all fine. Mama is well. It's nothing to do with the family. I have come to see you on another matter. An urgent one.'

'Wa alaykum e-salam, Ahmad,' he said, embracing him briefly. 'You had me worried for a moment. So what is it that is so important that you have dragged me away from my patients? And why couldn't it wait until Friday?' Qasim and his family always visited his mother on Fridays, after he'd been to the mosque with his brothers.

'I'm sorry Qasim. There is no-one else I can turn to. Can we speak somewhere privately?' Ahmad asked, looking across at the slave.

'Of course, if you think it's really necessary. I'm very busy today, you know. There's a young man who was thrown from his camel and has lost the use of his legs and a woman who is going through a very difficult labour. But I suppose I can always spare a few minutes for my little brother,' he said, his voice softening. 'Come with me.'

He led Ahmad through the hospital passages, past closed rooms where he could hear people groaning and sometimes a shriek of pain, past the recovery room with its familiar scent of aromatic herbs and flowers, past the operating room where the stench of blood was barely masked by the antiseptic plants they used, and finally out into the gardens.

Once they were seated under the bare branches of a willow tree, he turned to Ahmad and said, 'So tell me now, what is it that's so urgent, brother?'

'I need you to come with me to visit al-Hisham. He's very sick.'

'Al-Hisham? But he's in prison. I don't know what *I* can do to help him. They have their own doctor for the prisoners.'

'The prison doctor's useless. Worse than that, he doesn't want to get involved. Everyone is frightened that if they help al-Hisham they will get into trouble, be seen as traitors. I was there when he went to see him. He didn't even examine him. He just said there was nothing he could do. And then he left.'

'It's probably true. I doubt if he can cure him. From what I hear he has an incurable disease, brought on by his degenerate life style,' said Qasim.

'It's not your place to judge him,' Ahmad snapped. 'You're a doctor. You took an oath, the Hipposomething oath. Doesn't that mean you're bound to help people, anyone who needs you? Regardless of the life they lead.'

'The Hippocratic Oath. Yes, I did take that oath, although we don't swear to Apollo as the Greeks did. We swear to Allah. And yes, you're quite right, I am bound by that oath to give help wherever and whenever I can, no matter who the person is, but that doesn't mean I can work miracles.'

'Just come and see him, please. Then if you say there is nothing to be done, I will be satisfied. I promise. Please come, Qasim.'

His brother gave a deep sigh. 'Very well, I will come with you, but tell no-one. If they know that I've secretly visited the Khalifa, it would mean that I'd lose my post here at the hospital. You've never understood the world of politics, have you Ahmad? But even you must realise that al-Hisham is never going to rule our country. There are powerful men who want his throne. In fact I am amazed that he is still alive. I can only think that his enemies must believe that he is so ill and useless that he poses no threat. But all that could change and I don't want to get caught up in it. I have my family to think about as well as my career.'

'I understand, brother. I do, truly. But you are the best doctor in the city, Qasim. You studied with the great physician al-Zahwari, the father of surgery. I know you can help him, even if you can't cure him. That is all I'm asking. I can't bear to think of him dying there in that dank cell, all alone and in pain. Please help him.'

'I've said I will and I will. Now let me get back to work. I will meet you this evening outside the prison gates. I hope you know someone on the inside who will be discreet.'

'I do, brother.'

'Very well, at sunset then, after prayers. Now I really must get back to my patients. Alla ysalmak.'

'Ma'a salama, dear brother and thank you,' Ahmad said, embracing Qasim.

\*

When he had finished his duties at the Falcon House and been to the mosque to say his evening prayers, he set off for the prison. His only worry was if he ran into one of the night watchmen. The al-Darrabun were a law unto themselves. They would think nothing of arresting him first and asking about his business second. And if they knew he was visiting al-Hisham, he'd be taken straight to the Muhtasib, the officer in charge of the municipal police. He quickened his step. Unless he was very unlucky, the same guard should be on duty. By now Ahmad knew the man's routine and so only visited the prison when he knew he'd be there. He also made a point of always bringing a few of Aisha's homemade sweetmeats for him.

'Ahmad, is that you?' his brother called from the shadows of the prison wall. He emerged into the light of the street lamps carrying a small bag. 'Well, are we doing this or not?'

Ahmad could see that his brother was impatient to get it over with and he couldn't blame him. Each time he came here he experienced the same feeling of dread as the prison gates closed behind him.

## The Ring of Flames

'I know the guard,' he whispered. 'He knew Baba. Don't worry. Just keep close to me.' He walked up to the sentries at the gate, his heart pounding.

'Halt,' the first sentry commanded, pointing his lance in their direction.

'Is that you Ahmad?' asked the other one.

'As-salama alaykum, my friend.' said Ahmad.

'It's all right. I know this man,' he told his comrade-in-arms. 'He has come to see one of the prisoners.'

The other sentry stepped back and resumed his watch.

'This is my brother,' Ahmad explained. 'He's a doctor. He is going to examine the prisoner. These are for you,' he added handing over the sweetmeats wrapped in a vine leaf.

The sentry lifted his lamp so that he could see Qasim's face.

'I know you,' he said. 'You work at the hospital. You mended my nephew's broken arm. Last summer. A small lad for his age. He fell from a tree. Do you remember him?'

Qasim shook his head. 'No, I'm afraid not. We have lots of small boys with broken bones. How is he now?'

'Fit as a flea. You'd never know it'd been broken.'

'I'm glad.'

'Now, come along the two of you,' the guard said, opening the door so that they could enter. 'I don't know how you'll find His Royal Highness. He wasn't moving much this morning and didn't eat the food they gave him at dinner.'

They followed the guard through the damp passages. The prison was even worse in the winter, with green mould growing across the ceilings.

'It's a wonder anyone can survive in here,' muttered Qasim, his eyes darting about, taking it all in. 'If they come in healthy, I doubt they stay that way for long.'

'Here you are, boys,' the guard said heartily. He unlocked the cell door and pulled it open. 'Two visitors today, Your Highness. Aren't you the lucky one.'

Al-Hisham was lying on a mat in the corner. He didn't move and at first Ahmad thought they were too late, that he was already dead but then he slowly opened his eyes and looked at them.

'As-salama alaykum, Your Majesty,' Ahmad said. 'I have brought you the doctor as I promised.'

Qasim squatted down beside the Khalifa. He was a pathetic sight, unwashed, his clothes filthy and torn, his hair long and greasy.

'Why has no-one been caring for this man?' he asked the guard. 'Where is his servant?'

'Who knows? He hasn't been to see him for a month at least. It's not our job to wash the prisoners. We're here to make sure they don't escape.'

'Of course, of course,' Ahmad reassured him. He didn't want Qasim to upset his only ally.

'Well get me some water, man,' Qasim said. 'And some soap and some clean clothes.'

The soldier glared at him and left.

'Be careful Qasim,' Ahmad whispered. 'Don't antagonise him.'

His brother ignored him and turned his attention back to al-Hisham. He pulled the moth-eaten blanket off him and slowly began to examine him.

'It's not good,' he said at last. 'The disease has taken a firm hold of his body. I'm not sure what I can do for him. It's no good looking at me like that, little brother. I can only tell you what I see.'

'Surely you can make him more comfortable?' Ahmad said.

'Here. Will these do?' asked the guard, placing a bowl of water, a piece of soap and some clothes on the ground beside him. 'It's all we could find.'

'We must get in touch with his servant and find out why he hasn't been coming to see him,' said Ahmad. 'I'll do it tomorrow.'

'In the meantime, you can give me a hand here,' said Qasim.

He turned to the guard, who still stood in the doorway watching them. 'Can you bring him something warm to drink and some food. Not too much.'

'He won't eat it. Every day they give him food and every day they take it away untouched. But I'll see what I can find. There may be some hot broth left from the guards' supper.'

'That would be excellent,' said Qasim. 'Good man. Right, Ahmad, let's get these rags off him and clean him up a bit.'

They stripped and washed the unresisting body of the Khalifa and then dressed him in the coarse clean robes that the guard had found.

'That will have to do for now. Poor soul, he has sores everywhere. Pass me that ointment. It might help to ease them.'

Ahmad watched as his brother expertly rubbed the myrrh on the Khalifa's feet, his groin, his lips and even on his genitals. For all he admired his brother's skill and dedication, he could not imagine doing such a task himself.

'I know what it is,' Qasim said, feeling first the neck and then the armpits of the man. 'We call it nuar. There is nothing known to man that will cure it. The ignorant think it's a punishment from a djinn but it is just a terrible sickness.'

'Will the ointment help it?' he asked.

'This? A little. All myrrh will do is ease the pain. When I get back to the hospital I'll make up a potion of poppy seeds that will make him feel more comfortable.'

He leant over the Khalifa and asked, 'How do you feel, Your Majesty?'

'Like I'm dying,' said a croaky voice. 'In the name of Allah why doesn't someone bring me some wine?'

Qasim looked at his brother. 'Wine?'

'He likes to drink wine, lots of it.'

'Well bring him some.'

'Will it make him better?'

'No, Ahmad. I've told you. There is no cure for what ails him. But if he has some wine, then maybe he will eat and maybe he will get stronger.'

'It's forbidden.'

'I know it's forbidden but it might make a difference to him. I suggest that you find his servant first and talk to him. Ask your friend, the guard, to turn a blind eye. Do what you have to. It was you who wanted to make his dying easy. I'm just making some suggestions,' Qasim said. 'I must go now. Come and see me tomorrow and I'll give you some medicines for him.'

'Thank you, Qasim. I'll stay a little longer and try to get him to eat,' said Ahmad, hugging his brother.

'Ma'a salama, Your Majesty,' Qasim said and bowed to the supine Khalifa. 'Till tomorrow, brother.'

'Ahmad,' the Khalifa whispered. His voice was as hoarse as a dying crow. 'How are my falcons?'

'They are well, Your Majesty.'

'I want to see them. Take me to see them, Ahmad,' the Khalifa pleaded. 'Take me away from here.'

'I can't Your Majesty. But it won't be long before you can go home.'

'Here's the soup for our royal prisoner,' said the guard with a smirk. 'I do hope you find it to your liking, Your Highness.'

'Thank you. I'll see if I can persuade him to eat some,' Ahmad said.

'There's no point promising him that he'll be going home soon. That's not likely to happen this side of Eid,' said the guard. 'Haven't you heard the news?'

'What news?' asked Ahmad.

'Sulayman has defeated the new Khalifa. It's all change again. Al-Mahdi has retreated to Toledo with his tail between his legs, like the dog that he is.'

'So who is the Khalifa now?'

'Sulayman of course. He's on his way back already to take up his throne. They say he's going to live in the alcázar in Madinat al-Zahra.'

'So he's not coming to Córdoba?' asked Ahmad, trying to take in this new change of leadership, so soon after the last one.

'Not for the moment.'

'What do you know of this Sulayman?' Ahmad asked. 'Is he a good man?'

'The son of the Devil? I'm telling you now, he's far worse than any of the others. Al-Mansur was a ruthless man, but compared to Sulayman he was a saint. Mark my words, Sulayman and his Berber hordes are going to devastate our country.' The old guard pointed to al-Hisham. 'He won't last long once they get here. And as for going home, well that's the last place he'll be welcome.'

'What's he saying Ahmad? What did he say about my beloved Madinat al-Zahra?' the Khalifa asked, his voice trembling.

'Nothing of any consequence, Your Majesty. Nothing for you to worry about. Here, try to eat some of this broth and then I will see if I can find some wine for you,' Ahmad said in the same voice he used to persuade his children to do something they didn't want to.

'I'll see if I can find a drop of wine for him,' the guard said. 'But don't tell anyone it came from me.'

'Thank you. It will be our secret,' said Ahmad. So many secrets and he could be flogged if any one of them were revealed.

He watched as the Khalifa sipped at the broth. Whatever happened next the Khalifa's future looked very bleak. But what did the new change of regime mean for the rest of them? Was Sulayman as bad as the guard said? Were they about to experience a reign of terror? Suddenly he wanted to get home. He wanted to make sure that his family were safe. He desperately needed to see them.

## CHAPTER 13

Ahmad had only got half the story—yes, Sulayman had won and Muhammad II was licking his wounds in Toledo but the victor had no intention of by-passing Córdoba. He had an army of ruthless men who wanted payment for their services. What better way to repay them than let them loose in Córdoba's fine city. Hordes of Berber mercenaries rampaged through the golden city, looting and destroying everything in their way.

The library was once more barred and locked to the outside world and Salma and the other scribes were sent home to fend for themselves. And once again she and her grandmother sought shelter in Ahmad's house. At least there they felt safe, although she had no idea for how long. It had been so chaotic at the library —that haven of peace and tranquility—that she had no time to find Rachel and there had been no sign of Simon. She had no idea where either of them were and it worried her. With all the treasures in their shop, Rachel and her father were a prime target for the looters. Salma had seen inside and it was just like Aladdin's cave with silver rings, bracelets, amulets, plates, jugs, tiny silver jewellery boxes—some made by Rachel's father and others imported from Byzantium. She prayed her friends had got away in time. What did it matter if their silver was stolen, as long as they were safe? As for Simon, she hadn't seen him since yesterday. She was about to go to look for him and suggest that he come to Ahmad's house with her, but the Chief Scribe virtually pushed her out of the door, so desperate was he to get to safety. Safety. Was anywhere safe at the moment?

'Salma, come and help me with these children,' Aisha called.

Ahmad's house was crowded with neighbours and family. The women bustled about, putting down their sleeping mats and sorting out bedding. One family had even brought its goat with them. The animal was tied up on the patio with the others and bleated constantly, its voice mingling with the constant chatter from the women. Salma looked around her. Where would they all sleep?

'Salma.'

'Coming, cousin.'

Aisha had a two-year-old girl on her lap and was trying to get her to drink some goat's milk. An older boy was sitting on the floor, crying.

'See if you can calm this boy. He refuses to eat or drink. He just cries for his mother,' Aisha said.

'Where is his mother?' asked Salma, looking across at the other women. Surely one of them could look after him.

Aisha leaned closer so that the boy wouldn't hear her and whispered, 'Dead. All his family, save this little one. Killed by the soldiers. Ahmad found them sitting outside the remains of their father's shop, crying. He didn't know what to do with them, so he brought them home.'

'Where is Ahmad now?' Salma asked. None of the men were there. The house was full of women and children —no men. She would have felt safer if at least one of her cousins were there, but Rafiq was in Toledo and Qasim refused to leave the hospital, although he had sent his wife and children to stay with them.

'I don't know. He's been behaving very strangely lately, wrapping up left-over almori and honey cakes in vine leaves and sneaking them out. I can't understand what he's up to. He knows I would give him food if he asked. Who's he taking it for? And why doesn't he want to tell me?' Aisha said, wiping a dribble of milk from the child's chin. 'Anyway, I expect he's at the Falcon House. You can't leave the birds unattended, even if the city is under attack. Well that's what Ahmad says.'

Salma put her arm around the little boy. 'What's your name?' she asked.

The child snuffled and wiped his eyes with the back of his hand. At last he managed to whisper, 'Omar.'

'Well Omar, don't worry. We'll take care of you now,' Salma said, trying to reassure him.

'I want Mama,' he suddenly burst out. 'Mama. I want my Mama.' Tears ran down his face and his little body shook with sobs that threatened to tear him apart.

Salma tried to hug him to her, but he was lost in his grief and pulled away from her. She thought of his parents, butchered by the soldiers and remembered her own fear when she and Simon had been attacked. It could have been them. Had the child seen his parents killed? The look in his eyes said that he had. Poor little boy. She felt her heart would break for him.

'I don't know what to do,' she wailed to Aisha. She had no experience with small children. Unlike other young women of her age, she'd spent no time looking after younger siblings—she was an only child and brought up by her grandmother. Her young life had been spent studying and later, working in the library. That was all she knew. 'Why can't Fatima look after him?'

'Fatima is preparing the food for this evening. Everyone has something to do, Salma. How else do you think we're going to feed all these people?'

'But he won't stop crying.'

'See if he'll go and play with Qasim's children. I know they're a bit older, but he might feel more comfortable with them,' Aisha said. The child in her arms had fallen asleep, her head lolling on Aisha's shoulder.

'All right.' Salma bent down and spoke to Omar. 'Would you like to play a game, Omar? Shall we see if those children over there know any games? What do you think? I'm sure they do. Shall we go and ask them?' She waited until his sobs lessened, and at last he nodded and took her outstretched hand. 'Good boy. Let's find out which games they know.' She racked her brain, trying to remember some games from her childhood, but it seemed such a long time ago.

\*

It was already growing dark when they heard a loud knocking at the outer door. Nobody moved. Nobody spoke. Even the children were silent. The knocking continued, more urgently than ever. At last a voice called, 'Salma, are you there? Salma. It's me, Rachel. If you're there please let us in. Please, Salma. We've nowhere else to go. Salma.'

'It's my friend from the library,' she said to Aisha. 'What should I do?' She looked at the frightened faces around her.

'Let her in, of course. Be quick,' said Amina. In the absence of the men of the household, she was the oldest, the wisest and the one in charge.

'But there are so many of us already,' said Bayda. 'Where will she sleep?'

'Don't worry about that. Makoud unbolt the door and let her in. But be careful, in case it's a trick,' said Aisha.

'Yes, Mama.'

Together Makoud and Salma unbolted the inner door and then opened the spy-hole in the outer one.

'It's her,' said Salma. 'It's my friend Rachel.'

Makoud pulled the heavy bolts back and flung the door open. Salma wanted to cry with joy. There was Rachel and her father, and standing behind them, his fair hair covered with the distinctive blue zunar, was Simon.

'Come in and be quick,' Makoud said, pulling the visitors into the house and slamming the doors shut behind them. 'It's all right, Mama. There were no soldiers in the street. Just Salma's friends.' He slid the bolts back into place and then shut and bolted the inner door as well.

'Rachel, I'm so pleased to see you,' Salma said as her friend put her heavy basket on the floor and embraced her.

'You too, Salma. Thank God you were here. We've been hiding in the city, and didn't know where else to go. It's terrible. The Berbers are everywhere and they have no respect for anyone. Our shop is destroyed. Fifty years my father has lived there and now there is nothing. They took everything. We only just escaped with our lives,' she said, tears coursing down her cheeks.

'Don't cry child,' her father said. 'You're safe now.' He turned to the others and added, 'They were more interested in the silver than in us, thank the Lord.'

'Well, you are welcome to stay here as long as you need to,' Amina said.

'May God bless you and keep you safe from harm,' the old Jew said. 'You have done a wonderful kindness today, in helping us.'

'Peace be upon you,' Amina replied. 'My house is your house.'

\*

It was way past dinner time when Ahmad arrived home. Everyone was sitting down eating. He thought, not for the first time, how his wife was surely the most capable woman he'd ever met. He knew there was not a lot of food in the house—every day it was getting harder to buy fresh meat and vegetables because of the soldiers—but somehow she had managed to make enough to feed everyone.

'I'm starving,' he said. 'And that smells very good.'

'Mostly rice, I'm afraid,' Aisha said. 'Although I have saved some meat balls for you. The bread is yesterday's. I didn't want to send anyone to the farran to bake some fresh. Not with so many soldiers about.'

'You did right, dear wife. Better stale bread than an injured child.'

Ahmad looked about him. 'There are some faces that I don't recognise, wife,' he said.

'Of course, how rude of me. Let me introduce you to Salma's friends, Rachel and her father, Isaak,' Aisha said, beckoning for them to come forward. 'They brought the lamb I used for the meatballs, and many other things besides.'

'As-salama alaykum,' said Isaak, bowing politely. 'Thank you for your hospitality, sayyad.'

'Wa alaykum e-salam,' Ahmad replied. 'So you are Rachel's father? Salma has spoken of you and your daughter often, and with great affection.'

'Their shop was broken into,' Salma said. 'They had nowhere else to go, cousin. I was sure you wouldn't turn them away.'

Ahmad smiled and patted her head. She was a lovely girl; he thought of her like another daughter, she was so often in his home.

'So what news, brother-in-law?' asked Qasim's wife. 'Have you heard anything from my husband?'

'I have. He's well. But he's working very hard. I doubt if we'll see much of him for a while,' said Ahmad. He didn't mention his own plans to meet his brother the next day.

His wife put a steaming plate of rice and meatballs in front of him. It smelled of rosemary, thyme and garlic and already he could feel his hunger abating.

So that Christian friend of Salma's was here again. He could see a problem growing from that friendship. Aisha had already mentioned her concerns, how she thought they were becoming too familiar. It was unseemly for a girl of Salma's age to have close male friends, unless they were family. And besides which he was a Christian. Not that Ahmad had anything against the Christians, nor the Jews for that matter. Many dhimmis held responsible jobs, and some even converted to Islam. As far as he was concerned, if they obeyed the law they were no problem. But Simon was a monk—not someone who would renounce his religion lightly. If Salma persisted with this friendship she would be disappointed. Perhaps he should talk to Layla about finding a husband for her. Aisha had been nagging him about finding a good match for Fatima, he might as well find one for Salma while he was at it.

## CHAPTER 14

The next morning, before it was light, Ahmad took one of the horses from the stables at the Falcon House and set off for Madinat al-Zahra to look for Umari. He knew it was dangerous. Córdoba was crawling with Berber soldiers but he was sure that once he got away from the city he would have a clear ride to the old capital. At any rate, he told himself, he had no option. He'd already made enquiries about Umari's whereabouts in Córdoba and nobody had seen him for weeks. He remembered the man from his visits to the Khalifa. He was a devoted servant. He would never have abandoned his master. Or was Ahmad being blind? Not everyone had such a strong sense of loyalty as he had. And Umari was a slave after all. Who knows, this could have been his chance to disappear and become a free man. He wrestled with these conflicting thoughts as he rode on through the Andalusian countryside.

As he'd thought, once he was out of sight of Córdoba the road was empty. Nevertheless he turned off it and rode towards the sierra. He would follow the foothills until he was level with Madinat al-Zahra then he would enter through the west gate.

It was exhilarating riding west, with the sun coming up behind him and the sound of birds waking to a new day. A flock of meadow pipits flew up from a nearby field, startled by his approach, their calls ringing through the cold mountain air. He turned his horse's head to the right and rode through a copse of young cork oaks. He knew the area well; it was the route they took to a clearing where they trained the young falcons to return to the glove. He was climbing now and when he looked to his left he could see the plain spreading out below him, a dark swathe gradually turning to green as the sun's pale rays touched it. And there was something else—the glint of armour. He reined in his horse and looked below. An army was making its way to Madinat al-Zahra. Not a disciplined army, but a disorderly mob of soldiers, spread out across the fields as far as he could see. It seemed like thousands of them. Some had already camped south of the city—he could see their tents and the camels and horses—others were still trudging along the road from Córdoba. It was fortunate that he'd turned off that road when he did, or he'd have been seen.

'What now, my beauty?' he whispered to the horse. They were almost at the point where he had intended to ride down into the city. That was impossible now.

He jumped down from his horse and led her further into the copse.

'Stay here. I'll be back for you soon,' he said, stroking her nose. It would be easier to slip into the city undetected on foot. He tied her reins loosely to the branch of a tree, tucked the sword Rafiq had given him into his belt, and set off down the hill towards the west gate of Madinat al-Zahra. Once inside he knew exactly where to go. After all, he'd spent many years working and living here. It had been his job to teach the young Khalifa how to fly his falcons and he had presented himself at the palace every morning for seven years.

He thought back to those years. He'd only been a young boy, not much older than al-Hisham, but they had been worlds apart in everything except the falcons. It had been his father's idea. He thought the young Khalifa needed company, someone his own age. Well now, he was here again.

\*

Madinat al-Zahra had changed dramatically since he'd lived there. It was no longer the bustling, thriving, cosmopolitan city it had been, where ambassadors from all corners of the world came to kneel before their Khalifa. It was a husk of its former glory. He scuttled down the dirty, narrow streets, climbed over piles of rubble and eventually arrived at the alcázar. There were no guards at the gate, so Ahmad walked right in and made for the Khalifa's private rooms. There were a couple of young men lounging on the patio but still no guards.

'As-salama alaykum,' Ahmad said, approaching them.

One of them replied, 'Wa alaykum e-salam,' and turned away. The other ignored him.

'I'm looking for a man called Umari,' he continued. 'Have you seen him?'

'Umari? He's been gone a long time. Ran away,' the first young man said.

'Do you know where he's gone?' Ahmad was not giving up.

The young man shook his head while the other continued to stare at the dribble of water that came from a broken fountain.

'Do you have any food?' asked the first young man.

'No, I haven't. Is there anyone else here? Anyone that can help me?' Ahmad asked. He was anxious to find the servant and leave before the soldiers arrived, and it was obvious that these men were not going to be of much use to him.

'Why do you want him?' asked a high-pitched voice.

Ahmad turned round and saw a young man with a shaven head—Musa.

He pulled his hood away from his face so that Musa could see him and said, 'Do you remember me? I'm Ahmad. From the Falcon House.'

'Yes, I know who you are. Why do you want Umari?' he repeated.

'The Khalifa needs him. He's very ill and he needs someone to look after him. He keeps asking for Umari. If you know where he is, please tell me.'

'Dead. He's dead. They stopped him one night when he was leaving the prison and arrested him. The next day his body was found floating in the river.'

'Oh, poor man. May he rest peacefully with Allah,' Ahmad said. He remembered hearing about a body in the Guadalquivir. That must have been Umari.

'Is that all?' Musa asked. He looked gaunt, as though he hadn't eaten for some days.

'Is the Falcon House still standing?' Ahmad asked.

'It is.'

'Good. Come with me. If I can't take al-Hisham his devoted servant, then I'll take him his favourite falcon.' He looked at Musa. 'He's still alive isn't he?'

'Yes. Follow me.'

Together they walked through the palace grounds to the old Falcon House. Ahmad choked back a sob when he saw it. The roof had collapsed and the main door hung open.

'The falcons? Are they all right?' he asked, dreading how Musa would answer.

'They let most of them go,' he replied. 'But I kept back al-Hisham's favourites. They're in a cage through here.'

They walked through the open door, past the dilapidated cages, the piles of dirty straw and faeces and into a back room. There was a single cage and in it, sitting on their perches, a peregrine falcon and two young goshawks. Ahmad recognised them at once. It was Shamal and the goshawk chicks he had given the Khalifa.

'You have done very well, Musa. The Khalifa will be so grateful.'

'You must stop calling him the Khalifa, sayyad. It is forbidden. Sulayman is to be the Khalifa now. If anyone hears you, you will be executed. That is why they killed poor Umari.' Musa opened the cage and slipped hoods onto the birds then carried them carefully out. 'I will come with you, sayyad. You cannot carry three birds on your own,' he added.

'No, Musa. It's too dangerous.'

'It is more dangerous here. Madinat al-Zahra is to be Sulayman's new stronghold. He will be here any day,' the slave told him. 'I will come with you to Córdoba and help you to look after al-Hisham.'

'Very well, but we must hurry. I saw soldiers approaching the city. We must leave before they arrive.'

'Too late, my friend,' a rough voice said. 'Stealing the Khalifa's falcons are you? Wonder what Sulayman will say to that?'

Ahmad spun round to see a soldier lounging against the open door. He had a jug of wine in one hand and a short sword in the other. There was nothing for it, he slipped the hood off the peregrine falcon and tossed him out through the open door. The bird, who probably hadn't hunted for some time, didn't hesitate; he flew straight up into the cloudless sky and was out of sight within seconds.

'Now what did you do that for?' the soldier slurred. He was obviously well on his way to being drunk.

But drunk or not he was dangerous and he might not be alone. Where were his companions? Ahmad glanced across at Musa, who was pressed against the wall, terrified.

'That bird was worth a lot of money. I know all about falcons, you know. You shouldn't have done it. Not letting a valuable bird like that fly free. Now, why would you do that?' the soldier muttered, incoherently.

He pulled his sword from its scabbard and lunged at Ahmad. But Ahmad was too quick for him; he stepped to the side and the soldier blundered past him.

'Musa, look outside and see if you can see any more soldiers,' Ahmad called to the frightened slave. 'Hurry.'

The slave scuttled to the door and peered out. 'No. There's nobody.'

The soldier was coming at him again and this time he looked as though he meant business. Ahmad did not fancy fighting him with his sword—he had never really used a sword before. Instead he bent down and picked up a plank of broken wood and stood facing him.

'Prepare to meet your maker,' the soldier shouted and rushed at Ahmad.

Once again Ahmad stepped nimbly to the side and this time he swung the plank at the on-coming soldier. To his amazement he caught the soldier a tremendous blow on the side of the head and knocked him to the ground. He lay there, on his back, unconscious, a trickle of blood running down his face.

'Is he dead?' asked Musa.

Ahmad nudged the soldier with his foot. 'No, I don't think so. But he's going to have a dreadful headache when he wakes up.'

'Kill him. Use his sword,' said Musa. He bent down and pulled the sword from the soldier's unresisting hand. 'Kill him.'

'No. Come on, Musa. We need to get out of here. If anyone comes in and finds us with a dead soldier, they will kill us. So, come on. Leave him. He won't be awake for hours.'

'Shall I bring the goshawks?'

'Yes, put them in this bag for now,' Ahmad said and passed a leather satchel to his new companion. 'Now let's go.'

*

It took a while for them to get out of the city but they managed it without any more mishaps.

'Where are we going?' Musa asked. 'Córdoba is the other way.'

'I know, but that's where the soldiers are coming from. We're going up into the sierra.'

'It'll be cold up there,' whined the slave.

'You choose. Cold or dead? Which do you prefer? You can stay here and face the soldiers or come with me.'

Musa said nothing but continued walking north. After a while, he said, 'I'm sorry you lost the peregrine.'

'Not lost. He may come back,' said Ahmad. His trip had not been all that successful. Instead of one experienced, loyal servant, he had young Musa who was frightened of his own shadow, and instead of the Khalifa's favourite peregrine falcon, he had the two goshawk chicks. Well, at least he wasn't quite empty-handed.

They climbed back towards the spot where Ahmad had left his horse tethered. Although the sun was high in the sky now, it was getting colder and colder with every step. They were walking directly into a strong north wind, which came from the highest parts of the Sierra Moreno and he could taste the first flakes of snow in his mouth. He hoped they could get home before it got any worse.

'Here we are,' he said and was greeted with an answering whinny.

'A horse. You've got a horse,' the delighted Musa exclaimed. 'Why didn't you tell me, sayyad? I thought we were going to walk all the way to Córdoba.'

'I thought you'd like a surprise,' Ahmad said with a grin. It was the sort of trick he often played on his own children. As he thought of them his heart gave a lurch. If that soldier hadn't been alone. If he hadn't been drunk. If he'd attacked without warning. So many ifs and with any one of them, the outcome could have been very different. Tonight he would say extra prayers to thank Allah for saving him.

He untied the horse and swung himself onto its back. 'Give me the bag, Musa. Now, jump up behind me,' he said. 'Time to go home.'

As he turned the horse to head for home, he heard a hawk calling high in the sky—a falcon without doubt.

'Up there. Look sayyad,' shouted Musa.

High above them was a large bird of prey; he was a tiny black speck against the bright sky but to Ahmad it was unmistakably a peregrine falcon. Suddenly the bird swooped and with a loud whirring of wings landed on a nearby tree.

'Look at that,' cried Musa. 'That's the same bird. That's Shamal, the Khalifa's falcon. It's a miracle.'

'It's no miracle. He's just come back to us,' said Ahmad, holding out his arm and whistling softly. 'He wants to see if I have anything for him.'

Ahmad still had some pieces of rabbit in his bag and as the peregrine landed with a thump on his clenched fist he offered him one. While the bird wolfed down the meat, Ahmad grabbed hold of its jesses so he couldn't fly away again.

'Right, now we really can go home,' he said to Musa and slipped a hood over the falcon's head.

## CHAPTER 15

They trekked slowly along the foothills, keeping under cover of the cork oaks, until they could see the city of Córdoba below them. It was impossible to enter the city from the west—soldiers were still coming from there, laden with booty, all heading for Madinat al-Zahra. Ahmad and Musa would have to work their way round to the north side of the city and make directly for the prison.

'Quietly now, Musa. They mustn't know we're here,' Ahmad said, and as he spoke he saw one of the soldiers stop and stare right up at them. He froze, pulling his horse to a sudden halt. Luckily the horse was a placid animal, not easily spooked and he just dropped his head and began to eat some of the sparse grass.

'Get down slowly, Musa. Then back away into the copse,' Ahmad whispered.

'What is it, sayyad?'

'Just do as I say.'

Musa slipped off the back of the horse and was instantly no more than a shadow amongst the trees. The soldier was still looking their way and now he was gesticulating and shouting at one of the others. Had they been seen? Ahmad dismounted slowly and began to move his horse under cover. Now the soldier dropped his sack of booty and started towards them. A second soldier joined him and he too was looking up towards the trees. He must have seen the horse, or maybe a movement as Ahmad dismounted. Were they going to pursue them? It seemed so; a horse was a prize worth having when you were foot-sore and had a sack of stolen goods to carry. Ahmad waited spellbound as the soldiers began to climb up the steep incline towards him; he felt unable to move. Then, just when he'd decided it was time to make a run for it, he saw an officer ride along the road and shout up at the soldiers. The wind caught his words but the soldiers heard and understood. He was telling them to come back and to be quick about it. The soldiers slithered down the slope, back to where they'd left their booty. Without a word to the officer, they rejoined the rest of their contingent to walk to Madinat al-Zahra, but not before taking another long look at the spot where Ahmad stood, trembling behind the gnarled trunk of a cork oak.

Ahmad waited until they were out of sight and then he led his horse further into the copse.

'Musa. Where are you?' he called.

'Here, sayyad. What was it?'

'Some soldiers. They've gone now but I think we should wait until it's dark before we go any closer to Córdoba.'

'But, sayyad, it'll be even colder,' the slave said, then stopped when he saw the look on Ahmad's face. 'Sorry, sayyad. Better cold than dead.'

'Exactly. Here, wrap this around you,' Ahmad said, handing him the blanket he'd brought for the Khalifa.

They moved further into the woods until they came to a clearing which Ahmad recognised; this was where he had often flown the falcons.

'We'll wait here for a couple of hours. It should be safe for now. Musa, gather some wood and prepare a small fire. I'm going to send Shamal to find us some supper,' Ahmad said.

He slipped the hood off Shamal's head and spoke softly to the bird, who turned his head in all directions, taking in his new surroundings. 'You know this place, don't you Shamal. Good boy. Find us a nice fat rabbit.'

He held out his arm and the hawk needed no more encouragement; he flew straight up and circled over the top of the trees for a few minutes before heading for the fields below. It was dusk and the best time for catching rabbits. Within a few minutes Shamal had returned, a limp body held tight in his claws. The hawk dropped to the ground to eat his quarry, but before he could do more than tear off one of the legs, Ahmad had retrieved the rabbit and rewarded the falcon with a tit-bit.

He took the rabbit over to Musa, who by now had a small fire burning brightly on the edge of the clearing.

'Here. Start cooking this one. I'll let him catch us one more and that will be enough for tonight,' he said.

Once more Shamal flew down to the darkening fields and once more he returned with a fat rabbit in his claws. This time Ahmad cut off a larger chunk for him before tossing the rest to Musa to cook.

'Well done, my beauty,' he said to the falcon, stroking its head. 'Well done.'

He was pleased that the falcon had caught them some supper but more than that, he was pleased that despite being neglected these past weeks, Shamal had not forgotten his training—he had come straight back to the glove.

\*

It was a dark night, with no moon and few stars. They had entered the city from the north, as planned, and now they made their way through the deserted streets towards the prison.

'Good evening, friend,' Ahmad said, approaching the sentries. The usual guard was on duty tonight.

'As-salama alaykum, Ahmad. What brings you here so late in the evening?'

'Wa alaykum e-salam. I have brought a servant for the Khalifa.'

'I thought you were bringing him some medicine?' the guard asked, opening the gates and letting them through.

'Tomorrow. I will go to the hospital tomorrow and collect it.'

He couldn't explain to the guard that he'd been prevented from going to the hospital because they'd been hiding in the sierra for hours.

'And what's that you've got there?' the guard asked.

'It's the Khalifa's falcon. I've just brought it to give him some pleasure. I will take it away with me when I leave.'

'That you will. I don't want any vicious birds here in the prison. I've got enough to deal with all these prisoners.'

Ahmad saw the guard look at his bag and scowl. 'I have a little something for you, from my wife,' he said. 'Honey and sesame cakes. Do you like them?'

'I do indeed,' replied the guard, his usually sullen face breaking into a smile. 'I do indeed.'

'Excellent. I will tell my wife and she will make you some more,' he said, knowing full well that he wouldn't be telling Aisha anything about the guard nor his visits to the prison.

'Well, here he is again. As you can see, nothing has changed,' said the guard, throwing open the door to al-Hisham's cell.

As usual the Khalifa was lying on his filthy mat in the corner, facing the wall. He didn't move when they entered.

'Your Majesty, I have brought someone to see you,' Ahmad said. He waited until al-Hisham rolled over and opened his eyes then he added, 'It's Shamal.'

Instantly the Khalifa sat up. 'Shamal. You've found him. My beautiful Shamal. You are a true friend to me, Ahmad. A true friend.'

He stretched out his arm and allowed the falcon to jump onto his fist.

'He looks thin. Where was he? Where did you find him? Oh, my beautiful Shamal.' He undid the falcon's hood and slipped it off. 'He's lost some feathers.'

'Yes, Your Majesty. He was still in the old Falcon House but there were no falconers left to care for him. All the other falcons had gone, flown away or stolen; I don't know which. Luckily Musa moved Shamal into a separate room before anyone could take him, and he has been looking after him.'

'Was he the only one left?'

'Your new goshawks were still there as well. Look I have them here in my bag, but I think we'd better leave them be. If I take them out they will make such a fuss that the guard will come back.'

'Yes, yes, leave them where they are. I have my beautiful Shamal, that is enough,' he said, stroking the falcon's head. 'And what of Umari? Did you find where he'd gone?'

'Yes, Your Majesty. Umari is dead. He was killed by the soldiers,' Ahmad said. There was no point telling al-Hisham the reason for Umari's death. It would only make him worry. 'But I found Musa. Do you remember Musa? He will take care of you now.'

The slave, who had been standing there all this time staring at the Khalifa, now threw himself to the floor and bowed.

'Musa, yes I remember little Musa. A dear boy. You have done well, Ahmad. Very well.' He sighed, expelling the air from his throat with a deathly rattle. 'If only you could make me better, too.'

'Tomorrow I will come again, Your Majesty, and bring the medicine.'

'Good, good.' The Khalifa was getting tired now, and turned back to his falcon and stroked his head once more. 'Come and see me again, sweet Shamal. Soon I will be free and we will go hunting together,' he said.

'I will leave you now, Your Majesty but Musa will stay and look after you.'

'Very well, Ahmad. Take good care of my falcon.'

'I will take him home with me, Your Majesty and then I will be sure that he comes to no harm,' Ahmad promised. It warmed his heart to see how the Khalifa had changed when he saw the falcon. For a few moments the pain had lifted from his face and he looked like a young man again. 'I will bring him to see you again, insha'Allah.'

'Do not rely on Allah. He has deserted me.'

'Don't worry Your Majesty, I will bring your falcon back,' said Ahmad.'

'I will go and get some water to wash you, Your Majesty,' said Musa, turning his attention to his new charge.

Ahmad felt a surge of gratitude towards the young slave. He was giving up his newly found freedom to sleep in this hell hole and serve the Khalifa, but at least he could leave whenever he wanted. At the moment al-Hisham had no choice but to languish there at Sulayman's pleasure.

'Ma'a salama,' said Ahmad and left. Once again he could feel the prison walls closing in on him and he was desperate to get home to his family.

\*

It was almost midday before Ahmad had time to go to the hospital to see his brother. He went straight in through the main gate and this time the African slave recognised him and didn't try to stop him.

'Did you want to see your brother, sayyad?' he asked, giving a short bow.

'Yes. Please let him know I am here,' said Ahmad and sat down to wait.

The news about Umari had unsettled him. He'd known Umari for years, since he was a young boy. He'd always been a loyal servant to al-Hisham. But now there was another Khalifa and to continue to address al-Hisham as Khalifa was treason. What if the guard, or one of his comrades, told anyone about Ahmad's visits to the prison. They could easily have heard him talking to the Khalifa and calling him Your Majesty. Would that be considered treason too? The boy had been right to warn him. From now on he must take greater care where he went and what he said.

'Ahmad, I thought you were coming yesterday. I had everything ready for you. What happened?' Qasim asked, striding into the reception area with a leather bag over his shoulder.

'As-salama alaykum, dear brother.'

'Wa alaykum e-salam,' Qasim responded and then continued, 'So where were you? I waited until long past sunset for you.'

'I was looking for Umari.'

'So, did you find him? I need to tell him how to clean the Khalifa's sores,' his brother said.

Ahmad flinched when he heard Qasim refer to al-Hisham as Khalifa. 'Don't call him that,' he whispered. 'There is a new Khalifa now.'

Qasim stared at him. 'What happened?' he asked.

'Umari is dead. Executed for treason.'

'Poor man. So that's how his loyalty was repaid.'

'Loyalty to the wrong man, unfortunately,' said Ahmad.

'So there's no-one to look after al-Hisham?' Qasim asked, brusquely. As usual he was in a hurry.

'Yes. I went to Madinat al-Zahra and found Musa, another of al-Hisham's servants. He is with him now,' said Ahmad.

'So that's why you didn't make it last night?'

'We ran into some of Sulayman's soldiers and had to make a detour,' Ahmad said, dropping his voice so that the slave couldn't hear him. He didn't want to go into detail, especially about the soldier he'd attacked. The less his brother knew the better for everyone. 'It was late when I returned.'

'Well, you're here now. There's no point in explaining it all to you. I'll come to the prison again tonight and show Musa what to do. Now I must get back to work.'

'Thank you, brother. Ma'a salama,' said Ahmad. 'By the way your wife and family are well.'

'Alla ysalmak, brother. Thank you for caring for my family. Tell my wife I will see her on Friday.'

\*

It was late when Ahmad arrived home. The house was filled with sleeping bodies. Only Aisha sat by the fire, waiting for his return. His wife had allocated one room for all the children, another for the women and a third for the men. He groaned. Tonight he wouldn't be able to sleep next to his lovely plump, warm wife. Instead he'd have to sleep next to his son, an old Jew, a Christian monk and goodness knows who else. Still they were all safer here than outside in the city—he'd seen for himself what the soldiers were capable of. He worried for his brother Qasim, alone in his little house by the hospital. May Allah protect him, he prayed.

'Come and eat, husband,' Aisha said, putting a bowl of vegetable broth on the low table in front of him. 'Your mother made it. We've already eaten but I kept yours hot.'

'It smells good,' he said, picking up a spoon and taking a mouthful. The truth was that he had little appetite after his visit to the prison; he could still taste the sour odour of captivity in his mouth.

He reached up and touched the ring hanging on a leather cord around his neck. He'd hung the giant ruby there for safe keeping. Al-Hisham had been so grateful to see his precious falcon and have Musa to tend him, that he had rewarded Ahmad with the ring. He hadn't wanted to take it. In fact he'd been amazed that al-Hisham still had the ring and that it hadn't already been stolen or confiscated from him. Maybe the Khalifa wasn't as demented as he sometimes seemed; when he was arrested he'd removed the ring from his finger and hidden it in his clothing.

Nobody knew the true value of the ring. It was said to be priceless, but more than that, it was a symbol of the Omayyad power. The reigning Khalifa always wore it. It was the one piece of jewellery that al-Hisham was never without, which was why Ahmad had been astonished when he gave it to him. 'Take it,' he'd said to Ahmad. 'It has never brought me any good fortune. Maybe it will bring you some.'

Ahmad held the ring up to the light of the oil lamp and examined it. It burned a deep red, like a fire burning inside the stone. Fire. He had heard the legend but never given it much credence. They said that the ring could be used for good or evil. If the Khalifa was strong, the ring made him stronger and peace would reign. If he was weak then the ring would bring chaos and Córdoba would end in flames.

'What's that?' Aisha asked.

'A ring. Al-Hisham gave it to me,' he said, making sure to keep his voice low.

'The Khalifa gave it to you?' she gasped.

'Yes, but no-one must know.'

'Is that the famous ring that is handed down from khalifa to khalifa?'

'Hush woman. I don't want everyone to know I have it.'

'They say it is cursed.'

'Only in the wrong hands.'

'And yours are the right ones? What dangerous game are you playing Ahmad? Do you realise what could happen to you and to all our family, if you were found with that ring? It's too risky to keep it. Give it back to him.'

'Of course I realise what could happen. It's a priceless jewel and I'm sure al-Malik or Sulayman would feel that it was rightfully theirs, but al-Hisham gave it to me to look after. If he gets out of prison, if he gets better, then I will return it to him, but not now. Better to throw it in the river than give it back to him while he's a prisoner. He was very lucky not to have had it stolen already.'

'And what will you do if he dies in prison? You can't keep it.'

'I don't know. Anyway, he's not going to die. I won't let him.'

He knew how stupid his words were as soon as they left his mouth. There was little he could do to keep al-Hisham alive. If his illness didn't kill him then Sulayman's men probably would. What would he do with the ring then?

His wife turned away from him and said no more but he knew she was angry. Angry and scared. Everyone was scared these days. It was the uncertainty. You never knew whom to trust. She was right; it wouldn't do for people to know he had the ring. He'd be arrested and thrown in jail for certain.

'I saw Qasim today,' he said. 'He will come round on Friday to see his family. Be sure to tell his wife.'

'I will.'

'How is she?' he asked.

'Not good. She weeps most of the day and takes no notice of her children. Luckily Salma and some of the others keep them amused and your mother makes sure they're washed and fed. She says she wants to go back to her own home.'

'It's too dangerous at the moment,' Ahmad said, eating a bit more of the broth. If he left any he'd have to face his mother tomorrow.

'It's the pregnancy. It's making her tearful. Layla has made her a draught of herbs to steady her nerves but she won't drink it. I don't know what else we can do. Maybe Qasim can prescribe something for her.'

Ahmad tucked the ring back inside his shirt. It was only his imagination but it felt as though it burned against his skin. Would it bring him good fortune or, as Aisha feared, would it bring disaster on all of them?

# CHAPTER 16

Muhammad II stood on the ramparts of the city's walls looking down at the remains of his army, camped on the plain outside Toledo. What a defeated rabble they were. Less than half the men he'd started out with and most of them demoralised or injured. A full moon, almost at its zenith that night, lit up the camp as if it were day but its pale, cold light only made the scene more painful for him. Even the river Tagus, glinting in the moonlight could not charm him tonight.

The army had been completely routed by Sulayman's forces at Alcolea. They had almost arrived home, not twenty Arab miles from his beloved city of Córdoba, when they'd engaged with the enemy. What a disaster. He trembled with rage when he thought about it. They should never have lost that battle; his army was better trained, more disciplined and stronger than Sulayman's. The usurper would never have defeated them on his own but Sulayman had enlisted the help of that weasel, Count Sancho Garcia of Castille. The combined forces of the Berber-Castillian army had outnumbered them almost two to one. They'd stood no chance. Now some of his best men lay dead on the battle field. He'd only just escaped himself, abandoning the battle and riding north to Toledo with the remnants of his army.

And what price would Sulayman have to pay for Sancho Garcia's help? The Count never did anything without payment and everyone knew he'd had his eyes on taking back the Muslim lands adjacent to the County of Castille for some time. Muhammad couldn't allow that.

Well two could play at that game. He too had allies, strong allies. He was, after all, the Khalifa of al-Andalus. He would send a message to the Count of Barcelona and ask for his aid.

Muhammad II pulled his cloak about him and walked back towards the palace. The sentries on duty jumped to attention as he approached.

'Send for General al-Wahdi. Tell him I must speak with him at once. He is to come to my personal quarters,' he barked. There was no time to be lost. He would have that traitor's head on a spike for all the world to see before the summer was over.

\*

General al-Wahdi was the best general he had and Muhammad relied on him unreservedly.

'As-salama alaykum, Your Majesty,' the general said, bowing before his commander.

'Wa alaykum e-salam, al-Wahdi. We need to talk about mounting a counter-offensive against that scoundrel, Sulayman.'

'Indeed, Your Majesty, but the army is depleted and the men are tired and in low spirits. We need to recruit more soldiers before we can mount a counter-offensive, sayyad.'

'I understand that. But we cannot wait. It takes time to recruit and train new soldiers. We need battle-hardened men. Men who will not flinch in the heat of battle.'

'So what do you suggest, sayyad?'

'I am going to ask Count Ramon Borrell of Barcelona to come to our aid. Send a messenger to him immediately, this very night. Ask the count to come here to Toldeo and together we will ride to Córdoba and defeat the enemy.'

'Yes, Your Majesty.'

'And tell the other generals to inform their troops. That should put heart into the men.'

'Indeed, Your Majesty. I will see to it right away.'

'Your Majesty, there is a man with a message for you,' said a breathless servant, bursting into the room, unceremoniously. 'Please forgive me, but he says it is urgent and that he must speak to you right away.'

'Very well, send him in.'

He looked across at General al-Wahdi, who was about to leave and said, 'Wait, this may be of significance for you too, General.'

A dirt-spattered and exhausted messenger came in and bowed so low that Muhammad thought he would topple over.

'Your Majesty,' he said.

'Yes, what is it? You have a message for me?' he asked brusquely. It had better be important. He had no time to waste over some trivia.

'Yes, Your Majesty. I have ridden from Córdoba without rest to bring you the news that the city has been sacked. The Castilians have looted and plundered our beloved city. The people are hiding. They are frightened for their lives,' the messenger said, his voice breaking with emotion as he spoke.

'What? That barbarian, Sancho Garcia. So this is the infidel's payment. In return for his help, Sulayman has betrayed his own people. He has let the Castilians loose in our city. This will not go unanswered,' Muhammad said, his voice trembling with anger.

He was furious. Their beautiful city sacked by Christians. It was an insult, an outrage. The caliphate of al-Andalus stretched from North Africa to the river Douro and almost to the borders with the Kingdom of the Franks. It was the most cultured and powerful country in the West and yet the infidels had penetrated to the heart of the caliphate and sacked their capital city. How could that be tolerated? Sulayman would pay for this.

'And what of my family? What of my wives and children?' he asked.

'They are safe, Your Majesty. When we heard that the Castilians were attacking the city, they made their escape. They are in Málaga now.'

'Thanks be to Allah,' Muhammad said. At least his family was safe from that infidel. What a prize it would have been for him to capture Muhammad's family and hold them to ransom.

'But there is more, Your Majesty,' the messenger continued timidly.

'More?' roared Muhammad. 'More than that?'

'Yes, Your Majesty. The Berbers have elected Sulayman as Khalifa,' he said, the words so soft that Muhammad couldn't quite believe what he was hearing.

'Sulayman the khalifa? What, on the strength of one battle? Well that won't last long; mark my words. His days are numbered.'

He turned to General al-Wahdi, his eyes blazing. 'Send the messenger to the Count of Barcelona immediately. Promise him whatever he asks for, only make sure he agrees to help us. I will not rest until my sword lies in the belly of Sulayman ibn al-Hakem.'

*

Rafiq bound a clean rag around his leg. It wasn't a deep wound and the bone was not broken but it was taking a while to heal. He wished his aunt was there with her magical herbal remedies. She would soon have had it better. He racked his brain, trying to remember the names of some of the herbs she used. If only he'd paid more attention to her when he was a boy and she was tending to his childhood cuts and scrapes, but he was always in a hurry to be somewhere else and her explanations about the treatment she was applying were just so many words to him.

Each corps had its own doctor but theirs had been killed during the battle while attending to a young soldier with a lacerated throat. Rafiq could have gone to one of the other corps to be treated but he didn't think his injury was serious enough for that. Better to cure it himself.

Many of their men had died in that battle and more had been injured. It was one of the bloodiest that he could remember. It was hard to say who were the most bloodthirsty, the Castilians who hated them for being Muslims or the Berbers who hated anyone who was not of their tribe. He had lost some good friends and comrades at Alcolea, including Hannad, the quaid in charge of the archers. They had fought bravely but once the foot soldiers broke through their ranks they were cut down like sheaves of wheat, their arrows useless in close combat.

'Can I help you with that, quaid?' an old soldier asked. 'I used to be an orderly at the hospital in Córdoba before I became a soldier.'

'You can indeed. As you can see I'm not making a very good job of bandaging my leg.'

'Just give me a minute and I'll get some herbs to put on the wound. I won't be long.' The old soldier moved off through the rows of tents.

The mention of Córdoba made Rafiq think of his brother Qasim. Was he all right? Were the family safe? Rafiq tried not to think too much about his family when he was away on a campaign. There was nothing he could do for them and it only served to make him feel helpless being so far away. But as he told himself many times, he was a soldier and his place was here on the battlefield. Only now the battlefield had moved to the city and it wasn't just soldiers who were being killed but innocent women and children, old men; they were attacking the hospitals and the schools, sacking the libraries and the palaces. No-one and nothing was spared. That was not warfare. That was annihilation. The news about the sacking of Córdoba had spread around the camp like wildfire. He'd felt his blood run cold when he heard it.

'Here. I found some growing by the river. This will clear up any infection.'

The old soldier wiped the wound with a wet rag and then covered it with a handful of green leaves.

'What are they?' asked Rafiq. They looked vaguely familiar.

'Why it's just your common old willow leaves,' said the soldier. 'Always on the river bank they are.'

'Did you learn about them in the hospital?' asked Rafiq, feeling stupid for not recognising the leaves.

'No. My mother used to pick them and steep them in water to use as an antiseptic. She was one of those women who could tell the future. She delivered babies and cut hair and told fortunes.

She made potions for people who couldn't sleep and potions for men who couldn't get it up.' He laughed. 'You know what I mean, quaid.'

Rafiq smiled.

'That's why I thought I'd work in the hospital. But it wasn't for me. I didn't have the patience for all those sick people. I'm a man of action. I wanted to be a soldier. And here I am, forty years later and still alive. That's an achievement wouldn't you say?'

'I would indeed. Especially after Alcolea.'

As he'd been talking the old soldier had skilfully wound the bandage around Rafiq's leg. 'There you are, quaid. You'll be as good as new in a couple of days.'

'Thank you, soldier.'

'When are we going to Córdoba to kick those Christians out? The sooner the better, I say,' the old soldier continued.

'You'll know when we do, soldier.'

There were rumours among the quaids that Muhammad was planning a counter-offensive but nobody knew anything definite. He hoped it was true. The thought of those Christians looting and plundering his beautiful city ate at his heart. He was desperate to return. He didn't just want to kick them out; he wanted to slaughter them.

'Rafiq. Have you heard? Reinforcements are on the way,' said Asif, throwing himself on the ground beside him. 'What's wrong with you?'

'That? Oh, it's nothing. But what are you saying about reinforcements? From where?' asked Rafiq.

They had no more troops in the region. In fact, as far as Rafiq was aware this was all that was left of Muhammad's army.

'You'll never believe it, from the Count of Barcelona and his cousin the Count of Urgel. They will join us in two days and then we return to Córdoba,' said Asif, his eyes shining with excitement. 'The hour of our revenge is almost at hand.'

'That's very good news,' said Rafiq. He stretched his injured leg. It was stiff but it should be better in a couple of days, certainly good enough to ride. 'Yes, excellent news indeed.'

## CHAPTER 17

Ahmad climbed up to the roof terrace where his mother was having her afternoon snooze. It was the only place he could find any peace and quiet in order to think. Downstairs the women were preparing food, and the children were squabbling, as usual. His brother's children were bored being away from their home and their friends. They constantly quarrelled with each other and with the orphaned children he'd taken in, and when they weren't quarrelling they all charged about the house like caged beasts. He could understand their frustration but that didn't mean he had to put up with it day in, day out. Their mother did nothing to control them; she spent all day lying on her mat weeping. It couldn't go on like this. He had to do something.

With each day that passed he felt that it was becoming more and more his duty to assume the role of head of the family. Someone had to do it now that Baba was dead. It should really be Qasim—he was the eldest son—but he was too busy at the hospital. They barely saw him these days and his wife was constantly worried that something would happen to him. When he spoke to Qasim about her, all he said was, 'Not to worry.'

But he did worry. Rafiq was the second son but Rafiq was a soldier; he had to follow orders and he never knew where he would be from one day to the next. So it fell to Ahmad, the youngest son, to take responsibility. He couldn't just sit by and watch his family fall apart. They were living in dangerous times and if anything happened to him what would become of his daughters, of his wife, his mother and the rest of the womenfolk? No, there were too many things that had to be resolved.

'Is that you Ahmad?' his mother asked, sleepily. She opened her eyes and blinked in the sunlight, like a baby owl.

'Yes, Mama. I didn't mean to disturb you.'

'Is something troubling you, son? You seem worried.'

'I think it's time my daughters were married,' he said.

'Well Bayda is betrothed, is she not? Yusuf, isn't it?'

'Yes, Mama, but her husband-to-be is still a student. They plan to get married when he has finished his studies.'

'So what is the problem? You agreed to the match, didn't you?' his mother asked, propping herself up on her elbow and looking at him.

The sleep had refreshed her and she no longer looked so old and worn. The warm glow of the sunlight on her face made her seem years younger. She was still a beautiful woman despite her years. No wonder his father had never taken a second wife.

'I did. He is a fine young man and will make her a good husband.'

'And her dowry?'

'Yes, he has agreed to pay a substantial sum, almost one thousand dinars. There is no problem there. He has even agreed to Bayda having access to her own dowry, in case anything happens to him.'

'So what troubles you, my son?'

'The waiting, I suppose. I want her married and living somewhere away from the capital, away from all this fighting. I want both my daughters to leave Córdoba,' he said at last. 'It isn't safe here.'

'But this is our home. Why should we allow ourselves to be driven from our homes?' his mother demanded. 'Your father would never have sent his children away.'

'My father lived in different times,' said Ahmad. His mother didn't understand. She hadn't seen the butchery of the Berbers and the Castilians. She hadn't ventured outside the house in almost two years. The little she knew of what was happening to their beautiful city was what she gleaned from conversations with the rest of the family and everyone was careful not to frighten her. Perhaps that had been a mistake. Maybe it was time she knew exactly what atrocities were being committed by Sulayman and his troops.

'Why not tell the family that the wedding must happen sooner,' Amina suggested. 'Then she will have the support of their family as well as ours. No need to send her away.'

'Yes, that's a good idea,' said Ahmad. 'I will talk to Aisha about it. And then I will go and speak to Yusuf's father.'

'What about Fatima?'

'Yes, I will find a husband for her too.'

'Don't forget Salma,' his mother said. 'It's your responsibility to arrange a marriage for her as well, remember.'

'Ah. Now there I think I'm going to have a problem,' Ahmad said, thinking of the way he had seen Salma and Simon looking at each other.

\*

The falcons hadn't been flown for weeks. It was too dangerous to ride up into the sierra with them; there were soldiers everywhere. Most of the falconers, including Ahmad, had been sent home and only three men remained, sleeping and eating in the Falcon House. Ahmad was concerned how the birds were faring without their regular exercise and diet of fresh prey but there was nothing he could do about it. At least he had the Khalifa's favourite birds safe here, and could care for them.

He lifted Shamal off his perch and stroked his head. 'Here, my beauty, a treat for you.' He fed the falcon a chunk of raw goat's meat which he'd taken from Aishas's cold store. 'Eat that up, before we get caught,' he whispered.

Tomorrow he'd let the falcon hunt along by the river. They'd go early in the morning and, if they were lucky, they wouldn't bump into any soldiers. He couldn't keep feeding Shamal food that was supposed to be for them; there was hardly enough to go round as it was with so many mouths to feed in the house.

'Is he dangerous?' asked a little voice. It was the child he'd found, Omar.

'No, not at all. Well unless you try to take his food away from him. He wouldn't like that. Would you like to stroke him?'

Ahmad bent down and held Shamal closer to the boy. The falcon cocked his head on one side and stared at the child.

'Will he bite me?' asked Omar.

'Not unless you're a rabbit. Are you a rabbit?'

The child laughed. 'No, sayyad. I'm a boy. You know I am.' He reached up and gingerly stroked Shamal's head. 'It's very soft.'

'Yes, he's a beautiful bird,' Ahmad said. 'A bird fit for a Khalifa.' He watched as the boy ran off to tell the others about the falcon.

He hadn't been to see the Khalifa in weeks. It had been too dangerous with Sulayman's troops everywhere and the last thing he wanted to do was to attract attention to al-Hisham by going to the prison with a peregrine falcon on his arm. He hoped that the Khalifa had been forgotten, at least for now.

'Ahmad, what are you doing?' Aisha asked, looking at the remains of the goat meat.

'Just a little food for him, dear wife. Not much. And tomorrow he can catch his own supper.'

'I should think so too,' his wife replied. 'It's not easy making meals from next to nothing, you know.'

'Yes, my dear, I know.' Ahmad put the falcon back on his perch and sat down. 'I'm glad you're here, wife. I must talk to you. Come, sit beside me.'

Obediently, Aisha sat beside him. She looked worried.

'What is it, husband? Has something happened?'

'Nothing has happened. It's what I want to happen that concerns me,' he began. 'We have to choose a husband for Fatima.'

'But I thought you wanted to wait until Fatima had finished her studies to become a teacher. Then you were going to find her a husband, someone who wouldn't object to having an educated wife.'

'That's true. But things have changed. I think she would be safer if she were married as soon as possible. With so many soldiers roaming the city, no single woman is safe. I want both my daughters married.'

'Very well, husband, but to whom? Have you given any thought to a suitable young man?'

'I have. You know that last night I visited Hudhafa, the father of Yusuf.'

'Yes. Did it go well?'

'Yes, very well. I told him that we wanted Yusuf and Bayda to marry as soon as possible and he has agreed. The wedding will take place in two weeks' time.'

'Two weeks,' Aisha exclaimed. 'That's too soon.' She looked at him in horror. 'How can we get everything ready by then? There are her wedding robes to make, the family to contact, so many things, the food, the flowers. Oh Ahmad, why have you done this to me? Why do we women always leave these decisions to the men? They have no idea what is involved in organising a wedding.'

She placed her hands over her face and began to sob, whether from frustration or because suddenly her daughter was leaving her, he didn't know. Maybe he should have waited and spoken to her first about the timing of the wedding. But it was too late now.

Ahmad put his arm around her and said, as patiently as he could, 'Now, now, wife. Don't upset yourself. There are plenty of women in this house to help you. I hear that your sister-in-law is wonderful with a needle; ask her to sew the wedding robes for you. It will be good for her to have something to do instead of weeping around the house all day. My mother will help with the food and Makoud can let everyone know about the wedding. It's just a question of organisation.'

The more he spoke, the more he was pleased with his idea. The wedding would bring everyone together with a common purpose. It would stop them being so frightened about the future, give them something to concentrate on, instead of worrying about the soldiers all the time.

'I will leave it to you to tell Bayda,' he said, beaming at her.

'She won't be happy, you know. What do I tell her? They will have to live with his family you know, until he finishes studying,' Aisha asked.

'Tell her it's something she will have to sort out with her husband. I'm doing this for her own good,' he said, a little peevishly.

'And what of Fatima? What surprise have you for me there?' she asked.

'Yusuf has a brother, a couple of years older than him. He is a merchant and a widower. I have suggested to the father that the older brother considers taking Fatima as a bride. Of course he will have to agree but, in principle, the father thinks it is an excellent idea.'

'What happened to the older brother's wife? How did she die?' Aisha asked. He could see she was struggling with the idea of Fatima marrying a widower.

'In childbirth. The baby survived.'

'So there's a child. He wants someone to look after his child?' Aisha asked.

'I suppose so. That's natural isn't it? He's a young man still and he needs a wife and a mother for his child.'

'I don't like it, Ahmad. Sisters marrying brothers? That seems rather strange,' said Aisha.

'No stranger than everything else that is happening in the world,' Ahmad retorted. He thought it was a perfect solution. He knew the family. They were well respected, with Arab blood in their veins and both sons had sound careers ahead of them, one as a merchant and the other—when he finished his studies—as a lawyer. The fact that one of them was a widower was not an issue as far as he was concerned. It wasn't as though he was suggesting that Fatima become someone's second or third wife. Even if the man took more wives later on, she would always be regarded as the main wife. He couldn't understand why Aisha was raising objections.

'When do we meet him?' his wife asked.

'Tomorrow. We will go to their home in the evening, insha'Allah.'

'God willing? Allah will have to intervene if I am to arrange the wedding of one daughter and the betrothal of another all within two weeks. It won't be just Allah's will that we'll need but a miracle.'

'Rubbish, wife. I have every faith in you,' said Ahmad, giving his wife a hug. Now all he had to do was talk to Layla about finding a husband for Salma.

## CHAPTER 18

When Simon arrived back at his lodgings, the door was barred and there was no sign of anyone. He hammered on the door and then waited, listening for the sound of a footfall within. Nothing. Were they all still asleep? He banged on the door again. No response. Not a sound. Even the dog, who barked at every noise, was silent. Everyone seemed to have left.

'Can I help you, my son?' asked an old man, standing across the street. He was very bent, and wore long, dirty white robes.

'I live here,' explained Simon, 'but it's all locked up. Where is the mistress of the house?'

'Gone. She's gone to the home of her daughter, in Antequera. Left two days ago.'

Simon felt his heart sink. There was no way he could get through that heavy, barred door; it must be solid oak. How was he going to get to his manuscripts now? He'd been stupid to leave them there but, at the time, it had seemed the safest thing to do with them.

'You're one of those Christian students she has living there, aren't you?'

Simon nodded. He was in no mood to chatter with a stranger. He had to find a way of getting into the house.

'I thought I recognised you,' the old man said, nodding his head sagely. 'Seen you coming and going a lot over the years. You've stayed longer than most. They usually go back to where they came from after a few months. But I've seen you. You've stuck it out. She liked you. Made a point of saying so,' the old man went on, smiling a toothless smile at Simon. 'Said, if you come by, looking for your things, I was to let you in.'

'You have a key?' Simon asked in astonishment. 'She gave you a key? You can open the door?'

'Of course. She wasn't going to take it with her and leave her young foreigners stranded now, was she? Just a minute I'll go and get it.'

The old man disappeared down a narrow alleyway that ran alongside the house, leaving a surprised Simon waiting outside in the early morning chill.

So his landlady had left the city. He couldn't blame her. If it wasn't for Salma he would leave, too. It was too dangerous to stay, especially if you were a tall blond Anglo-Saxon like him. Even in this city of many races and religions he stood out, so nowadays when he ventured out, he kept the hood of his djellaba up in an attempt to hide both his blond hair and the blue turban he wore. Salma had suggested he throw away the zunar that the law obliged him to wear, but he was frightened that doing so would cause him even more problems. Anyway, he was a Christian and he was proud of his faith. Why hide it?

'Here we are,' said the old man, brandishing a bunch of heavy iron keys. 'I'll have to come in with you. I promised her that I wouldn't leave these keys with anyone.'

'That's fine with me. I just need to collect my belongings and then I'll bother you no longer,' Simon said.

He waited anxiously while the old man tried first one key and then another until at last he found the right one. There was another delay while he opened the inner door, but then they were inside and Simon bounded straight up to his room.

Everything was as he'd left it. He sighed with relief. He pulled open the trunk where he stored his clothes and there at the bottom were the manuscripts, hidden under his old monk's robes. Carefully he took the documents out one by one. This was the reason he had been sent to Córdoba. This was the fruit of his work at the library. In the time he'd been in Córdoba he'd translated nine books into Latin, books on medicine, philosophy, books of poetry and even one on astronomy which had survived the flames when Al-Mansur had ordered them all to be destroyed. They were all very precious to him but the most valuable of all were the three treatises he'd translated from ancient Hebrew. These the abbot would be very happy to receive. Simon had originally intended to take them all back to the monastery in person, but now he would have to trust them to the barid. He prayed that this messenger service was still functioning and had not been disrupted by the soldiers.

The door to his room opened. 'Have you found what you wanted?' asked the old man.

'I have but I will be a little while longer because I have to write a short letter to accompany this parcel,' he explained. 'Is the barid still running?'

'I wouldn't know,' said the old man. 'I never have the need to send any messages or parcels.' He scratched his head. 'Now you mention it, yes, I'm pretty sure I saw one of their men, only yesterday.'

Simon bent over his writing table and began to scribble a note to the abbot.

*'Esteemed Lord Abbot. Please forgive this hurried note but the circumstances here in Córdoba have changed. The library where I work has been closed now for many months because twice this year the city has been sacked by foreign mercenaries. I have become fearful of late for the safety of the manuscripts I have translated for the monastery, so, as a precaution, I am sending them on ahead by messenger. I will return in the summer, as promised in my previous letter.*

*I remain, in God's faith,*
*Your humble servant,*
*Simon of Norwich.'*

He folded the parchment carefully and placed it in the bag with the manuscripts then tied the package securely.

'Just one more thing and then I'm finished,' he said to the old man. He might as well take the rest of his possessions with him, few though they were, so he stuffed everything into another bag and slung it over his shoulder.

'That's everything now,' he said. 'Thank you for your help.'

Simon followed the old man down the stairs and out onto the street. He looked about him warily but there was no-one around—Salma had been right to suggest he come early in the morning.

'Ma'a salama, friend,' Simon said, bowing his head slightly to the old man.

'Alla ysalmak. May your God go with you,' the old man replied. 'And may Allah keep you safe.'

Well that should do it, both Allah and God would protect him. But would that be enough against the soldiers? For a moment Simon felt his belief waver.

\*

At first, the messenger had been reluctant to take the package. It was understandable. It was a long journey and would take him outside of his own land and away from his countrymen. And these were unsettled times; there were soldiers everywhere. In order to persuade him, it had cost Simon all the money he had and then he'd also had to promise the man that he would receive a silver piece when he delivered the package to the abbot. He hoped he was right in his assumption; the abbot was not known for his generosity.

Now, with the package on its way, Simon was torn with mixed emotions—anxiety for the safety of the manuscripts and relief that they were at last leaving the city. He murmured a prayer asking God to protect the books and give them swift passage.

His route from the barid back to Ahmad's house took him close to the library so he decided to see whether it was open. The front entrance was bolted and barred as usual, but Simon made his way round the building to where there was a side door. As he hoped, it was open. Cautiously he went in and headed for the Chief Scribe's office.

Bent over a desk, writing intently with a rather worn quill, was an old man with a long white beard—the Chief Scribe. So he was still here but he was alone; there was nobody else was in sight.

'As-salama alaykum, sayyad,' said Simon. 'I am surprised to see you here, in these troubled times.'

The Chief Scribe lifted his head and stared at Simon. 'Wa alaykum e-salam. What are you doing here, Simon of Norwich? I thought you'd returned to your own lands.'

'No. I was worried about what was happening to the library.'

He looked about him. There were no signs of vandalism but many of the shelves seemed emptier than before.

'We've been lucky so far, but I don't know for how long. I come here every day to work and check that everything is safe,' he said.

'Is that wise?' asked Simon. 'If the soldiers came they would probably kill you.'

'If the soldiers came and destroyed the library, why would I want to continue living? This is my life, my world. I intend to continue working here until the very end. Although I hope and pray that that is still a long way off. I pray that Allah will protect this beautiful place and all our lovely city,' the Chief Scribe said sadly.

'Is there anything I can do?' Simon asked. 'I could work at home on some of the books.'

'No. It's not safe to take the books out of the library. It is too dangerous. They must stay here.'

'What happened there?' asked Simon pointing to the rows of empty shelves. 'Where have the books gone?'

A crafty look spread over the Chief Scribe's face. 'What do you mean? It is all as it was before. Now, I suggest you go and don't come back here until the soldiers have left the city. It's not safe and there is nothing you can do.'

'But...'

'Alla ysalmak,' the scribe said, resuming his copying and taking no more notice of the young monk standing before him.

Simon knew there was no point staying. The books had been stolen, or more likely, the Chief Scribe had taken them and hidden them somewhere.

'Ma'a salama, sayyad,' said Simon and took his leave, pulling the door closed behind him.

\*

When Simon got back to Ahmad's house, Salma was sitting on the roof terrace copying the text from one of the books she'd smuggled home. She looked so beautiful sitting there with her delicately arched lips pursed in concentration and her long black hair, that gleamed like a raven's wing in the rays of the sun, tied back from her face. He could have stood there looking at her forever, lost in her beauty, but a tug at his robe awoke him from his reverie. It was one of the children.

'Will you play with me?' the boy asked.

'Maybe later,' Simon answered. He was quite unused to children and certainly didn't know any children's games.

'Simon. I didn't hear you,' said Salma, an enormous smile lighting up her face. He felt his heart skip a beat. No, he could never leave her and return to his own land. Never. This feeling that overwhelmed him whenever he saw her must be love. What else could it be?

'You're copying?' he asked. 'What is it that you're working at so diligently?'

'I'm worried that we will lose all our books if we don't do something to protect them,' she said. 'So I've decided to make copies of the ones I took from the library and I will hide them somewhere. Just in case.'

'I went to the library this morning,' Simon said. 'The Chief Scribe was there, working.'

'Is it open again?' she asked excitedly, putting down her pen and getting up as though she would go there right away.

'No. He was alone. I think he has been hiding the books. There were lots of empty shelves.'

'Good. I knew he wouldn't just leave our library to be looted like the rest of the city. I wonder where he's hiding them?'

'I don't know. When I tried to ask what had happened to them, he told me to leave.'

'He's protecting you. What you don't know, won't hurt you,' she said and turned back to her copying.

There was another tug at his robe.

'Please, sayyad. Will you play with me?' It was the boy again.

'Where is your mother?' he asked.

'She's busy. Sewing.'

'Oh, you haven't heard the news. Bayda's wedding is in two weeks. Everyone is running round like mad things trying to get prepared. The child's mother is making the wedding robes,' said Salma, without looking up from her work.

'Why the hurry?' he asked.

'It's cousin Ahmad's idea. He wants his daughters married as soon as possible. He thinks they will be safer if they're married.'

'Fatima too?'

'Yes, she is not very happy about it. Tomorrow she goes to meet her husband-to-be,' said Salma with a grimace. 'He's a widower. So she will have to take over the running of his household and take care of his child as soon as they're married.'

'Well that's normal, isn't it?' Simon was a bit unworldly when it came to talk about weddings and family matters. He had lived in a monastery for so long that none of that made much sense to him, but he did know that the woman's role was to care for her husband and his children, so he couldn't see why Fatima would object.

'But she wanted to be a teacher. How can she do that if she's married and has a home to run?'

Simon could see that he was about to enter a conversation where he would get very lost, so he turned to the little boy, who was still sitting there, looking at him, wistfully, and said, 'Come on. Let's see if we can find something for you to play with.'

## CHAPTER 19

Salma's grandmother dropped onto the couch beside her and sat there wheezing.

'Are you all right, Teta?' Salma asked, wiping the ink from her pen and laying it down next to the parchment. She stretched her fingers, wiggling them a little to restore the circulation. It was time she took a break from the copying before she started making mistakes. Anyway the sun had gone behind a black cloud and it was harder to see what she was doing.

'I'm fine, child. Just a bit of a problem with my breathing when I climb the stairs. You seem very busy.'

'Yes, I'm making copies of the books I brought home. Then when they're done I will take the originals back to the library and bring some more back to copy, but it's slow work.'

'You seem to have blotted that page,' Layla said, pointing to a small ink stain.

'It doesn't matter. Normally I would be worried about repairing the damage or might even start again, but now there's no time for perfection. Of course I want them to look good but the most important thing is to get the information copied. The knowledge we have in our libraries is vast. You've seen how people come from all over the world to read our books, to study, to translate our ideas and take them back to their own countries. If those books are destroyed all that knowledge goes with it, the ideas and research of thousands of scholars and professors. It would be a disaster far worse than the destruction of the palaces and mosques in our lovely city. That's why I want to copy as many books as I can before the worst happens. A few blots will not detract from what the book contains.'

'That's a very noble plan, my dear, but you are only one person. How can you hope to copy an entire library of books?'

'It's not just me, Rachel is helping me as well and Simon told me that he spoke to the Chief Scribe and he is doing the same. Maybe there are others trying to save part of it as well.'

'Well let's hope that all this effort is unnecessary and that the library remains untouched,' said Layla. She wiped the perspiration from her forehead with a small white cloth, and smiled. 'I'm glad you're here alone, Salma. I must talk to you about an important matter.'

'Yes, Teta, what is it?' She had an uncomfortable feeling in her stomach. Was this about Simon? He had been staying in her cousin's house for almost a month. Was her grandmother going to suggest it was time he moved somewhere else?

'You know, of course that your cousin Bayda is to be married very soon—how could you not with all the commotion that it has caused?' she began. 'Well, yesterday I had a long talk with Ahmad about your prospects. As you will have realised he is worried about the future of his own daughters and, as your father is dead and you have no brothers, he feels responsible for seeing you settled as well.'

'But I don't want to get married, Teta. I'm not ready to be a wife,' she said, panic welling up inside her. She knew that one day it was inevitable, but not now.

'I understand, my dear. You're still young and you don't want to give your life over to being a wife and mother. I do understand. I was much younger than you when my father decided I should get married. All my plans to go to the university were over as soon as he made his choice, but I was lucky in the husband he picked for me. My husband, your grandfather, was a kind man. He knew how much I wanted to study medicine so he allowed me to work in his father's pharmacy and learn how to make potions and ointments. Then later, I qualified as an apothecary and we worked side by side.'

'But how could you do that and be a good wife at the same time?' asked Salma. She had never heard this before. In fact she had never even wondered how her grandmother had become an apothecary.

'Ah well. After we'd been married a few years, my husband decided to take a second wife. I was very upset at first. I thought I had failed him in some way. But then I realised it was never going to change our relationship and, in fact, it meant that I had more time to devote to being an apothecary.'

'Why didn't I know all this, Teta? You never told me that Seedo had a second wife.'

'She died long before you were born, Salma, of the same disease that killed your mother.'

'And her children, my brothers and sisters?'

'Twin girls, who perished with her. Your grandfather was heartbroken. He never took another wife,' Layla said.

Salma thought she could see tears in her grandmother's eyes. How strange that she would cry for the other wife. Didn't she see her as a rival? Salma would hate it if her husband took a second wife. What was she thinking? She didn't want a husband. She loved Simon but she knew she would never be allowed to speak of it.

'What did Ahmad say?' she asked.

'He hasn't got anyone in mind for you, yet. At the moment I think he just wants to get Fatima and Bayda married and then he will find someone for you, but I wanted to speak to you about it, so you could accustom yourself to the idea.' She looked at her strangely.

'I'll never get used to the idea, Teta. Never.'

'Listen child, I know what you're thinking but it will never happen. That man is not for you. He is a Christian and you are forbidden to marry a Christian. And anyway, he's a man of God. It is as sinful for him to marry you as it is for you to marry him. You can have no future together. Don't waste your life dreaming impossible dreams.'

So she knew. Salma couldn't hold back her tears any longer. 'But I love him,' she sobbed. 'I love him.'

'Come here, my sweet child,' said Layla, putting her arms around her. 'I know it seems like the end of the world, right now, but one day you will understand that these laws exist for our benefit. You would never be happy with him. What would happen when you had children? Would you want your children to grow up as Christians and be excluded from the true faith?'

Salma shook her head sadly. It was cruel. Why had Allah let her fall in love with a Christian?

'Don't worry about it now. Just enjoy the celebrations for your cousins' weddings then we will talk about yours again,' she said, stroking Salma's hair.

Salma pulled away and turned to face her grandmother. 'You're not going to send him away, are you?'

'No, not if you behave yourself. It isn't fair on him or yourself to let him think that you care for him. One day he will go back to his own country and return to the monastery. Let him go with a clear conscience.'

'So he can stay?' Salma asked.

'Yes, he can stay for now. I'd hate to turn anyone away while the city is in such turmoil. Now pack up your things and go and help Aisha with the supper. I'm going to stay here for a while and watch the sun setting.'

\*

He'd been plagued by the same dream for nights now. The soldier was coming at him with his sword drawn. He could feel the sharp tip pressing into his chest. Simon was about to die, to stand before God. How would he explain to God about his love for an unbeliever, a Muslim woman? He had even considered abandoning his calling for her and now, before he had time to repent, he was about to meet his Maker. Then that's when the dream took a strange turn. His attacker stopped, arm posed to deal the death blow, and a look of surprise came over his face. He dropped to the ground, the sword falling from his grasp and blood oozing from his neck. It was at this point each night that Simon woke. He hadn't died. Somehow Salma had saved him. He resolved to speak to her, to find out exactly what had happened that afternoon.

'What is it, Simon? You look troubled. Is your head still bothering you?' Salma asked, her attention still on the book she was laboriously copying.

'My head is fine, thanks to your grandmother,' he replied.

'So, what is it?' She looked up at him, wrinkling her forehead in the delightful way she did when she was concerned about something.

'Tell me, Salma, what happened to the soldier who attacked me? How did we escape him? I need to know. Did I do something terrible? Did I kill him?'

Not only would that be a crime he would have to pay for with his life, but it would be a sin that would weigh on his conscience for eternity. He prayed that it was not so, but someone had stabbed the soldier—he had seen the blood—so if it wasn't him, then who could it have been?

'Oh, Simon, dear, sweet, gentle Simon. No, of course you didn't kill him. You were helpless, half-conscious and bleeding from your wound. You could hardly move, never mind kill anyone.

'Thank the Lord. It has been torturing me night after night,' he said and explained about his dreams.

'You are exhausted from the attack,' she said, resuming her copying. 'It will all fade with time.'

'But who attacked him? And is he dead or was he just wounded? Do you know? And what happened to the other soldier? Why didn't he come back and help him? You were there, Salma. Surely you know what happened?'

'So many questions,' she muttered, not looking at him. 'Too many questions.'

'But I have to know,' he insisted.

Salma put down her pen and looked at him. She was trembling.

'If I tell you everything, Simon, you must promise never to repeat it to anyone, not to your priest, not to a friend, not to the Chief Scribe, not to Ahmad. No-one. Promise me. The only one I have spoken to about that day is my grandmother.'

Simon was worried now. He'd never seen Salma like this before. She was always so calm and self-assured. Now she was on the verge of panic. What had happened that afternoon as he lay between wakefulness and oblivion?

'Tell me, Salma. Please. I will speak to no-one. I promise. But I have to know.'

The young woman covered her face with her hands and he thought she would weep, but instead she looked up, straight at him and said, 'It was me, Simon. I killed him. I stabbed him with my knife. I had to. He was going to kill you. I had no choice. I had to,' she repeated. 'I didn't mean to kill him. I just wanted him to stop. I couldn't let you die.'

At first Simon was too stunned to speak. Then he put his hand on hers and said what he knew she wanted to hear, 'You had no choice, Salma. God will forgive you.'

But even as he said the words, he knew they were not true. God would not forgive the taking of a life. It was a mortal sin. What was he to do? His heart felt heavy and it was as if all the sunshine had faded from his life. He stifled a sigh. All he could do was to pray for her Muslim soul and hope that God would listen to him.

## CHAPTER 20

They rose before dawn, as was customary on the day of a battle. Rafiq wandered through the rows of tents, checking that all was in order. Most of his jinetes were already dressed in their chainmail hauberks; some were with the horses checking that all was as it should be, others were cleaning and sharpening their weapons. He would finish his tour—more a walk of encouragement than inspection at this stage—and then he'd go and check on Antarah.

'Good day for a fight, quaid,' one of the men called to him as he passed his tent.

'Indeed it is, soldier.'

'What are those Catalans like, quaid? Do they know how to fight like good Muslims?' asked an old soldier.

'They're hard men, so I hear.'

'Good to have at your back, then, quaid?'

'Let's hope so, soldier.'

It would be a tough battle. Even with the Catalan reinforcements, Sulayman's troops out-numbered their depleted army. Today Rafiq's troops would be fighting under the leadership of the Count of Barcelona, a man nobody knew. The plan was for them to engage with the enemy at Guadiaro, near Ronda while Muhammad and General al-Wahdi reclaimed the city of Córdoba.

Rafiq strolled on, passing men still eating their breakfast, others knelt in silent prayer, some joking with their comrades, each with his own way of preparing himself for the battle ahead. He liked these moments before a battle, when everything was quiet and peaceful, the men chatting with each other, the horses munching their way through their breakfast. Soon all that would change, but for now he enjoyed the silence, the camaraderie.

'Cup of mint tea, quaid?' a young jinete asked.

'No thank you, soldier. Don't drink too much of that stuff or you'll be pissing yourself before the battle's half-way through.'

'We're going to show that bloody Sulayman who the real Khalifa is this time. That's right, quaid?'

'We are indeed, soldier.'

A streak of red appeared along the horizon. It would soon be light. Already the sea was turning silver and he could make out the dark shapes of fishing boats in the distance. His mouth began to water as he thought of the fresh fish they would eat tonight when the battle was over. They were camped upstream on the banks of the Guadiaro river. Further downstream were the enemy. They would meet on the wide plain of the Guadiaro valley. Flat and treeless, it was ideal for his jinetes.

He straightened his helmet and thrust his curved sword into the scabbard that hung from the baldric across his chest. His other weapons were a dagger he kept in his belt and a double-edged axe which tucked into Antarah's breast strap. That axe, though it had taken him a while to perfect his skills with it, had got him out of dangerous situations more than once. He picked up his shield and set off for the stables.

\*

They were in their usual battle formation, with the foot soldiers at the front, the archers behind them and Rafiq and his jinettes behind them. The Catalans were to their left. The river was to their right. The air was ripe with tension, the soldiers like taut springs. He felt Antarah tremble beneath him, her breath exploding in short sharp bursts, but she held firm. Rafiq murmured a word of encouragement to her and stroked her neck. Their horses were used to battle conditions and obeyed every word, every gesture their riders gave them and none was more obedient than Antarah. Men and horses alike awaited their commander's order, hearts racing, nerves strained, adrenalin pumping.

The battle lines were drawn. The enemy was in position. The Count of Barcelona, astride an enormous black stallion, waited behind them on a ridge from which he could survey the whole battle, his arm, holding the Catalan flag, was raised. They waited until the enemy was within range. Then the signal was given. Instantly the infantrymen threw their lances at the advancing troops. Then, without waiting to see how successful they'd been, each man dropped to one knee and lifted his shield, forming a tight barricade. Next the archers let fly a barrage of arrows that fell down on the enemy like rain. Men dropped to the ground, stopped in their tracks before they had even reached their goal. But still Sulayman's men moved forward. This was the moment Rafiq had been waiting for. On the commander's signal the archers and the infantrymen parted like a field of corn in a strong wind, and like that wind, Rafiq and his men rode through the gap straight at the enemy, swords raised, slashing and slicing at everyone in their way.

This was what he lived for. This thrill, the exhilaration as he rode straight at the enemy. He looked for the weaknesses, slashing at exposed arms and wrists, disabling his opponents' weapon hands, slicing at the neck whenever he had the opportunity. The jinete's style was fast and deadly. For what seemed to be hours, he slashed and cut and sliced his way through the enemy lines.

At last there was a lull in the battle and Rafiq had time to pause and survey the scene. His men were spread out now. The infantry were engaged in hand-to-hand combat. The archers had retreated to the rear, waiting for the opportunity to shoot again when their own comrades were clear. The Catalans on his left were fighting ferociously. The river on his right, ran red with blood and the ground around them was littered with dead and dying bodies.

Suddenly a tremendous blow caught him in the back and he was knocked right out of the saddle, his sword flying from his hand. For a moment he was winded and lay on the ground wondering how he'd got there. He looked up just in time to see an enormous man standing over him, holding a two-handed cleaving sword. He was about to be split in two. He rolled quickly to the right, just as the sword descended and buried itself into the soft earth. Rafiq jumped to his feet and looked about him for Antarah. Where was she? She would come if he whistled. But there was no time. His sword was lying on the ground where he'd fallen but it had been split in two. His assailant had extricated his own sword from the ground and now advanced towards him, the sword held above his head. Rafiq grabbed wildly at the first thing he could to defend himself, a wooden staff dropped by some peasant member of the militia. He lifted it before him and backed away from the swordsman. This wasn't going to end well. That sword would cut through his staff like a knife through butter.

Then all at once, a horseman was there. A flash of steel as he cut through the swordsman's wrist. A howl of pain and the sword fell to the ground. The enemy soldier spun round to face his new opponent, screaming some of the foulest oaths that Rafiq had ever heard. As he attempted to pull the young jinete from his horse, Rafiq hit him as hard as he could across the back of his head with the staff. The swordsman gave a grunt and fell to the ground, silent at last.

'Here, finish him off,' shouted the jinete and threw Rafiq a sword.

'There's no need. He'll never fight again,' said Rafiq, pointing to the lacerated tendons that hung from the swordsman's wrist. He whistled.

'Is that your horse?' the young jinete asked. 'What a beauty.'

'Good girl, Antarah,' Rafiq murmured and jumped up onto her back. He felt a whole lot safer in the saddle.

'You're a Muslim?' the jinete asked. 'And an officer, I see.'

'Yes. And you must be Catalan?'

'Yes, Marco is my name.'

'Well Marco, I owe you my life. But I'm not a rich man, so you will have to make do with my undying gratitude.'

'I can see you're no rich man. Whoever goes into battle carrying a staff, other than the farmers, that is? Don't they issue you with swords in al-Andalus?'

At first Rafiq felt insulted at the man's words but then he realised he was joking. He pointed to his broken sword and said, 'That's all that remains of my sword. A pity. It has served me well over the years.'

'Keep that one. I just took it off a dead soldier. You're welcome to it. You'll need it. Unless you'd sooner fight with the staff?'

'No, I'll keep the sword. My thanks and may Allah keep you safe.'

He touched Antarah lightly on the flanks and rode back into the battle. How had that swordsman crept up on him without him realising? That would never have happened when he was younger. He should never have dropped his guard. He told his men to be alert at all times, and yet he had let his mind wander and the consequences had almost been fatal. Thank goodness for the intervention of the Catalan. He was young. How old? Maybe eighteen, no more. Maybe Rafiq was getting too old for active service. Perhaps that was the simple explanation. He was past it. He shuddered at the thought. What would he do if he wasn't a soldier? That was all that he knew. Soldiering had been his life.

\*

Rafiq's blood was coursing through his veins. He could hear his heart pounding in his chest as though he had run twenty miles. He knew he should rest now that the battle was over but it was impossible. His body just wanted to carry on slashing and lunging at the enemy until not one remained, but his head told him that was not the way things were done. The enemy had surrendered and General Tayyab had ordered them to seek out and help the injured.

So now he led his men through the fallen bodies, identifying their own for burial, helping the wounded and rounding up the few enemy soldiers that had survived. Some would make good recruits for the army. Others might chose death instead. For now they were his prisoners.

He patted his horse's neck and tried to calm her. Her blood was up too. He pushed the hair out of his eyes; his helmet had come off in the battle and the wind whipped his long black hair around him like a scarf. In fact he was a sorry sight, covered in blood, his lance broken, his shield smashed. He wiped the blood from his face and looked about him at the carnage. The battlefield was littered with the dead and dying. It had been almost a total slaughter, with the Catalans giving no quarter to the enemy. Now, in the end, they were victorious and Sulayman was defeated.

But where was the Pretender now? No-one had seen the going of him. His body wasn't lying among the dead and wounded, so he must have escaped. Was that the end of it? Would the country see some stability again? Rafiq doubted it. There was something about Sulayman that said he'd be back. He'd had a taste of victory before and the lure of the Khalifa's throne was too strong for him to ignore. Despite their bloodthirsty allies, he felt that this battle was far from over.

'Finish me off, quaid. Don't leave me to suffer,' a weak voice called to him. 'For pity's sake, give me a soldier's death.'

Rafiq looked in the direction of the voice and felt his stomach turn over. How was it possible that this soldier still lived? He was barely twenty years old, his youthful face unmarked, his dark eyes burning with pain and his guts spilling on the ground beside him. He would never survive long enough for Rafiq to get him to a doctor.

'For pity's sake, quaid,' he begged.

Rafiq dismounted and bent over the youth. He was one of their own. An infantryman. A new recruit no doubt on his first and, now his last mission.

'What's your name, soldier?' he asked, averting his eyes from the man's horrendous wound.

'Ahmad,' the boy whispered.

Rafiq froze. Yes, that was it, the boy reminded him of his brother when he was young. That same innocent, trusting face. He pushed his sword back into his scabbard. He couldn't do it. Not now.

'For pity's sake, help me. End my misery,' the boy pleaded. 'In the name of Allah, I beg you.' His voice was weaker and it would not be long before he departed from this world.

If it were his brother, would he leave him to suffer? Of course not. Rafiq took a deep breath, pulled his sword from its scabbard once more, and murmuring, 'To Allah we belong and to Him is our return,' he thrust the sword through the young man's heart. The look of peace on the dead boy's face told him he'd done the right thing.

\*

It was almost a week before they reached Córdoba with the prisoners. As they crossed the plain towards the city they could see the pall of smoke hanging above it. Fire? What, in the name of Allah, had happened now? The news had reached them that Muhammad had regained the city and once again reinstated himself as Khalifa. So what had happened? Had there been another attack? Were all their efforts in vain? Suddenly Rafiq felt deathly tired. It was one campaign after another—they seemed to have been at war continually for years. It wasn't just Rafiq who felt like that, the men too were tired and had virtually given up all hope of ever seeing their families again.

'Soldier. Ride ahead and find out the reason for that fire. Then get back to me as fast as your horse can carry you.'

'Yes, quaid.'

He watched the young soldier ride across the Roman bridge into the city.

'Right men. We're going to wait here for a while to see what's happening. You lad, take the horses down to the river and let them drink. The rest of you can rest, but don't let down your guard. If the city is under attack again, we will need to respond quickly.'

'Yes, quaid,' the three junior officers under his command replied. One of them leapt down from his horse and led it to the river's edge, where he and the animal drank greedily from the muddy water.

Slowly Rafiq dismounted and led Antarah into the shade. She had been magnificent in battle, as fearless as ever. But she was getting old. How many more years would she have the strength and turn of speed that she had now? Maybe it was time she went into retirement and he got himself a younger horse. God knows, she deserved it. Or maybe it was time they both retired. He sat down by a large rock and closed his eyes for a moment. How long was it since he'd slept? A week? Two weeks? It was impossible to truly sleep while on a campaign. One part of you was always awake, always on the alert for danger. He sighed. How lovely it would be to have a whole night's undisturbed sleep, on a soft bed with the scent of jasmine around you instead of this constant stench of blood and faeces.

The sound of galloping hooves jerked him upright. It was the young soldier. Back already? Or had he actually fallen asleep?

'Quaid. I have news for you,' the lad said, excitedly slipping down from his horse.

'Well, spit it out, boy. What's happening in the city?'

'It's as you thought, sayyad. Muhammad II is now the Khalifa. He has installed himself and his court in the old alcázar.'

'So why is there so much smoke hanging above the city? Why the fires?'

'Oh, that's the Catalans, quaid. They're plundering the city.'

'What? Our allies, the Catalans are plundering our city? And Muhammad is aware of this?'

'Oh yes, quaid. It was he who gave them permission.'

'Allah preserve and save us. What manner of Khalifa allows foreigners to sack his own city?'

He turned away from the messenger so that he would not see the disgust on his face. This was the man he had fought for, the man who was now ruler of al-Andalus and it was he who had allowed these northerners to plunder Córdoba.

Well there was nothing Rafiq could do about it. As he reminded himself daily, he was a soldier and a soldier obeyed orders. As simple as that. He jumped onto Antarah's back and said, 'Right men. Let's take these prisoners to the dungeons and then we will return to the Dar al-Jund to see what our new orders are.' Maybe the General would explain this strange turn of events.

\*

The mutterings started almost as soon as he returned. The people of Córdoba were angry with Muhammad II and who could blame them? The city was a shell of its former self. First the Berbers had raped it under the command of Sanchuelo, then Sulayman and his Castilian allies and now, the final insult, the victor, the one who fought for them, for their city, had allowed his Catalan allies to plunder it. They were not in a mood to forgive him. The people were tired of war. They were tired of these power-hungry men who wanted to rule them. They were angry about paying such high taxes—all the money from which went on campaigns against the Christians—and seeing no benefit from it. Their city was in ruins and people scuttled about in fear of their lives. It was impossible to go about their daily business with so many soldiers roaming the streets, when fights could break out at any moment. Shops were closed, schools were shut, homes were barricaded; there were no visiting scholars, no itinerant merchants brought their wares and the caravans from North Africa skirted the city and made for Málaga or Seville instead. This was not the thriving city it had been when al-Hisham had been Khalifa and al-Mansur had ruled. The people of Córdoba had had enough. It was time to re-instate the imprisoned Khalifa, time to put al-Hisham back on his rightful throne.

'Have you heard the rumours?' Rafiq asked Asif, the next morning as they both waited for General Tayyab to arrive and give them their orders.

'They don't like him,' said Asif. 'And can you blame them?'

'But will they act on it?'

'If they have some support, yes.'

'But Muhammad is a member of the Omayyad dynasty. Surely they won't go against him?' Rafiq protested.

His friend shrugged. 'Here's the general now. Maybe he'll tell us more,' he said.

They both stood to attention as General Tayyab approached. He had been injured in the last battle and dragged his wounded leg as he walked, the pain etching itself on his face with every step.

'As-salama alaykum, men. Stand at ease.'

'Wa alaykum e-salam, General,' they both replied.

'You've heard the rumours, I take it?' he said straight away. As usual the general got straight to the point.

'Yes, General. But are they just rumours?' Rafiq replied.

The general smiled and stroked his beard, thoughtfully. 'Until we make them otherwise, soldiers.'

Rafiq looked at him in surprise. Was the general suggesting a coup d'état?

General Tayyab continued. 'I have been speaking to General al-Wahdi and he has proposed that we reinstate al-Hisham, who is after all still the rightful ruler of al-Andalus. That is what the people of Córdoba want. So you are to take some trusted men and go to the prison and release him right away.' He looked directly at Rafiq and handed him a roll of parchment. 'Take this with you. It has been signed by General al-Wahdi, who is now the Supreme Commander of our depleted army, and it authorises you to remove al-Hisham from the prison.'

Rafiq accepted the document and asked, 'But where shall I take the Khalifa? To the palace in Madinat al-Zahra?'

'No, numbskull. Sulayman has made that his headquarters. Our Khalifa would not last five minutes in the company of that traitor. No, he is to live in the old alcázar in Córdoba.'

'But Muhammad is there,' said Rafiq in surprise.

'Not anymore. No-one knows where the treacherous Muhammad is at the moment, but he certainly isn't in his palace. It's said that he plans to escape from the city,' replied the General. 'Probably with his Catalan friends.'

'That's one thing he is good at, escaping,' said Asif, bitterly. 'And what of his troops?'

'Don't worry about that, soldier. You have a new commander now. General al-Wahdi is a loyal soldier and a fearless leader of men. With his lead we may get out of this interminable whirlpool of internal warfare. Your job now is to send someone to prepare the alcázar for the arrival of al-Hisham.'

'Yes, General, at once.'

'And then I want you to take some men and find Muhammad. He is in this city somewhere.'

'Yes, General,' said Asif.

'When you find him, bring him to me or take him directly to General al-Wahdi. Is that understood?'

'Very well General.'

The general limped away from them leaving Rafiq stunned at the turn of events. Al-Hisham was to be Khalifa again. He thought of what Ahmad had told him about the Khalifa. He'd said al-Hisham was not a well man. So why put a sick man back on the throne? He'd always been a weak ruler. Why did the generals think that he would be any different now? Or maybe that was their plan. Put a weak figurehead on the throne to keep the people happy and then rule in his place. After all, that was what al-Mansur had done very successfully for twenty-five years.

'What do you think of that then?' asked Asif, interrupting his thoughts. 'Wait until the men hear about it. Fancy putting that old degenerate back on the throne. I can't believe it.'

'It's not my place to question the General's orders. I'm a soldier not a politician.'

'But you must have some opinion, man?'

'Yes, I think we should get on and do what the General has ordered us to,' Rafiq barked at his friend. If the truth be told, he was not happy with the way this was going. For years he'd served the same Supreme Commander, but since the death of al-Mansur he had served three different rulers and now it was back to al-Hisham again. Where did his loyalty lie now? With one of these ruthless, power-hungry upstarts or with the incompetent al-Hisham? It was best that he follow his own advice and leave the politics to others while he obeyed orders.

One person would be happy with the news, he was sure of that. His brother Ahmad would be delighted to hear of al-Hisham's release. Well he would hear about it soon enough and, if all went well, maybe Rafiq would be able to go home tonight and sleep in a decent bed. He pushed any further thoughts of politics and duty out of his mind and set off for the Dar al-Jund.

## CHAPTER 21

Most of his corps of jinetes were lounging near the stables. Rafiq picked two of his most able men and shouted across at them. 'You two. Smarten yourselves up and come with me, and make sure your swords are serviceable; we don't know what we may encounter. We've a job to do for the Khalifa.'

They looked at him in surprise but said nothing. They too had heard the rumours. Well it wouldn't hurt to keep them guessing for a while longer.

'And bring an extra horse. A quiet one.'

The two jinetes were on their feet in seconds. If there was one thing he could rely on from his men, it was their unquestioning obedience.

Within ten minutes they joined him at the main gate, mounted and leading a docile grey mare.

'Follow me,' he said.

'Where are we going?' asked the younger man.

'To the prison, soldier, to release our Khalifa. So let's be on our way, sharpish.'

They rode though the deserted streets, passing the barricaded doors of shops, the empty market place and on, up to the Great Mosque. Here Rafiq called a halt.

'We will say a prayer to ask for Allah's blessing before we continue,' he said.

The three men removed their weapons and their shoes then washed themselves in the usual cleansing ritual. Once they were ready they entered the mosque together. Stepping from the bright sunlight into the darkened mosque, it was difficult to see at first but as his eyes became accustomed to the soft light of the oil lamps he noticed a woman kneeling before the mihrab. It was not one of the normal hours of prayer and he was surprised to see anyone there at all, especially a woman—they normally prayed in a section at the back of the mosque—and there was something strange about her. She was very large, but not fat and rounded like most women, more muscular, almost like a man. In fact as she bent over to pray he could have sworn she was a man. Well, it took all sorts to make the world. He had more important things on his mind.

Rafiq laid his prayer mat on the ground facing the mihrab and knelt in prayer. The two soldiers did the same. Rafiq was not a very strong believer but he knew he'd led a charmed life as a soldier and who else could he thank but Allah? It didn't hurt to acknowledge Him from time to time. For some reason he felt compelled to offer up some extra prayers today. Maybe Allah was looking out for their city at long last. As he knelt and repeated the time-old prayers a feeling of peace came over him and by the time they had all finished their devotions he felt refreshed, a whole man again.

As he rolled up his mat he noticed that the strange woman had gone. Outside Antarah, who had taken a liking to the grey mare, was contentedly nuzzling her. She whinnied softly as he approached. The soldiers followed him.

\*

The sentry at the prison gates leapt to attention when he saw them arrive. It was obvious that the men on duty were left very much to their own devices. He knew from the gossip that no-one wanted to be put on prison detail; it was poorly paid, extremely boring work and the food was disgusting.

'Quaid,' said the sentry. 'What can I do for you?'

'Take me to the prisoner, al-Hisham,' he said, thrusting his scroll of authority under the man's nose.

The man looked at the document in surprise then nodded at his companion who opened the gate wide enough for the three soldiers to enter. They followed the guard down a dingy passage where the walls dripped a greenish water and the air was as stale as an old boot. No fresh wind had entered this hell hole for many a year.

'This is the man you want,' the soldier said, stopping outside a darkened cell. 'I don't know if al-Hisham is awake.'

'Well wake him up and tell him we've come to take him out of this cesspit,' Rafiq snapped.

'Yes, quaid.'

The guard opened the cell door and went inside. 'Wake up, Your Majesty. There is someone here to see you. Wake up.' He seemed reluctant to touch him.

Rafiq watched as a bundle of rags unfolded itself; first a leg emerged, then another, then a hand reached out and pushed against the wet floor. Was this al-Hisham? Rafiq had only seen the Khalifa once, many years before. He couldn't believe that this was the same person. Despite what his brother had told him, he never expected to see such a ruin of a man.

'Who are you?' a quavering voice asked him. 'What do you want? Have you come to execute me? If so, be quick. Draw your sword and be done with it. I am ready to meet my maker.'

Rafiq bowed. 'No, Your Majesty. I have come to take you away from here. I have come to take you home. You're free.'

'Who are you?' the Khalifa repeated. He remained where he was, huddled in the corner of the cell.

'My name is Rafiq ibn Makoud. You have nothing to fear from me.'

'Makoud? I know that name.'

'Yes, Your Majesty. My father was Makoud ibn Qasim. He served you for many years, until his death.'

'Yes, yes. I remember him well. So you are his son? Then my dear Ahmad is your brother?'

'Yes, Your Majesty. You have nothing to fear. I have come to take you to the alcázar.'

A crafty look came over the Khalifa's face and he drew back into the shadows. 'It's a trick. How do I know you are who you say you are? You have come to take me to my execution.'

'No, Your Majesty. I have come to take you home.'

'No, no. I won't go with you. Where is Musa. Bring Musa to me,' the Khalifa cried. He was becoming distraught.

'Who is Musa? Rafiq asked the guard.

'He is his servant.'

'Well send for him and be quick about it,' he snapped. He should have realised that the Khalifa would be reluctant to leave his cell. He had been living with the threat of death hanging over him for over a year. Now he believed that the moment had come. Rafiq couldn't take him by force. He was the Khalifa and his wishes had to be respected, no matter how ridiculous they were.

'Soldier, go and find my brother, Ahmad. He lives in a big house by the river, close to the cattle market. Tell him that the Khalifa needs him, urgently. Don't take no for an answer. Otherwise we're going to be here all night,' he told the man standing outside the cell. 'And make haste.'

'Yes, quaid.'

The soldier turned and fled from the dungeon as though all the bats in hell were after him. Rafiq couldn't blame him. They were all used to death and the stench of dying but this smell was different; it was the odour of something corrupt and rotten, something hidden in the darkness away from the light and the air. Better to die on the battle field than rot in a prison, that's what all soldiers thought. That was why so many defeated soldiers elected to join the enemy and fight rather than go to prison.

Rafiq turned to the guard and said, 'I'm going to wait outside. Tell the Khalifa's servant to get the Khalifa ready to travel. I cannot take him to the alcázar looking like that. Is that understood?'

'Yes, quaid. Would you like me to show you the way out?'

'No. I can manage,' Rafiq replied, walking as normally as he could and holding back a childish desire to run out of that hellish place as fast as possible.

\*

He recognised Ahmad as soon as he came in range of the lamplight. He wore his usual long brown djellaba and carried a large hawk on his right hand.

'Ahmad. Over here,' he called.

'Rafiq. I came as quickly as I could. What's happened? Has something happened to the Khalifa? Is he worse? Or is he just having another of his tantrums?'

'Calm down, little brother. Nothing has happened to him. I am trying to release him and take him to the alcázar but the half-wit thinks I've come to execute him. I can't get him to leave his cell. You will have to persuade him.'

'I'll try but what makes you think he'll listen to me? You realise he's not always in his right mind? Sometimes he's completely coherent but other times he hears voices and sees images.'

'Images?'

'Yes, usually of his mother and sometimes of his father. Once I caught him talking to our own father, al-Jundi. And he often mistakes poor Musa for his former servant Umari.'

'Well, whatever happens, he has to leave the prison. Those are my orders and I intend to fulfil them. He can bring his ghosts with him for all I care.'

Musa had received the message about preparing the Khalifa to leave and by the time they re-entered his cell he was sitting there —still in the same corner but now his face had been washed and his beard combed. A clean white turban was wound round his head and he wore a white djubba and a djellaba that seemed three sizes too large for him. When he saw Ahmad, he stood up and a spectral smile crept over his face.

'As-salama alaykum, Your Majesty,' Ahmad said and bowed. 'I'm glad you're ready. We have no time to lose. This is your chance to get out of this awful place. I am taking you to the alcázar.'

'You have brought Shamal with you,' al-Hisham said.

'Of course, Your Majesty. He is to go home with you now.'

'Very well. If you are sure this is no trick, Ahmad.'

'No, Your Majesty. This is not a trick. This is your deliverance. This soldier is my dear brother. He has come to escort you to the alcázar.'

'But you will come too, Ahmad?'

'Of course, Your Majesty. I will come with you. I will not leave you until you are safe.'

The Khalifa stretched out his arm for the falcon and Ahmad lifted it from his own hand and placed it on al-Hisham's.

'I am ready,' the Khalifa said.

Rafiq was impressed with the way his brother handled the Khalifa, almost as though he were a child—which in many ways he was.

He led the motley group out of the dungeon, through the foul passageways, out the main gate and into square opposite them. There they paused for a moment while Rafiq's men collected the horses. What a contrast this must be for the Khalifa. Rafiq watched as al-Hisham stood in the centre of the square and breathed deeply, inhaling the perfume of the jasmine and myrtle bushes. Then he lifted his head and stared at the sky, a canopy of black silk, studded with stars and a sliver of moon that cast a pale light over them all.

'We must go now, Your Majesty. Let me help you mount your horse,' Rafiq said. He eased the sick man into the saddle and placed the reins in Musa's hands. 'Lead him carefully and follow me closely,' he added.

He was still anxious for the Khalifa's safety and wanted to get him to the alcázar as soon as he could. Muhammad's men might still be around. Even now they could be on their way to kill al-Hisham. He could take no chances. 'Ahmad, jump up behind me and let's get moving. There is no time to be lost.'

\*

Rafiq's orders had been to release the prisoner and take him to the alcázar. No more and no less. But what should he do now? He couldn't just leave al-Hisham in the alcázar unprotected. The

Palace Guard were an unknown force. Until today they had been protecting Muhammad II, now they were to guard al-Hisham II. Could they be trusted? He decided that he and his men would wait at the alcázar until they received new orders from General Tayyab.

Ahmad had followed the Khalifa and his servant into the inner part of the palace. So while he waited for his brother to reappear, Rafiq wandered through the courtyard. He had never been in the old alcázar before—it was called the old alcázar because it had once been the home of Abd al-Rahman III. It was an elegant building, not as sumptuous as the palace at Madinat al-Zahra was said to have been, but to him this was luxury beyond his reach. The tapestries alone were worth more than he could make in a year of lucrative soldiering, and the marble columns rivalled even those in the Great Mosque.

'Would you like anything, sayyad?' asked one of the palace servants, offering him a tray with bread, olives and oil on it.

'That would be fine, and something to drink,' Rafiq replied.

'Wine, sayyad?'

'No, just some mint tea.'

As the servant left, Asif came rushing into the courtyard. 'Rafiq. I have news. But why are you still here? Is the Khalifa safe?'

'Yes, Asif. All is as the General asked for. And what of you? You looked excited. Come sit down and tell me what has happened.'

'Well, it's done,' said Asif, throwing himself down on the bench beside Rafiq. 'There's no need to stay here now. We'll have no more trouble from him.'

'Muhammad?'

'Who else?'

'Did you find him? Tell me what happened,' Rafiq said.

'Pass me some of that bread and I'll tell you everything.' He broke off a hunk of bread and dipped in the dish of olive oil. 'I'm famished.'

'Stop feeding your ugly face and tell me what happened.'

'There's not much to tell. We caught him trying to slip across the Roman bridge, dressed as a woman.'

'What? Dressed as a woman? I can't believe it,' said Rafiq.

'It's true. I swear on my wife's life. He wore a woman's robes and a cloak over his head. And he'd shaved off his beard. As if that would make any difference, with his ugly mug. He didn't get far. The sentries on the bridge knew it wasn't a woman straight away.' Asif helped himself to another piece of bread and a few olives. 'How stupid can you be? Did he think a lusty soldier wouldn't know the difference between a man and a woman. Our soldiers spend half their time—when they're not fighting—looking at women. They know how a woman moves. They don't need to look at a person's clothes to decide if it's a man or a woman; they can tell by looking at their bums. And Muhammad was never going to be able to wiggle his hips like a woman.'

Rafiq's mind flashed back to the strange woman he'd seen in the mosque. Had that been Muhammad, getting up his courage?

'So he was arrested?'

'Yes, and taken straight to General al-Wahdi.' He laughed. 'He was more like a woman then, crying and begging for mercy.'

'So where is he now?' asked Rafiq.

'Well, his head is on a pole on the gates of the city, right next to the rotting skull of Sanchuelo. I imagine they threw his body to the dogs.'

The servant entered and poured out two beakers of tea for them. He had heard Asif's words but made no comment, although his hand shook as handed them the tea.

'It's over, Rafiq. The Khalifa is back on the throne and the Pretender is dead. Maybe now I can go home and spend some time with my wife.'

'I wouldn't be too sure about that,' said Rafiq, sipping the mint tea. 'Sulayman will take heart from Muhammad's death. He is not the man to run away from a fight. No, this isn't over by any means.'

The Ring of Flames

# PART TWO

# The siege of Córdoba
# 1011 -1013

## CHAPTER 22

The rain hadn't stopped for weeks. It rained all day and all night. The sun seemed to have deserted them because it remained stubbornly hidden behind heavy black clouds day after day. At first the rain soaked into the parched ground, which lapped it up like a thirsty camel, but then it could drink no more and the rain pooled into gigantic puddles and cascaded down the mountain streams and ravines in torrents. It washed the streets of the city clean and blocked the drains and gutters; it took everything before it and deposited it in the river. There was nowhere else for it to go. It flooded the fertile plains, tearing up the newly planted crops and turning the area into a morass; it soaked the cattle and sent the goats scurrying for whatever shelter they could find; it swelled the Guadalquivir until its banks could no longer withstand the pressure and the muddy river spilled out across the land. It was a monster that could not be contained.

Ahmad watched as the flood water rose higher and higher, turning the road into a river and lapping at the door of his house. This spot, where he had built his house so many years before, was once so tranquil and safe; now it was about to become the centre of a maelstrom. A dead goat, its stomach swollen, its eyes staring at nothing, swirled past. Soon it would be them being carried downstream. Everything he had built would be swept away if they didn't do something to stop it.

'Makoud, Simon, come here and help. See those logs. Bring them here and help me to build a barricade. We have to do something to hold back this water. A few more hours and the house will be flooded.'

They toiled for a while, heaving the enormous trunks of wood into position but it was obvious that it was going to make no difference. The water was already creeping under the door and sending Aisha into a state of panic.

'Ahmad. What are we going to do?' she wailed. 'The water is going everywhere and it is so filthy. I will never get this house clean again.'

'Move as much as you can off the floor and take some of the stuff upstairs. You two as well,' he said, pointing at Simon and Makoud, who by now were soaked to the skin.

'If the river keeps rising you won't be able to stay here,' Simon said.

'What choice do we have? Layla's house is in a worse spot than ours.'

'You could stay in my house. We could go there now. It's a bit small for all of you but at least it will be dry,' Simon said.

'What about your landlady? The Christian woman. Won't she object to you filling her house with strangers?'

'She's gone. Left the city. Even the old man who was looking after the house has gone to live with his son in Seville. He gave me the keys before he left. So, you see, the house is empty; I'm the only one who lives there now.'

'Let's see what Aisha has to say. It sounds as though it would be a good idea, just until the river goes down.'

He stared at the fast flowing river; it had risen by a good hand's breadth while they had been talking. By tonight their home would be under water. If only he'd built more rooms upstairs, instead of that silly terrace. That had been the women's idea. We need somewhere to dry the washing, they said and somewhere to sit in the cool of the evening. Well they'd have a job drying any clothes today. He pushed his wet hair out of his eyes and straightened his cap. Simon was right, it would make sense to move into the city. Since al-Hisham had been back on the throne, Córdoba had been more peaceful. Rachel and her father had moved back home, as had Qasim's family, and Simon —although he seemed to be here every day—had returned to his lodgings. Only Salma and Layla had stayed with them—which was the reason that Simon was always bringing books here for Salma to copy. He ought to say something to him, but what? It wasn't proper for a young man to spend so much time with an unmarried woman, even if he was a monk. But so far the Christian hadn't done anything out of place and everyone found him a very pleasant young man, so Ahmad held his tongue.

He pulled at one of the logs that was on the point of floating downstream, and shoved it against the wall. Then he went inside to see the extent of the flood water. It was bad. Aisha and the others had tried their best to remove things before they got too wet and dirty but the ingress of water was unstoppable. Wet rugs and blankets hung over the lines that the women had strung across the room. His mother was futilely trying to brush the water back out the door.

'Stop. We can do no more,' he said. 'The river is rising very fast. We must leave before we get washed out of our home. We're going to Simon's house. Apparently the owner has left and Simon says there is plenty of room for us all.' Simon hadn't said that exactly but if Ahmad told them that the house was small then Aisha would object and want to remain in her own home. As it was she didn't look happy.

'But Ahmad, we can't abandon our house just like that. What if robbers come? What if something happens to everything we have worked for? We can't leave our lovely home,' she protested. 'No we can't leave. The rain will stop soon. You'll see.'

'Stop your bleating, woman. We're leaving. Salma, Makoud, start loading all that we might need onto the donkey. Mama, find a rope and tie it to the goats. They're coming with us. Aisha, you had better sort out the rest. Go through each room and pack as much as you think we can carry. I hope we will be gone only a few days but we must be prepared for the worst.'

The worst? The worst was that the mill race, just upstream from them, would break its bounds and their house would be swept away. He prayed to Allah that it wouldn't come to that.

# The Ring of Flames

'What about your falcon, Baba?' asked Makoud. 'Shall I let him go?'

'No. He's coming with us. Wait while I put his hood over his eyes. I don't want him spooked by all this confusion.'

He stroked the falcon's head then slipped the leather hood over his eyes. He was a bird he'd hand-reared from a chick, many years ago. The mother had been killed and the chick would not have survived if he hadn't taken it home to care for it. With hindsight he knew that he probably shouldn't have done that—it was tantamount to stealing the bird—but he was only thinking of saving the tiny bundle of fluff. Then when he was grown, Ahmad couldn't part with him.

'I'll take him with me,' he added, placing the falcon on his shoulder.

Everyone worked in silence, constantly aware of the steadily rising water level. Even Aisha had become resigned to leaving her home but that didn't stop the tears that ran down her face.

'Enough of that crying, woman. We'll be back soon enough.'

'What about Mama? I don't think she'll be able to walk all that way,' Aisha said.

'I'll be fine. Don't you worry about me, my dear,' said Amina. 'I've seen worse than this in my time. A drop of rain isn't going to keep me from my family. I'll be all right.'

Ahmad took one last look through the rooms of his house. He too, was sad to be leaving but what choice did they have? They couldn't fight against the river.

'Come, we must go now. If not we will be cut off from the road. Makoud, you take the donkey first and we'll follow.'

What a sorry, bedraggled group they were. They splashed through the flood water until they reached the road that ran along the city wall. Here the river merely lapped against the stone ramparts and the going was easier. As they reached the West Gate, Ahmad stopped and looked back towards his home. By now the river was up to the level of the Roman Bridge and, in the distance, he could just make out the white facade of his house, like a small island surrounded by the swirling black waters of the Guadalquivir.

'Lead us to our new home, Simon,' he said sadly, as he wondered if his poor house could withstand this onslaught.

One by one they followed Simon into the city, Makoud leading the overladen donkey, then Layla with the goats, Aisha bowed down with panniers and bags, Salma with a sack of books over her shoulder which should have been by rights in the library and Amina leaning on her son's arm. They were wet; they were cold; they were dirty but at least now they were on dry land. As they trudged past the Great Mosque, Ahmad murmured a prayer to Allah, asking him to keep his family safe.

*

Within a few days it was as though they had always lived in the Christian woman's house. Aisha and Amina wasted no time in organising the household and Ahmad was able to leave his family and return to the Falcon House.

Although the number of birds in the Falcon House was considerably less than a few years before, now with the return of al-Hisham to the throne Ahmad hoped that they would soon be able to increment their depleted numbers. They had been instructed to breed as many of their own falcons as they could and to add to their numbers by buying from abroad. In time the Falcon House was going to be, once again, a thriving part of the palace.

'We need to get some of these birds out. It's not good for them cooped up in here all the time. They need to fly, to stretch their wings and hunt,' said Ahmad, looking at the falcons sitting on their perches, gloomily grooming their feathers. 'You can see they're bored.'

'They don't like the rain. You know that. Look if you're so bothered, take one of them up to the sierra but you'll get soaked and he won't catch anything. The rain will stop soon and then we can get back to normal,' said his friend, Amir.

'We've been saying that for weeks and it's still raining. The falcons aren't the only ones bored with this weather.'

'How are the love birds getting on?' asked Amir. He meant the peregrine falcons that had mated recently. The female had laid three reddish-brown eggs and for the last twenty-five days she had been incubating them.

'They seem to be devoted. The male hardly leaves her side.'

'Not much longer until they hatch, then?'

'Another week.'

'Are all the eggs fertile?'

'I think so. She doesn't seem to have rejected any,' said Ahmad. He checked every day to see if the female had pushed any of the eggs to the edge of the nest, a sure sign that something was wrong with them, but so far she had kept them all. If everything went well they would have three new peregrines soon. They should be magnificent birds. The father was a peregrine falcon from the same area as Shamal, in the north of Portugal, a region renowned for the quality and speed of its raptors. The mother was a home-bred falcon, and a beauty. They had been mates for almost five years and produced some splendid chicks in that time. He was sure that these young peregrines would be no exception.

'Don't you think it's strange how they always stick to the same mate?' said Amir. 'I mean, you'd think it wouldn't matter to a bird whom he mated with.'

'They mate for life.'

'Well so do we, but we don't always limit ourselves to one mate,' laughed Amir. 'I mean, how boring would that be?'

Ahmad knew that his friend had four wives, the maximum that was allowed under Islamic law. He couldn't understand how he could afford to have so many nor why he wanted more than one. Ahmad was happy with Aisha. She fulfilled all his needs and he didn't relish the idea of having more than one woman in his house to control. It had been bad enough when Bayda and Fatima had been living at home. Now they were both married and living with their husbands—although in Bayda's case they still lived in her parent-in-law's house—he had no need to worry about them. In fact he was pleased that he had brought their marriages forward. Fatima now lived in Málaga, where her husband had a thriving business importing spices from the East and Bayda and her student husband lived in Seville. As far as Ahmad was concerned, they were both out of danger and it meant he had two less family members to worry about, and two less women in the house.

'You're incorrigible,' said Ahmad with a laugh. There was no use getting annoyed with Amir. He was a good man but he had a lust for the women that Ahmad couldn't understand.

'Who was it that said, go forth and multiply?' Amir asked, grinning at his friend. 'Isn't that what I'm doing?'

Before Ahmad could think of a witty reply, the door burst open and one of the younger falconers rushed in.

'It's stopped raining. Praise be to Allah. They say that the Guadalquivir is beginning to drop.'

'That's excellent news,' said Ahmad. He would be able to take his family home in a few days at most.

## CHAPTER 23

If Ahmad had plans to return to his flooded house outside the city walls, he soon realised that this wasn't going to happen. Within a few days there was an influx of refugees from the countryside. At first he thought they were running from their sodden fields and ruined crops but then he heard the true reason. Sulayman's Berber troops were roaming the countryside and ravaging the land while Sulayman, ensconced in the alcázar in Madinat al-Zahra, did nothing to control them. The people came in their hundreds, starving, injured, in tattered clothing and carrying what little possessions they had managed to hang on to: a few chickens, a sack of grain, a mangy dog, a bag of olives. Some rode donkeys, a few had camels but the majority walked, carrying all they could on their backs. They sought out their relatives and moved in with them while those who had no family in the city camped on the streets and on the steps of the mosque.

'Ahmad, the rain has been stopped for a week now. When are we going home?' asked Aisha. 'Do we even have a home to go to?'

'The house is still there. I walked down there yesterday. The river water has gone down and our home is still standing but it's going to take a while longer for it to dry out. I don't want to take Mama back to a damp house, not while she is so weak. It won't hurt to wait a little longer. You're comfortable here, aren't you?'

He silently praised Simon's forethought. It had been an excellent idea to move into the Christian woman's house. If they hadn't done it, then some other family would have. It was happening all around them, people taking over empty buildings and making them their own.

Aisha looked at him sadly. 'Yes, I am comfortable here. I'm very grateful to Simon for bringing us to this house, but it's not my home. I would like to go home.'

'I know, my dear. I too would like to be back in our house, after all I built it with my own two hands. But the time is not right. Just be patient. The weather is changing and soon the winds and the sun will dry everything out and we can go back there.'

'As you wish, husband.'

Aisha went out to the back patio. He watched her cut a bunch of thyme from the bush and begin to chop it into fine pieces.

'Dinner?' he asked. He loved goat cooked with thyme and rosemary.

'No, I'm making this for your mother. She has a fever and Layla says if I make an infusion of thyme it should help the fever to break.'

'Is she that bad?' Ahmad asked. 'I thought she was just tired out after moving. It was a long walk for her and she got very wet; we all did.'

'Yes, I thought that as well, but she isn't improving. In fact I think she's worse. She has no energy and just lies on her sleeping mat all the time. Even Makoud can't persuade her to get up. I'm worried about her. Do you think we should ask Qasim to come and see her?'

'I'll speak to her first,' said Ahmad. He was supposed to be on his way to the Falcon House—the chicks were due to hatch this morning—but seeing to his mother was more important. He sometimes forgot how old she was because she was usually so sprightly and always busy doing something around the house. It was very unlike her to lie in bed all day.

Just as Aisha had said, his mother lay in the darkened room she shared with Layla, Salma and his wife. She didn't move when he entered.

'Mama. Are you all right, Mama? Aisha says you have a fever.' He bent over her and placed his hand on her forehead. It was burning.

'Don't worry about me, Ahmad. I'll be all right soon. I just need to rest, to get my strength back,' she whispered. She didn't sound well at all.

'Are you in pain, Mama?' he asked.

She shook her head.

'Would you like me to get you something to eat? Or some water?'

'Nothing. I just want to sleep.'

He stroked her hair back from her face. She was so hot. Aisha was right. This was more than tiredness. He would have to send for his brother.

'I'll ask Qasim to come and look at you, Mama,' he said, opening the window so that the cool breeze could come in.

'Don't fret, son. I told you, I just need to rest.' She closed her eyes and turned to face the wall.

Ahmad quietly moved away. His mother needed something more than thyme tea if she was to get better. If he hurried he could call at the hospital and speak to Qasim on his way to the Falcon House.

\*

When Ahmad arrived at the hospital he was surprised to see how many people were waiting outside—most of them refugees from the countryside, by the look of their attire. He pushed his way through the crowd and headed for the entrance.

'Take your turn,' shouted a man with a dirty bandage around his arm. 'There're plenty of people before you. Take your turn, like everyone else.'

'He doesn't even look ill,' shouted another man. This one leaned on a makeshift crutch and his right foot was a livid purple.

'Maybe he's a doctor,' said a woman holding a small child in her arms. 'Are you a doctor, sayyad?'

At this, the crowd moved closer to him, surrounding him and clamouring for help.

'He's a doctor.'

'Doctor, my child is dying.'

'Doctor, please help my son. He's burning up.'

'Doctor, help me.'

One by one they joined in. 'Help me, help my child, he's dying.' The voices swelled and merged together, becoming a single cry of pain.

'I'm not a doctor,' Ahmad shouted. 'Get out of my way. I have official business here. Out of my way.' It was a lie but it served to make those nearest to him stop long enough for him to squeeze through and get to the sentry on guard. 'Let me pass. I need to speak to Doctor Qasim ibn Makoud. I am his brother.'

'Yes, I know you. You can go in. Hurry, before this mob tears you apart, but you'll have difficulty seeing him.'

'Why's that?' Ahmad asked as he slipped past the guard and through the great wooden door that led into the hospital grounds. 'Where is he?'

But the guard wasn't listening. He had slammed the door behind him. Ahmad could hear him shouting at the crowd, trying to bring some order to it. People were becoming more and more impatient and that impatience was turning to anger.

Once inside the hospital grounds, Ahmad set off to look for his brother. He had a vague memory of the hospital layout and was sure he would come across Qasim working in one of the wards.

'Who are you?' a voice demanded. 'You can't just walk in here without permission.'

The man looked like a doctor; he wore a white robe, its hem stained with blood and on his head was the usual white ghifara. He looked exhausted.

'I'm looking for Doctor Qasim. I'm his brother. I've come to tell him that our mother is ill. She has a fever.'

'Have you seen the crowd outside?' the man asked. 'Well, there are twice that many people inside. All waiting for treatment. We are only treating the most urgent cases at the moment. We don't have enough doctors to do any more. I will take you to your brother but I don't know that he will be able to help you. Follow me.'

As Ahmad followed the doctor along the corridors and past the normal tranquil gardens, he saw for himself the truth of the doctor's words. The gardens were full of people seeking treatment; they lay or sat where they could, old men and women, children, pregnant women, their faces full of despair. Those that were able, stood in the corridors and talked amongst each other in low voices.

'Your brother is in the operating theatre. Wait here and I'll tell him you're here,' the doctor said. He disappeared through a doorway and left Ahmad waiting and wondering if he should leave. The smell of blood and sickness was overpowering. Even the aromatic plants that grew in pots in every room couldn't reduce the stench. One thing was plain; his mother couldn't come here.

'Ahmad. Something is wrong with Mama?' his brother asked. He looked on his last legs. He was usually so clean and immaculate in his white robes, his hair cut short and covered with a ghifara, his hands and nails spotless. Qasim was obsessed with cleanliness. He told them it was the best way to avoid sickness. Today he looked as though he hadn't even had time to clean his teeth.

'Yes, brother. She is very weak and she has a fever. She won't get up. Just lies in her bed and says she wants to sleep. It's not like Mama.'

'No, that doesn't sound good. But she is old, remember.'

'I know, but she was perfectly fine until we moved into the city. I thought she was tired from the exertion of moving but it has been going on too long now. If you could come and look at her, we'd all feel happier,' Ahmad said, feeling a twinge of guilt at trying to drag his brother away from all these sick people.

'I'll see what I can do, but... well you can see for yourself. We weren't built to cope with so many,' he said wearily.

'What's wrong with them?' Ahmad asked.

'Most of them have a strange sickness. It's nothing that I've seen before. We're putting those patients in a separate part of the hospital—keeping them apart from the rest, in case it's contagious. Then there're stab wounds and lacerations, the usual aftermath of the battles—that we can cope with—and we sew them up or operate, amputate a limb or two and then send them on their way. It's the sickness that's difficult to control.'

'So what shall I do about Mama? Shall I bring her here?'

'No. Not here. Haven't you been listening to anything I've said, Ahmad? She may have the sickness. And if she doesn't have it then I don't want her to catch it. What I haven't told you is that most of my patients have died from it. All we can do is to give them something to bring down the fever and help with the pain,' Qasim said, wearily.

'So where has this sickness come from?' Ahmad asked.

'Nobody knows. Nobody has seen anything quite so virulent before. It's possible it's because of the floods. Dirty flood water can carry disease. Who knows? Maybe one of the foreign soldiers carried the disease. We'll never know for sure.'

'Mama hasn't any pain. I asked her. She says she's just tired.'

'And you think she'd tell you if she had?'

'Maybe not.' Ahmad had been in such a hurry to get to the Falcon House that he hadn't bothered to press his mother about her symptoms. He thought he could leave that to Qasim. 'So what should I do?' he asked.

'Have you asked Layla to look at her?'

'Aisha asked her. Layla prescribed some thyme tea. But what good would that do? You need to see her, Qasim. She is your mother, after all.'

'Very well. I'll come in an hour. I'm due to have a break then anyway. I've been here…' Qasim paused, silently calculating the hours, 'for two days and nights. I need to go home to see my wife and children. And to sleep. But I'll visit Mama first. Don't worry, little brother,' he said, putting his arm around Ahmad. 'She's an old woman and it's probably as you thought, that she's exhausted from moving from her home. Now I must get back to my patients. I'll see you later.'

'Ma'a salama, brother,' Ahmad said but his brother didn't reply; he was already on his way through the door to the operating theatre.

As Ahmad wound his way through the hospital corridors he was stopped by the other doctor.

'Did you arrange something with your brother?' he asked.

'Yes, thank you. He's going to try to visit her later today,' Ahmad replied.

'Come with me. I'll let you out through our back door, then you won't have to fight your way through that crowd again,' the doctor said, leading Ahmad through a number of adjoining rooms where every bed was occupied. 'Pull your kufiya across your mouth and nose. Just in case. These are the patients with the sickness that I'm sure your brother told you about. They are in isolation.'

Ahmad did as he was told, copying the doctor who had pulled a mask of muslin up over the lower part of his face. He rarely wore a kufiya but today he was glad of it as he passed the silent beds. The sickness seemed to have drained all life from those inflicted with it. They lay there, pale and unmoving, and the only sounds uttered were an occasional groan or a wheezy cough.

'Here we are,' the doctor said, opening a small door and letting Ahmad out.

Before Ahmad had time to thank him, the door was closed and the doctor gone. Ahmad was in a narrow alleyway that ran past the hospital. He'd walked down here many times but never noticed the door before. He pulled his scarf away from his face and breathed deeply. He was glad to be out of there. How on earth could Qasim stand it, day in, day out?

He hesitated. What to do? Should he continue to the Falcon House? Or should he return and see how his mother was? What if she had this awful sickness? She could pass it on to the others, to

Aisha. At the thought of his beloved wife catching this disease, he knew he had no choice; he would go home and warn her.

As he walked back towards their temporary home, he found himself looking more closely at the strangers he passed. They all looked under-nourished and many were ragged and dirty. Could they be the carriers of the disease? He pulled his kufiya closer around his face and hurried his step.

There seemed to be a lot of soldiers in the street today, members of the city's militia. What was that all about? Was there going to be another battle? He prayed not.

'Ahmad. I'm on my way to your new home now,' said a familiar voice. It was his brother, Rafiq.

'As-salama alaykum, brother. This is a surprise.'

'Wa alaykum e-salam, Ahmad. Are you going there too?'

'I am. Mama is ill and I've been to speak with Qasim about her. But what are you doing here? And why are there so many soldiers in the streets?'

'It's bad news, I'm afraid, brother. You won't be able to go back to your house for some time. In fact it's very fortunate that you moved into the city when you did.'

'But we have to go back soon. Someone will move in and then it will be the devil's own job to get them out. The house will be dry in a few more days and then we must go back to it. Everyone wants to go home, Rafiq; we're all tired of living in someone else's house, and I'm tired of living in the city. I want to go back to my peaceful house by the river.'

Rafiq threw back his head and laughed. 'By all that's Holy, I swear that you are the most ill-informed man in Córdoba. Your peaceful house by the river, is now a Berber out-post. Sulayman has surrounded the city. No-one can get in and no-one can leave. There is a blockade. We're all prisoners. You should go to the mosque this evening. There you will hear all about it from the imam and read the notices that have been posted. We all have to work together on this. Get your head out of that shit-hole that you call the Falcon House and think about your family for once.'

Ahmad was speechless. First war, then the flood, refugees and sickness and now Córdoba was besieged. Allah was punishing them all for their sins.

'But...'

'No buts about it, brother. If we don't pull together we won't survive.'

'What about the Khalifa?'

'What about him? He's all right for now in the alcázar. He's safe enough. General al-Wahdi is in command. He's cancelled all leave. That's why I've come today, to tell you what's going on.'

Ahmad knew he should be worried for his family and he was. But his over-riding emotion right at that moment was disappointment. He wasn't going back home, not for some time, if ever.

'How long will this blockade last?' he asked.

'Ahmad, your guess is as good as mine. Sulayman is determined to overthrow Córdoba and we are just as determined to stop him. It will last until one side surrenders or Sulayman is dead.'

'Best not to tell Mama. She really is not well. Qasim says there's a sickness in the city that can't be cured,' said Ahmad.

If what Qasim had said was true, then they were not only trapped inside the city but they were unable to escape the sickness.

## CHAPTER 24

Aisha's smile of welcome for her husband and her brother-in-law vanished when she heard what they had come to tell her. So they wouldn't be going back to their home after all; they were to stay in Córdoba, maybe forever. She felt tears spring to her eyes but she bit them back. How could she let her brother-in-law know how upset she was with the news.

'Some food, Rafiq?' she asked, feeling a strong need to do something practical.

'Just some tea would be lovely, Aisha. I'll go in and see Mama first.'

'No,' said Ahmad, firmly.

'What do you mean, no?'

Both Aisha and Rafiq looked at him in surprise.

'No, you can't go in to see her until Qasim has been,' said Ahmad. 'We don't know if she has this sickness that is spreading throughout the city. Qasim says it is very infectious. We must wait until we know what is wrong with her.'

'Rubbish, husband. She hasn't been anywhere since we arrived. How could she have caught an infectious disease? Anyway I've been with her day and night since we moved in. If it was infectious, I would have it by now,' said Aisha.

'Nevertheless I would be happier if we just waited until Qasim arrived. He's on his way now,' Ahmad said.

'Just make the tea, Aisha and we'll wait until Qasim arrives,' said Rafiq.

'This blockade, will it mean that we won't be able to bring any food in from the countryside?' asked Aisha, putting the water to boil on the stove.

'Absolutely. Nothing will come in and nothing will go out.'

'But how will we eat?'

'We must grow as much as we can inside the city. You will receive more information on what we must do to survive, but for now, let me tell you that it is best to save as much grain and flour as you can. Keep your goat and any other animals safe,' instructed Rafiq.

'Why?' Aisha asked. 'Who would want our animals?'

'When the food supplies begin to run out and you can no longer buy flour to make bread, when the markets no longer sell honey and sweetmeats, when the butcher has no more meat, when we cannot get fish from the river, then people will steal whatever they can. You have to be prepared for that,' said Rafiq.

She saw him look directly at Ahmad when he spoke. Did he think Ahmad wouldn't be prepared?

'Will it last that long?' she asked. Fear was creeping up her throat like a cold hand. How was she going to feed her family if they could no longer buy food? In their own house by the river they had a garden. There they grew melons, corn and oranges. They even had sugar cane growing alongside the riverbank. Here there was only a square patch of land and a patio. Not enough to grow food for a rabbit.

'As I said, you have to be prepared. Nobody knows how long it will last. It could be over tomorrow or it could last years,' her brother-in-law replied.

'Years?' she cried, unable to keep the panic from her voice.

'Don't worry, dear wife,' said Ahmad, putting his arm around her. 'We will find a way. Allah looks after his people.'

'I'm not depending on Allah to help feed my family,' Aisha said, indignantly. 'We will have to find our own way. Rafiq is right. We must be prepared. And the first thing I think we should do is dig up that patio. We will save as many seeds as we can and use them to grow our own food.'

'That's an excellent idea,' said Rafiq.

'But, it's not our house,' said Ahmad.

'You heard what your brother said, husband. Nobody can come in and nobody can go out. We're unlikely to get a visit from the Christian woman. If she has any sense, she'll stay where she is in Antequera.'

She didn't often speak to her husband like that and no doubt he would be annoyed at her attitude but she had to be practical. She was the one who had to feed her family.

'Very well. I'll tell Makoud to do it tomorrow,' Ahmad said meekly.

'And see if they have any seeds at the Falcon House that we could use,' said Aisha.

'Falcons don't eat many seeds you know—they prefer meat,' her husband said.

'Don't we all,' said Rafiq with a smile.

There was a loud banging at the door.

'Is that Qasim?'

'You stay here. I'll check,' said Rafiq, drawing his sword.

Rafiq opened the door cautiously, his right hand gripping his sword in readiness.

'Open the door, Rafiq. I haven't all day,' snapped their eldest brother.

'And a very good day to you too, Qasim,' said Rafiq, letting his brother in and bolting the door behind him.

'Sorry. I shouldn't be here. I have patients waiting for me in the hospital,' Qasim explained. 'So how is Mama?'

'Not good. We're waiting for your diagnosis, brother.'

'Well, let me see her then. As-salama alaykum, Aisha, Ahmad.'

'Wa alaykum e-salam, dear brother-in-law,' said Aisha. 'Come with me. Your mother just lies there and doesn't speak. It will revive her to see you, I'm sure.'

Amina was lying in the same position as before, her face turned to the wall.

'Mama, here is your son Qasim. He has come to make you better,' said Aisha.

She saw her brother-in-law frown at this remark. So even before he examined her he was thinking the worst, was he?

'As-salama alaykum, Mama,' said Qasim. 'I hear you are unwell.'

Amina turned slowly towards them. The light from the oil lamp in Aisha's hand fell on her face and now they could all see how thin and gaunt she was. Their mother seemed to have aged a hundred years since she'd taken to her bed. Aisha heard Ahmad gasp.

'Wa alaykum e-salam, my son,' Amina said, lifting her hand and touching her son's face.

'Tell me what ails you, mother,' Qasim said, gently pulling the cover back so he could see her better.

'Nothing, my son. Just tiredness. All I need is some sleep and I'll be all right in the morning.'

'She has been burning up with fever,' said Aisha.

Qasim touched his mother's forehead. 'Yes, you do seem a bit hot, Mama.' He turned to the rest of the family and added, 'Can you leave us now, please. I'd like to examine Mama in private.'

'Oh, yes, of course,' said Ahmad, blushing with embarrassment. 'How thoughtless of us. Come Rafiq, Aisha. Come with me.'

'I'll make us some tea,' said Aisha. 'Then we can talk about getting this patio dug up.'

'Get Makoud to do it. He's not doing much these days, is he?' said Rafiq, walking ahead of them to the kitchen patio. 'I thought he was going to work in the Falcon House.'

'They wouldn't take him now, even if I could persuade him to do it. They got rid of a lot of the falconers when al-Hisham was in prison. We just don't have that many birds any more. I've only kept my job because of the Khalifa.'

'He could always enlist,' said Rafiq. A black look from his sister-in-law told him he should say no more.

'Actually, he's been helping Layla. She's teaching him about herbs and plants and that sort of thing. I told him that he needs to go to the university to learn these things properly, but he says he hasn't time to do that,' said Ahmad.

'I hope Layla's teaching him which herbs he can eat,' said Rafiq. 'That would be more useful.'

'Oh, Rafiq, you're frightening me,' said Aisha. 'Surely you don't think this blockade will last very long?'

'Let's hope not, dear sister-in-law.'

Qasim came out onto the patio and washed his hands in a bowl.

'How is she?' asked Ahmad. 'Does she have that disease you spoke about? Will she have to be kept in isolation?'

'She is very weak. But I don't think she's contagious. She has a slight fever, but the thyme tea is helping to bring that down.'

'So Layla was right, after all,' said Ahmad.

'Yes, you should listen to her, brother. She knows what she's doing,' said Qasim.

'So what is it?' asked Aisha.

'She's old. Her heart is weak; that is why she's so tired. Mama is right. What she needs to do is rest. Make sure she eats, something easy for her to digest, a little fruit, some broth.'

'So it's good news?' Ahmad asked, looking unconvinced.

'She is not contagious, and she doesn't have to go into isolation. That's good news isn't it?'

'But will she get better?'

'As for that, I don't know. As I said, her heart is very weak and she has lost a lot of weight. She is old. Her body is worn out. I cannot tell you how long she will live. Her spirit is strong so maybe she will live many more years. But I cannot promise you that. Now I must go. I'd like to make sure my wife and children are all right before I return to the hospital.'

'Some tea before you go?' asked Aisha, offering him a glass of mint tea.

'No, thank you Aisha. I really must leave.'

'Thank you, dear brother-in-law,' Aisha said, gripping his hands in hers.

'Ma'a salama, my brothers,' Qasim said. He picked up his bag, pulled his djellaba around him and was gone.

After Qasim had left, Aisha went into the room where her mother-in-law still lay, unmoving. She was relieved that the old woman did not have the sickness that they were all talking about but sad that Qasim appeared to be unable to help her. Well if she was going to die, then Aisha intended to make her as comfortable as possible. She had always been the best of mother-in-laws, kind and caring. There were many times when Aisha had been grateful for her company and support.

'Mama, are you awake?' she whispered.

'Yes, child.'

'Shall I bring you a little cold tea? Nice and sweet?'

Amina nodded her head. 'Thank you, my dear.'

\*

Rafiq had seen many sieges in his years as a soldier. None of them had ended happily. None had ended before the besieged city was reduced to rubble or the populace starving and the children dying of disease. The people of a besieged city had not just one adversary, but many: disease, malnutrition, cold, thirst, infection, bombardment from the enemy, marauding soldiers, attrition, internal fighting, theft and fire. They defended their homes from the enemy without and the enemy within. With nowhere to go they died where they lay. Rafiq tried to forget the sieges he had taken part in but the stench of the dead and dying bodies still remained with him. Now this time, he would be on the inside, one of the besieged.

'I had better go to work,' said Ahmad.

'Don't you think you'd be more use here, making sure that nobody can break into your house? Look at that door, for example. A strong man could kick that in easily.' Rafiq rattled the door, to emphasise his point. Ahmad really didn't understand how dangerous things were becoming. This door wouldn't keep out a child, never mind a starving mob.

'Yes, you're right. I'll check all the doors and shutters. And I'll get Makoud to help me dig up the patio. But for now I must go to the Falcon House.'

'Do you have a well?' asked Rafiq.

'Yes, we do. It's not a very deep one but it's full at the moment.'

'That's good news. But ration the water carefully. And start now. Don't wait until it's running low. You can live for quite a while without food but not without water. I've seen grown men kill each other for a flask of water,' Rafiq said. 'And use the oil for the lamps sparingly. You will need it when winter comes.'

'I will, brother and thank you for your advice.'

'I must get back to the Dar al-Jund, now. If I get time I'll call by tomorrow. Ma'a salama, little brother.'

'Alla ysalmak, Rafiq. May Allah protect you.'

*

Rafiq had not told Ahmad and Aisha everything. There wasn't any point in worrying them unduly. At the moment there was very little they could do, except try to conserve food and water. For now there were no real shortages, but after the last two years of civil war the plentiful supplies of corn were diminished. The crops had been destroyed and many of the livestock rounded up and killed by Sulayman's soldiers. It wouldn't be long before the people of Córdoba began to realise that their abundant source of food in the countryside had been cut off. Then the trouble would begin. People would start hoarding food. Prices would rise. The bakers would ration the amount of flour they sold. And the thefts would begin. Luckily there were plenty of fresh water wells within the city, some public but also a number of smaller, private wells, such as the one in Ahmad's house. If people were careful they could probably survive for a couple of years, especially after the heavy rains that they'd just had. But when did people behave sensibly in a crisis? General al-Wahdi had already set up a force of soldiers to monitor stores of wheat and corn, and guards had been placed at all the public wells. The bath houses were closed until further notice. The water was turned off at all the fountains and ponds that ornamented the city. Even the Khalifa had been asked to conserve water. Better to start now, the General had said, then wait until everything had run out. All this Rafiq had explained to Ahmad and Aisha. The look on Aisha's face when he told them what could happen haunted him still.

'Where have you been? Chuckles has been asking for you,' said Asif as soon as he entered the Dar al-Jund. 'He says the horses must be guarded day and night. You're to organise some men to do it.'

'What about the Falcon House? Do you know if we're to guard that too?' Rafiq asked. Surely they wouldn't leave it to the falconers to defend.

'He never mentioned anything about the falcons. I expect they'll end up in the pot,' Asif said with a laugh. 'You know, a nice tagine of royal falcon.'

'They belong to the Khalifa,' Rafiq reminded him. 'Anyway what are your orders?'

'My men are to defend the city walls. They're already in place alongside the archers and slingshots. In fact I can't stand here gossiping. I need to make sure they've made the naphtha.'

He picked up his red cloak and headed for the door.

'Hang on, I'll come with you,' said Rafiq.

The two friends climbed onto the ramparts and surveyed the scene below them. Sulayman and his men were camped on the far bank of the Guadalquivir, their tents in serried ranks.

'It's the same from the north wall, and the west and the east,' said Asif. 'They have the city surrounded.'

'What's that coming towards us?' asked Rafiq. 'A siege engine? They're going to use siege engines? Surely not.' In the distance he could make out a giant wooden structure being dragged along by a team of oxen. Their own machine, turned against them. 'Why, in the name of Allah, would he do that? He'll reduce the city to its foundations if he uses that monster.'

'It's a threat. He won't use it. Well not yet, at least. Sulayman wants the city intact. He doesn't want a pile of rubble.'

'Have you two men got nothing better to do than gossip?' barked a familiar voice. 'Quaid, you were supposed to report to me two hours ago.'

'Sorry, General. I was on my way to the stables, right now,' said a chastened Rafiq.

'Quick about it, soldier. You're not retained to stand about admiring the enemy's uniforms,' said General Tayyab. 'The next time I pass by here, I want to see this wall manned by well-armed archers. I want to see the naphtha distributed to all of them. I want them ready so that when the time comes, every flaming arrow will reach its mark. Surprise is the enemy's best attack. We are *not* going to be taken by surprise. Is that understood?' General Tayyab glared at Asif and Rafiq, who quickly saluted and climbed down from the wall.

'Yes, General,' they both replied.

The use of naphtha was common and Rafiq was sure that Sulayman's archers would also be firing flaming arrows at them before long. As the General said, it was best to be prepared.

'General al-Wahdi has already received a messenger from Sulayman. The traitor demands an immediate surrender. He demands we open the gates and let him in,' said the General. 'Well he can make as many demands as he wants. Córdoba is not surrendering. Remember that. Córdoba is not surrendering.' With those words, the General marched away.

They knew the tactics of a siege. Both were seasoned soldiers and Asif, like Rafiq had taken part in a number of them, usually in the north of the country. They would surround a city under the rule of a Christian king, cut off the exits and entries to the city, block the supply lines and then wait it out. The intention was to force the occupants to negotiate a surrender rather than destroy the city—undoubtably this was what Sulayman intended now for Córdoba. However sometimes the king was stubborn and refused to surrender. In that case, they would wait until the inhabitants were tired and weak from hunger and then they would attack, using the siege engines to hurl flaming balls of pitch over the walls or catapult huge boulders into the city. They would ram the gates with enormous trunks of oak and try to scale the walls. If none of that worked and they were still unable to breech their defences, then they would continue to wait until the dead piled up in the streets. It was a slow, expensive method of warfare and not one that Rafiq relished. For him there was something much nobler about fighting man to man on the battlefield than starving out men, women and children and reducing their homes to rubble. Sometimes, not often, they'd been forced to retreat because there wasn't enough food to sustain their own army but usually it was the besieged city that was made to surrender. What would happen here in Córdoba? The surrounding countryside, made desolate by Sulayman's army, would recover in a few months and become fertile again. It would sustain their enemies while they starved inside the walls. Patience was the key in a siege and Rafiq felt that Sulayman had plenty of that.

## CHAPTER 25

Assured that there was nothing else he could do for his mother, Ahmad left her in Aisha's care and headed for the Falcon House. The doors were barred and bolted and he had to wait quite some time before anyone came to let him in.

'Where the hell have you been? Nasir's been shouting for you. The Khalifa wants to see you,' said one of the falconers.

'Have the eyases hatched?' Ahmad asked, pushing past him and striding into the back room.

'Did you hear what I said?' the falconer asked. 'The Khalifa wants to see you.'

'I heard, but first I must look to the chicks. Are they healthy?' he asked.

'You and the bloody chicks. Yes they've hatched and yes they're healthy but for how much longer I don't know. The mother needs to get out and hunt or they'll starve to death.'

'I know. We must talk to Nasir about what we're going to do.' Reluctantly he tore his eyes away from the eyases. There were three of them, covered in a white down that was still damp, their beaks gaping as they angrily demanded food. Eyases ate an incredible amount of food, especially in the first few weeks so Amir was right, the mother would have to hunt.

'Better to see the Khalifa first. If Nasir asks for you again I'll tell him where you are,' said Amir.

'Very well.' Ahmad reached across and stroked the female falcon's head. She was a beautiful specimen, one of the finest falcons in the falconry, and her chicks would be the same if they survived. What were they going to do if this blockade lasted as long as Rafiq suggested? The birds needed to hunt or be fed. If there was going to be a shortage of food then it was unlikely there would be enough for the birds.

On his way to the Falcon House he'd seen how scared people were—it amazed him that he hadn't noticed the signs before. Everyone was boarding up their shop fronts and barricading their homes. It was just as Rafiq had said, people were preparing for a long siege. It had been chaos in the market when he walked past it; women, and some men too, were loading their bags with as much food as they could carry. The stall holders were shouting and trying to keep them in order but the women screamed at them and demanded they give them what they wanted. But what they wanted was what everyone else wanted and he witnessed two women fighting like lunatics over a small sack of corn. What was it going to be like when the siege had really begun to bite? As soon as he'd seen the Khalifa he'd go home and help Makoud dig up the patio. Rafiq was right, as usual, he had to think of his family now.

\*

The Palace Guards let him go straight through to the Khalifa's quarters. Since al-Hisham's release from prison Ahmad was treated like an honoured guest in the palace.

'Sayyad, the Khalifa will only be a moment,' said Musa, bowing when he saw Ahmad. 'Can I bring you some tea? A little wine?'

'No, thank you Musa. I will wait in the garden.'

He walked through to the gardens and sat under the shade of an orange tree. The ornamental ponds were full of fish, large golden carp which swam lazily about, oblivious to the fact that one day soon they could be served for the Khalifa's dinner. He smiled ruefully to himself. Since talking to Rafiq, he found himself looking at everything around him in terms of whether he could eat it or not.

'My dear Ahmad,' said the familiar voice of the Khalifa. He sounded upset.

'As-salama alaykum, Your Majesty,' replied Ahmad. 'You wanted to speak to me?'

'Yes. I have urgent need of your advice. Come, sit beside me.'

He led Ahmad to a shady bower where they could both sit and talk undisturbed. Since his release al-Hisham looked more like his old self. He was still as thin as a stick, but dressed in his white cotton robes and turban, with his sores concealed under a flesh-coloured paste, he was once more the Khalifa. Nevertheless, Ahmad could see from the way he walked that he was still in a great deal of pain and he knew, from what his brother Qasim had told him, that there was nothing that could be done to cure him.

'You have heard about the blockade?' al-Hisham began. 'This traitor Sulayman now lives in *my* palace, in Madinat al-Zahra. But that is not enough for him. He wants this city too and *my* crown.'

'Yes, Your Majesty. My brother is a soldier. He told me about Sulayman.'

'Well then, you know that this cannot be allowed. This is civil war. This is *fitna*. We will destroy Sulayman and recapture my beautiful city,' he declared angrily.

'Yes, Your Majesty. But how can I help?'

Al-Hisham wiped a tear from his cheek. 'I have been advised by the Grand Falconer to get rid of the falcons. I have been advised to do many things: turn off the fountains, drain the ponds, close all but essential bath houses. They have even suggested I dig up these beautiful gardens and grow vegetables. Can you imagine it? All of that I will consider if it means that we can defeat Sulayman, but get rid of my falcons? How can I possibly do that?'

'But why, Your Majesty? Why has he asked you to do that?'

'He says there is no place for such birds in a city besieged by enemies. He says they must go.'

'But you are the Khalifa, Your Majesty. Surely it is your decision whether the birds stay or go?' said Ahmad.

That was typical of Nasir. He cared nothing for the birds. To him being Grand Falconer was nothing more than a job, a well paid, prestigious job.

'Ah, my dear friend, if only it were so. They know I'm not a well man and do not have the strength to go against them. There is nothing I can do. He asks me to agree because it is protocol but the reality is that he will do with the falcons whatever he chooses.' His voice dropped to a whisper. 'I cannot go back to that prison, Ahmad. I cannot go back.'

'Your Majesty, you won't go back to prison. The people wanted you for their Khalifa. It was the people of Córdoba who demanded your release. They won't allow you to go back there.'

'But these men are so manipulative. They can persuade people of anything. No, I dare not go against the Grand Falconer. He says that it would be imprudent to have a falcon house full of expensive birds when the people are starving.'

'But no-one is starving yet, Your Majesty. The blockade has only just begun. It may last only a few months. My brother assures me that the city has enough food to last out for a year at least. Suppose you destroyed all the birds and then the siege was over? That would be dreadful,' Ahmad said, trying to speak calmly and not show his anger in front of the Khalifa.

'Yes, I have thought the same, Ahmad. That was why I wanted to speak to you. I know you will find some way to help.'

Ahmad looked at him, in amazement. What on earth did the Khalifa think he, a lowly falconer, could do?

'But what can I do?' he asked.

'Take the birds and hide them somewhere.'

'Your Majesty, it's impossible to leave the city. I would take them gladly if I could.'

The Khalifa looked as though he would weep again. 'Please Ahmad. There is no-one else I can ask.'

'Well, what we could do is bring some of the best birds here, into the palace. He wouldn't dare touch them then,' suggested Ahmad.

'Yes, let's do that,' said the Khalifa, looking more animated. 'But what of the others?'

'We leave them where they are for now and when I hear that the Grand Falconer is going to destroy them, I will release them. They can fly free and fend for themselves.'

'When will you bring them to me?' asked the Khalifa.

'Tonight. After the Falcon House is closed for the night I will bring you the first one. Then each night I will bring you one until all the best birds are safe,' Ahmad promised. It seemed the only solution but he wasn't happy about it because if he were caught then he could be accused of stealing the royal falcons—a crime that meant imprisonment or possibly death.

'I knew I could rely on you, dear friend,' said the Khalifa, offering him his hand. Ahmad swallowed his distaste at touching him and bowed.

'The ring, Your Majesty. Now you are a free man, I must return your ring,' said Ahmad, looking at the hand where the ring was normally worn. 'It is a Khalifa's ring.'

'No. I gave it to you, Ahmad. You have always been a loyal and dear friend. One day that ring may open doors for you, maybe even save your life. It is of no use to me. My days are numbered. Keep it safe, dearest one and use it wisely. Now go and return tonight with the falcon.'

As Ahmad made his way back to the Falcon House he thought about the ring that the Khalifa had given him. It was worth a fortune but here in this besieged city it had less value than a sack of grain. So far he had told nobody about the ring, except Aisha. He kept it on him at all times, hidden in the lining of his djellaba; he was terrified that someone would see it and accuse him of stealing it. Maybe the Khalifa was right, maybe one day he would be glad he had it, maybe it would indeed save his life. Or maybe it would be the cause of his death.

\*

Ahmad waited until everyone had gone home for the night and he was alone in the Falcon House. Most of the falcons were asleep, their heads tucked behind them, resting on their backs; they were birds who liked to hunt during the day. At night they slept. Only the female with her three eyases was awake. She watched him nervously as he approached the nest and began making an agitated ee-chup sound. The chicks squawked angrily at him and burrowed deeper under their mother. They knew something was wrong. He had decided that the first bird he would take to the Khalifa was the mother and her chicks. Then he would take her mate. They would be safer with al-Hisham than here in the Falcon House. But before he could do that he needed to quieten the falcon, whose calls were getting louder and louder.

'Here, now. No need for that,' he said gently stroking her grey and white mottled breast. 'No-one's going to hurt you, or your babies. There now.'

He slipped the hood over her eyes and instantly she was quiet and he was able to lift her off the nest and put her on her perch. Then he gathered up the three chicks, taking care to collect as much of their nest as possible. Luckily peregrines were not fussy nest builders, any old scrape in the rocks or on a ledge was sufficient for them. He placed the chicks carefully in a wooden box and put it in his bag. Then, placing the female falcon on his wrist, he set off for the alcázar. Tomorrow he would explain to Nasir that al-Hisham had requested him to bring the new hatchlings to the palace for him to see. It wasn't a lie, after all.

## CHAPTER 26

The library was open once again, but for how long? Nobody could answer the question that was in all their minds but Salma had decided to take advantage of this opportunity to work on something new. The copies of the books she had smuggled out were now finished. She needed more.

A noise at the far end of the reading room distracted her from the manuscript she was copying. Her friend had come in and was looking through the books on the top shelf—the section on Judaism and Hebrew poetry.

'Rachel? How are you?' she asked, laying down her quill pen and going across to her. She hadn't seen Rachel since they'd moved into Simon's house. 'Is everything all right?'

'Yes, I'm fine. As-salama alaykum, my friend.'

'But where have you been all these months?' asked Salma. 'I was worried about you. Your house was boarded up and when I knocked there was no-one there.'

'We've been living close to the synagogue. My father thought it would be safer. If we were attacked we could take refuge inside. He seems to think that the Berbers would respect our holy place,' she said scornfully. 'I think he is deluded. Sometimes I feel that my father doesn't really understand what's going on.'

'So have you come back to work?' Salma asked. 'There is so much to do.'

She looked around her, at the rows and rows of shelves, all closely stacked with precious books. The knowledge they contained was immeasurable. In here you could share the thoughts and ideas of some of the greatest minds in the world. What was to become of it all?

'I fear for the library,' she continued. 'The Chief Scribe says that if the soldiers enter the city, they will steal the books or worse, burn them.'

'So what's the point of sitting here hour after hour copying manuscripts?'

'I take them home and hide them. If the library is destroyed, at least some of the books will survive,' Salma explained.

'But how do you decide which books to copy? Even you can't copy them all; they say there are four hundred thousand books in this city,' said Rachel. 'How do you choose?'

'I have been selecting the ones on medicine. I think they will be the most useful for people in the future. It was my grandmother's idea. She says it would be awful if all that knowledge was lost. But you're right. My efforts are but a drop in the sea of time. It makes me want to weep when I think what could happen to this place.'

'There will be very little you can do, if the worst happens,' said Rachel. 'You should think about how to save yourself, not the books. That is what occupies my mind to the exclusion of all else. My father thinks the soldiers will massacre all the Jews if the city surrenders.' She began to cry. 'And all he can do is spend his days praying. What use is that? Prayers have never helped the Jews from persecution. We need to have a plan. We need to escape.'

She pulled out an embroidered cloth and wiped her eyes. 'Let's talk of happier things. Tell me about Simon? Are you still in love with him?'

Salma could feel herself blushing. 'No, of course not. We're friends, that's all. You know very well he's a Christian and a holy man at that. He has been very kind to my family, letting us live in that house with him.'

'I thought he was going back to his own land?'

'He was, but he left it too late. Now he can't even get word to the abbot about what is happening here. He's very unhappy about it.'

Rachel looked disappointed that her friend wouldn't tell her any more, so Salma added, 'You know Ahmad wants to find me a husband?'

'I didn't but I'm not surprised.'

'I've told him; I've told them all that I don't want to get married. I'm dedicating my life to the library,' said Salma.

'But you have to get married one day,' said Rachel. 'It's only natural. That's the way the world works, a man and a woman and a family. That's what I want. That's what most women want.'

'Well not me.' She almost said that if she couldn't have Simon then she would have no-one, but she didn't want to hear those words spoken aloud. Something inside her still clung to the fragile hope that one day she and Simon would marry, some day in the future, when all this was over.

As though summoned by her thoughts, Simon came rushing into the reading room, a heavy tome under his arm.

'We were just talking about you, Simon,' Rachel said, with a smirk.

Simon nodded in Rachel's direction but spoke straight to Salma. 'Have you heard? They're selling off some of the books.'

'What? Who's selling the books?' demanded Salma. This was exactly what she had feared.

'The Chief Scribe, of course. He says the library has run out of money and this is the only way to raise it. There is also talk of closing the library again, at the end of the month.'

'Then we have no time to lose. We must remove as many of the books as we can and all the materials we will need for copying,' said Salma.

'But what if we're caught?' asked Rachel. 'It's a crime to steal books from the library.'

'We aren't stealing them. We're just taking them home to copy. We can bring them back when everything gets back to normal,' said Salma.

'If it ever gets back to normal,' said Simon.

'No, I can't do it. It's too dangerous. You're a Muslim Salma, but I'm a Jew and Simon's a Christian. We will be treated much worse if we're caught with stolen books,' said Rachel. 'I don't want to spend the rest of my life with only one hand.'

Salma looked at her friends. It was true. She had less to lose than they did.

'I'm sorry. You're right. In that case I will just carry on as before, taking a couple of books back home each night and copying them there. It's best if you two don't get involved.'

'Have you thought about what you will do with the copies?' asked Simon. 'They need to be hidden somewhere.'

'In your church, perhaps? That's a strong building,' suggested Salma.

'No, that's the first place the soldiers will go. They know that the Christians keep all their gold and valuables in their churches.'

'Yes, and it's the same with the synagogue,' said Rachel. 'You'll have to find somewhere else. Somewhere dark and dry.'

'What, like a cave? Where will I find a cave in the city of Córdoba?'

'I must go. I just came to tell you the news. I'll see you later at the house,' said Simon. 'Ma'a salama, my friends.'

'Alla ysalmak, Simon,' said Salma. It was time she returned to her copying. The work was more urgent than ever.

Once Simon had left, Rachel followed Salma back to her desk.

'I'm going to talk to a soothsayer this evening,' she said. 'Why don't you come with me? Maybe she can tell us something about the future.'

'A soothsayer? I've never been to one before,' said Salma. 'Do you think she can really tell what will happen in the future? Ahmad says they're all tricksters. He says they just tell you what you want to hear.'

'They don't just tell the future,' said Rachel. 'They can also ward off evil.'

'I'm surprised that you believe in such things, Rachel. But yes, I will come with you. It could be interesting.'

'We can go straight after we finish work,' said Rachel. 'Before it gets too dark.'

'All right.' It sounded fun, something different to lighten the gloom that hung over the city.

*

The two girls looked carefully up and down the alleyway before slipping through the open doorway into a small patio.

'You do realise this is against the law?' whispered Salma. 'My religion forbids me to have anything to do with soothsayers. They say they do the devil's work.'

Salma didn't really believe all that nonsense about devil's work. There were lots of these women in the city, none of them Muslim. They often came into her grandmother's pharmacy to buy herbs and potions because their main occupation was delivering babies for those who couldn't afford a doctor. Some of them also cut hair and painted henna patterns on the feet of those about to get married. They seemed harmless enough to her.

'It's just a bit of fun,' said Rachel. 'Maybe she will tell you who you'll marry.'

'I hope not,' snapped Salma. She was getting tired of Rachel's insistence that she would marry one day.

A bead curtain was suddenly pulled back and a short, stout woman with henna-coloured hair came towards them.

'Two young women who want their fortunes told. Am I right?' she said with a smile that revealed a row of silver teeth. 'If there is a rich man waiting to marry you? Is that what you want to know? Yes?'

'Well,' Salma began, staring at this strange apparition in front of her. The woman was wearing a long tunic of vivid colours and on top of that an orange robe sewn with brightly coloured beads. Around her neck and wrists hung silver chains, and as she shuffled towards them the bells on her ankles tinkled softly and the many rings on her fingers glowed in the light of the oil lamps already lit.

'Yes, you are quite right,' said Rachel, boldly. 'How much will it cost us?'

'A young lady who gets straight to the point, I see,' the woman said, flashing her silver teeth at them. 'A silver dirham for the two of you. A special offer for two lovely young ladies.'

Salma looked at Rachel. It seemed a lot of money, but Rachel was desperate to go ahead with it now that they were there. She opened her purse and took out the coin.

'Here. That's for both of us.'

'Follow me, my dears.'

She led them into a small dark room, lit only by a single candle. Unlike the candles they sometimes used in the library, which were made of tallow and reeked of animal fat, this candle was made from beeswax and burned brightly, giving off a sweet, pleasant smell. The soothsayer must make a lot of money telling fortunes if she could afford beeswax candles, thought Salma.

'Who wants to go first?' the soothsayer asked, pulling a huge shawl over her head so that it covered most of her body as well. It had the most surprising effect, covering her multi-coloured person and transforming her into a dark spectral being.

Salma felt a shiver of fear run through her. It wasn't good to meddle with the unknown. Maybe there was a reason why Hadith law condemned the soothsayers. She glanced across at Rachel, who was looking scared now.

'I'll go first,' she said. If the woman was a charlatan she would soon know.

'Sit down here and give me your hands,' the woman said, seating herself on a low couch. She took Salma's hands in her own and stared at them for what seemed an inordinate length of time. Her grip was firm and warm and Salma gradually felt herself relax.

'Well child, I can tell you are a brave, resourceful girl and those qualities are going to help you survive because very bad times lie ahead for you,' the soothsayer began. She paused. 'And I can see you have a secret. A dark secret that you can tell no-one.' Again she hesitated, then added, 'This secret must never be revealed. This secret could destroy your world. Blood. There is a lot of blood.' She stopped, her head bent as though she was thinking, or listening.

She knew about the soldier. How could that be? Salma had told nobody, only Simon and her grandmother knew. She was petrified the soothsayer would say more and Rachel would know what she'd done. She wanted to pull her hands away and run out of that oppressive room but she couldn't move.

'And you have something hidden on your person that does not belong to you,' the soothsayer continued. 'It too could bring you serious harm. Beware child. Do not do these foolish things. You must take care that your heart does not rule your head.'

Salma felt that the book she'd hidden in her bag was burning into her side. Was it so obvious? Could she see it? But the woman wasn't looking at Salma's bag, she was still staring at Salma's hands. 'You will go on a very long journey from which you will never return,' she said after a long pause.

Salma said nothing, just waited. A long journey? What did that mean? Was she was going to die? She could hear Rachel suck in her breath sharply. The light from the candle seemed to be growing dimmer and there was a glow around the woman's head that seemed to have nothing to do with the candlelight.

'There is sadness ahead for you and unrequited love. I'm sorry to tell you this, child. I feel you deserve better,' continued the woman in the same soft voice.

Suddenly she let go of Salma's hands and looked at her. 'There's nothing else I can tell you, child. Your future is laid out for you as plain as day.'

Salma wanted to ask her what all this meant but she had already turned to Rachel and asked, 'What about you, now, my dear?'

'I'm not sure if I should,' Rachel stammered. 'What if it's something I don't want to hear? Maybe I'll just go home.'

'I cannot tell you if it will be good news or bad, my child, unless you give me your hands so I can read what your future says.'

'Come on Rachel. This was your idea. You'll regret it if you go home now,' said Salma. She stood up and let Rachel sit next to the woman.

As before, the soothsayer took the girl's hands in her own. The atmosphere in the room was growing oppressive. At last she began. 'I see marriage for you, my child, and a baby. But before that, there is something else.' She waited a moment and then added, 'There is hardship and pain. You too are going on a journey. You will cross the sea and travel through deserts and over mountains until you reach your destination.' Her voice dropped to a whisper and she continued, 'There is suffering ahead for you, my dear, and a death. But you will survive.'

Then she dropped Rachel's hands as though they burned her and said, rather brusquely, 'That's all girls. I have no more to tell you.' She stood up. 'I think you should both go home now. Leave before it gets too dark.'

'Ma'a salama,' both girls chorused and almost ran out of the door.

'Well, what did you think of that?' asked Salma, holding Rachel's hand as they ran down the alleyway.

'Stupid old woman. What did she mean about all that hardship and death? I just wanted to know if I would have a loving husband and lots of children. And how can either of us be going on a long journey when we're trapped in this city?'

'Well she did say there was a marriage and a baby. That's good, isn't it?'

'And what was all that about you having secrets that could cause you harm? I think she just made it all up to scare us. I wish we hadn't given her any money until she'd finished. It wasn't worth a silver dirham.'

## The Ring of Flames

They were close to the synagogue now, so Salma left Rachel to make her way home and she set off for the Christian area where they were now living. It was almost summer and the cicadas were in full voice. It was a beautiful evening, the air heavy with the scent of jasmine and stars appearing in the darkening sky, one by one. But Salma had her mind on other things; she couldn't get the soothsayer's words out of her head. Did the woman really know about the soldier that Salma had killed? Or was Salma reading too much into what she'd said. She tried to remember the exact words. They had been very vague, something about a secret and blood. It could have meant anything. Maybe most of the people who came to her had secrets. That was why they wanted to know their future. Yes, that was it; she was just playing on people's fears. But she seemed to know about the book in her bag and also why she had it. And what about the journey? A journey from which there was no return. How she wished she had never gone to see the soothsayer. For Rachel she had talked about a husband and a baby, but not for her. Well she was probably right about one thing; all that was waiting for Salma was unrequited love.

## CHAPTER 27

A tremendous crash woke Ahmad from his sleep. He leapt up from his sleeping mat, confused and disorientated. Then he remembered. The bombardment had started days ago and each morning as soon as it was daybreak the enemy renewed its attack. Six months had passed since the blockade. Now Sulayman had tired of waiting for them to surrender. Now he was trying to break through their defences.

Ahmad's thoughts turned to his brother. He hoped Rafiq was safe. He didn't want to lose another member of the family. His heart was still heavy from the loss of his mother. Amina had turned her face to the wall of her room and lain there until death took her in her sleep. Neither Layla, nor Qasim had been unable to do anything for her. His brother said she was old and she no longer wanted to live. It was as simple as that. Ahmad had been angry. He didn't want his mother to die. He wanted her to fight for every breath. But Amina had other ideas. She ignored the entreaties of Aisha to eat what little they could offer her and, towards the end, even refused to drink.

They had buried her in the traditional manner. Aisha and Layla had washed her body, closed her eyes and lips and tied her favourite scarf around her face to hold her chin in place. They had covered her with a simple shroud and laid her in a shallow grave —Makoud had dug it in their vegetable patch as there was nowhere else—with her head towards Mecca. She lay on her side, her feet neatly placed side by side while her family knelt and prayed for her soul. Although Ahmad had asked him to, the imam hadn't been able to come to their home to repeat the tenets of their faith, as he would normally have done: he had too many dead and dying to attend to. Now Amina's grave was covered with the herbs she tended with such loving care, and it was the saddest and sweetest smelling place in the house.

'How long can this go on?' his wife groaned. She stood in the doorway, wrapped in a grubby robe. There was no water for washing clothes unless it was absolutely necessary. That alone upset him, to see his beautiful wife reduced to looking like a street beggar.

'Come, dearest one. Let's pray together today,' he said, for wont of anything more comforting. The truth was that he asked himself that same question every day. It was almost two years since the siege of Córdoba had begun. They rationed the water from their well between the six of them and they ate one meal a day and thanked Allah that they were able to do that. They were the lucky ones. Many were far worse off.

'What good will praying do?' snapped Aisha. 'I have prayed to Allah all my life and now, when we need his help he ignores our prayers.'

'You don't know that, my dear. We're still alive, after all. Maybe we have a job to do. Maybe Allah wants us to suffer a little. It is not for us to question the Almighty. By His grace we live. To Allah we belong and to Him is our return.'

He took her hand and together they knelt and prayed. And Ahmad said a silent prayer beseeching Allah to keep his brothers safe.

\*

There were no Palace Guards at the entrance to the alcázar when Ahmad arrived. Now that the Falcon House was closed, he visited the Khalifa every morning to check on his hawks. They were probably the only ones left in the city. As he had promised, Ahmad had set as many birds free as he could before the Grand Falconer could destroy them. He and some of the other falconers had done it between them. What a sight it had been to see the birds fly away. Many had hesitated, unsure what to do with their unaccustomed freedom—some of the birds hadn't hunted for over a year and their feathers were in poor condition—but after fluttering around the yard of the Falcon House for a bit they took off, the bolder ones leading and the others following. Soon the sky had been full of hawks, their screeching calls echoing throughout the city. It hadn't taken long for Nasir to come running to investigate. Needless to say he had not been pleased but what could he do? He couldn't dismiss the falconers; they had already been fired. He had blustered and raged and said they must get the birds back, but even he knew that it was impossible. The falcons were on their own now, and no doubt would eat better than the citizens of Córdoba.

Ahmad pushed open the unguarded door and went into the alcázar. It was eerily quiet. Had something happened to the Khalifa? Was that why there was nobody guarding the palace?

'Sayyed, you are early. His Majesty is not dressed yet but I will tell him you're here,' said Musa, coming into the entrance hall from the palace gardens. 'Can I bring you some tea while you wait?'

'No, thank you, Musa. Tell me, why are there no guards on the door, this morning? Has something happened?'

The servant shook his head. 'No, sayyed. I didn't know that they had left already. I'm sure the Khalifa will explain everything to you.'

So something had happened. But what? He kept remembering what his brother had said about him being the most uninformed man he knew. He really should try to remedy that. Nowadays knowing exactly what was happening in the city could mean the difference between life and death.

He had barely sat down in his favourite spot in the garden when the Khalifa came rushing out to see him. For once he hadn't waited for Musa to comb his hair and arrange his turban; his straggly grey hair hung down his back in greasy strands and his robe flapped open.

'Ahmad, thank Allah that you have come. Have you heard the news?' he said, sitting beside Ahmad and gasping for breath.

'As-salama alaykum, Your Majesty. You seem very agitated. What has happened?' Ahmad asked, standing up and bowing to the Khalifa.

'Wa alaykum e-salam, dear friend. Yesterday I had a visit from General al-Wahdi. It is over. He says the people of Córdoba are starving. The army is depleted and we have no more armaments. In other words we cannot continue to fight Sulayman and his Berber hordes. It is time to surrender.'

Ahmad couldn't quite take it in. What was the Khalifa babbling about? Surrender? The city was going to surrender after all that they had endured?

'But what will happen to you?' he asked.

'I will have to go into exile and Sulayman will be the new Khalifa,' al-Hisham said. 'Unless they decide to chop off my head, instead.' He tried to smile but he was too upset and his lip trembled. 'I fear it will be the latter, Ahmad. It looks like my time has come.'

'But General al-Wahdi would never let that happen,' Ahmad protested.

'Do you really think Sulayman is going to let any of us live? General al-Wahdi's future is as bleak as mine.'

'What did the general say? What does he advise you to do?'

'Nothing. He just came to inform me that, unless there was a change in fortune before the end of the month, he would be officially surrendering the city of Córdoba to Sulayman. After that it will be out of his hands. Ahmad, I'm frightened. I know I must die sometime and when I was in the prison I prayed for Allah to take me from this world. But now I don't want to die and I certainly don't want to die at the hands of that traitor. You have to help me.'

'How can I help you, Your Majesty? I have no power, no arms, no soldiers. What can I do?' asked a distressed Ahmad.

'You are the only one who cares if I live or die, Ahmad. You have seen how already General al-Wahdi has removed the Palace Guard from the alcázar. There is no-one left here to protect me.

What am I to do? How will I defend myself? I am a sick man. How I wish your father was still alive. He would have known what to do.'

Ahmad felt annoyed when al-Hisham mentioned his father. It was true. His father would have known what to do, but his father was a soldier with much experience and he had known people of influence. Ahmad was a simple falconer. He had never pretended to be anything more.

'Don't do anything rash, Your Majesty,' he said, at last. 'I will talk to my brothers and see what they say.'

It wasn't just the Khalifa who was in danger, what about the people of Córdoba? If the gates of the city were opened to Sulayman and his army there would be death and destruction everywhere. His soldiers would rape their women and plunder their homes. No-one would be safe. He thought of his wife and his niece, Salma, and his blood ran cold. Surely General al-Wahdi wouldn't subject his city to that?

'Go now. There is not a moment to lose. We have to escape before the enemy arrive,' said al-Hisham. He looked like a wild man now, with his long hair hanging over his face, his staring blue eyes and his uncombed beard that still retained the reddish colour it had in his youth.

'Yes, Your Majesty. I will come again as soon as I have some news.'

As he walked back towards the Christian woman's house, he struggled with thoughts of what he should do. There were very little options to choose from. It was obvious. If Córdoba was going to surrender, the best option they had was to run away. But how? For two years they had been captive in their own city. He knew there was no escape. Is that what he had to tell his wife? They would be trapped in their homes, waiting for the enemy to come and kill them. They could try and hide but sooner or later the soldiers would find them. And what of Rafiq? He would be killed. Or maybe he'd change sides and join the army of Sulayman but somehow Ahmad couldn't see that happening. He needed to speak to his brothers as soon as possible. This was not a problem he could solve alone.

## CHAPTER 28

Rafiq had been awake since long before dawn. He stood on the ramparts watching the lights in Sulayman's camp for any movement. A ground mist obscured his view but he knew that enemy troops surrounded the city. Was this the final day? Would Córdoba fall today? It was difficult to believe that the city could withstand much more from the enemy. Yet here they were. They had withstood pestilence and floods, the people were starving and many were dying but still they would not surrender. He felt a fierce pride for the people of Córdoba. After failing to starve them into submission, now Sulayman had decided to reduce their lovely city to rubble by a war of attrition.

'Hold your places, men. Archers, get ready,' he commanded. 'Water buckets and sand ready.'

The men were exhausted. He was exhausted and desperately trying not to show it. An army fought on its stomach, so they said. This army fought on desperation.

As the mist began to clear he could make out the lines of enemy soldiers stretching as far as he could see in both directions; there were archers with their arrows already flaming from the burning naphtha, tiny flashes of light that surrounded the city like a ring of fire. The sun crept slowly along the horizon and suddenly the sky was alight with flames as thousands of arrows flew through the air. Instinctively the soldiers lifted their shields to protect themselves and the water carriers rushed to dowse the flames. Where water wasn't available they used buckets of sand. Where sand wasn't available they stamped out the flames with their feet or threw their cloaks over them. Everyone, men, women, even children were desperately trying to extinguish the flames before they spread, but despite all their efforts some eluded them and soon buildings were burning and the air was filled with acrid fumes.

'See to that one, soldier. Quick. Over there. Hurry man,' Rafiq barked, making his way along the line, encouraging and directing the men.

These were not his own men, his jinetes—the cavalry no longer existed since they had killed all the horses. What a terrible day that had been for all of them, but there had been no other solution. There wasn't enough food for the men, never mind the horses. His noble Antarah was no more. He hadn't allowed the men to kill her; he had done it himself. What a horse she had been, proud and noble until the end. For that, if for no other reason, he hated Sulayman with all his soul. He would never surrender to him. Rafiq had been transferred to the wall after the death of one of the other quaids—his friend, Hasan. There were only three quaids left under General Tayyab's command now: Asif, Isa and himself—and half the men there used to be.

'Prepare to shoot,' he shouted to the archers under his command. He waited until he was sure the enemy was within range and bellowed, 'Shoot.' A hail of arrows rained down on the enemy and for a moment the sky was black with them. As deadly as any other weapon, but not tipped with naphtha—that had run out months before. Still the men were good marksmen and he saw many Berber soldiers fall under the onslaught.

Then there was no time for thoughts, no time to think of his fallen comrades, no time to regret the loss of Antarah. That would all have to wait. As the morning mist lifted he saw the siege engine again as it slowly trundled into range. Arrows were useless against this monster. Nevertheless he directed the men to shoot directly at it in the hope of killing some of its operators or at least one of the oxen. A few arrows reached their mark and he watched as the enemy soldiers fell to the ground but it was not enough to make any difference. An arrow struck one of the oxen, which bellowed in pain but continued to pull the siege engine relentlessly towards the city walls, rumbling and thundering its way towards the weakest part. Previous attacks had broken through the wall, but they had repulsed the enemy and all night the Cordobeses had toiled repairing the breach. Now it would be rent apart again. But his soldiers were ready. Once there was a break in the wall, they knew what to do. It always came down to hand to hand fighting, the bloodiest and the best way for a man to die. You could look your adversary in the eye before you killed him.

There was an almighty crash as the first boulder hit the wall. Then another flew further and crashed into the ramparts, sending both soldiers and masonry hurtling into the sky. Then another and another. A flaming ball of tar crashed into the Dar al-Jund, sending the whole building up in flames. The enemy was relentless. He looked at the devastation around him. Soon the bombardment would stop and the soldiers would attack.

'Fall back,' he shouted at his men. He needed them alive to repel the enemy, not crushed under flying masonry. 'Fall back and be ready.'

\*

Qasim wiped the sleep from his eyes. For the first time in days he had managed to get home to his family. The children had been happy to see him and clung to him, chattering like a flock of magpies but he had been so tired that he'd fallen asleep over his meal. He felt sorry for them. They weren't getting enough food. Their limbs were like sticks and the sparkle had gone from their eyes. Growing children needed good food, fresh fruit and vegetables. His wife did what she could but every time she tried to grow anything in their tiny patch of ground, someone came in the night and stole it. The chickens too had been stolen. They knew she was alone with just the children for company, with no man to protect her while he was at the hospital. It seemed so unfair for people to behave like that, when he gave every waking moment to helping the sick. But everyone was starving. All of Córdoba watched their children grow weak from lack of food. They brought their pitifully thin children into the hospital everyday, some sick from disease—although the infectious disease that had plagued them the previous year was now in decline—some injured in the bombardment but most of them suffering from malnutrition. It broke his heart to see them. He and his staff did what they could but it was never enough. What most of them needed was a full stomach.

Aisha, his sister-in-law, sometimes brought them some fruit from her garden, but she didn't have much to spare. Sometimes it was an orange, or a bunch of mint. She even brought them some bananas once. And before the goat died, she would bring them a jug of milk every day. She was a good woman. He wished his wife would agree to move back into their house then he wouldn't worry about her and the children quite so much. But she said she wanted to be near him. It was ridiculous; he was never at home.

'Qasim, I think you should have a look at your son before you go back to work. He has had a very sore throat for a few days now. I've given him a potion that Layla made up for me, but he's no better.'

'He seemed fine, last night,' said Qasim.

'He was excited to see you, that's why. He has been awake all night coughing and now he has a rash on his body.'

'All right. Where is he?'

'He's still in bed. I thought it was the best place for him.'

His wife fussed over the children rather too much. Maybe it was because she had been quite old when they were born or the fact that their last child, another son, had died when he was only two weeks old. At one point in their marriage he'd begun to think she was barren and even considered taking a second wife, but then a miracle happened and she had two daughters in quick succession, and then Bakr. For a while he'd still clung to the idea of having another wife—he'd even seen the one he wanted, a lovely girl from a good family, with wide child-bearing hips—but in the end he decided against it. Now he was glad he only had one family to worry about.

'Well Bakr, Mama tells me you have a sore throat. Let Baba have a look at it. Open wide,' Qasim said, sitting down beside his son.

He placed a spatula on his son's tongue. The throat was red and inflamed.

'That looks painful, my little one. Can you swallow?' he asked.

His son nodded.

'He has a rash as well,' his wife interrupted. 'See, how red his skin is.'

'Yes, my dear. Don't worry.'

'But what is it? Can you cure it?' she asked, her voice rising in panic.

'I have read of something like this. It is an infection that attacks the throat. It is important to keep everything he touches very clean. I know, I know, that is not easy at the moment with the shortage of water, but you must do your best.'

Suddenly his wife burst into tears. 'I am doing my best, husband. It is hard. I am here on my own all day and all night. I do what I can for the children but it is never enough.'

'Dry your eyes, woman. Tears won't help. You have to be brave for the children's sake. If you can't cope alone, go to my brother's house.'

'They barely have room for themselves in that pokey house,' she snivelled.

'Well go to your sister's.'

'No, husband. I'll stay here, in my own home. If I leave, who knows what will happen to our house. I must stay here and keep it safe for my family.' She wiped her eyes and added, 'So will he have to go into hospital?'

'No. He is more likely to get better here. The hospital is far too crowded. Anyway this infection is likely to be contagious. It is better that you keep him here, in bed and keep Ulla and Muña away from him.'

'So what can you give him to make him better?'

'I'll ask Layla to make up some lohock for him to drink; it will soothe his throat. And you can give him thyme tea. I'll see if I can find some willow for you to add to the water to wash him. It is imperative that he is kept clean and willow is an excellent antiseptic,' he told her.

She looked at him, her eyes wide with fear for her child. 'Will you be home tonight,' she asked.

'I'll try, my dear. You just have no idea how much I long to be home here with you and the children, but people need me and it is not easy to leave when someone is crying in pain.' He put his arm around her. 'Be brave, my dear. One day all this will be over and our lives will return to normal.'

Was that true? Would everything return to normal again? He was beginning to doubt it.

## CHAPTER 29

Simon opened the door of the church and slipped inside. He didn't want to be seen by the bishop who would surely ask why he hadn't returned to England when he had the opportunity. Betraying his promise to the abbot weighed heavily on him, but now it was too late; he couldn't leave even if he wanted to.

The church was empty, stripped bare of all its rich adornments. Had they been stolen? Or merely hidden away for safekeeping? The bishop was a crafty old man. Simon was sure he'd hidden the gold and silver plate and the silver candlesticks somewhere secure. That was what Simon was hoping. It was true when he'd told Salma that the church was the first place the soldiers would sack but that only meant that the Christians had to become cleverer at hiding their riches. There would be somewhere in this building that could be used to hide the books that Salma had copied. Some loose panel, some hidden door, somewhere that only the priest would know about. All he had to do was find it.

There were many Christians living in Córdoba and the cavernous size of the church reflected that. It was an old church and plain in style, but it had a thriving congregation and its own bishop as well as two priests. Yet it wasn't even recognisable as a church from the outside as it was forbidden to display a cross on the building, but that hadn't stopped the soldiers identifying it and stripping it of all that they could. For almost four years the city had been embroiled in a civil war and the ravages of that war had taken their toll on the church of St John. Simon was saddened to see it so desolate.

He walked the length of the nave, stopping every so often to examine the floor for loose stones but there was nothing that looked like a hiding place on the ground and nothing on the bare walls, so he went down the stone steps into the vaulted crypt. It was cool but dry in there, the perfect place to store valuables. The reliquaries that were normally displayed for the faithful to see had been removed and now all that remained were a few coffins and the bones of the dead. The skulls and skeletons of the departed were stacked against the end wall, directly below the altar, a reminder to all that life was transient.

'Can I help you, my son?'

Simon turned round, startled to find an old priest standing behind him.

'I was looking for somewhere quiet to say a prayer,' he said, blushing with embarrassment.

'And you preferred to do that down here in the crypt?' the old priest asked, with a smile. 'You're Simon of Norwich, are you not?'

'Yes, I am.'

'I heard you had left the city, to return to your monastery. We haven't seen you in church for some time.'

'I was about to leave when the blockade happened,' Simon said, trying to convince himself he was not lying to this priest, that he had indeed intended to return to England.

'Why don't you tell me the real reason you are rooting around in the crypt, my son? Maybe I can help you.'

Simon hesitated. What did he have to lose? If there was a safe hiding place in here, the priest would surely know about it.

'You're quite right, Father. I do have another reason for being here. I'm looking for a place to hide something valuable,' he admitted.

'And you think the church is the best place to do that? Look around you. We have nothing of value any more. It has all been stolen. All that we have left of value is our love for the Lord Jesus Christ. That they cannot steal from us,' said the priest, a little bitterly.

'It is sad to see the church so empty, so desecrated,' said Simon. He remembered the first time he had visited the church. The altar was hung with embroidered silk cloths and behind it stood a magnificently carved altarpiece, depicting scenes from the New Testament. There had been silver candlesticks and a chalice and plate to celebrate the eucharist. Now he doubted that there were even bread and wine to offer the faithful. 'But what of the Bible? Where do you keep it?' he asked. Surely the church would have its Bible carefully guarded.

'Ah, yes,' said the old priest. 'You are right. We have to hide a few things so that we may continue to do God's work.'

'But where do you hide it?' asked Simon.

'Tell me first, the nature of this valuable you want to hide,' said the priest.

'You have heard, no doubt, that the government are selling the books in the libraries. I want to hide some of the books, so that when the civil war is over, this city can reclaim its reputation as a centre of learning. That would not be possible without books.'

'So you want to hide stolen books in this church?' the priest asked angrily. 'You break the seventh commandment and then you want me to assist you in hiding the stolen goods?'

'No, of course not. We haven't stolen them. They are copies of the originals. We just want to preserve the knowledge that is in them. Surely you don't want to see the libraries desecrated by Berber soldiers and all the books destroyed?'

'How do I know you won't disclose our hiding place to others?' he asked.

'Look, I just want somewhere to hide a few books until this awful war is over,' said Simon. 'I'm not going to tell anyone about it.'

'Do you have the books with you?' the priest asked.

'Yes, there are ten. And a few more at home.'

'Come with me. I think we have room enough for a few books.'

Simon followed him through the crypt until they were standing directly under the altar, facing the wall of skulls.

'You will have to help me,' the priest said and bending down, began to remove some of the skulls. 'My back is not as strong as it once was. But be careful. If you remove the wrong skulls then the whole pile will collapse and the entrance will be exposed.'

They worked together for half an hour, removing the skulls and carefully placing them to one side until they had cleared a space large enough for a man to enter.

'Now you must remove that stone,' the priest said, pointing to a block of stone set in the wall. 'It's far too heavy for me.'

'But what is this?' asked Simon. 'Did you build it?'

'Behind that stone is a small cave. It's always been there. I expect it has been used to hide the church's valuables for many years, long before my time. The skulls used to be stacked at the other end of the crypt and so it was much easier then to get into our hiding place, but the bishop thought it would be better to use the bones to hide the entrance to the cave. Nobody likes to handle skulls, not even the Berbers.'

It was ingenious. Simon tugged and pulled at the stone until at last he could get a firm grip and hauled it out onto the floor. It was as the priest had said. Behind the stone was an opening just big enough for a man to wriggle through.

'Well go on. You have to crawl in there and then you can put your books where you want to,' said the priest. He took an oil lamp down from the wall and handed it to Simon. 'You'll need this.'

Simon took the lamp and reaching into the opening, placed it on the ground. Then he squeezed through the gap and tumbled into an Aladdin's cave. There were paintings, sculptures and the missing candlesticks and chalice, even the altarpiece had been dismantled and hidden there. Not only that, there were Muslim artefacts too, carved ivory pyxis and caskets, metal drinking vessels and marquetry. He looked about him in amazement. So this is what the priest considered nothing of any value.

'Well?' asked the priest. 'Have you seen all you need to? Hide your books and come out. There's no need for you to stay in there gawping.'

'Just a minute.'

Simon lifted the oil lamp higher so that it threw its light on the back wall of the cave. That looked like a good place to store the books. He pulled them out of his bag and began stacking them carefully. The wall seemed dry enough. He ran his hand along the surface to be doubly sure—mould would ruin the books as surely as the soldiers would. Yes, it was completely dry. A perfect place to leave them. Salma would be delighted. He stopped. Something was not right. He could feel a faint current of cold air on the back of his hand. How was that possible? He was in a closed cave inside the church. He looked at the oil lamp and saw the flame flutter slightly. Was it possible that there was an opening behind the wall? He ran his hands over it again. It was perfectly smooth. He rapped against it with his knuckles and his heart almost stopped when instead of the noise of a solid stone wall he heard a hollow sound. Behind the wall there was another space. What on earth did that mean? Was there another cave? A bigger one?

'Are you finished? We need to hurry,' said the priest.

'I'm coming out now.' He clambered out of the cave and handed the lamp back to the priest. 'Is this the only cave under the church?' he asked, casually.

'It's the only one I know about.'

'There are no more catacombs?'

The priest shook his head. 'No this is the only burial chamber we have in the church.'

'But maybe before? Is that possible?' asked Simon.

'Why do you ask, Simon of Norwich? What is going through your mind?'

'Nothing. I was just curious. And the bishop, where is he?'

'The bishop left two years ago, just before the blockade. He was off like a scalded cat as soon as he heard about Sulayman.

Left his congregation, his priests and his church behind,' said the old man rather bitterly.

'Maybe he thought it was the best thing to do,' Simon said, although that was not his true opinion of the cowardly bishop's actions.

'Maybe. Maybe it is God's will that we are abandoned here in this God-forsaken land, where all they do is fight over who should rule.'

'It's not our place to question God's will,' Simon replied.

'You're right, my son. Come on now, help me to replace these skulls.'

\*

Simon set off to find Salma, his heart racing with excitement. Maybe this cave would be large enough for them to hide in if Sulayman won. There was air down there. They could possibly survive there for a few weeks, until things had quietened down. He couldn't wait to tell her about it.

Salma was at home, talking to her friend Rachel when he arrived. She was sitting at a table, her books spread out before her and the light from the open window shimmering on her dark hair. There was a smudge of ink on her cheek and she looked thin and tired, but he felt she had never looked so beautiful. He wanted to pick her up in his arms and take her away from this beleaguered city.

'I have good news,' he said, throwing himself on the couch beside them. 'I've managed to hide the books and there's room for more.'

'Oh Simon, that's wonderful,' Salma said. 'Where? Where have you hidden them?'

'I can't tell you that, yet. I have promised to keep its location secret, but be assured they are safe. When you want me to take some more, let me know because there is space enough.'

He was disappointed to see Salma pout at his words.

'But surely you can tell me? I'm the one who has been doing all the work, copying them. I ought to know what you've done with them.'

'Yes, and you will one day, but for now I am sworn to secrecy. You will just have to trust me.'

She smiled at him. 'Of course, Simon. Forgive me. Thank you for hiding the books. My heart can rest easy that at least some of our treasures will survive.'

'Show me what you're copying now,' he said, moving closer to her. She smelled of jasmine.

Salma passed him the open book. The original was beautiful, with a delicate script and detailed drawings of the human body. He turned the parchment pages carefully. It was a book of herbal medicine and each plant had been carefully drawn and its uses documented.

'Your grandmother would love this book,' he said. 'You should give a copy to her.'

'Maybe I will.'

Suddenly the door opened and Ahmad appeared. 'As-salama alaykum, children.' He looked around the room. 'Salma where is Aisha? I must speak with her.'

'Wa alaykum e-salam, cousin. She is upstairs drying the washing.'

'Tell her to come down right away.'

'Very well.' Salma put down her pen and hurried up the stairs to find Aisha.

'Wa alaykum e-salam, Ahmad,' Simon said. 'You seem worried. Is something wrong?'

He ought to tell Ahmad about his theory regarding the cave but now didn't seem to be the moment; he would speak to him later.

'Wrong? Yes, something is very wrong. Be patient and I will tell you what I have heard.' He looked at Rachel. 'How is your father, Rachel? Is he well?' he asked.

'As well as can be expected, thank you. He is coming here soon to eat with us, so you will see for yourself.'

'Good. He needs to hear this too.'

'Needs to hear what?' asked Aisha, bustling into the room. 'What's happened, Ahmad? Why all this panic?'

'Where is Makoud?'

'I'm here, father.'

'And Layla?'

'She is at the hospital,' said Salma.

'Well this cannot wait until she returns. Sit down all of you and listen carefully. I have some very bad news for you. As you know, my dear,' he looked at Aisha as he spoke. 'I went to see the Khalifa this morning, as I always do.'

'Yes, yes, but what is the news?' his wife asked impatiently.

'I hoped I would never have to say these words, but we cannot hide our heads in the sand any longer. It is over. The Khalifa told me that General al-Wahdi had been to see him to tell him that our army is about to surrender. We cannot withstand Sulayman's forces any longer. Unless a miracle happens soon, the city will fall.'

A stunned silence greeted Ahmad's news. Then Aisha began to wail and cry. 'They will massacre us,' she cried over and over again, ringing her hands in anguish. 'Massacre us. Massacre us. What of my family? My son? Thanks be to Allah that our daughters are safe. At least they will survive.'

'Stop that now, woman. We cannot panic. We must do all we can to survive. We all know what will happen when the gates are opened and the Berber soldiers come rushing in; we have seen what they can do. We need to talk to Qasim and Rafiq. They will know better than I what must be done,' said Ahmad.

'We must escape,' said Rachel. 'That's what we must do, escape or they will slaughter us. We have to escape.'

'But how?'

At that moment there was a loud knock at the door. They all froze, for a moment it seemed as though the Berbers had already arrived.

'It'll be my father,' said Rachel.

'I'll let him in,' said Makoud. Of all of them, he seemed the least concerned with the news.

'Simon and Salma, you must go to the hospital and tell Layla and Qasim that I need to speak to them, urgently. Makoud, you find your uncle Rafiq and tell him the same. They must come here tonight. Don't take no for an answer but do not tell them what you know. If others get to hear that we are about to surrender, they will panic and that could make things worse. After all there is still hope. Miracles do happen.'

'What are you saying, my friend? The city is going to surrender?' asked Isaak, coming in, closely followed by Makoud. He looked like a man dying on his feet.

'Isaak, dear friend, come in. Sit down. You look exhausted. Here, let me take your cloak,' said Ahmad, coming across to embrace the old man.

'When did you last have something to eat?' asked Aisha, eyeing him carefully. She turned to Rachel. 'Is there no food in your house, child?'

'Very little and my father always says he ate something at the synagogue. I'm sorry. I didn't realise.'

'He has been saying that so that there would be more for you, child. Can't you see how yellow he is? His skin is as bright as that yellow turban he always wears. Here, Isaak, drink a little water. I will heat up some nettle soup for you. It's not very filling but it is good for you,' said Aisha, bustling about.

Whenever there was a crisis Aisha would busy herself with looking after others. Simon had seen her do it before.

'Thank you. You are very kind.'

'Please sit,' said Ahmad.

Isaak looked at him. The law was clear, a non-Muslim could not sit if a Muslim wanted to sit. Simon was well aware of that; he had fallen foul of that aspect of the law before.

'Here, old man. Sit here. I have to leave soon, anyway,' said Simon, getting up from the couch.

'Thank you.' Isaak almost fell onto the couch, his legs buckling under him. 'Now, tell me about this rumour,' he said.

'It's no rumour, I'm sorry to say,' Ahmad replied. 'The Khalifa told me himself, this morning.'

'You know what will happen to us if the Berber soldiers enter the city,' Isaak said. 'They will kill all the Jews.'

'Not just Jews. They will massacre everyone,' said Ahmad. 'That is why we have to have a plan. We have the advantage that al-Hisham has been forewarned and he has warned me. We must use that time to do something to help us survive.'

'But what?' asked Makoud. 'All we can do is fight them.'

'We can't even do that. Surrender is exactly what it says. Our army lays down all its weapons and we rely on the mercy of the victors,' said Ahmad.

'What mercy? There will be no mercy for the likes of Rachel and me,' said Isaak. 'We have to escape.'

'Escape? How is that possible when the city is surrounded? Do you mean, once the gates are open we should try to slip out unnoticed?' asked Makoud.

'Now that would take a miracle,' said Ahmad.

'People have escaped from this city in the past,' Isaak said.

'Which people? Jews? How did they do that?' asked Makoud.

'I don't know. I assumed they were Jews. All I know is that there were a group of dhimmis who built a tunnel and used it as an escape route.'

'But where was this tunnel?'

'I don't know. Nobody knows. This was many years ago, before I was born.'

'It could be true,' said Simon, who had been listening to everyone and so far had not told them about the cave. He looked at their hopeful faces. What should he do? Tell them what he suspected and betray his word to the priest or keep silent. He sighed. What good was his word if he let his friends die? No, he couldn't keep this to himself. He would pray for forgiveness if he survived. And if he didn't, then he hoped that God would understand. 'Today I took some of Salma's books and hid them in an underground cave. I promised I wouldn't tell anyone about it, but that was before I knew the city was on the point of surrendering. We could hide in the cave. It has a supply of fresh air and it is dry and cool.'

'Where is this cave?' asked Ahmad.

'It is behind the crypt of the Church of St John. They use it to hide all the church's valuables.'

'It will be the first place the soldiers will look,' said Ahmad, dismissively.

'Maybe, but the church looks empty. It is not easy to find the hiding place. I would never have seen it if the priest hadn't shown me,' said Simon.

'But we could just be postponing the inevitable. We would have to come out sometime and then the soldiers would still be here,' said Ahmad.

'Why did you say it had a supply of fresh air?' asked Salma. 'Surely caves are closed. Where does the air come from?'

'I don't know, but I think there is another cave behind the one where I stacked the books. When I was in there I could feel a draught on my hand. It was coming through a crack in the rocks. If we can break through into that area then maybe we could live in the inner cave.'

'Oh, I don't like the idea of being shut up in an underground cave,' said Aisha. 'It would be like being buried alive.'

Ahmad suddenly turned to Isaak. 'Could this be your underground tunnel?' he asked.

'It's possible. They were dhimmis who used it. I always thought they were Jews but they could easily have been Christians.'

'Yes,' said Simon excitedly. 'Maybe it's not a cave at all, but the entrance to a tunnel.'

'So we could escape?' asked Rachel.

'Not so fast. We need to have a look at it. Is that possible, Simon? What about the priest?' asked Ahmad.

'We could go at night. There will be no-one there then, but we will need to take a dark lantern and something to move the rocks.'

'Good. First we will speak to Qasim and Rafiq and then we will go to the church.'

## CHAPTER 30

Rafiq was surprised to see his brother, Qasim hurrying along the road in front of him. 'Hold on, Qasim,' he called.

His brother stopped and waited for him to catch up.

'So, you've been sent for as well,' Qasim said, as they continued on their way to Ahmad's house. 'Just because our brother has no work to do these days it doesn't mean that the rest of us are idle. What is so urgent he has sent for us both?'

'I know as little as you, Qasim. But he's never done this before, so I think it must be important. Like you, it was bloody difficult for me to get away. We need every man we have at the moment. I shouldn't have left my post; it's lucky I've got men I can rely on.'

'It's bad, is it?'

'Very bad. Sulayman is increasing the assault on our city every day; I don't know how much more we can take. We've lost a lot of soldiers.'

'Yes, I know. We get your injured, remember. The hospital is struggling to cope with the casualties that come in daily. And that's not including the civilians who are starting to die from lack of food and water. But it's the old and the very young who are suffering the most. I tell you, it's pitiful to see some of those little children. They should be laughing and running around with their friends, instead they are lying on the ground, with distended bellies and too weak to move. All because some power-hungry maniac has decided that he would make a better ruler than al-Hisham. I wish someone would put an arrow through his heart.'

'That wouldn't make any difference. All that would happen is someone else would see their opportunity and take his place.

Until we get a strong leader, we will never have peace,' said Rafiq.

'We need another Khalifa like al-Rahman III. He knew the wisdom of having a country at peace. Nothing good can come of a country divided against itself.'

'Well I think the Omayyads are finished. Whoever wins, it won't be al-Hisham.'

A rat ran across the path in front of them.

'Is that a portent, brother? Rats out in broad daylight,' said Rafiq.

'I expect even the rats are starving these days.'

'How is your family?' asked Rafiq. 'Are they coping?'

'My family are starving, like everyone else. It breaks my heart to see how lethargic my children are now. My wife is a good woman; she does what she can but there are days when there is nothing at all to eat. The little one lies in her bed, crying with hunger most of the time. The boy has been sick but he's better now. He caught a pigeon the other day. He rushed home with it as proud as if it were a side of lamb.'

'Pigeon is very nourishing,' said Rafiq. He hadn't eaten since the day before and the thought of a fat, juicy pigeon on a plate of rice made his mouth water. He sighed. The best way to beat hunger was not to think about food, but that wasn't easy. When he wasn't in the heat of battle, it was food that was uppermost in his mind.

'Yes. You'd be surprised to see how far my wife stretched that one, scrawny bird. It made a beautiful broth. Now Bakr spends all his time scouring the streets with a net, hoping to find another one.'

'This is one of those times when I'm thankful that I don't have a family to worry about. It must be very hard for you.'

'It's hard for everyone, Rafiq. Come on, let's see what our little brother wants this time.'

Qasim knocked at the door and waited. They could hear the sounds of furniture being pulled across the floor, then the bolts drawing back and finally the door was unlocked and opened.

'Uncle Qasim, uncle Rafiq. As-salama alaykum. Come in please.' said Makoud.

'Wa alaykum e-salam, nephew,' they both replied. 'As you can see, we have come to see your father, as requested.'

'Is that them?' called Ahmad. 'Bring them in quickly, and bolt the door.'

Their brother was not alone. It was like a family conference, with Layla, Salma and her Christian friend, Aisha, Makoud and the Jewish family.

'What is it, this time, Ahmad?' Qasim asked rather curtly. 'We're busy men. I can't just come running every time you have something that worries you. I don't even get time to see my own family. Can't I get that through to you?'

'I'm sorry, Qasim. I know your work at the hospital is very important but I thought you should hear this. And you too, Rafiq, although you may already know about it.'

'Well what is it?'

'Ahmad, why don't I make some mint tea for everyone first? I grew the mint myself but there's no sugar I'm afraid. The last got used up yesterday,' Aisha said, looking at Qasim and Rafiq.

She seemed worn out and scared. Rafiq looked around the room. All faces were turned towards the brothers, frightened and expectant. Something had happened. But what?

'No thank you, Aisha. Both of us have little time to spare. It's better if we hear what Ahmad wants as soon as possible.'

'Well sit down, at least,' said Ahmad.

He waited until Rafiq and Qasim had become seated then he began. 'You know I go to see al-Hisham every day to tend to his falcons?'

'Yes, we know that, Ahmad,' snapped Qasim. 'Get to the point.'

'Today when I arrived, he was distraught. General al-Wahdi had been to tell him that the city is about to surrender.'

'What?' said Qasim. 'But it can't. Everyone will be slaughtered. They can't surrender. Are you sure he understood the General? You know al-Hisham can get things muddled. It's a symptom of his disease. His mind is not clear.'

'There is no doubt. That's what General al-Wahdi said. Unless there is a miracle, the city will surrender by the end of the month. Al-Hisham's servant was there. He heard it too.'

'But that's only two days away. Rafiq, is this true?' asked Qasim.

'I haven't heard anything, but I'm not surprised. Our defences are greatly weakened. Our troops are hungry, tired and demoralised. I doubt that we can motivate them to continue fighting much longer. If anything, I had expected General al-Wahdi to surrender sooner than this. He has held on as long as was humanly possible.'

'So it's true?' said Qasim. 'It's the end.' He stood up. 'Well thank you, little brother for letting us know. I will go and see to my family then I'll return to the hospital.'

'No. Don't go yet. That isn't all I have to tell you,' said Ahmad. 'We think we may have found a way to escape.'

'Escape? From the city? That's impossible. We would know about any escape route,' said Rafiq. This was astonishing news. But then Ahmad often surprised him. 'Tell us more.'

'Simon has found a cave hidden behind the crypt of his church. He went there today to hide some books. It's big enough to hold many people and he thinks there could be another cave or a passage behind it.'

'That's your escape plan? That we hide in an underground cave? For how long? Until we all die of hunger or suffocate? Or until the soldiers discover us and kill us?' said Qasim, starting to get up again.

'Sit still, Qasim. Let Ahmad finish,' said Rafiq. He had heard of tunnels and caves that the dhimmis had constructed in the past.

Most of them had been used to hide their gold but it was possible that some of them could have been used as a way of getting out of the city undetected.

'Our Jewish friend here, remembers hearing about some dhimmis escaping through a tunnel that went under the city wall. Isaak, tell them what you told us,' said Ahmad.

The old man related all that he knew about the tunnel and when he'd finished, Ahmad said, 'So you see, this cave could be the entrance to a secret tunnel.'

'It's a possibility. We need to have a look at it,' said Rafiq.

'That's why I wanted you here. We need to do this together.'

'And right away. If what you say is true, there is very little time to open up the tunnel and prepare to leave,' Rafiq continued. 'The first thing is to see if there really is anything behind that cave.'

'I suggest we go tonight, as soon as it's dark,' said Simon. 'The church will be empty after sunset. There is only one priest left; the others have all gone.'

'But won't it be locked?' said Ahmad.

'No. The church is always left unlocked, so that the faithful may enter at any time to pray. There is nothing in it to steal anyway.'

'I can't go now,' said Qasim. 'I have to get back to the hospital. But send for me later and I will come and help.'

'What about your family?' asked Aisha.

'I won't tell my wife anything yet. Best not to worry her until I know exactly what we can do. Ma'a salama everyone. I will see you later tonight. If you do not send for me, I will return here anyway to see if there is any news.'

'Alla ysalmak, Qasim.'

'I too must get back to my post before I'm missed,' said Rafiq. 'I know where the church is and I will meet you there after sunset. I'll bring some tools, in case we have to break down any walls. Ma'a salama. Until tonight.'

'Alla ysalmak, Rafiq. Makoud, lock the door behind your uncle,' said Ahmad.

As Rafiq walked away from the house, he could hear Makoud slide the heavy bolts back into place. His head was spinning with the news that Ahmad had told them. Surrender was something that was at the back of every soldier's mind but not anything that you dared consider. To think of surrendering sapped your resolve. The men had to focus on winning, on the prizes they would receive when the enemy was defeated. Surrender was never to be contemplated. Surrender could mean death, but death with dishonour. Every soldier knew that death awaited him sooner or later, but all wanted a noble death, on the battlefield. What about him? What did he want? He could change sides again. He had done it before. He could fight alongside Sulayman's men. No. His heart filled with hatred for that man. He thought once more of his beloved Antarah, fearless and loyal. She was dead because of this bloody siege. No, he would not fight for Sulayman. He would sooner die.

\*

As soon as the sun began to set, Ahmad, Simon and Makoud set off for the church. The night was dark, the sky cloaked in heavy clouds that hid both moon and stars. Each carried a dark lantern and Makoud had an iron pick hidden beneath his cloak. They shrouded the lanterns and kept close to the shadows. They wanted no-one to question them tonight.

It was just as Simon had said. The heavy wooden door to the church was closed, but unlocked. It squeaked loudly as it swung open, causing them to stop and wait to see if anyone was lurking in the shadows and had heard them. But the square was deserted, the only sign of life a few lights flickering inside the neighbouring houses. Nobody roamed the streets at night, unless it was with the hope of stealing some food from an unguarded huerta.

They slipped inside the church and were just about to close the door behind them when a voice whispered, 'Not waiting for me then, brother?'

'Rafiq. Come in and close the door quietly,' Ahmad instructed. 'Did you bring any tools?'

'I've got a pick and a shovel. And my sword, in case it's needed.'

'Let's hope not. Now Simon, where's this burial chamber?'

'Follow me,' said Simon. He led them down the stairway into the crypt. 'The entrance to the cave is there at the far end, behind all the bones.'

'Bones?' Ahmad lifted his lantern so that the light shone on the rows of grinning skulls. 'By all that's holy, what's that?' he asked.

'It's where they keep the bones of the dead. The entrance is behind them. Clever, isn't it?' replied Simon.

'It's macabre. Are you saying that we have to move all those skulls? There must be a thousand of them or more,' said Ahmad, a wave of disappointment rising in his throat. It would take them hours to move all the bones and then what? Their escape route would be easily discovered, if there was even a tunnel behind there.

'No, we don't have to move them all. The only thing is that I'm not sure exactly which ones we moved last time.' Simon edged closer to the wall of skulls and shone the lantern along them. 'It was somewhere here, on the end.' He bent down and pulled at a skull.

'Stop. You'll have the whole lot falling down on you. There has to be something to indicate where you start,' said Rafiq. 'You're sure it was in this corner?'

'Yes. We made a gap that stretched from the floor to about the height of my waist.' He stretched out his arm to show them.

'All right, then we must look here for a sign.'

'I can't see anything,' said Makoud. 'They all look the same to me, like faces from Hell.'

'But they're not all the same. Look carefully. Most of them have teeth, but not all. Some are larger than others. This one looks like a child,' said Ahmad.

'But which is the one we can remove without the others tumbling down?' asked Rafiq.

'What's that?' said Simon, shining his lantern on a small skull set half-way up the wall. 'There's a blue mark on that one.'

'Why would there be a blue mark? It has to be the one.'

They looked at it for a moment, unsure what to do. The skulls seemed to be finely balanced. Removing the wrong one could bring them all down. Even Rafiq looked hesitant about disturbing them.

'You three try to hold the skulls in place with your bodies while I remove this one with the blue dot. If you feel them start to move, shout out and I'll put it back,' said Ahmad.

They did as he suggested and Ahmad gradually withdrew the skull from its niche.

'Is everything all right?' Ahmad asked.

'Nothing seems to have moved. I think there's a wooden frame holding the skulls up,' said Rafiq.

'So we've found it,' said Makoud, excitedly. 'Come on, let's get some more out.'

'Yes, it looks as though this is the entrance, but go carefully,' said Ahmad. 'They still don't look very stable to me.' The thought of the skulls falling on top of them filled him with horror. If they weren't so desperate to find a way out of the city, he would have turned and left that depressing place. The dead should be left in peace, not moved about like so many chess pieces.

They removed the skulls one by one until Simon said, 'That's it. That's the stone I have to take out so we can get into the cave.'

He reached in and prised the stone free with the pick axe. A blast of cold air entered the crypt. 'See what I mean. There's air in there. Fresh air.'

'Makoud, you go in first. I'll hand you the lantern and the tools once you're in,' said Ahmad.

'But what if there's something in there, Baba?'

'If there's anything alive in there, I'm sure it will be more frightened of you than you are of it. Go on, boy. We haven't all night.'

Makoud wriggled through the gap. At first it was quiet. Then he saw the glow from Makoud's lantern and heard his son gasp in astonishment. 'It's full of treasure, Baba. It's a treasure cave.'

Ahmad squeezed through the hole and tumbled into the room to find Makoud sitting on the floor surrounded by gold and silver objects.

'This must be worth a fortune, Baba. It's the Christians' treasure. People always said that the Christians had hidden their valuables somewhere. This must be where they hid them.'

'They're not very valuable now, son.'

'What do you mean, Baba? How can treasure not be valuable?'

'Can you eat it?'

'Well no.'

'Can you drink it?'

'No.'

'Can you even use it to buy something to eat?'

'No, there's nothing to buy.'

'Exactly. So how is it valuable?'

'Your father is right. Our world has changed. What we value most now is our freedom, our lives and a good meal,' said Simon, pulling his pick and dark lantern into the cave.

'If Simon is right and there's a tunnel behind this wall, then everything will change. We will gain our freedom and stay alive,' said Ahmad. He was feeling more positive now. He turned to Rafiq, who had had trouble squeezing through the narrow gap. 'Tight fit brother?'

'Just a bit.'

'Now where did you feel the current of air? Where should we break through?'

'It's here, somewhere,' said Simon, tapping along the wall until he found the place where it sounded hollower. 'That's it, I think.'

'Well, let's give it a go. I'll start,' said Rafiq.

He swung the pick over his head and buried it into the wall. It looked easier than any of them had hoped. With each blow that his brother made, large chunks of rock fell to the floor, sending up a cloud of dust that soon had them coughing and sneezing.

'We all need to help,' Ahmad said.

The men tied their scarves around their faces and soon the three of them were attacking the wall with picks and bare hands. Suddenly the wall collapsed in front of them, the rocks and stones falling through into a black chasm. They had found the tunnel.

'You were right, Simon. There is a way out.'

'Old Isaak was right, you mean.'

'So what do we do now, Baba?' asked Makoud.

'We need to see how far it goes. If it's been here as long as Isaak says then it's possible that it's become blocked up over time.'

'Where do you think it goes?'

'He said it went under the city walls.'

'But then it might come up in the middle of Sulayman's troops,' said Makoud. 'That wouldn't be good.'

Rafiq laughed. 'No it wouldn't. So we'd better be sure we know what we're doing. Makoud, you go back into the church and keep guard. If anyone was to discover us down here we'd be caught like rats in a trap. Here take this and don't lose it.' He handed Makoud his sword. 'If you have any trouble with anyone, run him through. Don't hesitate. Your only strength will be surprise. Simon, you stay here in case the tunnel collapses and we need help. Ahmad and I will go and see how far the tunnel leads us.'

'But.'

'No buts. We need to see where this tunnel goes to and it could be anywhere. A Christian monk isn't going to be much use if we come up in the middle of the Berber camp, is he?' Rafiq turned to Ahmad and said, 'I'll lead the way. Bring the shovel in case we need to clear away any debris.'

'Here, take one of the lamps,' said Ahmad. He wasn't sorry that Rafiq had taken charge. Even sitting in the cave he could feel the walls closing in on him. It would be much worse inside the tunnel.

'God go with you,' said Simon, handing him the shovel.

The passage was wide but only high enough for a child to stand upright. It had been lined with ashlars and the floor had been semi-paved. Whoever had constructed it had meant it to last. They would have to crawl into it on their hands and knees. Rafiq took off his red cape and hitched up his robe.

'Take off your djellaba, Ahmad. You'll never be able to crawl in that,' he said, then bent down and wormed his way into the tunnel.'Good job I didn't eat much dinner today. It's a tight squeeze in here.'

Ahmad laughed at his brother's feeble joke and did as he suggested, then grasped the dark lantern and followed him into the darkness.

'Are you all right?' Simon called after a few minutes. 'Rafiq? Ahmad?'

'Yes,' Ahmad replied.

The monk began to prayer in his own language. The voice was faint and even though Ahmad couldn't understand the words, it was comforting. Soon he could hear nothing, just the panting of his brother as he crawled ahead of him. He could feel a breeze of cold air on his face. Somewhere ahead there was an opening. He breathed a sigh of relief; at least they wouldn't suffocate.

'Are you all right, Ahmad?' asked Rafiq.

'Yes, I'm fine.'

'We must be outside the church now. I think we're heading east.'

'Away from the river?'

'For now.'

They soon lost all idea of which direction they were travelling because the tunnel seemed to bend first one way and then the other. After a while the ceiling was higher and they were able to walk, although Rafiq still had to bend a little. Twice they had to stop to clear rubble that had fallen from the roof, but most of the tunnel was sound.

'I think we're going uphill,' said Rafiq. 'I'm sure of it. And I can see a light up ahead. We must be coming close to the end. Cover your lantern.'

At first there was nothing but unrelenting blackness and then as their eyes became accustomed to the dark, Ahmad could make out a grey patch ahead of them, which became gradually lighter and lighter as they approached. He could hear the sound of rushing water and smell the scent of mint and watercress. The paved floor beneath him was now wet and slimy.

'We're near the river,' Rafiq said. 'Wait here and I'll go ahead and have a look.'

He put down the shovel and the dark lantern, took his knife from his belt and slid forward on his belly.

'I'm coming with you,' said Ahmad. He didn't want to be alone in there. Better an enemy he could see than face his fears in the dark.

'Keep quiet then and keep low,' whispered Rafiq.

Ahmad lifted his head cautiously and looked about him. It was hard to make out where they were but he could hear the river close by and the scent from the watercress beds was stronger than ever; the tunnel had ended abruptly beside the river bank. If only they could see the sky then they could work out which side of the river they were, but the clouds hid all from view. With Sulayman camped on the south bank, it was vital to know exactly where the tunnel came out. Ahmad could see the lights from the enemy camp in the distance and hear the faint sound of voices but what lay between them?

He turned round and slid back down the tunnel, closely followed by Rafiq.

'We can get through. We can escape,' he said, relief and exhaustion making his voice tremble. 'It's a miracle. Allah is watching over us. We must tell the others. We must be prepared to leave as soon as we can.'

He felt Rafiq put his hand on his shoulder.

'Yes brother, we can get out, but we don't know where Sulayman's men are camped. We might be delivering ourselves straight into their hands.'

## CHAPTER 31

Ahmad's heart was racing. For the first time in two years he felt that he could at last do something to help his family. It had been eating away inside him, this feeling of impotence, the inability to do all that he wanted to for his family. He knew it wasn't a failing on his part but that had made it no easier. Now he had found a way to bring hope to them all.

By the time he, Makoud and Simon had returned home, the rest of his family were already sitting down to their meagre meal.

'Ahmad. Where have you been? I've been so worried about you. And why are you dirty?' Aisha asked, coming to greet them. She hugged Makoud so hard, he yelped, 'Mama, you're hurting me.'

'Let me wash and then I will tell you all. Where is Layla?' said Ahmad.

'She's lying down. She wasn't hungry. She said she ate something at the hospital, but I don't believe her.'

'Well tell her to come here. I need to speak to you all. And Salma, run down to Rachel's house and tell her and Isaak to come here right away.'

He went to the well and pulled up a full bucket of water and began to wash himself.

'Ahmad, what are you doing? That water has to do all of us and … Don't spill it. I can use it to water my plants after you've finished with it,' said Aisha, looking at him in horror.

He smiled at her. What did it matter? After today they wouldn't be taking water from the well anyway. He felt lightheaded as though all his cares were floating away.

'Don't worry, wife. Allah will provide.'

'You've gone mad. Makoud, your father has gone mad. Come son, wash your hands and eat and leave your father to his madness.'

Aisha went to the table and poured out three bowls of greyish broth.

'What's this Mama?'

'It's vegetable broth. Eat it up. It tastes better than it looks,' she said, sitting beside him and putting her head in her hands.

'It's very nice,' said Simon, drinking his down in one go.

'I'm sure it's lovely, dear wife,' said Ahmad, drying his hair and sitting down beside them. 'I think you must be a witch. You manage to make us meals every day out of nothing. You must have some special spells in your cooking pot.'

'If I were a witch, husband, I think I would conjure up something more appetising than vegetable broth. Now are you going to tell us what you've been up to?'

'You know where we were. We went to look for Isaak's tunnel.'

'And did you find it?' asked Layla, coming out of her room to join them.

'We did, aunt,' he said and looked at their faces. What were they feeling? Excitement? Fear? Disbelief? 'We can escape from the city but we must go very soon—maybe even tonight.'

'Tonight? That's impossible,' cried Aisha.

'I want you to get things ready, wife. Don't bring more than we can carry. The tunnel is wide enough for one person to enter at a time but there are parts of it where it's necessary to go on your hands and knees. We must only take the essentials,' Ahmad continued, ignoring the anguished look on his wife's face.

'What about the bird?' Makoud asked.

Ahmad felt his chest tighten. This was a decision he kept putting to the back of his mind. No more. Now he had to act. He got up and went straight out to the patio. His falcon was sitting on his perch, his head tucked round on top of his wing but when he heard Ahmad, he sat up and looked straight at him, his eyes gleaming.

'Hello, my beauty,' Ahmad said, lifting him off his perch. He scratched the top of his head, gently. He was a fine bird, a good hunter and he came back to the glove at the first call. He was the reason they had managed to survive as well as they had. He often came back with a rabbit in his claws, and sometimes small birds or rodents. He was the real magician who provided the ingredients that made Aisha's soups tasty. 'Time for you to have a taste of freedom, my dear friend. Fly free and find yourself a mate.'

With a heavy heart Ahmad climbed up to the roof terrace. He could see the lights of the enemy camp in the distance. They stretched around the city like a second wall, a ring of flickering flame.

'Alla ysalmak, dear friend,' he said and launched the falcon into the sky. The bird flew straight up and was instantly swallowed by the night. He would find a place to roost and tomorrow, if he returned, they would be gone.

He could hear a man's deep voice as he walked sadly down to join the others. It was Qasim.

'So you found it?' his brother said. 'There really is a tunnel.'

'Yes, there really is one. It hasn't been used in a long time, is my guess, but it's quite serviceable.'

'Where does it come out?'

'That's the problem. We're not sure.'

'I thought that was the whole point of going down there, to find out if it really went anywhere?' said Qasim.

'Oh it goes somewhere, all right. We know that. We just didn't know where we were when we came out of it and we could hardly ask anyone,' said Ahmad. 'It was dark. We could see the enemy camp but we couldn't make out how far away it was.'

'It could be risky then?'

'It's all risky, brother-in-law,' said Aisha.

'But you're going?' asked Qasim.

'Yes, we're going. It's the only chance we have.'

'I'm not going with you,' said Layla. 'I'm too old to be leaving my home. When I die I want to die here in Córdoba, with my ancestors.'

'We all want to do that, aunt, but we don't want to die now, by the hand of Sulayman and his Berber army. We will come back when this war is over,' said Ahmad.

'No, I'm staying. I'm needed at the hospital. I shall spend the last years of my life here, where I belong, helping those who need me.'

'But I need you,' cried Salma. 'You can't stay here, Teta. It's not safe.'

'Don't worry about me, child. I'll be fine. Allah will protect me and if he doesn't then I will be by his side all the sooner.'

'I want to ask you a great favour, Ahmad,' said Qasim.

'Of course, brother. What is it?'

'I can't go with you, either. I cannot leave the hospital. It is my duty to stay and care for the sick and the dying. They need me.'

'But what of your wife and children?' asked Aisha. 'Don't they need you, too?'

'That's what I wanted to ask you. Will you take them with you? There is nothing for them here but starvation or death. Please take them with you. I beg you, Ahmad.'

Ahmad put his arms around his brother. 'Of course we will. Tell them to be ready to leave at a moment's notice. I will send someone for them. But you know it will be soon.'

'Yes, I'll go home now and talk to her. It won't be easy but I hope she will realise it is for their own good.'

Ahmad looked across at Aisha. Could he do what his brother was doing? Could he send his wife and family away to safety and stay here without them? No. He knew he couldn't be parted from her like that. Only death would part them now.

'Alla ysalmak, brother. May Allah bless and keep you,' he said, hugging Qasim again.

'Ma'a salama, Ahmad. Allah protect and keep you all safe. You will be in my prayers every night,' said Qasim, struggling to hold back his tears.

'I will see you later at the hospital,' Layla said. 'First I must help Aisha pack.'

'Very well, aunt.'

'I must go, too. I must tell al-Hisham to be prepared,' said Ahmad.

'The Khalifa? Is he coming with us,' asked Aisha. 'In the name of Allah, won't that put us in more danger?'

'More or less. What does it matter? We can't leave the Khalifa here to be assassinated. I will be as fast as I can. Make haste all of you. You must be ready to leave when I give the word.'

\*

As soon as Ahmad had left, Aisha began to gather together all that she thought they would need. She piled everything on the sleeping mats and then stood looking at it. How could they make an escape carrying cooking pots and plates, sleeping mats, blankets, clothes, containers for water, so many things? It was impossible. There was no donkey to carry it all. She'd have to chose more carefully.

'Here, let me help you,' said Layla. 'I'm sure someone said something about having to go part of the way on your hands and knees. You must only take the essentials. One change of clothing, one sleeping bag and everyone must carry their own things. That way people take what is essential to them.'

Aisha smiled, 'Like I'll carry the cooking pot?'

'Yes, something like that.'

'Oh, I wish you'd come with us, Layla. I can't imagine what it will be like without you.'

'You'll be fine. You will have your husband and your son. And Salma is going too.'

'Yes and Rachel, I hope.'

'Ah here they are now. Why, what on earth is the matter, child?' Layla asked as Rachel began to cry.

'It's my father. He's dead,' she said, between her tears.

'Come, sit down. Now tell me what happened,' said Layla, putting her arm around the sobbing girl.

'Her father had a heart attack,' explained Salma. 'It happened this morning. One minute he was talking to her about where they would hide when the city surrendered, and then he had a tremendous pain in his chest and died.'

'It was so sudden,' wept Rachel. 'I didn't even have time to say goodbye to him. I just stood looking at him. I didn't know what to do.'

'Where is he now?' asked Aisha.

'They've taken him away to bury him. I told the rabbi what had happened and he saw to everything. Oh, what am I going to do without my father? He was all I had.'

'I'm so sorry, my child,' said Aisha. 'You will have to stay here with us, now. Has Salma told you that your father was right about the tunnel? We've found it.'

'Yes. She said you're leaving soon.'

'We're all leaving very soon, maybe tomorrow,' said Aisha. 'And you're coming with us. You can't stay here alone.'

'I've brought all that I need,' said Rachel. 'Salma said to bring everything. And I found some money that my father had hidden.' She pulled a small bag of gold coins out of her pocket. 'If we manage to escape it will be useful to have some money.'

'If we escape,' said Aisha. She was fearful of Ahmad's plan but what was their alternative? Stay here and throw themselves on the mercy of the Berbers? 'Salma, can you pack a small bag with whatever you will need for the journey.'

'Yes, cousin.'

'And I mean small. You can't take all those books you've been writing in. You won't be able to carry them.'

'She's right, Salma. It won't be easy to get them through the tunnel. But you could hide them in the cave with the others. At least that way they will be safe, until you return,' said Simon.

Return? Did any of them really believe they would return? Aisha's heart was heavy. They were about to leave their home, their friends and their city and go, Allah alone knew where.

'You're coming with us, aren't you, Simon?' Salma asked.

Aisha could see the pleading in her eyes.

'Yes, of course I'm coming. There's nothing to stay for now.'

When she saw the happiness on Salma's face, she realised it was just as well Ahmad hadn't arranged a marriage for her; it would never have worked. She was in love with the Christian, even if it was against the law. Sometimes you just couldn't control your heart.

'It's time you both got ready to leave. Remember, whatever you take you will have to carry a long way.'

'Where are we going, Mama?' asked Makoud.

'You'll have to ask your father. I hope he has some plan that extends beyond getting through the tunnel,' she said, and although she tried to sound positive, her own doubts were obvious to everyone.

Once Aisha had packed all she could, and hassled her son until he eventually put what he wanted in a small bag, she went out to her garden and picked all the remaining fruit, vegetables and herbs.

'Let me help you,' said Layla. 'Why don't you cook the ripe ones and you can take them in that earthenware pot—you'll need some food on the journey. I'll pack the others in a bag.'

'Do you want to take some to the hospital?' Aisha asked.

'No. They have a big garden. One thing we do have there is plenty of vegetables. No meat. No fish and no bread, very little medicine but plenty of vegetables. I'll be fine.'

'I'll miss you, Layla.'

'And I'll miss you too, my dear. But you must go with your family. Nothing awaits you here but death and misery.'

'I know, but it is hard to leave the place that you love. I was born here. My children were born here and I always thought I would die here.'

'If you don't hurry up, Mama, you may get your wish,' said Makoud, grinning at her. At least he was relishing the adventure.

'I'll miss you too, Teta. I wish you would come with us,' said Salma, tears streaming down her face.

'My place is here, my little one.'

'Don't forget me, Teta,' she sobbed. 'We'll come back after the war is over. I promise.'

Salma pressed the book of herbs that she had copied into her grandmother's hands. 'This is for you.'

Layla opened the book and looked at it, turning the pages carefully. 'It's very beautiful. Thank you, my child. I will treasure this forever. It will be of great help to me in my work.'

Amina looked around the patio; everything was ready. All they had to do was wait until Ahmad came back for them. She chopped up the ripe vegetables and put them in the pot to cook. There was no point leaving any food for the soldiers. She hoped they would starve.

\*

Qasim knew his wife would not take the news well, but he didn't expect her to break down completely in front of the children.

'Qasim, you can't send us away. I won't go. My place is by your side,' she wailed. 'Have I been a bad wife to you? Is that why you want rid of me?' She was becoming hysterical. 'You're taking a new wife, aren't you? That's it. I am to be divorced and sent away into danger, while you set up home with a new wife. Well I won't go.'

'Pull yourself together, woman. You're talking rubbish. Of course I'm not trying to get rid of you. Don't you think it is hard for me to part with you and our lovely children? You have always been the best wife a man could have. Why would I divorce you?'

'But you're sending us away.'

'Yes, with a very heavy heart. It will be too dangerous for you and the children to remain here. The city is about to surrender. Do you understand what that means?'

He tried to keep his voice calm, to reassure his wife, but inside he was angry with her. Why couldn't she understand that he was doing this for them? Why did she think everything was about her?

'It means you don't love me any more,' she said with a pout.

'Dearest one, of course it doesn't. It's because I do love you, that I want you safe,' he said.

'How will I be safer in the company of strangers than with my own husband?' she asked. 'I will be in danger and there will be no-one to protect me.'

'You won't be with strangers. You'll be with Ahmad and his family. They will look after you and the children. Remember I'm doing this for you,' he said. 'It won't be for long. Once everything has calmed down, you will be able to return and we will be together again.'

'But until then? Where will you be? Why can't you come with us? If Ahmad is leaving with his family, why can't you take yours?'

'My dear wife, you know that I must remain at the hospital. We are very few doctors. How can I leave now when every bed is full and there will be more suffering to come? I cannot abandon my colleagues nor my patients. You must see that.'

'All I can see is that your hospital is more important to you than we are. It's always been the same. The hospital first.'

He tried to put his arm around her but she pulled away from him. Qasim could see that it was going to take a long time to convince her to leave and he didn't know how much time they had. Ahmad could send for them at any moment. He would have to change his approach.

'Dry your eyes, wife. I have had enough of this. I am the master in this household and you will do what I say. My children are not staying in this city to be slaughtered by Sulayman's troops. Do you hear me?' He saw her nod, reluctantly. 'They are leaving. Ahmad and his wife are taking them to safety and you should be grateful for that. You should go down on your knees and thank Allah that your brother-in-law has found a way to escape and is willing to help my family too. If you don't care enough for your own children's safety then you can stay here. It is up to you. You can stay in this house and wait for the soldiers to come. But I want the children to be ready to leave as soon as Ahmad sends word. Is that understood?'

'Yes, husband,' she whispered.

'Good. There is no time to lose. Get the children fed and pack a small bag for each of them.'

He didn't like chastising his wife like that but it was the only way to make her break out of her misery. Unlike some men, he never beat his wife and he didn't expect unquestioning obedience from her. It hurt him to have to speak to her like that but there was no alternative.

'Did you hear me?' he asked, his voice cold. If he relented now, she would never go.

'I will go with them,' she said quietly. 'I will not leave my children to be looked after by strangers.'

'Good. I'm glad we agree. Wait here and I will come for you when it's time. Now I must return to the hospital.'

His wife turned away from him and began looking through the children's clothes. Why did she have to be this way? He loved her but there were times when he couldn't understand her. Surely she realised how difficult it was for him to be parted from his family?

He picked up his djellaba and set off for the hospital. He would have liked to have stayed with his family longer, played with the children a bit, talked to Bakr about how he must take care of his sisters now, tried to explain to them why their father wasn't going with them, but he was needed at the hospital. His wife was right. The hospital always came first. How could it not when people were in need of a doctor? His duty was to help them. He couldn't turn his back on the sick and wounded, not even for his own family.

Would he ever see them again? Was this going to be the last he saw of his beautiful daughters? And Bakr, plucky little Bakr, who wanted to grow up just like his father, when would he see him again? He didn't even know where Ahmad was planning to go. He ran his fingers through his hair in frustration. Had his brother actually got that far in his plan of escape?

## CHAPTER 32

Ahmad knew it would make their escape more complicated if al-Hisham came with him, but what choice did he have? Sulayman would either throw the Khalifa back in jail, where he would surely die a slow and painful death, or he would have him executed and place his head on a spike at the entrance to the city. He couldn't allow either of those things to happen. Al-Hisham was a sick man; he was weak and degenerate, but he was the lawful Khalifa of Ahmad's country. If no-one else could do it then he would save him.

The door to al-Hisham's inner chambers was closed but, as before, there were no Palace Guards on duty. Ahmad rapped as hard as he could on the door. He could hear someone scurrying about inside and then the door opened a crack.

'Who is it?' asked Musa.

'It's Ahmad. Let me in. I must see the Khalifa.'

'As-salama alaykum, sayyad. I am very glad to see you. The Khalifa is sleeping. He won't leave his harem,' said the slave. 'He says he feels safer in there.'

'Are there still people in the harem?' Ahmad asked, surprised. 'Men and women?'

'Only the men, now. They don't know about the city surrendering.'

Ahmad shuddered at the thought of what the soldiers would do to the occupants of al-Hisham's harem when they arrived.

'Wake him up. Tell him, it's important.'

'Very well, sayyad.'

The Khalifa was lying on a velvet couch and lifted his head when he heard Musa say that Ahmad was there. 'Well, have you a plan?' he asked, sitting up. 'Have you come to help me?'

## The Ring of Flames

'Yes, Your Majesty, I have a plan. I've found a way to get out of the city.'

Al-Hisham waved his hand to dismiss his servant but Ahmad stopped him, 'No, Your Majesty, it is best if Musa stays. He needs to know what we're going to do.'

'Very well, Ahmad. But before you tell me your plan, you should know that General al-Wahdi sent word that the city will surrender in the morning.'

'In the morning? By all that's holy, so soon.'

'Is that a problem?' the Khalifa asked.

'No, Your Majesty. It just means that we must leave tonight. Right away.' He turned to Musa. 'Please get the Khalifa dressed now, but not in his usual clothes. Find some old clothes, nothing conspicuous and cut his hair and beard. He must wear a ghifara and a dark djellaba, so that he blends in with everyone else.'

'What about Shamal? Can he come with us?' asked al-Hisham. His eyes were shining as though he'd been drinking wine.

'No, Your Majesty. The escape is going to be difficult. We must take only what we can carry and a falcon would draw too much attention to us. You should let Shamal go now.'

'No. I cannot do it.'

'You must, Your Majesty.'

'Are you sure there is no other way?' asked al-Hisham.

Ahmad knew the Khalifa would be upset about losing the falcon but even he couldn't jeopardise the safety of his family for a bird. 'We will find another one when we reach our destination,' he said. It was strange that nobody had asked where they were going, not even Qasim. Just the fact that they would escape the city seemed to be enough for them.

'Very well.' Al-Hisham got up from his bed and shuffled across to Shamal, who was fast asleep on his perch. 'He won't like me waking him at this hour.'

'He'll understand,' said Ahmad.

The Khalifa picked up Shamal and carefully removed his hood. The falcon blinked in the light of the oil lamps and swivelled his head, taking in everything with his enormous black eyes. 'Time to go,' said al-Hisham. He walked out into the garden with Shamal on his hand, and Ahmad and Musa followed him.

The air was rich with the scent of myrtle. Ahmad felt a great sadness all of a sudden. Even if he came back to Córdoba when the civil war was over, it would never be the same. It was unlikely that al-Hisham would survive many more years; his illness would take him even if he managed to escape the soldiers. And who would be on the throne when they returned? Would it be Sulayman or another? A pain in his heart told him not to delude himself; they were never coming back.

Al-Hisham had stopped in the centre of the gardens. He was stroking Shamal's head and talking to him. Tears were streaming down his face.

'You are everything I wanted to be and failed,' al-Hisham whispered to the falcon. 'You are fierce, brave and noble. And now you will be free.'

Ahmad moved forward to help him but the Khalifa waved him away. As gently as he could, and despite his shaking hands, al-Hisham removed the jesses from Shamal's legs. The bird waited, his head cocked to one side, watching him.

'Ma'a salama, dear friend,' the Khalifa said and then extended his arm and threw the falcon into the air. In a moment Shamal was gone. Although there was nothing to see in a sky, blacker than the darkest night, al-Hisham remained looking at the spot where he had last seen his beloved falcon.

'What of your other hawks?' asked Ahmad.

'I let them go, yesterday, after General al-Wahdi told me of the surrender. I knew they had to go. But I had hoped that I could keep my beloved Shamal,' he said accusingly.

'Your Majesty, we must go,' said Musa. 'The soldiers will be here soon. Sulayman will be here.'

The name seemed to arouse the Khalifa and he said bitterly, 'Sulayman. I should stay and confront him, not run away like a woman. I am the Khalifa of al-Andalus, son of al-Hakim II and grandson of the mighty al-Rahman III. I am the rightful ruler of this country. I shouldn't run away from my responsibilities.'

'You are indeed, Your Majesty, but your army is about to surrender. There will be no-one to defend you or your city,' said Ahmad. 'You must come with us. Then later, when the army has recovered, maybe you can return.' He knew his words were hollow, but the last thing he wanted at this late hour was for al-Hisham to have a change of heart and stay to face Sulayman. He had to get him to safety.

'Ah, if I had half the courage of my beautiful Shamal, I would remain here, but I haven't. I am a weak man. A sick man. I cannot fight Sulayman, although I wish with all my heart that he was dead.'

'Your Majesty,' Musa pleaded. He looked scared.

'Very well. If we must leave then let us do it,' al-Hisham said.

He took Musa's arm, and leaning heavily on him, followed him back into the alcázar.

'As soon as you're ready, you must bring the Khalifa to the church of St John. Bring as little as possible with you and keep to the shadows. Tell no-one. Nobody must know he's the Khalifa,' said Ahmad.

'But where will you be?' asked al-Hisham. 'Why aren't you going with me, Ahmad?'

'I have to tell my family that the city will surrender tomorrow morning. They are waiting for me. Don't worry, Your Majesty, I will see you at the church.'

'I don't know, Ahmad. It is not seemly for a Khalifa to enter a Christian church,' al-Hisham said.

'Wait outside until I arrive. You won't really be in the church, but in order to reach the entrance to the tunnel you must pass through it. I'm sure Allah will forgive you, Your Majesty,' said

Ahmad as once again he spoke to his Supreme Commander as though he were a small child.

'Do not worry, sayyad. We will be there,' said Musa.

\*

Rafiq walked along the ramparts, trying to cheer his men. They had had enough. The bombardment had not ceased all day, only now with the fall of night, did they have some peace but that didn't mean rest; they still had to remain vigilant. This was the time when Sulayman would try to send men over the wall to slit a few throats.

'Take a break, soldier. You look all in. Go down and see if the cook has anything left to eat. We'll keep watch,' he said to a young soldier who looked as though he was about to drop to his knees.

'Thank you, quaid. I won't be long.'

'And you too, go with him. See if someone can put something on that wound.'

'Yes, quaid,' said a burly man with an open gash down the side of his face. It oozed blood that dripped down his neck and stained his tunic.

Some of the soldiers were still fighting the fires started by the tar boulders that had landed earlier; they were hard to extinguish especially as the men had been told to use as little water as possible. They shovelled dirt and sand on them until they were reduced to smouldering lumps. The smell was awful but no worse than the usual stench of blood and guts that came from the battlefield.

No wonder General al-Wahdi was going to surrender. The men were weak with hunger, and morale was at the lowest he'd ever known it. They'd lost half the army and were almost out of weapons. If it went on like this they'd be fighting the Berbers with their bare hands. The forge, which had been going day and night for two years, was almost out but still they laboured on, producing arrow heads and spears, reconstituted from the enemy's own weapons. But what was the point of fighting on?

They would all be slaughtered if they continued. If they surrendered then at least some of them would be saved and given the opportunity to join Sulayman's army. That young soldier for example; he was too young to die. Perhaps General al-Wahdi was right to surrender.

He sighed. Below him in the distance he could see the lights of the enemy camp and the huge, dark tower of the siege engine. Last night the Berbers had scaled the walls and nearly gained entry to the city. It had been a hard and bloody battle. Some of the dead still lay where they had fallen, the survivors too exhausted to take them away. He knew his place was here with his soldiers; men whom he had fought beside and who had died under his command, but part of him said that he should take this opportunity to flee with his family. At least he could protect them. Once the call to surrender had been given then there was nothing he would be able to do for his men. At that point it would be every man for himself.

Rafiq thought back to when he'd first become a soldier; it was to follow in his father's footsteps. He had idolised his father, who had had a long and successful career. Al-Jundi had saved the life of the Khalifa's son and as a reward he'd held a privileged position in the court of al-Rahman III, but his father had never seen as much action as Rafiq had. It was a wonder he was still alive, he'd fought in so many campaigns. Had Allah protected him all these forty years just so he could surrender now? It was time he retired before his luck ran out.

'Uncle Rafiq,' a voice whispered.

He looked behind him; it was Makoud, scarcely recognisable under the hood of his all-enveloping djellaba.

'What the hell are you doing here? You could get yourself killed.'

'Baba says the surrender is tomorrow morning. We're leaving tonight,' he whispered. 'He wanted you to know.'

'Good. Thanks for telling me, boy.'

'You will come with us, won't you, Uncle?'

## The Ring of Flames

He looked at the boy's anxious face. They would have a hard journey ahead of them, even if they managed to get away undetected. Who would protect them? Ahmad was no good with a sword. He smiled to himself as he remembered his young brother's first attempt to wield one; he'd nearly cut his own leg off. And who else was there? This young boy and a Christian monk.

'Why are you smiling, Uncle?' Makoud asked.

'It's nothing.'

'You will come?'

'If Allah spares me, I will come with you. After all someone has to look after that brother of mine, with his head filled with falcon feathers.'

'Right away, Uncle. We're going right away,' Makoud whispered, insistently.

'Yes, yes. Run along, Makoud. I'll be with you when I can. Don't wait for me. If I'm late, I will find you.' He hesitated and then added, 'May Allah go with you, child.'

He watched as Makoud disappeared into the shadows and then continued his walk along the ramparts. He would just check that all his men were awake and then he'd go.

'Rafiq,' his friend Asif said, making him start; he had approached so quietly.

'What is it? You nearly gave me a heart attack, creeping up on me like that.'

'General Tayyab wants to talk to us. He's waiting in the Dar al-Jund.'

So this was it. He was going to tell them about the surrender.

'You're to come with me, now,' said Asif.

'What about my men?'

'Leave them. His orders were for us all to go to him,' he said.

'Who was that?' He nodded in the direction that Makoud had gone.

'My nephew.'

'He seemed very agitated.'

'Are you surprised? All the city is agitated. Or hadn't you noticed?'

Asif scowled at him. 'You've got a plan, haven't you? I know you, you devious bastard.'

'Do you know what he wants, so urgently?' asked Rafiq, ignoring Asif's jibe and wondering if he should tell Asif what he had heard.

Asif shook his head and turned and marched off in the direction of the Dar al-Jund.

Well this would make it easier. If the general said they were going to surrender, he could leave his post with a clear conscience.

As he ducked through the archway into the Dar al-Jund, he noticed the young soldier sitting on the ground.

'Feeling better, soldier?' he asked, although the lad still looked half-asleep.

'Yes, quaid,' the soldier said, hurriedly getting to his feet and standing to attention.

'Well run along now; get back to your post.'

'Yes, quaid.'

Rafiq headed for the general's office, where he found Asif and Isa already waiting.

'Be seated, men,' said General Tayyab. He too looked worn-out. His usually immaculate uniform was torn and blood-stained, and there was an angry-looking burn along his forearm.

'General.'

'I've just had news from General al-Wahdi that we will give the order to surrender at dawn.'

'But General,' Asif protested, both surprised and distressed by the news.

'The decision is final, quaid. There is no sense in continuing this war. We have lost more than half our army and have hardly any weapons left. The people are starving and there is hardly any water. It is in the best interests of everyone if we surrender. I pray that Sulayman behaves in an honourable way and treats the people of Córdoba with respect.'

'He won't, General. It'll be a massacre. You know it will,' protested Isa.

'What I know or think has nothing to do with it. I have my orders, quaid. And now you have yours. At dawn tomorrow, you will tell your men to lay down their weapons and surrender to the enemy. I want no heroics. That would only lead to a blood bath. The gates will be opened and Sulayman will be allowed to ride into our city unmolested.'

'What about the Khalifa?'

'General al-Wahdi has said that he's to stay in the alcázar until Sulayman sends for him.'

'He'll be executed.'

'Probably. But then he won't be the first Khalifa to be executed, will he?'

'He'll be the first legitimate one,' said Rafiq, angrily. Why was General Tayyab taking all this so calmly? Had he and al-Wahdi made some deal with Sulayman?

'Remember whom you're talking to, quaid. I will not tolerate insubordination. I'd hate to have to throw you in prison right now, when we need every man we have to make sure this goes smoothly.' He looked at each of them in turn as though he were trying to assess their feelings about his announcement. 'Now, if I have made myself clear, go back to your posts and see to your troops.'

'Yes, General,' they said.

As soon as they were out of the general's earshot, Rafiq turned to the others and said, 'What are they up to? Have they made a pact with Sulayman? I've never seen General Tayyab so relaxed about anything before.'

'Maybe, like the rest of us, he's just fed up with this damn siege,' said Asif. 'You can't blame him. I can't remember the last time I had a good square meal. My stomach has thought my throat had been cut for months now.'

'It's been the same for everyone,' said Isa.

'Do you think we should warn our men?' asked Rafiq. He was beginning to feel guilty about leaving them with no leader.

'No. If General Tayyab found out, you'd be courtmartialed. You can't tell anyone anything until just before dawn,' said Isa. 'Then they'll have to make up their own minds about how they want to spend the rest of their lives—in prison or in Sulayman's army.'

'What, serving under General Tayyab again?' asked Rafiq, bitterly. He knew this was the way things went. Most of the soldiers were mercenaries. It was a job for them and they fought for the highest bidder. But the general? That was different. He should have some loyalty to al-Hisham.

'Yes, probably. What's the matter with you, Rafiq? You were happy enough to dump Sanchuelo and fight for Muhammad.'

'Yes, but Sanchuelo had murdered his own brother.'

'And Muhammad would probably have done the same if he'd had the chance. Don't get so involved, Rafiq. With all your experience, you should know how it works. I, for one, would be grateful if Sulayman took me into his army,' said Asif.

'Anyway, it's time we got back to our men,' said Isa. 'See you at dawn, my brothers. May Allah keep and protect us.'

'Ma'a salama.'

As soon as Isa was out of sight, Asif turned to Rafiq and hissed, 'You knew, didn't you? You knew about the surrender and you didn't tell me. I thought we were friends.'

'What does it matter? You know now.'

'You're up to something, Rafiq. I can smell it.' He pushed his face close to Rafiq's, so that he could smell his sour breath, and glared at him.

This siege was affecting them all.

'Don't be ridiculous, Asif. Nothing's going on,' he snapped and marched away.

As Rafiq left the Dar al-Jund, he looked for the young soldier again, but he'd gone. What was he going to do? He'd told

Makoud that he'd go with them but he couldn't find it in his heart to just walk out on his men.

## CHAPTER 33

Ahmad and his family were the first to arrive at the church, accompanied by Simon and Rachel. There was no-one about, so they slipped inside, closing the door behind them.

'Will we wait for the others in here?' asked Simon.

'Yes. Go down to the crypt and start removing the skulls from the entrance to the tunnel. Makoud, you go with him.'

'What shall we do, cousin?' asked Salma.

'Well you can take those bloody books down into the crypt for a start. I don't want any delays just because you're looking for the best place to leave them.'

'I won't take long, cousin. I promise,' she said, and followed the two men down the stairway into the crypt.

'Where's Qasim? I thought he was bringing his children?' asked Aisha. His wife looked tearful but resolute. She had that look on her face that he'd seen before, when she was determined to do something and nothing was going to stop her. He thanked Allah that he had such a loyal and brave wife.

It had been hard leaving their home—because after two years the Christian woman's house had become their home—but no-one had complained. They had gathered together on the patio and prayed to Allah for forgiveness for running away and for his protection on the long journey ahead of them. Then they had each taken the small bag that they had been allocated and left. Nobody had spoken a word. They locked the door behind them and trudged down the street towards their new life. And still no-one had questioned him about their destination.

'That sounds like someone, now,' said Rachel. She opened the door a crack and looked out.

'Let us in,' whispered Qasim. 'Quickly. I think I saw someone in a doorway.'

'Cover the dark lantern, first,' instructed Ahmad.

Rachel did as she was told and let the newcomers in. Qasim's wife had a face that seemed set in stone. She spoke to no-one, but the children began to chatter excitedly to each other.

'Wife, take the children down into the crypt. If there is anyone hanging about, I don't want him to hear them,' said Ahmad.

'Come with me,' Aisha said, putting her arm around Qasim's wife. 'We'll feel safer down there.'

'Safe?' she snorted. 'There is nowhere safe now. I might just as well kill myself and my children right now.' She pulled away from Aisha and grabbed little Ulla by the hand. 'Come with me, children. And be quiet.'

Ahmad saw his brother open his mouth as though he was about to say something to her, then change his mind. 'Don't worry, Qasim. We'll look after them. She's frightened. We all are.'

'Yes, but some of us make an effort to control our fear,' Qasim said. 'She is angry because I won't go with you.'

'Of course.'

'Where are the others?' Qasim asked.

'They are opening up the entrance to the tunnel. I hope Aisha has warned your wife about the skulls,' said Ahmad.

There was a strangled scream from the crypt.

'Obviously not,' said Qasim with a smile. 'Oh well, something else she will blame me for. I'll go down and help. Are you coming?'

'In a moment. Rafiq isn't here, yet. Nor is al-Hisham.'

'But Rafiq's coming?'

'He told Makoud he was.'

'He's probably delayed.'

'It will be dawn soon. We need to get everyone into the tunnel before then. Where on earth is the Khalifa? We can't leave without him.'

'What's that?' Qasim said, covering the dark lantern.

They waited in silence and then they heard it again. Someone was outside. There was a gentle knock on the door.

'Open it,' said Qasim, drawing a sword from his belt.

Ahmad looked at him in surprise. Since when had Qasim taken to carrying a sword? His hand went automatically to his own short sword, which he now wore all the time. It was as well to be armed when you didn't know who was friend and who was foe. He carefully pulled back the bolts on the door and opened it. Musa stood on the steps, covered in blood. Behind him, leaning on a stout staff, stood al-Hisham.

'Quickly. Quickly. Come in. What on earth has happened, Musa? Where did all that blood come from?' Ahmad asked, staring at them open-mouthed.

'We were attacked,' the slave said. 'Just out there. A man jumped out on us and demanded money. I tried to explain that we had no money but he pulled back the Khalifa's hood and then he recognised him. He was going to take the Khalifa away. He said he'd get a good price for him from Sulayman. I couldn't let him do that. I had no choice.' The slave was babbling now and tears were streaming down his face.

'What happened? Are you hurt?' asked Qasim.

The slave shook his head.

'What about the Khalifa? Is he hurt?'

'No. But I couldn't let him take him away.'

'Of course not. Now calm down, Musa, and tell me what happened to the man,' said Ahmad.

'He's out there,' Musa gasped, pointing to the door.

'Wait here.'

Silently the brothers crept out into the night. The darkness was slipping away to the west and in the east the sky was grey; it was almost dawn. Ahmad leaned over the body. 'I know that man. He's one of the palace servants. He must have seen you leaving. What if he's told anyone else? There could be more men coming for the Khalifa. What are we going to do?' All their plans would be ruined if they were found now.

'Well we can't leave him here for someone to find. Grab his legs: we'll hide him in the church,' said Qasim.

'What was that?' asked Ahmad, turning towards the house opposite just in time to see a figure slip away into the darkness. 'Someone's seen us.'

'Go after him. Hurry. I'll drag the body inside.'

'But…'

'Hurry. If he tells anyone what he's seen, we'll all die.'

Ahmad sped off in the direction the man had taken. The area was a maze of narrow passageways and alleys. He would never find him, not on this dark night. He could have gone down any of them. It was a waste of time. They should just try to make their escape before anyone came back.

He turned and ran back to the church. There was no sign of Qasim or the dead man, so he tapped gently on the church door. Instantly it opened.

'Well?' asked Qasim.

'Impossible to find him. We'll just have to hope he didn't realise it was the Khalifa. He could have thought it was just been a brawl or a robbery and decided he didn't want to get involved.'

'Well, let's hope you're right, but it's even more important to cover our tracks now and for you to leave as soon as possible,' said Qasim.

'What are we going to do with him?' asked Ahmad, looking at the man who was lying on the stone floor like a crumpled doll.

'Let's take him down into the crypt. We'll leave him in the cave then no-one will find him. He wanted treasure, well he can be buried with it.'

'Musa, help the Khalifa down the stairs into the crypt. You're going to have to help him through the tunnel. Give your bags to one of the others, Simon or Makoud; you won't be able to manage them and the Khalifa as well,' Ahmad instructed. 'And be as quick as you can. If that man decides to tell anyone what he saw, we won't have much time.'

He looked across at al-Hisham. He seemed to be in a dream and just followed the slave as meekly as a lamb.

He and Qasim took the body down into the crypt. Luckily Simon and Makoud had already removed the stone and the women and children were sitting patiently in the cave; they would never need to know about the dead man. He knew that even Aisha would panic if she heard that one of the palace servants had tried to rob the Khalifa. Perhaps she'd been right, bringing the Khalifa with them was a tremendous liability.

'Leave him here for now,' said Qasim. 'I'll push him through the gap when you've all gone and then I'll close up the wall behind you.'

They dumped the man unceremoniously beside the pile of skulls. Inside the cave he could hear the children's excited chatter about the treasures that they'd found. They fell silent when Musa helped the Khalifa crawl through the hole and they saw that they were in the presence of the ruler of al-Andalus. He wondered what they were thinking? Al-Hisham didn't look much like a khalifa at the moment. Musa had done his job well and his master looked more like another servant than the man they all served.

'You will have to go now, Ahmad. You can't wait any longer. It will take you a long time to get everyone through the tunnel,' said Qasim. 'I'll clean up the blood.'

'But what about Rafiq? We have to wait for him.'

'He's not coming. Anything could have happened to him. He could be dead. You can't risk everyone's lives on the off-chance that he'll go with you.'

Ahmad was about to protest but Qasim was right. Who knew what had happened to Rafiq? The surrender was at dawn. Already Sulayman would be making his way to the city gates and General al-Wahdi would be getting ready to abandon their beautiful city to that barbarian. If they left now, it would be perfect timing because no-one would be looking for them. All the soldiers would be at the gates of the city and then ... He pushed the thought from his mind. There would be time enough to dwell on the fate of the citizens of Córdoba once they were safe.

'Very well, brother. Thank you for your help,' he said, embracing Qasim. 'We will miss you.'

'Alla ysalmak, Ahmad. I will always be grateful for what you're doing for my family. If Allah wishes it, I will see you all again, one day, when this dreadful war is over.'

'Take care, Qasim. These are dangerous times.'

'Don't worry about me. But before you leave, tell me one thing. Where are you going? I need to know where to find my family when I am no longer needed here.'

'To Ardales. To the birthplace of our grandfather. It seemed the best place to go; it's possible that we still have family there who will help us.'

'Well then, dear brother, I will see you in Ardales, one day.'

The brothers embraced and Ahmad squeezed himself through the gap to join the others. It was time to go.

\*

Rafiq stood on the ramparts, watching the sky grow lighter and lighter. The clouds of the previous night had disappeared and soon the sun would light up a bright blue sky. His men had taken the news philosophically. He could see that many of them were glad that the fighting was over and there was a look of relief on their faces when he told them to abandon the ramparts. Now they all stood on the parade ground, awaiting their new commander. What a tattered, rag-bag of an army they were now; emaciated, dirty and bloody, they stood to attention as he walked along their lines. What should he do? He had to make a quick decision because at any moment General Tayyab might reappear. He had already inspected Rafiq's corps and was now at the far end of the parade ground. Now was the moment. Rafiq walked to the end of the line and, without altering his stride, made straight for the officers' quarters.

It was empty, as he had expected. Everyone was on the parade ground waiting for General al-Wahdi. All he had to do now was get to the church before they left. He slipped out of the Dar al-Jund and began to run. He'd brought nothing with him, except his sword, his dagger and what remained of his pay; there had been no opportunity to collect his belongings from his room. He would have to manage without them. The main thing was to get there before they blocked up the tunnel. If he couldn't escape with the others and it was realised that he had left his post, then he would be arrested for desertion. To die in battle was one thing but the thought of execution made his blood run cold. To know the moment of your death and be powerless to prevent it was something everyone feared.

The city was eerily silent as he raced through the streets and it didn't take him long to get to the church, but the door was locked. Surely Ahmad had said that it would be unlocked, that it was always unlocked. He rattled the handle but it held fast. He tried putting all his weight against it but the door was made of solid oak and could withstand more than his puny efforts. He looked around him. There was no-one in the street, so he banged as hard as he could with his fists. 'Ahmad,' he called. There was no sound from within. Had they already left? It was now daybreak. He was too late. He saw a small rock in the road and picked it up. The church had windows set high in its walls. If he was careful he could throw the stone through the nearest one. He aimed carefully and threw the stone straight at the window. The glass shattered with a sharp crack. 'Ahmad,' he called again. 'It's me. Rafiq.' If they were in the cave or even down in the crypt no-one would hear him. He walked back to the front of the church and banged on the door again. Loudly. What did it matter if anyone in the street heard him? This was his last chance.

The sound of bolts being drawn back made him stop hammering. At last. Someone knew he was there.

'Rafiq? Is that you?' asked Qasim, peering round the door. 'Where the hell have you been? The others have gone. I was just closing up behind them. Come in, quickly before anyone sees you. It's a wonder you didn't wake up the whole street with your noise.'

'What have you done with him? He was my brother. You killed him. I saw you,' yelled an angry voice.

Rafiq spun round, just in time to see a figure brandishing an axe running straight at him. Instinctively he drew his sword, stepped to one side and thrust the sword into the man's chest. He fell to the ground without a sound, the axe clattering down the steps.

'Who the hell was that?' he asked Qasim.

'I think it was probably the brother of the man who followed the Khalifa. He's dead.'

'He's just a boy,' said Rafiq, looking down at the dead body.

'Bring him in here, before anyone sees him,' Qasim said. He led the way into the crypt. 'I'm glad you're here. You can help me with him, as well.' He pointed to the body of a dead man, propped against the wall of skulls.

'Who is devil is he?'

'Don't know. It sounds as though he's that one's brother. All I know is that he was skulking around outside and then decided to rob the Khalifa. He got a knife in his side for his pains.'

'Who did it? Ahmad?'

'No, of course not. You know Ahmad, he'd have tried to talk him out of it, either that or given him all he had. No, it was Musa, the Khalifa's servant. And a good job too. He knew too much. Musa said he'd recognised the Khalifa.'

'And this one?' Rafiq asked, dropping the body of the youth he'd just killed on the floor of the crypt. He was still shaking from the attack. It always took him that way. It was the adrenalin kicking in so quickly. He looked at the boy's face. Now that it was no longer contorted with rage, it was clear that he was only fifteen or sixteen years old. All his life before him and now snuffed out in a moment of mindless rage.

'I think he was watching us from the shadows when we were dragging the body into the church. Ahmad ran after him but lost him. Don't give it too much thought. It was you or him. And I know which one I prefer,' he said, putting his hand on Rafiq's shoulder. 'Come on now, give me a hand to stuff them through the hole and then you can follow them in. You'll soon catch up with the others. With the women and children in tow, they weren't really hurrying.'

The first man was cold. It wouldn't be long before he began to stiffen. Between them they pushed him through the gap, legs first and let him fall where he might. What a punishment for him, to be buried in a Christian tomb. There would be no vestal virgins for him. Then they pushed the youth in after him.

'They'll be pleased to see you,' said Qasim. There were tears in his eyes as he spoke. 'They need a strong man to protect them. I'm glad you decided to go with them.' He put his arms around his brother and hugged him. 'Take care of them, brother and may Allah go with you.'

'I will, Qasim. I will guard them with my life,' Rafiq said. He had never seen his brother so emotional before. Normally he kept his feelings tightly under control, but today he had said goodbye to his children, his wife and his family. Even he couldn't hold all that inside.

'Hurry up now. Remember we still don't know what they will face when they leave the tunnel.' Qasim gave Rafiq a friendly push. 'I'll replace the stone and the skulls once you're inside. Do you have a lantern?'

'No. I didn't have time to get anything,' Rafiq said.

'Take this one. I can manage in the dark. It will be easier once the sun comes up.'

At this reminder of how quickly the day was starting, Rafiq struggled through the hole and into the cave.

'Look after yourself, my brother,' Qasim said as he slid the stone into place.

Rafiq looked about the cave. There was plenty of treasure but it wouldn't be much use to them as it was all far too bulky to carry through the tunnel. He took a deep breath and bending double began to crawl into the passage.

\*

He'd been wriggling through the dark for what seemed an age, when the tunnel suddenly grew wider and he found he was able to stand upright again. What a relief to stretch his muscles, if only for a moment. The floor of the tunnel was levelling out now. Suddenly he heard a noise. He stopped. A rat perhaps? There had to be rodents in the tunnel. He took a few more steps and then stopped again to listen. Yes, there was definitely something or someone behind him. He tucked the lantern under his cloak to hide its light, drew his sword in readiness, and waited. Then he heard a tiny sigh of frustration. It was no animal. Someone was following him. He held his breath and waited, straining his eyes in the gloom. A figure gradually materialised out of the blackness. Rafiq waited for the moment and then uncovered the lantern. The figure stumbled, blinded by the sudden blaze of light.

'Asif?' Rafiq couldn't believe his eyes.

'Are you planning to kill me with that thing?' Asif asked.

Rafiq lowered his sword, but didn't replace it in its scabbard. 'What are you doing here?' he asked.

'I could ask you the same thing,' said Asif. 'Deserting, by the look of it. I'd never have thought you were capable of desertion, Rafiq. Not such a loyal soldier now, are you?'

'What do you want?'

Rafiq's mind was racing. What was he going to do? The others needed him. Ahmad needed him. Now this stupid soldier had decided to poke his nose in. He should just run him through with his sword right now and be done with it.

'I want the same as you, to get out of this bloody city before Sulayman's men arrive.' Asif looked about him. 'How did you find this tunnel? That dhimmi tell you about it? And who were those dead men? Fresh, I'd say. Had to kill them did you?'

'You're not coming with us, Asif. Go back to your family. They need you.'

'They're dead. And if they're not dead already then they soon will be. As will I, if I stay.'

'You could fight for Sulayman.'

'I'll take my chances with you. That seems a much better option. Anyway, I've got enough to keep me going for a few years,' he said with a laugh, dragging a heavy sack out in front of him. 'I'm sure you've taken your share of the treasure, already. Such a pity that we can't manage to carry any more. Still we know where it is now and when everything's quietened down, I'm coming back for more. I expect you will too.'

Rafiq's heart gave a lurch. Qasim? Did he get away before Asif turned up? Had he been hurt?

'My brother, did you see him?' he asked.

'The doctor. Yes, I saw him. He was just putting the skulls back in place when I arrived.'

Rafiq stepped towards Asif, his sword pointing at his throat. 'Where is he now?'

'How should I know. I left him busily hiding our tracks.'

'What do you mean? What did you do to him?' The point of his sword was now touching Asif's skin.

'I didn't do anything to him,' Asif said, pushing the sword away with his hand. 'I just said you had told me to come along if I could get there in time. He wasn't sure whether to believe me at first, but I said that you wanted another fighting man to protect them. He just pushed me down the hole and told me to hurry. Actually his words were, "I hope Rafiq hasn't invited any more of his bloody friends along."'

He laughed.

'So Qasim is all right? You didn't hurt him?'

'Of course not. Why would I hurt a doctor? It was him who sewed up my arm that time. Look, don't you think it's time we got moving. It'll be daylight soon.'

'All right, you can come, but you do what I say.' He motioned him to go ahead of him. 'You go first, where I can keep an eye on you.'

'Well give me the lantern then.'

'No, you'll manage.'

What were the others going to say when they saw Asif? They'd think he'd betrayed them. Or maybe they'd be pleased to have some extra protection. His biggest worry now was whether they'd catch up with the others before they exited the tunnel. It would be difficult to trace them once they were out because as yet he still had no idea where Ahmad planned to take them.

## CHAPTER 34

Salma had hidden her books in the cave, all except one; she just had to keep one for herself. She prayed that they would be safe, that no-one would find them until the city was at peace. It gave her a sense of satisfaction and even pride, that she had done this small thing for the city, that she, an insignificant scribe, had tried to save something of their heritage while others had done nothing.

At first she thought she would panic when she entered the tunnel. It was so dark in there and the walls pressed down on her, making her feel that she couldn't breathe, but after a while her eyes became accustomed to the dark and she crawled steadily forward, following the flickering lantern with which Simon led the way. Rachel was directly behind her and she could hear her praying softly to herself in Hebrew. Aisha had made her remove all symbols of her Jewish faith and throw away the yellow star. She said it was safer for her that way.

Salma's knees were sore, her back hurt and she was tired of crawling through the dark. Her nose itched from the dust and the tiny bits of gravel that fell from the ashlars that lined the roof and she desperately wanted to sneeze. She was glad that Aisha had given her and Rachel some old clothing that had once belonged to Makoud; it made them look like a couple of boys but at least it was easier for them to crawl along the stone floor. However Salma wasn't so pleased when her cousin insisted that they cut their hair short and remove their jewellery, but she had done as she was instructed; Ahmad said it was for their own safety. Now she felt like a shorn lamb and kept the hood of her djellaba up whenever possible. She wondered what Simon thought about her new appearance.

They had been travelling downhill since they'd left the cave but now the tunnel levelled out and they were able to stand up.

'Oh, that's much better,' she said, stretching her back. It had been exhausting dragging herself along the ground like an animal.

'No talking,' hissed Ahmad from behind her. 'We don't know where we are or who could be listening.'

He was right. Even the children made no noise. Everyone was too frightened to speak. Was this what the soothsayer had meant when she said they were going on a long journey, never to return? A deep sadness filled her heart when she thought of her grandmother; she would never see her again. Last night she'd tried to persuade Layla to come with them but it was hopeless; her mind was made up. How was Salma going to manage without her? Her grandmother had cared for her since her parents died. It was Layla who encouraged her to follow her dream and work in the library; it was Layla who refused to have Salma rushed into an early marriage—the usual solution for an orphaned girl. Even last year, when Ahmad had found husbands for his daughters and wanted to find one for Salma, Layla had said it could wait. She had told her that she must follow her heart. She would miss her grandmother sorely. Now she would have to fight her own battles

'Ahmad, can we rest for a minute?' whispered Qasim's wife. 'Please? I have cramp in my leg. Just for a minute.'

'Very well. But no talking. We'll have five minutes and then we must move on.'

Salma could hear a sigh of relief from the other women. It wasn't easy to crawl through a narrow tunnel in a long robe, even if it was hitched up around your waist. One of the children began to cry.

'What is it, little one?' she asked Ulla.

'I want Baba,' she sobbed. 'Where is Baba? Why isn't he with us?'

'Don't cry, sweetheart. Your father will come and see you later, when he's finished his work at the hospital. He's a very important man. They need him to stay at the hospital.'

'But how will he find us?'

Salma sighed. What could she tell this child to make her feel better?

'Your Baba knows where we're going,' said Ahmad. 'He will find you; don't you worry. It might not be soon, but he will come and find you one day.'

That seemed to be good enough for the little girl, at least for now. She rubbed the tears from her face and smiled at Salma.

'You'll stay with us, won't you?' she asked.

'Yes, I'll stay with you. We'll all stay together and look after each other,' Salma said. Everyone had been so fixed on escaping from the city that nobody had mentioned the future. Maybe it was best that way. Maybe it was best to let the future unfold in its own way.

'Time to move on,' Ahmad whispered. 'We're getting close to the exit now, so be as quiet as you can.'

'What's that?' asked Musa. 'I can hear something. In the tunnel. Someone is following us.' He pulled out his dagger and turned to face the darkness.

'Quiet. It's probably nothing; just a rat I expect.'

Everyone held their breath and listened. Their fear was palpable. Then they could all hear it. Whatever it was, was approaching and approaching fast. They could hear regular, heavy footfalls getting closer and closer, then suddenly a dark shape appeared before them, doubled over as though in pain, closely followed by a second shape.

'Qasim?' his wife called out, 'Is that you, dear heart?'

'No. It's me, Rafiq and my friend, Asif. Thanks be to Allah, we've found you,' said Rafiq, throwing himself down on the floor. 'I thought we were going to get stuck in that bloody tunnel. My back feels as though it will never be straight again.' He rubbed the dirt from his tunic.

'I'm so pleased to see you, brother. We were worried about you,' said Ahmad. He stared at Asif.

'I thought we could do with an extra sword,' Rafiq explained. 'Asif was one of General Tayyab's quaids, like me.'

Salma could see that Ahmad was not wholly convinced, but he turned to Asif and said, 'Ahlan wa sahlan.'

'Thank you,' said Asif, bowing slightly. Salma noticed him looking at the Khalifa.

'But now we must make haste,' said Ahmad. 'There will be time to talk later. Rafiq, make your way to the front and join Simon. When we arrive at the exit you will need to survey the scene. Asif, you defend the rear.'

'Very well, Ahmad.' Rafiq edged his way past Qasim's family, the Khalifa and his servant, past Aisha and Makoud, until he stood beside Simon. She was so thankful that Rafiq and his friend had joined them and that it would be Rafiq and not Simon who would crawl out of the tunnel first. Simon was a brave man and it was obvious he would do everything he could to help them, but he was a monk not a soldier. She knew that they would all feel much safer now that Rafiq and his friend had arrived.

\*

He lifted himself up out of the tunnel and fell flat in the long grass, where he lay motionless for a few minutes while his eyes adjusted to the glare of the sun. He listened for any sound that would tell him what was around him but all he could hear was the gentle babble of the river and the warbling of some tiny birds in the reeds. Cautiously Rafiq lifted his head and looked about him. He heaved a sigh of relief; they had come out on the south side of the river, about an Arab mile from the enemy's camp. He could see no sign of life either around the camp or in the fields. As he had hoped, all the soldiers were now in the city.

'It's all clear,' he called down the tunnel. 'And we don't have to cross the river.' That was a blessing because he was sure Ahmad had never considered how he was going to get the women, three children and a sick Khalifa across a river that was, at this point, both wide and deep.

Ahmad's head appeared out of the long grass, his eyes blinking in the sunlight.

'No-one around?'

'No. I can't see anyone. So, little brother, what is your next move? You have thought of a next move, haven't you?'

'Of course. You forget that I know this part of the countryside like the back of my hand. Before the siege, I rode out here every day with the falcons.'

Ahmad looked back at the tunnel anxiously. 'Why did you bring your friend with you?' he asked. 'Does he know the Khalifa is with us?'

'It wasn't my idea. He followed me. I haven't told him anything about the Khalifa. What do you think I am, an idiot?'

From the look Ahmad gave him, that was exactly what he was thinking.

'But how did he get into the tunnel?'

'He told Qasim I'd invited him to come with us.'

'And Qasim believed him?'

'Apparently. Anyway, he's here now.'

'I've seen him looking at the Khalifa. Are you sure he doesn't know anything?'

'I'm not sure about anything. All I know is that he's a greedy man and not to be trusted. I thought we were friends but now, I'm not so sure. Be careful of him, Ahmad. I'm hoping that once we're away from Córdoba, he will go his own way.'

'I hope so, too.'

'So, what is your plan?' asked Rafiq.

'We head for the Sierra Morena and once we're in the mountains we move west.'

'Then what? Where the hell are you planning to take these people? Or do you intend that they spend the rest of their lives living with the wolves and the bears?' asked Rafiq.

'Of course not. We're going to Ardales. To our roots.'

'Ardales? But that's due south of here.'

'Well, brother we could head south straightaway, but I think we might get caught by the Berber soldiers. They won't stay in Córdoba forever. My plan is not to head south until we are well out of Sulayman's way. I know it's longer, but I'm hoping we can buy a donkey or two to make the journey easier.'

Rafiq clapped his hand to his head in amazement. 'You astound me, Ahmad. How can we afford to buy a donkey, never mind two? All we have are the clothes we stand up in and a bit of loose change.'

'But I have this, brother.' Ahmad dug deep into his djellaba and pulled out an enormous ruby ring. As he held it out for Rafiq to see, the sunlight caught it and it glowed with a redness that took his breath away. It was the red of freshly spilled blood and it burned like fire. He had never seen anything like it before.

'Where did you get that? Was it in the cave with the rest of the treasure?' asked Rafiq.

'The Khalifa gave it to me. It was his grandfather's.'

'But why did he give it to you? It must be worth a fortune.'

'It was when he was in prison. The ring was all he had and he wanted to thank me. I tried to tell him to keep it, but he thought he was going to die in there and he didn't want the guards to find it.'

'Well what about later, when he was freed? Didn't he ask for it back? After all it belongs to the Omayyad dynasty. It probably once graced the hand of al-Rahman III.'

'No. I offered to give it back to him but he refused. So, in the end, I thought it might come in useful,' Ahmad explained.

His brother had been carrying around the Khalifa's ring in the pocket of his djellaba all this time and hadn't mentioned it to anyone. Ahmad was certainly full of surprises.

'Here,' he said, handing the ruby back to Ahmad. 'Put it somewhere safe and whatever you do, don't let Asif know that you have it. Come on. It's time we got away from here. So we're going north, you say?'

'That's right, brother.'

## CHAPTER 35

Ahmad would not let them rest until they had reached the tree line. Here they could stop and not be seen by any prying eyes. Nobody spoke as they stood there, watching their city burn below them. The soldiers had taken their revenge on Córdoba and the black smoke from the fires they had set rose straight up into a cloudless sky. They could even smell it from their lofty position in the sierra.

'Will they burn the whole city?' asked a tearful Salma. 'Everything? The library? The hospital? The university?'

'Maybe not everything,' said Rafiq. 'They won't burn the hospital. But even that's not certain. Once the soldiers are allowed to sack the city, there is no stopping them. They will take everything that is of value and lay waste to the rest until there is no more they can destroy. They will not stop until this lust for revenge is satiated. Even Sulayman cannot halt them now.'

'What of Qasim and Layla?' asked Aisha, tears streaming down her face. 'Oh, why didn't they come with us? Why did they have to stay?'

'Hush, wife. They will be fine. Qasim will look after Layla. They will be in the hospital. Why on earth would the soldiers be interested in burning down a hospital?' said Ahmad, looking at Qasim's wife and children. Since she had realised that Qasim was definitely not coming with them, his brother's wife had become calmer and was trying hard to be brave for her children's sake. His young nephew was biting his lip, trying desperately not to cry and the two girls were clinging to each other and sobbing as though their hearts would break. He could hear their mother telling them to be strong, that Baba was safe and would join them soon.

'Praise be to Allah. May he guard and protect us all,' said Ahmad. 'Let us take a minute to thank Allah that he has allowed us to escape from these cruel men.'

He knelt down and led them in prayer. After a few minutes, during which a calmness settled on them all, he said, 'We have a long way to go and it isn't safe to stay here. We'll climb further up the mountains and find somewhere we can rest. Tomorrow we will set off for the town of Ardales. There we have relatives who, I hope, will take pity on us and give us shelter. But I must warn you, we still have a long journey ahead of us.'

He was worried about the Khalifa. Al-Hisham was trying hard to keep up with the others but now that he was away from his court and all his servants, Ahmad could see just how sick he was. If he was to survive this journey, they would have to find some transport for him.

'Baba, look,' called Makoud. 'Is that one of ours?'

Perched on a tree ahead of them was a peregrine falcon. Al-Hisham saw it immediately and raised his arm. 'Shamal, my beauty. I knew you'd come back to me,' he said as the bird flew down and grabbed his scrawny hand. The bird's talons tore his flesh but he didn't seem to care. Tears of happiness streamed down his worn face.

'That's good news. Now we will get some fresh meat,' said Ahmad, although he knew Shamal would have to work hard to catch enough prey to feed all of them.

\*

All day they toiled up the mountain. Ahmad wouldn't let them stop until he was sure they were far enough away from the city to be safe. At last they came to a clearing. It was the very same place where an attempt had been made on the Khalifa's life many years before, when Ahmad had ended up in hospital with an arrow in his chest. If al-Hisham recognised the spot, he gave no sign and Ahmad decided not to mention it to anyone. Instead he instructed Aisha to unpack her cooking pot and they all set about preparing the food. He and al-Hisham had taken it in turns to hunt with Shamal during their climb and now they had three pigeons and two rabbits to eat for their supper. Ahmad felt happier and more positive than he had done for weeks. It was good to be out of that claustrophobic city, breathing in the mountain air. More than that, the return of Shamal had given the Khalifa a burst of energy and Ahmad felt renewed hope that he would last the journey after all.

'Makoud, collect some wood for a fire and Simon, see if you can find any water. There should be a stream nearby. I know this place,' he said.

The women, aided by Musa, had already started gutting the rabbits and plucking the pigeons. Aisha set her cooking pot on the fire to warm up the vegetables Layla had cooked for her, ready to add the meat as soon as it was prepared.

'We'll eat well tonight, husband,' she said, smiling up at him.

Despite having had no sleep the night before, despite dragging her plump body through the tunnel and walking for hours up the mountain, his wife seemed happy. It did not seem to matter to her that she was squatting in a clearing in the middle of the forest, half-way up the Sierra Morena, preparing a meal for her family from left-over vegetables and prey taken from a falcon, nor that they had not brought any cutlery or plates with them, nor that they would soon be eating straight from the cooking pot and drinking water from a mountain spring. Her family were hungry and she would make sure they were fed. He smiled to himself. He had done it. He had got his family out of the city. Ahmad leant across her and helped himself to a rabbit leg.

'Here,' he said to al-Hisham. 'Give this to Shamal. He deserves it.'

\*

For the next three days they trekked through the mountains, gradually making their way westwards until Ahmad and Rafiq both agreed that it was safe to make their descent. They could see the city of Seville in the distance, its turrets and domes glinting in the sunlight.

'We must find some transport,' said Ahmad. 'The Khalifa is holding us back; he walks so slowly.'

The energy burst that Shamal's return had brought him had disappeared and now al-Hisham appeared to be weaker than ever.

'We will have to leave him,' said Rafiq. 'He's a sick man. We can find him somewhere to stay and leave him to die in peace.'

'Impossible. Maybe you could do that—after all death is your trade—but I cannot leave him to die alone.'

'He'll have Musa to care for him.'

'No. I said I would help him and I intend to keep my promise. We must buy a donkey.' He thought about the ring in his pocket. He didn't really want to exchange the Khalifa's ring for a donkey but what else could he do?

'You are as stubborn as a mule, little brother. All right. I will go with you into the village and we'll see if we can find anyone foolish enough to sell us their donkey.'

'I can go alone,' Ahmad said, a bit too sharply. It annoyed him when his brothers always referred to him as 'little brother.'

'No, it's safer if we go together. If anyone sees you with that ring, you could be attacked.'

'What about Asif? Is it safe to leave him here with the Khalifa?'

'I told him that he was an old uncle of ours and we couldn't leave him behind.'

'Did he believe you?'

'I don't know. He seemed to,' said Rafiq, unconvincingly.

'Very well. I hope you're right about him.'

Ahmad instructed the others to stay well hidden and promised to be back as soon as they could, but before he left, he called his son to one side.

'Makoud. If we're not back by nightfall, you must go on without us. Follow the road south until you come to Ronda. Then ask for the road to Ardales. I'm trusting you to look after your mother and your cousins.'

'But what about the Khalifa?' Makoud whispered.

'He will have to go as far as he can. If he cannot continue, try to find somewhere safe for him to stay. Musa will look after him. Here, take my sword. It's never been much use to me,' he added with a smile. 'And keep an eye on Asif. I'm not so sure about his reasons for being here. Don't let him know the Khalifa's real identity, whatever you do.'

'Come back, Baba,' Makoud said, his face grim. 'We need you.'

It was hard to go down to the village. Up here in the mountains, away from people, Ahmad felt safe but if they were to ever make it to their new home, then he had to find some way of carrying the Khalifa.

'Are you ready?' asked Rafiq.

'As ready as I will ever be,' said Ahmad with a grin.

'You really are a mad man. What if there are soldiers in the village?'

'No, there won't be. We're too far away from Córdoba.'

'Maybe, but we're quite close to Seville. Do you know who holds Seville?'

Ahmad shook his head. He barely knew what was going on outside his own family and the Falcon House; how was he to know what was happening in a city so far away from Córdoba?

'I suppose it's the Khalifa, the same as the rest of al-Andalus.'

'Yes, but which one? This civil war has split the country in two. How do we know which side these people will support?'

'I hadn't thought of that,' Ahmad said, looking suddenly grim.

'Are you sure you want to go down there? If anything happens to us, how will the others manage?' asked Rafiq.

'They'll be all right. I've spoken to Makoud. They will continue without us.'

'Oh, very well, I can see that you have set your mind to this, but let me go first. If I see anything that suggests they support Sulayman, we turn round and head back to the others. Is that agreed?'

'Yes. Now come on. Let's go,' said Ahmad. The longer they talked about it the more he began to question the wisdom of going to the village. For a moment he wished he hadn't given his sword to Makoud.

They climbed down the windy path that led to the white village, keeping as close to the trees as possible. Ahead everything seemed quiet and normal. There was no sign of any soldiers. They could see a couple of men in the distance, collecting olives. They had spread a large cloth on the earth beneath the tree and were beating the branches until the ripe olives fell to the ground. Two donkeys stood patiently in the shade, empty panniers on their backs.

'Do you see the donkeys?' said Ahmad.

'Of course I can see them, but they're not going to sell you one of them. They need them. How else are they going to get the olives to market?'

'You don't know that. If we offer them enough money they might sell us both of them.'

He heard his brother groan. 'No, we'll keep to the plan and make enquiries in the village,' said Rafiq.

Ahmad made no more protests. If they had no luck in the village, then they could always come back to the two men. They continued along the path for another half an hour until they saw a white-washed village ahead of them.

'Right, you stay here and I'll go and make enquiries,' said Rafiq.

Ahmad was going to protest but a look from his brother told him it was useless. 'All right. Don't be long,' he said, sitting down under an ancient al-kharrūba tree. He picked up a fallen pod and opened it to see if there were any beans inside. Only one. He popped it in his mouth and chewed it slowly.

Two children came skipping down the lane. They stopped when they saw him and stared.

'As-salama alaykum, my children,' he said, with a smile.

The children giggled and ran on. They didn't seem frightened of anything. It made him realise how different it was here. In Córdoba the children were becoming like wild animals, scavenging the streets for food. They would have come straight to him, demanding to know what he was eating, scooping up the open pods and stuffing them in their mouths, whether they contained seeds or not. These children were not hungry and they weren't afraid. He stood up. There was nothing to fear in this village; he was sure of it.

'Ahmad. Come on,' said Rafiq, as soon as he rounded the corner. 'There are no soldiers here. I spoke to a man who had heard about the siege of Córdoba but he didn't know it had fallen. He says there's an old woman with, I suspect, an equally old donkey, who wants to sell it. He will take us to see her.'

'Praise be to Allah,' said Ahmad. At least there would be no fighting.

He followed Rafiq up the winding streets until they came to a small square where people were setting up a local market. He tried not to stare at the sacks of peppers, courgettes, pumpkins, at the oranges and limes, the pots of honey, at the bags of spices: turmeric, chilli, nutmeg and cardamon, at the fresh bunches of herbs: mint, parsley, rosemary and thyme. His mouth began to water and the realisation of just how long it had been since he had eaten a decent meal dawned on him. This was what it would be like when they reached Ardales. No more eating watered-down soup made from nettles and parsley and no more of that awful gruel that Aisha encouraged them all to eat rather than starve.

'Here he is,' said Rafiq. He bowed politely to the man selling loaves of freshly baked bread. The smell of the bread made Ahmad's stomach rumble.

'As-salama alaykum,' said Ahmad.

'Wa alaykum e-salam, strangers. I hear you're looking to buy a donkey?' the man said.

'You have one for sale?'

'My sister wants to sell her donkey. It's a good animal, docile and strong, but I must admit it is a bit old now. But still capable of a solid day's work.'

'We are travellers. We need a donkey to carry some of our luggage,' said Rafiq.

'We have money,' said Ahmad, about to take the ring from his pocket, but Rafiq's hand on his arm stopped him.

'Where is your sister? We would like to see the animal and agree a price with her,' said Rafiq.

'Not far. Continue along this road until you come to the last house. She lives there. You will hear the donkey before you reach it. Some days the stupid animal thinks he's a guard dog.' The man smiled at them. 'I would come with you but I must sell my bread. Alla ysalmak, my friends.'

'Ma'a salama and thank you,' said Ahmad.

It was exactly as the baker had said. They had barely left the square when they could hear the donkey braying.

'Well he's got good lungs on him,' said Rafiq, with a laugh. The donkey was tied up outside a rather dilapidated house, where an old woman sat in the doorway, wrapped in a black shawl.

'As-salama alaykum,' said Ahmad.

'Who are you? You're strangers to this village. I've never seen you before,' she screeched at them. 'What do you want? I don't have any money. I'm just a poor widow.'

'Calm yourself, woman. We are indeed strangers, but we haven't come to do you any harm. Your brother sent us. He said that you have a donkey for sale. Is that the beast?' said Rafiq.

At the mention of the donkey, or maybe that her brother had sent them, the woman relaxed. She even managed a toothless smile. 'Yes, indeed. That animal is for sale. I have no need of him now. I am too old to collect olives and I never go to the market any more. What do I need a donkey for? He's a good beast. He has served me and my late husband well. Look at him. Not a bit of fat on him.'

The donkey was indeed on the lean side, his shoulder blades looked sharp enough to cut through wood. But he seemed lively enough. When Ahmad went over to examine him he shied away, baring his teeth at him aggressively.

'Let me take a look,' said Rafiq. He ran his hand along the animal's back then picked up his hooves and examined them. 'He'll do. I don't think he's got many more years in him. You saw his teeth. He's not a youngster.'

'As long as he gets us to our destination, that's all that counts,' whispered Ahmad. He turned back to the old woman. 'I'm not sure. How much do you want for him?'

'Ten dinars,' she said, sharply.

He bit back the desire to laugh. That was more than a year's pay.

'No, sorry. He's a bit long in the tooth, for what we want,' he said, and turned to walk away.

'Five then.'

He walked over to the donkey again and studied him. 'No,' he said, shaking his head. 'He's only worth five dirhams, and I'm not sure I even want to pay that for him.'

'Are you trying to rob a poor widow? How could I live on five dirhams. Very well, give me thirty dirhams and you can have him.'

Ahmad looked at Rafiq. What should they do? He had no money, only the Khalifa's ring.

'I can see you are an honest widow woman, so I'll give you twenty-five dirhams,' said Rafiq, pulling the remainder of his pay from his pouch and holding it in front of her.

It was like magic. No sooner had the words left Rafiq's mouth than the woman had untied the donkey, handed the rope to Ahmad and pocketed the twenty-five dirhams.

'Have a safe journey and may Allah go with you,' she said and disappeared inside her house. clsoing the door firmly behind her.

'Well, you have your donkey,' said Rafiq.

'Yes, but why do I feel that we have been duped by that old woman. She couldn't get away from us quickly enough.'

'I've still got a few quirats left. Enough to buy some bread. What do you think?' asked Rafiq.

'Excellent idea. But why wouldn't you let me offer her the Khalifa's ring? Then you could have kept your money.'

'What good would that ring be to her? She wanted money to buy food. You saw her; she was as thin as her donkey. No, we will keep that ring. After all, it's not really yours.'

Ahmad put his hand into his pocket to touch the ring and reassure himself that Rafiq was right that he should hold on to it. But he felt nothing.

'It's gone. The ring. It's gone,' Ahmad cried. He scrabbled about in his pocket but there was no sign of it. He tried the other pocket. He took off his djellaba and shook it, hoping to see the ring fall from its folds. Nothing.

'I thought you had it sewn inside your djellaba?' asked Rafiq.

'I did. Inside the pocket. But it's not there now. And look.'

They examined the pocket. There was a small tear in the wool, as though someone had ripped the ring from the pocket.

'So it's been stolen?'

'Yes.' He'd been so stupid. He should have kept it somewhere much safer than in his djellaba.

'Who knew you had the ring?' asked Rafiq.

'Only Aisha, and the Khalifa, and you.'

'Did you have it out for any reason? Could someone have seen you with it?'

Ahmad thought back over the last few days.

'After I showed it to you, I thought it might get lost just sitting in my pocket, so I asked Aisha to sew it in there. Maybe someone saw her.'

'We have to get back to the others. I have a bad feeling about this,' said Rafiq.

They bought their bread and toiled their way back up the mountain as quickly as they could, but before they reached the clearing, a worried-looking Salma ran down to greet them.

'You're safe. Praise be to Allah. We've been so worried about you,' she said.

'What is it, Salma? Why are you so upset?'

'Thank goodness you're back,' she said, a tear running down her face as she spoke. 'We're so sorry. there was nothing we could do to stop him.'

'Stop who? What's happened, Salma?'

Rafiq didn't wait for her answer. He strode past her and into the clearing. Musa was crying. Aisha was bending over Makoud and Qasim's wife was trying to keep the children occupied as far away as possible from the others. Something had happened in their absence.

'Where is he? Where is Asif?' Rafiq thundered.

'He's gone, and he's taken the Khalifa with him,' sobbed Musa. 'There was nothing I could do to stop him.' The slave had an ugly bruise on his face and a cut lip.

'Did he do that?' Rafiq asked.

The slave nodded and said, 'He stabbed Makoud.'

'What?' Ahmad let go of the donkey and rushed over to his son. 'Are you all right, son? Where are you hurt?' he asked, bending over him.

'It's fine, Baba. Just a flesh wound in my arm. Mama has cleaned it and bandaged it for me.'

'I'll kill him,' Ahmad shouted, leaping to his feet.

'We have to find him first,' said Rafiq. 'Which way did he go?'

'He went back towards Córdoba. He said Sulayman would pay a good price for the Khalifa,' said Musa. 'I tried to stop him. I told him he was mistaken, that he was just an old man, but he knew. He'd seen him before. And he had his ring.'

'So he's got the Khalifa and the ring,' said Ahmad.

'And a bag of treasure he took from the cave,' Rafiq said.

'We have to stop him. If he tells Sulayman that Qasim helped the Khalifa to escape, he'll kill him.'

'Don't worry. He won't get far. The Khalifa can hardly walk. Unless he carries him, they'll be making slow progress,' said Rafiq.

'What if he kills him and just takes the head to Sulayman?' Ahmad asked.

'No, he won't do that. I know Asif. He's not a bad man, really. He wouldn't do that. He could have killed Musa and Makoud, and Simon. Where is Simon?' he asked, looking around him.

'He took him to carry the Khalifa,' Salma said. 'They'll kill him when he gets there. I know they will.'

'So much for my theory,' said Rafiq. 'We'll never catch them now.'

'When did they leave?' Ahmad asked.

'Just before midday. We were just about to pray.'

'Not long after we left then?'

Makoud nodded. 'You have to find them, Baba. They'll send the soldiers after us, once they know it was us who helped the Khalifa.'

'Yes, and Asif knows where we're headed. You told him this morning,' said Rafiq.

'Don't worry. Aisha, get us some water and here, take this bread. We bought it in the village for you.' He turned to his brother and said, 'Rafiq, we can catch them. I know a much shorter way back to the city. Asif won't risk going along the valley, in case he meets any soldiers. He wouldn't risk losing his prize. He will go back the way we came, through the mountains. If we hurry, we can cut them off. Take Makoud's djellaba and put it over your uniform. You don't want anyone realising you're a soldier.'

'What about the donkey?'

'We'll take it with us. It'll be good cover and it means we can bring the Khalifa back on it.'

Rafiq wrapped himself in Makoud's djellaba and took the flask of water from Aisha.

'Just one more thing,' said Ahmad. He went over to the falcon and put him on his hand. 'We may need Shamal's help.'

'Take good care, husband,' said Aisha, putting her hand on his arm.

'I will. Makoud, look after the others. If you hear anything, go and hide in the forest. We will find you when we return.'

'Come back soon,' Aisha whispered.

'I will, dear wife.'

He leant over and kissed her.

'Come brother, we must go,' said Rafiq. 'That weasel is not going to escape with his prey, not if I can help it.'

Ahmad took a last look at his family and grabbing the donkey by its halter, led the way down the mountain.

\*

They made good progress along the road towards Córdoba, stopping occasionally to hide if they saw anyone suspicious. Most of the time the road was empty. No-one in their right mind was heading for the city. And nobody had been able to escape the blockade.

The stench of the fires got worse the closer they got, and their clothes became covered with a thin film of white ash. Ahmad tried not to think of what was happening in his beloved city. It broke his heart to think of the flames engulfing its beautiful palaces and homes. At least the Great Mosque would be safe. No Muslim leader would dare to destroy a mosque.

'I think we're almost at the point where we turned off into the mountains,' Ahmad said.

'But we haven't been going very long,' said Rafiq in amazement. 'You certainly took us a long roundabout route the first time.'

'We didn't get stopped, though, did we?'

'No. I suppose not.'

'I think it will take them at least another couple of hours to get down here,' said Ahmad.

'So what do we do?'

'We go back up the mountain path and wait for them in hiding.'

'But what if you're wrong and they've already passed this point?'

'Ah, that's why I brought Shamal. I will release him and we'll watch where he goes. If he sees the Khalifa he'll go to him. If not, he'll return to me. I hope.'

'What do you mean, I hope?'

'Well you can never be sure with a falcon. He might just decide to go off and do a bit of hunting.'

'That's not a such a bad thing, especially if he brings his prey back to us.'

They turned off the road and stood in a small clearing. 'All right. Watch carefully which way he goes.'

Shamal flew from the glove and soared straight up into the sky. At first it was hard to see him because of the clouds of smoke that were drifting their way, but then there he was, circling above them.

'He's seen something,' Ahmad said. 'Watch what he does.'

'He's coming back again. No, he's coming down over there.'

Ahmad heard a sharp whistle, followed by a harsh call. 'That's the Khalifa, calling him and Shamal has answered.'

'They're over there, just above us. They're much closer than I thought. Get down. Quick, hide the donkey in those trees.'

Luckily the donkey was not of a stubborn nature and allowed himself to be led into the densest part of the forest and tied to a tree.

'He'll be all right there. There's plenty for him to eat.' Already the donkey was steadily munching at a patch of thick grass.

'Now, follow me and keep quiet,' Ahmad said. He led them to the path where he hoped Asif and the others would pass by. 'We

## The Ring of Flames

must hide here in the bushes and wait for them. They're not far away.'

As long as they could surprise Asif, there would be no problem. If Simon was still with him, it would be three to one. Asif wouldn't be expecting them to have got ahead of them. If anything, he'd be looking behind him. All they could do now was wait and pray that Allah would help them.

\*

They didn't have to wait long before they saw them coming down the path towards them. Simon walked in front, with the Khalifa on his back. Asif followed them. Every so often he prodded Simon with his sword. They could hear Asif berating them, his voice reverberating through the still mountain air.

'Get a move on, you lump of pig's fat. Can't you move any quicker than that. That excuse for a human being that you carry on your back will die before we get there at this rate. And I don't want that to happen. I want to present him to Sulayman in one piece. If he dies then so do you,' said Asif.

'Here, take this and use it, if you have to,' whispered Rafiq. He handed a curved knife to Ahmad, its handle embossed in silver. It was really a ceremonial knife, given to him after a particularly successful campaign, but it would have to do. It was sharp and he could stab and slice with it, if necessary. 'And mind you don't cut yourself,' he added with a grin. His little brother was almost as useless with a knife as he was with a sword.

'Haven't you got anything better than this for me?' Ahmad asked.

'It's just for you to defend yourself. I'll attack Asif. Your job is to get Simon and the Khalifa away from here as quickly as possible. Get the donkey and go back up into the mountains. I will catch you up after I've dealt with Asif.'

'What if you get injured?'

'Don't worry about me. You have the Khalifa to worry about and your family. You need to get back to them as soon as possible, before anyone finds them.'

They had picked a spot where the ferns and bushes had grown thick and lush, and where the path narrowed so that anyone coming along it could walk right past them without seeing them. They crouched as low as they could and peered through the bushes until the others reached them: they could see the hem of Simon's brown robe just in front of them. They were so close now that they could hear his laboured breathing as he struggled with the weight of the Khalifa on his back. Rafiq put his hand on Ahmad's arm to restrain him. His brother was shaking, either with fear or excitement; he didn't know which. As soon as Simon had passed and Asif was level with them, Rafiq leapt up with a roar that could be heard throughout the forest.

The shock on his old friend's face was a delight to behold. Before Asif could recover, Rafiq had him pinned to the ground, his foot on his chest and the point of his sword pressing into his neck.

'Ahmad, go. Now,' he shouted, picking up Asif's sword and throwing it away from him.

Simon was so surprised at their sudden appearance that he immediately stood upright and let the unfortunate Khalifa slip to the floor.

'Are you all right, Your Majesty?' asked Ahmad, running towards al-Hisham and bending over him.

'Ahmad. Dear Ahmad. You are always there when I need you,' the Khalifa whispered. He looked as though he would not last much longer.

'Come, Simon, help me get him up. We've brought the donkey. Just carry him this last short distance and then no more.'

'How did you find us?'

'Later. I'll tell you all, later. Now we must get him away.'

Rafiq waited until his brother and the others were out of sight and then turned to Asif. 'You tricked me. You betrayed me. You stole from my brother and you stabbed my nephew.'

Asif tried to get up, a faint smile on his lips, but Rafiq pushed him down again, and continued, 'Nothing to say? I'm not surprised. How many years have we fought side by side? Thirty? More? You were a man I thought I could always count on. A man who was loyal to his comrades. How can an army function if the men cannot share a common loyalty? It is your betrayal that hurts more than anything.'

'Don't talk to me about loyalty and betrayal, quaid. You were making your escape, deserting your post. You never gave a thought to your comrades. All you were interested in was saving your own skin.'

'You had the chance to come with us. We welcomed you. My family welcomed you.'

'Only after you realised you had no option.'

'You could have had a good life, made a new start.'

'What spend the rest of my days in Ardales, grazing sheep? Do I look like a man who'd be happy with that sort of life?'

'You look like a defeated man to me,' said a voice.

It was Ahmad. He bent down and picked up Asif's sword. 'You were going to hand the Khalifa over to Sulayman. You betrayed the man you fought for, the anointed leader of your country. You stole his ring, the symbol of his power and the emblem of his dynasty. And you would have betrayed my family to the soldiers. You do not deserve to have a new life. You do not deserve to live.'

'Ahmad, no. Leave this to me,' shouted Rafiq, stepping away from the man on the ground. What was his brother trying to do? Why didn't he leave it to him to deal with Asif?

'You can't let him live, Rafiq. I know he is your friend, but he will tell Sulayman who helped the Khalifa. They will kill Qasim. They will hunt us down. We will always be looking over our shoulders, wondering when they will come for us. I can't allow my family to live like that. I'm sorry Rafiq, but if you can't do it, then I must.'

He lifted the sword and drove it straight into Asif's heart before Rafiq could stop him. It was over. Asif was dead. Blood dribbled from the side of his mouth and his unseeing eyes stared at the darkening sky above.

Ahmad had been right. They could not afford to let him live. Yet Rafiq hadn't been able to find it in him to kill his friend. They had shared too many memories together, too many hardships and battles, victories and defeats. Ahmad had realised that. That was why he had come back. He'd known that Rafiq could never bring himself to kill Asif. If he'd been able to do it then he would have killed him in the tunnel, as soon as Asif had discovered their escape.

'Here's the ring,' Ahmad said, pulling the ruby from Asif's tunic. 'And here's the treasure he took.'

'Well that'll come in handy.' Rafiq opened the bag and looked inside. He let out a low whistle. 'There's enough there to keep you going for a few years, little brother.'

'What will we do with his body?' Ahmad asked.

'Just roll it into the bushes. If anyone finds him, they will just think it was an ambush. Another unlucky deserter.'

'We'd better hurry. It'll be dark soon and there's a long way to go.'

They dragged the lifeless body into the undergrowth. As Rafiq covered his old comrade with dead branches, he felt sad, but more than that; he felt disappointed in his friend. Despite the years they'd known each other, his greed had overpowered any sense of loyalty and friendship.

## CHAPTER 36

Makoud stopped, dropping the firewood he'd collected. He could hear voices, men's voices and they were going up the path towards the clearing. He turned and ran back to the others.

'Quick,' he said. 'Someone's coming.' He turned to Qasim's wife and said, 'Take the children into the trees and keep them quiet. The rest of you, grab what you can and hide. Don't come out until you hear me call for you. Is that understood?'

He took the sword from his belt and hid behind a thick thorn bush. Two men entered the clearing. They were dressed like soldiers, but their uniforms were ragged and filthy. Deserters.

'I thought I could smell rabbit,' said one of them. He was the older of the two, and he still wore his red cape. The other wore a torn djellaba over a bloodstained tunic.

'I'm starving. My stomach thinks my throat's been cut.'

'It would have been if the quaid had got to you.'

The other laughed. 'Yes, instead it's him lying there with his throat cut.'

He walked over to the pot of stew that Aisha had been unable to remove in her hurry and spooned some out to try. 'Good. It's bloody good. Come and try it.'

They looked about them, torn between sitting down and eating the stew and looking for whoever had made it.

'We know you're there. Come out. We won't hurt you. We're just a couple of travellers, down on our luck.'

'Hungry travellers,' added the one in the bloodstained tunic.

Makoud watched them, praying that the children wouldn't make any noise. These men weren't travellers. They were thieves and murderers. And if they were deserters, then they were also desperate men. Please don't let anyone move; don't let them make a sound.

'Come out, come out, wherever you are,' the older man called. 'Well, if you don't come and join us, we'll have to eat on our own.'

The men sat down by the fire and started to eat the stew.

'Hey, there's some bread, too,' the younger one said, breaking off a huge chunk and dipping it into the stew.

Makoud could hear his stomach rumbling; it was so loud he worried that the deserters could hear it as well. He was famished and seeing them eating his family's food made him angry. He wanted to rush out and stab them both.

'It's not worth it, Makoud,' whispered Salma, creeping up behind him. 'We'll eat later. Come with me. I've sent the others further into the forest. We'll come back later when they're asleep.'

As quietly as they could they crawled away from their camp and ran to join the others.

Aisha was standing guard when they reached the clearing where the others had hidden. They were safe here; it was at least an Arab mile from their camp.

'Well?' she asked.

'Two men. Probably deserters,' panted Makoud. 'They've eaten our food.'

'What all of it?'

He nodded sadly. The thought of them wiping the pot clean with that lovely bread that he'd been longing to eat ever since Baba had given it to them, made him angry.

'So what do we do?' asked Qasim's wife. 'We don't have much with us. I left most of our things at the camp. The children will be cold later without a blanket to keep them warm.'

'We must stay here until Baba returns,' Makoud said. 'But I'll go back later, when they're asleep and see what I can get.'

'I'll go with you,' said Salma.

'In the meantime, I think we're safe enough here. The men looked exhausted. I don't think they'll be going far until tomorrow and maybe Baba will be back by then.'

'All right, Makoud. Here, eat this.' His mother handed him a small piece of bread.

'You brought some with you,' he said, in surprise. 'I thought those bastards were eating it all.'

'Makoud. Mind what you're saying.'

'Sorry, Mama.'

He stuffed the bread into his mouth in one piece and tried to chew it slowly. 'That's the best bread I've ever tasted,' he said when he'd finished.

'Really?'

'Except for yours, Mama. Except for yours.'

'Well I think you and Salma should have a rest now, if you're planning to go back down there when it's dark. I'll keep watch,' said Aisha, who'd armed herself with a thick wooden staff.

\*

It was dark when Aisha woke them.

'Here, Salma, take my staff and this knife.' She handed her the knife she used to skin the rabbit. 'And this might come in useful.' She gave her the axe they used for chopping firewood.

'Thank you Aisha. We'll be as quick as we can.'

'Wait,' said Makoud. 'I'm going to take the rope.'

'Where did you get that?' his mother asked.

'Baba said to bring it, in case we needed it for anything.'

'So, what do you need it for?' she asked, as he wound it round his waist.

'I don't know yet. But it could be useful.'

'Get on with you. And be careful. Remember, if they're still awake don't try anything. Rafiq and your father will be back soon. It won't hurt us to hide here a little longer.'

'What if they don't come back?' Makoud said, his eyes clouding over.

'They'll be back. Your father wouldn't leave us here alone, unprotected. He'll be back. Don't ever doubt it.'

'All right, Mama. Keep the others hidden until we return.'

Aisha reached up and kissed her son. 'Off with you now.'

They moved through the forest like shadows, careful not to stand on twigs or crash through bushes. Once they stopped, holding their breath, sure that they'd been spotted, but it was just a deer who leapt away, flashing his white rump at them.

There was no sound from the camp except that of a man's deep snoring.

'They're asleep,' said Salma. 'What do we do now? Do we kill them?' Her face told him that she was not really prepared to tackle these two and certainly not to kill them.

'I don't think so. I thought we could just tie them up and leave them for Baba and Rafiq to deal with. What do you think?' He unwound the length of rope from his waist.

'So that's what you wanted the rope for?'

'Yes, but how can we do it, without waking them?'

The soldier snoring his head off, was lying on his back, his arms flung out above his head. The other was curled up like a hedgehog.

'I also brought the net Baba uses for trapping small animals. We could drop that over that one and tie the other one up.'

'But as soon as we tie one up, he'll wake and then the other one will know we're here. It won't work,' said Salma. 'I know what we'll do. We'll take that one first.' She pointed to the one curled up into a ball. 'You throw the net over him and I'll keep an eye on the other one.'

Makoud's stomach was churning. It was dangerous. They were asleep now but any noise would wake them and then how would they defend themselves against two experienced and armed soldiers?

'Where are their swords?' he asked.

'Right by them. I don't think we could get them without waking them up.'

Just then the one on his back gave a loud grunt and rolled over onto his side. Makoud thought his heart had stopped; he was so scared.

'It's too dangerous,' he said. 'We'd better go back.'

'No. We can do it,' said Salma. She grabbed the staff in both hands. 'I'll use this to make sure he doesn't wake up. You take the knife.'

Makoud looked at her in amazement.

'Come on. Give me the rope. You tackle that one with the net. Hurry before they hear us and wake up,' she whispered.

Reluctantly, Makoud handed over the rope to his cousin.

Salma crept across to the snoring soldier and lifting the staff hit him across the back of the head. There was a grunt and he lay still. Quickly she wound the rope around his body, pinning his hands against his sides and then tied it off around his ankles. He looked like a goat ready for the slaughter.

Meanwhile Makoud was creeping closer to the second soldier. Suddenly the man stretched and stood up. Makoud froze. Salma quickly dropped down behind the trussed soldier, hoping not to be noticed.

'It's bloody cold up here in the mountains,' the soldier muttered. 'What's happened to the fire?' He picked up some small branches and staggered over to the fire and threw them on the dying embers. Instantly the fire burst into flames casting its rosy light around the area. 'What the fuck is that?' he shouted and reached for his sword. He laughed. 'A girl? Well this is my lucky night.'

He knew no more. Makoud was on his back driving his mother's vegetable knife into his back. The soldier screamed and tried to throw the boy off but Makoud clung on, stabbing and stabbing until the soldier collapsed on the floor.

'What have you done?' asked Salma. 'Is he dead? Have you killed him?'

'I don't know. I think so.' Makoud was shaking. He hadn't planned to kill anyone. He just wanted to capture them. How had this happened? What would Baba say? It was a sin to kill someone. Would Allah forgive him?

He bent over the man he'd stabbed and turned him on his back. He was definitely dead. His mouth hung open and his blank eyes stared into the darkness. 'I think he's dead.'

'What about the other one? He's waking up now,' said Salma. The man was groaning and struggling to free himself from the rope.

'Leave him. Baba can decide what to do with him later. Come on, let's take what we need and get back to the others.'

He had to get away from this place. The smell of the dead man's blood was all over him. He felt sick. What was he going to tell his mother? And Baba, what was he going to tell him?

'Makoud. You did a very brave thing there. You saved me,' said Salma, putting her hand on his arm.

'But I killed him.'

'If you hadn't killed him, he would have killed you and goodness knows what he would have done to me. You did the only thing you could.'

'Let's get away from here. I think I'm going to be sick.'

*

It was morning by the time Ahmad's group arrived back at the camp.

'What the devil has happened here? said Rafiq, striding over to the trussed-up man and kicking him with his boot. 'Wake up.'

'There's another one here. He's dead,' said Ahmad. 'What's been going on and where are the others?'

'You. Wake up. What's happened here?' Rafiq said, kicking the man again.

'Untie me, please,' the deserter pleaded.

'When you tell me what happened.'

'I don't know what happened. I was asleep and when I woke up I was trussed up like a goose for the slaughter. And I've got a bloody great headache as well.'

'What are you doing here?' asked Ahmad. 'Where are the others?'

'What others. I don't know what you're talking about. We were looking for somewhere to spend the night and we found this place. It was abandoned. I'm telling the truth. There was no-one else here. Untie me please.'

'So who did this to you?'

'I don't know but whoever it was also killed my mate.' He nodded towards the dead body lying amongst the ashes of the fire.

'And you didn't see anyone?'

The man hesitated.

'Well? Did you see anyone or not?' barked Rafiq.

'I thought I saw a girl, but I must have been dreaming.'

'On her own or was someone with her?'

'There might have been a boy with her? I'm not sure. My head was spinning. I think someone hit me with a boulder. Then I passed out again.'

'Makoud?' Ahmad said, turning away from the man on the ground. 'It must have been Makoud. So where are they now?'

'Well they won't have gone down towards the village. They'll be deeper in the forest. Come on. We need to find them. We don't know how many more soldiers there were,' said Rafiq.

'What do we do with these two?' asked Ahmad.

'Nothing. Leave them where they are. The vultures will see to that one. We'll come back for the other one later.'

'No. Don't leave me. Just untie me. Please. I beg you,' the man whimpered.

The others took no notice and ignoring his cries, they turned right and headed further into the forest.

\*

'They're coming,' shouted Makoud. 'I can see them. And they have Simon and the Khalifa with them.'

He shinned down from his lookout post and ran down the path towards them.

'Baba, you're back,' he shouted. 'You're safe.'

'Of course we're back. Now tell me what's been going on. Who are those two men in our camp? And why is one of them dead?'

'Baba. I didn't mean to do it, honestly.'

'He saved my life,' Salma interrupted. 'He had no choice.'

'All right. You can tell me all about it, later. For now I need to rest. We've been walking all night.' He looked at the happy faces before him and added, 'Where's Musa? Tell him to come and see to the Khalifa. As for the rest of you, get some rest because we're moving on as soon as it's dark.'

'A moment, brother,' said Rafiq, putting his hand on Ahmad's shoulder. 'We need to speak.'

'What is it?'

'The deserter.'

'You think he's a deserter?'

'Well he's a soldier; that's obvious. If we let him go he may follow us and put us all in danger. I think we should kill him.'

'But we can't kill an unarmed man. That would be murder,' said Ahmad, a look of horror on his face. 'Don't you think there's been enough killing?'

'It's the way of the world, brother. Remember we are wanted men. If our enemy finds us, he won't hesitate to kill all of us, even the women and children.'

'No. You can't kill him in cold blood. I won't let you,' Ahmad insisted. 'It was enough that we had to kill Asif. We can't kill anyone else.'

'Very well, very well. I'll go back and disarm him and let him go. But if I see him again I will kill him. Is that good enough?'

Ahmad nodded. 'Now I must lie down and sleep. My head won't think straight; I'm so tired.'

'You do that brother. I won't be long.'

Rafiq turned and headed back for the camp. As he approached, a fox ran out from the clearing. Above, in the tops of the trees, he could see the vultures already gathering.

He walked over to the deserter, who was still twisting and turning, trying to escape his bonds. Rafiq pulled out his dagger and sliced through the ropes around his ankles.

'Now, I'm going to let you go, but here's my advice. Get as far away from this place as you can. I never want to see you again. If I see your ugly face anywhere near us, I won't hesitate to kill you. Understood?'

'Just untie me please. Then you'll never see me again. I give you my word.'

'Roll over.'

He sliced through the ropes, one by one until the man was free. Rather unsteadily, the deserter got to his feet, and stretched. 'Thank Allah that you came along,' he said. 'I could have died from starvation.'

'More likely the wolves would have got you,' said Rafiq. 'Now get out of my sight and I hope never to see you again.' He turned as if he was moving away.

'I'm going. I'm going,' the soldier mumbled. 'Just let me get this stiffness out of my legs.'

He bent down and started to rub his leg. 'No, you won't see me again,' he said and pulled a slim dagger from inside his boot.

But Rafiq was too quick for him. He turned and thrust his sword straight through the man's chest. The deserter let out a low groan and fell back.

'I knew you wouldn't take my advice,' he said to the dying man. 'It didn't have to be this way.'

'Rot in hell,' the soldier said, and expired.

Rafiq gave him a kick with his boot. He wasn't going to bother burying either of them. He'd leave it to nature to clean up after him. He'd met men like these many times before. They had no honour. They couldn't be trusted. Ahmad wouldn't listen to him, but he knew that they would always be looking over their shoulders if he'd let the man live. He'd given him a chance to leave but, as he knew would happen, the idiot thought he could trick him. Well, it was done now and hopefully they could get on with their journey.

*

Once the sun had begun its descent over the horizon, they packed up their meagre belongings, installed the Khalifa on the donkey and set off down the mountain.

Thanks to Ahmad's encouragement and constant chivvying they reached the road before it was night and set off in a south-westerly direction.

'No need to go through the village,' Rafiq said. 'We'll just keep to the road. If we're lucky, we won't meet anyone and we'll be well on our way before morning.'

'Aren't we going to stop somewhere and sleep?' asked Aisha.

'Not until morning. It's safer to walk at night, now that we're not in the mountains with wolves and bears to worry about.'

'We're lucky, there's a full moon tonight,' said Simon. He was walking beside Salma and Rachel. Behind them came Musa, leading the donkey and the Khalifa. It wasn't much of a beast of burden. In fact, as Salma had whispered to him earlier, it looked as though someone should be carrying the donkey. Still they did seem to be moving slightly quicker than before. Personally, the slower they travelled, the better; it would put off the inevitable. Soon he would have to make the biggest decision of his life and he was still no closer to doing it than when he was in Córdoba.

Ahmad had already explained to him that he could get a ship to England from Cádiz. All the big sailing ships stopped at Cádiz. All he had to do was follow the Guadalquivir to the sea; he could even get a boat to take him. He knew that already. That was how the bishop had arrived and that was, presumably, how he had returned. Simon had one, possibly two days left to decide whether he would continue with his vocation and go back to the monastery—where they had been expecting his return for the last four years—or travel on with Salma and the others to Ardales. He stole a glance at her. The moonlight favoured her, making her skin glow milky white and emphasising her large dark eyes.

Tonight she had her beautiful shorn hair covered with a scarf, but a single strand, like a wisp of black silk, hung over her face. It was no good. Whenever he looked at her his heart beat so wildly that he was sure she could hear it. How could he leave her? He searched in vain for other reasons why he shouldn't go back to the monastery but always he returned to the single, undeniable fact that it was his love for her that had kept him here for four years and continued to keep him here. His choice was simple really. He had to chose between Salma or his vocation. He groaned.

'What's wrong?' Salma asked. 'Are you in pain?'

How could he tell her that his pain was terminal, that it cut through him like a sword?

'I was thinking about England,' he said.

She didn't reply.

'The abbot will wonder what has happened to me.'

'Ahmad says you will be leaving us soon,' she said. He wondered if he could detect a touch of sadness in her voice.

'You will be going south,' he said. 'If I am to reach the sea, I must turn west.'

'Will you be happy to return to your land?' she asked. 'Have you missed England?'

'I have been happier here, in al-Andalus, than I have ever been,' he said, solemnly. It was true but this happiness of his, did it come from something good or from the Devil's lust? His mind was so confused he could not be sure. Was this a temptation? Was God testing his faith? It certainly felt like it.

'I thought you said we wouldn't meet anyone at night?' Aisha hissed at her husband. 'Who are they?'

Ahead of them was a group of people sitting by the roadside.

'Wait here,' said Rafiq. He drew his sword and marched towards the people while the rest of them stood in the road wondering where they could run to if these were indeed their enemies. For what seemed an inordinate length of time, Rafiq stood talking to them. Then they saw him sheath his sword and beckon for them to join him.

'It's all right. These good people are travellers like us. They are heading for the coast,' he said.

'Welcome,' said one of the men. He was a Jew; Simon could see the yellow sash around his waist. 'Please sit and join us in some food.'

'We cannot delay for long,' said Ahmad. 'We have a long way to go.'

'Not as far as us, I think,' said the Jew. 'We are going to Palestine.'

'Really?' said Rachel, who up until that point had hung behind Salma, staring at her countrymen.

'Yes. We know that the good times are over. We have lived in peace here for more than three hundred years, but now, the tide is turning. The Jews are no longer welcome. It is time for us to find a new home. And what about you, sweet child? Why are you travelling with a group of Muslims? Where is your family?'

'My family are all dead. These are my friends. They have helped me to escape from Córdoba and the army of Sulayman,' she said. Simon heard Ahmad gasp. They were not supposed to tell anyone where they had come from.

'So these Muslims helped you to escape?'

'They are my friends,' she repeated.

'I see,' the Jew said. 'So we are all fleeing from someone. When we have eaten, let us walk part of the way together.'

'Gladly. There's strength in numbers,' said Rafiq, sitting down and accepting a plate of chickpeas from one of the women.

\*

They walked with the Jews for a day and a half, until they came to the point where the road made a sharp fork to the right.

'This is where we must part,' said the Jew, whose name they now knew was Jacob. He signalled for his group to stop and then looked straight at Simon and said, 'You're welcome to walk with us to the coast. There you will find a ship to take you back home.'

At first Simon was too surprised to speak then he said, 'I'm not sure that is where I'm going.' He looked across at Salma, but she was bending down speaking to one of the children.

'Why would you not take this opportunity to return to your homeland, to your vocation? You are a fortunate man; you have a homeland. You do not have to wander the earth hoping to find somewhere you can worship your God without hindrance, somewhere you can feel truly at home, somewhere that people treat you with respect and do not set their dogs on you or spit at you in the street. Why throw all that away?' He didn't wait for Simon's reply, instead he turned his attention to Rachel and said, 'And you, child, are you coming with us?'

Rachel looked at him, her eyes shining with expectation. 'I can go with you?'

'Of course you can. You belong with your people. Come on this adventure of your life. Come with us to the land of your ancestors.'

Rachel looked at Ahmad.

'You can go with them if that's what you want, Rachel,' he said and then added, 'Jacob, I trust you will care for this girl as if she were your own daughter?'

'You have my word. She will live with my wife and I until she finds a husband and has a home of her own.'

'Is that what your father would have wanted, Rachel?' Ahmad asked.

'My father wanted me to be happy but more than that he wanted me to be a good Jew. He always said that one day we would travel to the home of the Jews.'

'Is it far away?' asked Salma.

'Yes, very far. We have to cross the sea and travel over mountains and deserts before we arrive. But it is a fair land, with green pastures and plentiful water. She will be happy there,' said Jacob.

'It is just as the soothsayer told you,' Salma said, then blushed.

'Yes. It is written in my destiny,' said Rachel. 'Thank you, dear friends, but now I must leave you and go with these people. If God is willing, we may meet again one day; if not in this world then in the next.'

She threw her arms around Salma and hugged her. 'God go with you, dearest friend.'

'And you, Simon?' asked Jacob. 'Will you accompany us on part of our journey?'

Simon looked at the people around him. He had been living with them for two years. They were his family now. It didn't matter that they were Muslims and he was a Christian; they had treated him as a friend, more than that, as a son. He couldn't leave them now. He knew in his heart that he would never be able to marry Salma, no matter how much he loved her. Her religion was too important to her just as his faith was to him. No matter. It was enough that he could see her and be her friend. He would continue to worship God and follow the scriptures, but he wouldn't return to the monastery. His life was here now, in al-Andalus.

'No, but thank you for the offer. As Rafiq said, there is strength in numbers; I am needed here,' he said and was rewarded with a hug from Makoud and a beaming smile from Salma.

'In that case, we will say goodbye,' said Jacob.

'Ma'a salama, friends. May Allah watch over you on your journey,' said Ahmad.

*

They journeyed in silence for a while then stopped by a small stream to rest. It seemed quiet after the company of the noisy Jews, who had chattered nonstop as they walked and when they weren't chattering, had sung their own songs. Al-Hisham could still hear Ahmad humming one of them to himself, over and over.

He looked at his friend and tears filled his eyes. He knew Ahmad was not of the persuasion to love him as he would have liked, but he could never have found a truer friend in all of al-Andalus. Ahmad had stood by him through everything. A mere falconer and he had proved himself to be braver than the bravest soldier, and more than that, a loyal supporter of the Khalifa and the caliphate.

'Your Majesty,' said Ahmad. 'I think you must take this ring back now. It belongs to you and your family. What could I do with it? I could never sell it and I could never wear it. I think you should have it back.' He handed the ruby to al-Hisham.

The ring of the Omayyads. Al-Hisham slipped it on his finger. He could see his father wearing it, as he walked in the gardens and read aloud to him. What a long time ago. He'd been happy then. But all that had changed once the ring became his. It had brought him nothing but misery and sickness. Soon it would bring him death. He knew he would never return to Córdoba, even if Sulayman was killed. Another pretender would spring up in his place. There was no peace for his country any more. So, his reign as Khalifa was over. And he was not sorry.

'Your Majesty,' Ahmad said, bending over the reclining Khalifa. 'Is there anything you need? Would you like some water?'

'No, Ahmad. I have all that I need. Tell me, when will we arrive? When will this torment be over?'

'Another couple of days, Your Majesty. Look over there. Those are the mountains of Ronda and over there, to the right is the road that will take us to Ardales.'

'What sort of place is this Ardales? I have never heard of it.'

'It lies at the foot of the Sierra of Ronda, in a pleasant green valley. There are lakes and woods and fertile land. It is a quiet town, I believe and we will be able to live there in peace.'

'A good place to die, then,' the Khalifa said, calmly.

'A better place to live, Your Majesty.'

'True. Good hunting, would you say?'

'Excellent hunting.'

'Good, then Shamal will be happy.' The Khalifa lay back on the grass, the ruby glowing on his hand.

'Ahmad. Promise me that when I die you will bury this ring with me,' he said.

'I hope you live for a long time yet, Your Majesty.'

'Promise me.'

'Of course, Your Majesty. The ring will not leave your finger.'

'Good. The ring has not brought peace nor happiness to my land. It is time it went back into the earth from whence it came.'

'Yes, Your Majesty.'

'I will sleep now, for a while,' he said and closed his eyes.

\*

It was as though a tremendous weight was lifted from Ahmad's shoulders. He no longer had the ring. And now their journey was almost over. Ahmad felt at peace. He had brought them away from the dangers of Córdoba, from almost certain death at the hands of the enemy and now they could begin a new life. Even Rafiq looked different, less tense, more relaxed; he moved slower and he took time to talk to the children. Earlier Ahmad had heard him tell them that when they arrived in Ardales, he intended to buy some horses to breed. He remembered how that had been his brother's boyhood ambition. Perhaps now they could all fulfil their dreams.

How long the Khalifa would live was uncertain, but at least he would end his days in peace, surrounded by people who respected him and some who even loved him. Ahmad could do no more for him. He looked fondly at his family. Salma was sitting next to Simon and the children, making a daisy chain for the girls. They too seemed happy. What was it she'd said about a soothsayer? Women. Only women would believe in that rubbish. He looked across at his wife.

'Aisha.'

'Yes, Ahmad?'

He went over to her and put his arms around her. What did it matter if anyone saw him? 'Are you happy, dear wife?'

'Very happy, husband. you have done well.'

'Yes, little brother, you have done very well,' said Rafiq, punching his arm, just like he used to do when they were boys.

# POSTSCRIPT

It was just as Ahmad had feared. Once General al-Wahdi surrendered, the destruction of Córdoba began. The city was sacked and plundered by Sulayman and his Berber soldiers. The citizens were massacred, the libraries and universities disappeared and sixty eminent scholars were murdered in one day. Sulayman took on the title of Khalifa and became Sulayman II, but he didn't rule for long. His policy of giving concessions to his Berber, Arab and slave troops reduced his caliphate authority. His was a reign of terror, killing and looting and the Berbers treated Córdoba as a city under occupation. Sulayman's generals were given provincial governorships as rewards, and in 1016, just three years after he became Khalifa, Sulayman was deposed and murdered by one of them, the governor of Cueta. Then began the rule of the Hammudid dynasty who ruled Córdoba until 1023. The Golden age of the Omayyads was over.

The Ring of Flames

# **GLOSSARY**

*al-Andalus* the Islamic name given to Moorish Spain
*alcázar* palace, fort or castle
*alcazaba* walled fortification
*alla ysalmak* response to goodbye
*al-kharrūba* carob tree
*ammu* uncle
*as-salama alaykum* Hello
a*rab mile* is between 1.8 and 2 kilometres
*baba* father
*Barid* postal service
*Dar al-Jund* soldiers quarters in the palace
*Dar al-'ilm* house of knowledge
*Dhimmi* Jews and Christians
*al-Darrabun* night watchman
*dirhams* units of currency
*Djellaba* a hooded cloak
*Djubba* long robe
*Djinn* a mythical being from the spirit world
*Farran* communal bakehouse
*Fitna,* civil war, period of instability
*Ghifara* a crocheted cap
*Hadith* reports of the deeds and sayings of Mohammed
*Hajj* a respectful way of addressing an old man
*Hamman* baths
*huerta* allotment
*Imam* holy man
*insha'Allah* God willing
*jihad* holy war
*Jinete* horseman
*kufiya* a scarf
*Lohock* linctus
*Ma'a salama* goodbye
*Mihrab* niche in the wall of the mosque

*Muhtasib* officer in charge of municipal police
*Nuar* an incurable disease, possibly syphillis
*Quaid* officer in charge of a corps of 10,000 men
*Quran* the central religious holy book of Islam
*Sayyad* master or sir
*Sayyida* queen, queen mother
*Seedo* grandfather
*Tagine* North African stew of spiced meat and vegetables
*Teta* nickname for grandmother
*Wa alaykum e-salam* Peace be upon you
*Zenana* the innermost apartments where the women live
*Zunar* a blue belt or turban worn by Christians

Property of Beavercreek Schools
Loaned to
Dayton Islamic School
3662 East Patterson Road
Beavercreek, OH 45430